AT THE BAT

THE STRIKEOUT THAT SHAMED AMERICA

—A NOVEL—

DEL LEONARD JONES

First published by Casey Strikes Out Publishing in 2020
Copyright © Del Leonard Jones, 2020

ISBN print   978-1-7326052-4-4
ISBN ebook   978-1-7326052-5-1

To my loving wife Dianna, my children Ciera and Douglas,
and to my mother and father

"Hope springs eternal in the human breast."—Alexander Pope

*April 20, 1888—minutes after sunset
It's a Friday*

CHAPTER ONE

three seconds after the strikeout

Casey's swing leaves him twisted. He drops to one knee. The bat slips from his calloused grip and rests on home plate. The soil beneath him is soft, tilled by his spikes. His mighty swing has loosened the soil of his grave.

Gasps from the crowd, then utter quiet, as if he's fallen from a trapeze without net. Dead air fills the ball yard. Casey's Niners have lost and the Oaklands heap atop their pitcher with both celebration and disbelief in their eyes. The ball club cheers but the jubilation is buried in that eerie quiet. Mighty Casey has dug more than a grave, he's dug a *mass* grave.

The last pitch of the game nestles in the catcher's glove. Five thousand expected it to be crushed over the War Monument and to be bounding into history. The catcher Grasshopper Nova ignores the jubilation of his clubmates. He stays in his crouch. He hands the Strike Three ball to me backward over his shoulder. Smooth and cool, the one pitch old. I squeeze it for comfort. I won't let it go.

"*Vámonos,*" the catcher hollers, and when I don't move he turns to face me square. His voice is urgent. "Let's go ump. They want you dead."

"Who does?"

"Everyone."

No place seems safer than another, but my feet obey and I follow him. Grasshopper Nova stops to collect a burlap sack at his bench. "My gunny sack of shit," he says.

1

I glance back at Casey. He's still on knee, a shock of red hair curling from beneath his cap, a wad of tobacco in his cheek, a dribble down his chin, a dirt smear across the MUDVILLE NINERS stitching of his jockey silks. I shouldn't be following after Grasshopper Nova or any player, umpires never want to give a reason to suspect favoritism. Strictly square. But the survival instinct is strong. Casey's dead eyes turn angry, then wild like a Nevada dog. They find me. He picks up the bat at his feet and rises like Thor with hammer. A fanatic charges onto the field from the grandstand. He leaps and steals Casey's cap from behind and Casey can't decide which villain to bludgeon, me or the thief. His mouth begins to froth. He beats his bat on the marble plate. I expect the lumber to shatter into splinters, but all I see is Casey's anger and pain vibrating back at him through solid wood.

His tantrum takes long enough for the catcher to hurry me into a tunnel that leads to the visitor's clubhouse. Grasshopper Nova wedges a wooden wheelbarrow against the inside door handle. Satisfied with the barricade, he pulls a four-barreled Sharp's pistol from the gunny sack and tucks it in the waist of his knickers. Another reach into the sack extracts a knife, a flask, and a cloth rag. He takes a long drink, pours liquor on the rag, cleans the cut above my eye.

I flinch at the sting. I'd forgotten my wound at the hands of the Oakland coacher Old Reliable Jake. I'd forgotten everything before the strikeout. I remove my shoes and shake coarse sand from them.

"Old Jake almost murdered you a half inning ago," Grasshopper Nova says. "He's the happiest man in California now."

"Coachers are happy when they win," I say. "Every day we umpires make half the world happy, the other half we make miserable."

I startle at the fists upon the door. I startle again at the pounding of what sounds like a bat. Grasshopper seems not to notice. He nods as if I've spoken an indisputable fact. "Sins are forgiven by the winning clubs, winning coachers and winning fanatics," he says. Then, he changes his opinion. "You have a world of enemies today, *ese*. All of San Joaquin Valley. All of California. Casey has fanatics from here to Denver to New York. We Oaklands have none. You've put the world into utter despair."

Casey hollers from outside the door. "C'mon, open up." He sounds like he's in a barrel.

Grasshopper takes a step back to admire me. "That was something, *cabrón*, really something. You're an odd man, but a brave one. I can't wait to tell my little boy, my *mijo*." He speaks English with a Spanish word here and there. Maybe he really is a Mexican as he claims to be but his accent seems a bit off. "You're a damn gutsy umpire. One with *cojones*, that's for sure. *Estúpido*, but gutsy."

"I call what I see," I say. "I don't call what I don't see. Simple as that."

"Nothing's simple as that," Grasshopper says. "You could've called a ball or two. You could've let Casey hit the shit out of it. You could've made life easy."

Casey hollers. "I'll feed your nuts to my dog."

Another drink pours down Grasshopper's throat. He sprinkles the last drops of whisky on the sore cracks of his catcher's hands. The whisky sinks into the fissures and I wince for him.

He laughs. "Do you know what *cojones* are?"

"Balls," I say. "Nuts. What Casey wants to cut off. He called me a eunuch on the yard, he thinks I have none."

More bat pounding. "He knows you have some now," Grasshopper says. The wheelbarrow budges. He reaches for the handle of his pistol. "Courage, that's what *cojones* are."

I don't understand why testicles are courage. Must be a figure of speech. I don't get figures of speech. I know what people mean when they say it's raining cats and dogs, but I wish they'd a-just say it's raining a lot. I'm a disciple of plain English. A disciple of plain everything. I don't get sarcasm. Like when my mentor The Judge says, "Now, Walter, that's just terrific," when he really means is that it's just awful.

"I wish The Judge had umpired this game," I say. "He was supposed to."

"I don't know The Judge. They say he's the game's second best, but no other umpire would've declared those first two strikes, not even Honest John Gaffney." Grasshopper stuffs the empty flask next to the pistol in the waist of his knickers. "Even before the strikeout, you stood up for me, *también*. No other umpire would've done that, either. I'll never forget you *ese*."

A mob pushes against the door now, shouting curses, budging the wheelbarrow another smidgen. About three picas, a half inch.

"Maybe we should let them in," I say. "See where courage takes us."

"Face the music?"

"What music?"

"Shit, you're odd." Grasshopper picks up my shoes and pushes them into my hands. He hurries me through the players tunnel that leads outside The Home of the Mudville Niners and into a one-horse cab.

I resist. "My Papa wouldn't want me to run. He always said, 'When you're up to your neck in shit it doesn't hurt to piss your pants.'"

"That's funny," Grasshopper says. "You're a funny man, you said some funny shit out on the yard. You said those exact words when you were half conscious." He glances at my head and then at his pistol. "I point this at a man to make him piss his own pants."

"I can't run away. I've got two more games to umpire tomorrow."

"You've kicked an anthill," Grasshopper says. "You'd best scat."

"It's unprofessional to leave a job undone."

"Live to fight another day. The game needs fearless umpires like you."

He pushes me into the cab. "Save yourself. Hope springs eternal. I wish you could stand behind me again some day, but this is the last game I'll ever play." He slaps April pollen from the horse's rump. "*Vaya* con *Dios*, good luck *ese*. Tap it light."

"Tap what light?" I say, but he doesn't hear over the cabman's whip and the horse's lunge.

As I ride off, most of the crowd is still in the grandstand and the cheap seats—the bleaching boards. The people are motionless, stunned in disbelief. A few hooligans have busted through the wheelbarrow and run after my cab with obscenities and howls. They throw rocks and dirt clods as I put on my shoes.

Ahead of the traffic, I arrive at the train station in minutes. Four minutes precisely. The seven o'clock releases its brakes. "You'll have to run hell for leather," the cashier says. I think that means run fast.

I have an awkward gait and I'm the last one to jump aboard the straining train, my mask tight under my arm. My blue suit and mask give me away, anyone can tell I'm an umpire, but aboard there's no need to hide my identity. The Friday train is jammed with salesmen going home to San Francisco, they're oblivious to the strikeout thirteen minutes old, oblivious to the end of the world, oblivious to the end of the Niners' nineteen-game winning streak the train leaves behind. Word will swamp barbershops tomorrow, but for now no one takes notice of me, of my line of work, of my many oddities, of my bow tie caked in dried blood.

I'm lucky to find the last seat near the engine. The windows are wide open due to the heat. I close my eyes to the smoke and sparks and listen to air drawn through the flues and out through the smokestack that drowns out the rustling of afternoon newspapers. I recall the breeze of Casey's miss on my sweaty face. That's all I choose to remember for now.

Grasshopper Nova was right to get me out of there. The mob of hoodlums and cranks would've done to me what they did to The Judge a couple of days ago in Santa Cruz. And yet, I feel I should return. Two more games tomorrow. Unfinished business that I won't be finishing. Then I feel I'm chasing after someone, I don't know who, and I will the chug to chug faster. Unfinished business in both directions. Past and future. I'm thirsty and I have to pee at the same time. My toes cramp in a curl, the mask under arm digs into my ribs. My throat feels like I swallowed an old belt, I haven't urinated in hours, my head aches, the cut oozes. I'm holding the base ball, the last pitch. The cat-gut stitches throb in my fingertips. The base ball has a heartbeat. Edgar Allan Poe could've written a story about it.

All there is to do is to stay out of trouble, "stay low" as base ball pitchers say. Casey's strikeout will be on Page One in all the San Francisco papers in the morning. *The New York World*, too. Before the game, the tally-keeper picked up his megaphone and hollered that Nellie Bly was in the grandstand. The same girl reporter Nellie Bly who six months ago convinced a judge that she had psychosis or delirium and acted her way into Blackwell's Asylum. She wrote an exposé about it in the *World*, and then a book, about spoiled meat served at mealtime, patients tied together with rope, freezing cold baths. Ladies young and old were made to sit on hard benches with rats crawling over their feet.

Nellie Bly, not yet twenty-one, has prompted reforms in all thirty-eight states, including California where my Moms is at the Marine Hospital that Houses Crazy Seamen. Nellie Bly's my heroine. She's also America's sweetheart. The St. Regis offers eggs *a la Nellie Bly*. When she was introduced at the game she stood and waved to cheers. Umpires aren't allowed to cheer or wave back, and so, I just gawked. I couldn't help myself. She's smart as a whip, whatever that means, and she's lovely, thin and prettier than the tobacco shop girls I try never to notice.

In a few hours, people will be alarmed to learn that the Niners were stopped from breaking the record for consecutive wins by the ragtag Oakland club. But it will be a two-day story at most. When Casey pounds out his revenge tomorrow, a fresh Niners streak will be underway. All will be forgotten. That's the beauty of the game—and of newspapering. Few things hold a reporter's attention for three days and base ball's last pitch is consumed by the next.

The Judge says that end-of-the-world strikeouts float away like dandelion seeds in the outfield. Strikeouts don't float, but Casey's did. The pitch Mouse Mathews threw at Casey spun and twirled unpredictably left, right, to the ground, and then upward.

It's hot near the engine. A man sitting across from me reads his newspaper. Cables move faster than trains, and I worry that a reporter might ambush me at the San Francisco depot. I rise and walk the aisle, step between noisy cars. The only light is the red glow of a warning lantern. The train's sound turns hollow as it crosses a high trestle. I throw my bloody cap into the gray wind, heave my mask into the cry of escaping steam. I do it to stay incognito, but the second I let go of my mask I want it back. Without it I feel naked. I crave its protection.

I get that urge to throw myself off next, just for that instant, to hurl myself into the wind where I will float about with the seeds. I haven't had that urge for a long time, since before I started umpiring three years ago. Back then, I suffered a misery so deep I wanted to turn myself inside out. I was sad about everything and nothing. I'd split wood for cookstoves until I had cracks in my hands like the catcher's. The external pain brought peace to my insides. Still does. I'm a small man, but hard as a rock. I don't carouse all night like ball players. I'm healthy, I'll try to live to a hundred and give myself time to sift it all out.

I have a zest for umpiring, that much I've sifted. No one understands my odd passion except The Judge. The Judge understands, but he's half-dead in Santa Cruz now. He makes my head wound seem like a picnic. He may never umpire again.

I remove my blue jacket and bloody bow tie next. They kite away from the red of the lantern and into the dark. Casey swung, thank God for that. I wonder if I would've dared declare Strike Three had he not. Maybe. The pitch was up in the zone. Mouse Mathews didn't stay low. I could've declared it either way, but declaring a third strike without a swing would've been suicide. Yes, if I thought it was a strike I would've declared it. At least, I hope that's what I'd have done. That's what an umpire with *cojones* would've done.

The train rattles on. The moon is up and sliced in half. I almost throw the ball at it, change my mind, grip it tight, feel its pulse, inhale a breath of night air that's still warm from the day. There had been only wisps of clouds all afternoon at the yard, but now they billow above dragon-breath air. It smells of the dry lightning storm that aches to pour upon the Sierra Nevada a hundred miles off. I imagine the mountains crawling with cats and dogs.

Casey twisted down of his own accord, and I leave all three strikes in the valley loam as the train chases westward. It wants to catch the last faint strip of color in the sky, but there is no color left to chase. It was blown into blackness with Casey's swing.

Me and the train long for a hint of red. "Red sky at night, sailor's delight," I say and I close my eyes. I know what that means; Papa explained it to me when I was small. Way back on Papa's side is William Brewster, a pilgrim on the Mayflower. He named his daughters Fear and Patience and his sons Love and Wrestling, it's all in the Bible that Papa left behind. If Papa knew I'd grown to be an umpire he'd be surprised that a living can be made in such an odd line. I'm grateful that Papa named me Walter Brewster, a solid name to disappear behind. Love Brewster wouldn't survive an inning. Sailors like calm weather. Umpires like calm games. Our job is to make order out of chaos. But that's as impossible as controlling the weather, as impossible as quieting a baby with colic.

Moms did the best she could, but melancholia is the same as drowning, it causes you to grab onto the people who love you most and drag them under. She fought for life's balance for fourteen years after Papa left. I was nineteen when I found her in the attic. She'd been missing two days.

"I've seen this before," the doc said. "Another woman suffering hysteria and the general paralysis of isolation."

She was taken to the Marine Hospital that Houses Crazy Seamen. My sister, Annie Katharine, was fourteen and moved east to live with relations. She's married by now, no doubt.

Moms calls melancholia "being in the weeds," or "being out of sorts." I'm in the weeds sometimes. Not often, though, since I started umpiring. The Judge says I'm more and more in the clover, but I still have whatever it is that makes me odd. I have that all the time. Moms isn't odd. Just sad. I can be odd and out of sorts at the same time, but I want to stay out of the weeds. I don't want to be sad. I want to stay in the clover. I love umpiring, I can be surrounded by a yard full of people and yet be no part of them.

My hand kneads the pulsing ball for three hours until the train slows. A dozen men are waiting on the platform at the foot of Market Street as the train clanks in, car by car. I watch out the window for one of the men to crush his cigar, free his hands for pencil and paper, but all keep on smoking. None are reporters, it's past deadline. I know a lot about deadlines. I know about newspapers. I know a lot about typesetting and I know a lot about pill bugs.

From the train station, I tramp along damp wooden sidewalks and take refuge in my room for a long time, days and days. I know none of my neighbors at my boarding house, I avoid the meal table. I won't let one food touch another. I always eat alone so that I don't get teased. I often long for company but never seek it. After any game, I'm tired. Tired of being yelled at. After a day at any yard I crave the luxury of silence. I have a globe and I sit in my room and pretend to go around the world, from east to west, west to east, and sometimes up over the North Pole.

I usually don't stay in my room for days and days. I like San Francisco, I can walk among 300,000 people without bumping into anyone. That serves my nature. But I decide it's best this time to stay low. I sleep without knowing how long, nurse my concussion, grow sick of tinned tomatoes and stale sourdough until I have no appetite at all. I spend voiceless nights thinking about stuff, about strike one and strike two. I think about the audience's Strike Three gasp. Gasps as if the world's strongest swimmer just drowned in a waterfall's vortex. They couldn't stop Casey from drowning, but they had to do something. They jumped in with all their hearts and drowned with him.

I stay in bed, toss the ball up and down. I wonder how The Judge's recovery is going. He never misses a call, but he missed one in Santa Cruz. That's what he told me when I stopped by on the way to the San Joaquin, the Home of the Mudville Niners, the very morning that Casey struck out. The Judge said he made a bad call, that he's never been perfect like Honest John Gaffney. I've never seen Honest John Gaffney, but coachers and players throw his name in my face. When they disagree with my decisions they say, "You're no Honest John Gaffney." They say it most every day.

The Judge is a justice of the peace in San Francisco. He has a light schedule in summer that lets him umpire. He judges balls and strikes better than any man I've seen. He's in his sixth season in California. Before that he umpired in the big leagues. He won't say where. He won't talk about it.

The Judge got me into umpiring, we see each other three or four times a year when we meet up for Chinese and beer. I sit across from him at the grogshop. He faces the window to the local hall where drunken men lose wages at billiards and poker. I peer through the dark blue swirl of cigar smoke at an oil painting. I study it whenever The Judge gets up for a pee, which is always. The grogshop is seedy. Not seedy like dandelions, another kind of seedy. The beer is belch, the chop suey's made of chicken gizzards, bamboo and tripe. I don't like Chinese. It's all mixed together, but we never encounter sozzled players that high up on Filbert Street.

The Judge is thirty-seven, only eleven and a half years older than me but far wiser. The painting is modern of the Indian Wars in Montana. A lone cavalry commander sits astride a horse in a meadow, thickets of yellow flowers, early May, no new leaves yet on a mountainside of aspen. The white aspen bark has a wisp of blue because of the cigar smoke. The rider's gaze follows a snowmelt crick out into the horizon. I wonder if there's a waterfall out beyond the horizon past the end of the painting. There are rocks by the crick, and I wonder if there are pill bugs under them.

Pill bugs are armadillidiidae; they can roll themselves into a ball called *conglobation*. It helps them survive. I can go on and on about pill bugs. You won't find them beneath waterfalls in the roar.

The walls of my boarding house are painted blue, which envelops me in coolness. I have no artwork on the walls. The musty moose antlers nailed over the door are from a previous occupant. He'd been to Alaska. When I look at the antlers, I want to go to Alaska, too. My finger always travels through Alaska and the Yukon when it circles my globe. I'll get there for real someday, I'll take The Judge along, if he survives his beating. I'll survive mine, but he looked awful when I stopped by to see him on my way to the San Joaquin the day Casey struck out.

My shades are drawn, there's nothing to see from my bed except those antlers, my globe, a stove still choked with winter ashes, chipping blue wall paint, a bucket of water, clothes hanging on nails, a bookcase, two rusty rail spikes for bookends. Between the rail spikes is Papa's King James and two or three other tattered books. I don't read them. I like rulebooks. I don't read fiction. Edgar Allan Poe keeps me awake.

The room's untidy, but everything's where it's supposed to be. Calm. Orderly. Most people would take down the moose antlers, but I have things the way I want them. I get cross when things get changed. I shave each day. Other men don't, but I do. They're always changing the rules. I often wonder why they put first base down the right side instead of the left. The game swirls counterclockwise. I stare at my globe and wonder if it swirls clockwise in Australia.

On Monday, I open my cupboard to the last can of beans. I'm tired of living like a bat. The strikeout must be forgotten by now. I break my vow of isolation and shop for supplies at the bakery and market. I tip my hat at my landlady, Widow Buckman, and pray to God that I don't come across a ball player. Of course, most players and coaches don't know me without my blue suit and mask, but if I come upon one in town I always forgive and forget what was said at the yard. Players don't reciprocate. They say I cost them every game without exception. I never mention their mistakes, how a grounder scooted through their wickets, or how they rounded third, imagined themselves as fast as an antelope, and got thrown out at the plate by three feet.

Casey made two mistakes. He failed to swing. Twice. He should've let the third one go. It would've been ball one. He made three mistakes but he'll always blame me. That's what players do.

Sometimes I come across a player who acts cordial. I'm cordial back, but I don't fraternize. I'm nobody's buddy. I got hugged by a drunk player on the street once; I think it was part of a bet. I shoved him away. I never want to give a reason to suspect favoritism or the reverse. Strictly square. The sozzled player called me a weirdie. I'd never heard that before. I've heard *retard* and *spastic. Imbecile* and *ignoramus. Mongoloid* and the *village idiot.* A *pea-brain,* a *numbskull, flapdoodle, yokel,* a *dolt,* a *dummy,* a *dotard,* a *dunderhead* and a *dunce.* I'd been called all of these things even before I was an umpire. None are precisely accurate. I'd be a wallflower if I were a girl. My sister Annie Katharine's a girl, but isn't a wallflower. She's outgoing.

I was once called *Frankenstein,* though I bear no resemblance at all. Frankenstein's monster is taller than even Casey. I'm somewhat short. Some say I'm handsome. Odd and short, but handsome. Frankenstein's monster's ugly. Has a scar. I'll have a scar, too, from the cut on my head. Some say my head's full of bosh; they say I must've been pulled out of Moms with forceps. But my head's got its normal shape, or I wouldn't be handsome.

My head still hurts from the game, but I walk fast so I can get back to my room. I buy the *Chronicle* and *Examiner* and learn that the Niners swept two from the Oaklands on Saturday. A volunteer umpire was pulled from the grandstand, "one with vision," the *Chronicle* says.

The *Chronicle* says that the game I worked has been overturned. Base ball minister William Rufus Wheaton said the Oaklands used an illegal player. The catcher Grasshopper Nova is disqualified. The Mudville Niners win. I thought it was the right thing to let Grasshopper Nova stay in the game, but the minister overruled me.

Papa once said there is only one hard-and-fast rule. The one about pissing your pants when you're up to your neck in shit. That's the only rule in black and white, he said, but almost all base ball rules are in black and white. Rules that aren't in the book are up to the umpire's discretion, but those can be appealed to the minister of the Northern California Base Ball Association. My decision was appealed and overturned. The three Niner wins secured the record at twenty-two straight.

Some umpires get mad when they're overruled, but it's OK by me. It's the minister's prerogative, not the end of the world. The strikeout will be forgotten, I'll be back to work. There's an umpire shortage, always will be The Judge says. I may have to go back to the D-league where they play crappy ball. I'll pay my dues another season until my next break.

I find myself hungry for the ten-cent risotto across the street from my boarding house at the *Fior d'Italia*. Girls of ill fame live in the pitched-roof bordello above the restaurant. When I come home from games they wave underthings at me from their windows. They cackle and call down, "Hey, mister shy man, in the mood for some sparking?"

I've always wanted to protect girls. I've never saved one for real, but as a boy I walked the tracks every day with a bucket to pick up coal for Moms' stove. The tracks would shake and I would imagine Suzie Jefferson screaming, the stiff sole of her shoe caught in the timbers of a trestle. Suzie Jefferson was a girl in my grammar school. She dropped her pencil on purpose and I'd pick it up. I woke up every morning hoping for a chance to protect and keep her safe. I'd imagine the coal scattering from my bucket. Steam and sparks from the engine's whistle showered Suzie Jefferson's golden hair. My sister Annie Katharine said I was *obsessed* with Suzie Jefferson.

I have an urge to rescue the girls of ill fame above the restaurant, to protect them from their ways, but I don't go to *Fior d'Italia*. Italian food's always touching other Italian food and the girls don't seem to want a rescue. I might as well hang upside down bat-like forever. I recline in bed and toss the base ball into the air. I catch it over and over. Four hundred and thirty-two times precisely until I nod off.

A knock startles me. I hear knocks at neighboring doors from time to time, but this is only the second knock ever on my door. The first was several days ago when a wire arrived from William Rufus Wheaton telling me The Judge was beaten nearly to death in Santa Cruz. He was supposed to umpire the Niners series, but I had to do it.

This second knock is loud enough to vibrate the moose antlers. Too loud to be one of the sinful girls wanting a rescue. I ignore it, I give the door knocker a chance to change his mind. When the knock's repeated, I holler "Hold your horses!" That means have patience.

I get my trousers from a hook, put them on and throw open the door to my life. I'm expecting nighttime, but I'm hit by a bombshell of daylight, warm and bright for a foggy day. I've been asleep for hours and hours, maybe days and days. I hate not knowing.

"You're the umpire." Male words like bare knuckles. A reporter. "Been looking for you all over, it's like you don't exist."

"Sure I exist."

"You're funny," he says.

My eyes are squinty. I'm in the shadow of my stoop and he's standing in broad daylight. Or, what's trying to be broad daylight as the sun works to burn off the fog so that afternoon can begin.

It's hard to see in the morning fog, just as it's hard to umpire in the late afternoon when sun and shade touch each other on the yard. If I'm facing the sun and the play happens in the shade, that's about the worst of all. Before Casey struck out, it was the pitcher Mouse Mathews who was looking directly into the setting sun. His shadow stretched far behind him. His giant shadow ears reached the shortstop and the second baseman. Casey and I were both in the shade of the grandstand. Grasshopper Nova, too. The three of us had no sun in our eyes, we had a damn good look at all three pitches.

The reporter's looking into the sun. My angle is superior, which is all an umpire can ever ask. Perfect order from utter chaos is an impossible ambition, but a good umpire strives to get the best angle.

October 12, 1887
It's a Wednesday morning

CHAPTER TWO

one hundred eighty-nine days before the strikeout

N ellie Bly spends her last penny on five sticks of Adam's Black chewing gum. She folds four sticks into her mouth and wanders for hours about Manhattan, black saliva dripping down her chin, the curl gone from her bangs. She wears taped and undersized eyeglasses from her childhood, her most dreary dress, and size five shoes on size-three feet.

At long last, she is taken by two Irish policemen, big and strong.

Justice Duffy says she is somebody's darling. "She's too pretty to be abandoned. Someone must be searching for her." He calls in reporters. "Maybe she has a husband who cast her away. We must protect her from becoming a woman of the town."

Nellie Bly wants to slap in the face any man who wants to protect her, but she smiles into space as reporters look her over. She's new to the city and two days of publicity brings no claims on her. Insanity doctors are brought in for an examination. She insists that she's in her right mind, but Justice Duffy says she has a far-away expression and over-sized pupils to match her over-sized shoes. He commits her to Blackwell's Island Insane Asylum.

Justice Duffy isn't the first judge she's fooled, and he won't be the last. At fourteen she hoodwinked another in order to win her mother a hard-fought divorce, reaping revenge on the scales of justice, upon her stepfather—and upon men in general.

At the asylum, nurses slap noncompliant patients and drag them about uncarpeted halls by the hair. The kitchen stench compels her to hold her breath. Patients eat oatmeal gruel, slices of unbuttered bread, saucers of exactly five prunes and boiled potatoes that have made no acquaintance with salt or pepper. Nurses wear heavy garments while patients go without shawls. Clothing is pulled from them when it comes time for icy baths in water used repeatedly by girls with body sores.

When the saga's over, she watches Joseph Pulitzer, publisher of *The New York World,* read her item aloud to himself.

> The nurses said, "rub, rub," behind bits of soap to scrub all of me until I was an unfortunate with nothing left of my pride and former glory. One could weep and plead for release, and to no avail. Were I to put up a struggle, one touch of a bell would bring in male assistants before I could cover myself with a flannel gown.

Mr. Pulitzer pumps his fist into the air. "This is destined for Page One! This is worthy of a prize!" He continues reading.

> Many of the girls inside Blackwell's are as sane as myself, they need only to dry out from the red liquor. Others have nervous disabilities and are human wrecks. Fiendish nurses encourage them to make advances on ugly old doctors, and a baby with a nice Jewish face was born in the basement.
>
> The ugliest nurse, armed with a bunch of keys, asked me if I would like to marry a doctor of my own. I daresay, one or two young and handsome physicians became flirtatious.

Joseph Pulitzer raises his thick eyebrows. "You need to make it clear that the flirtatious doctors struck out with our new, fresh-faced correspondent."

The edition runs out in record time. That's all that really matters. Letters ask her to write more about her encounters with the handsome doctors. At twenty-one, she already knows that effective journalism is as much about what is left out as what is put in. She decides then and there that mystery will be a trademark of her work as much as chaos has been a trademark of her life.

She was an 1864 war baby, born Elizabeth Jane Cochran in Cochran Mills, a Pennsylvania town founded by her father. She's the youngest of his fifteen children, ten of which were from his previous marriage. At some point she tacked on an "e" to make herself a Cochrane and to set herself apart from the gaggle. She had no close friends but the closest ones called her Pink. Others knew that she despised Lizzie, and that's what they called her.

Cochran Mills girls wore bland frocks to hide the town's black dirt, but Pink's mother, Mary Jane, dressed her in pink to stand out, hence the nickname, though her nature wasn't frilly, and she often came home covered in Kiski River mud.

Boys couldn't resist her and the first proposal came at age five. Booker Stevens visited his grandfather in Cochran Mills in the summer of 1869. He knew the rules of card games and I Spy, he knew it all because he was from Pittsburgh, and he was twelve. One hot afternoon Pink and Booker went beneath an unpainted porch where the ground was cool and dark. She was already well on her way to perfecting her smile and her ability to walk with the grace of Queen Victoria. She had, in fact, honed her charms enough to get Booker to eat dirt.

Booker spit his proposal from a mouthful of grit. "Betrothed girls show their bottoms," he sprayed, and she promptly hiked her pink frock and took a bow. Even then, she knew the angle of the sun, she knew to leave the lower half of her butt in the shade of a slat, and Booker could only pretend that he was rewarded for eating worm poop.

He lied and said he had seen everything, and laughed that her bottom had no freckles. She refused to play with him again. He returned to Pittsburgh when summer ended to be forgotten except for the letters he sent. Pink, an early reader, became weary of circling Booker's misspellings and grammatical errors. She eventually got sick of his letters altogether, and that was years before she received her sack of adoration every day at *The New York World*. Years and years before her ugly episode with the base ball hero Casey.

As far back as she could remember, she never thought any boy could best her. At age six, she borrowed a leather-bound medical book from her daddy's library and showed a group of stupid boys the illustrations. A town scandal, but all was forgotten when her daddy, Michael Cochran, died of a crippling malady when she was seven. His last words to her were, "Don't let anyone ever feel sorry for you. You're more clever than the boys. Promise to stay that way."

He left behind a fortune, but no will and a mob of adult children by his first marriage. They looted everything before his body was cold and sued to force the mansion's sale at auction. The court awarded his widow sixteen dollars a week and some pennies for Pink's piano and riding lessons. It was enough, but Mary Jane was humiliated and married the first man to consider a woman in her forties.

Pink was nine when the war hero Jack Ford limped into her life. Her stepfather said "done it," when he should have said "did it," and "I have saw" when he should have said "I have seen." When she corrected his grammar, Mary Jane shushed her and Jack Ford said, "I expect to go to heaven all the same."

He claimed to have been shot in the ankle with a Minnie ball; his foot had fallen from the hospital train to be eaten by coyotes. Whenever her mother wasn't home, Nellie Bly taunted Jack Ford. She'd stand beyond the reach of his cane, chew gum, braid her hair and echo back his flawed lexicon. She'd run when he stumped after her in frustrated pursuit. The house would seem to shrink, but he never thought to look in the straw hamper where she'd stay until, driven by hunger or boredom, tip it and wiggle free.

He nearly caught her once. He broke her eyeglasses and tore a piece from her pink frock before she escaped out the back. "I'd like to plant a kiss on the Rebel who shot off your foot," Pink shouted and when her mother came home Jack Ford said, "This house needs a hickory stick more than it needs a piano." He attacked the instrument with his cane, ordered Pink to her room, beat his wife for Pink's sass, and then had his way with Mary Jane on the keys. Pink listened as the two played unorganized chords a half beat behind Jack Ford's grunts. After he had drank himself to sleep, Mary Jane stayed up to conceal her bruises with rouge, sew repairs to Pink's frock and tape her glasses. The neighbors never knew.

Cochran Mills boys wrestled for Pink's attention. At thirteen she added breasts to her repertoire and their wrestling escalated to bare knuckles. She lived up to her Papa's request to stay more clever than the boys. She denied every one a kiss. Denial gave her power and power gave her a craving for risk and danger that would one day lead her into Blackwell's Asylum—and later into Casey's mansion on the outskirts of Golden Gate Park.

Nellie Bly had precisely two childhood girlfriends at a time. One would be somewhat pretty and jealous of her. The other would be fat or plain or both and ostracized. Other girls resented her for one asinine reason or another, usually for poaching boyfriends for sport. They called her Lizzie to her face and a tart behind her back. The entire town resented that Cochran Mills was named for her dead daddy and she resented them back for populating her daddy's town with dullards. Every hometown male was as uneventful as the men who later approached her on trains.

Mary Jane at long last sued for divorce and the fourteen-year-old Pink testified on her mother's behalf. She smoothed her dress and told the magistrate that her stepfather was a drunken man of determination and stumbled about calling out "Lizzie! Lizzie!" until he grew exhausted and settled for his wife.

"Mama ran from him, too," Pink testified, "but he broke furniture and threw it into the yard until she became afraid of what the neighbors might think."

Pink knew the magistrate wanted to know if Jack Ford ever caught her, but he was too proper to ask. She kept the mystery, and she kept her power.

"Your story is impossible to believe about a man with the decency to marry a widow with a precocious daughter," the magistrate said.

"My daddy, Michael Cochran, taught me never to lie."

"You're not your daddy," said the magistrate. "You're a sprite and these are wild tales without corroboration. You aren't the first young lady to lie. You won't be the last."

"I have never lied in my life and I never will," Pink said.

The magistrate remained skeptical, so Pink removed her glasses and told him what he wanted to hear. "The cripple never caught me, thank my stars, but he dragged Mama into the mop closet and grunted out 'Lizzie, Lizzie, Lizzie' like the chug of a double-header train."

The magistrate praised Mary Jane for tending to her wifely duties and tidy housekeeping and said he had no choice but to rule in favor of the hero Corporal Ford.

"Wounded veterans are to be believed and respected," the magistrate said.

Pink burst into tears, wiped them, and smiled a sexful smile she had long practiced to the mirror but had never once employed.

"Sweetheart," said the magistrate, "do you have any knowledge of adultery or desertion."

Pink nodded her head yes, it was a necessary fib. "Jack Ford dragged me into the mop closet. Once when Mama was to market."

Gasps filled the courtroom. "I never done that," Jack Ford said.

"Then he laid me on the piano, his heaving notes play in my ears."

"It's a lie. I've done nothing but protect the child."

Nellie Bly turned red with anger. "He saw my freckles you know where."

"It's a blame lie," Jack Ford said, and it was, but the hero was going to hell all the same.

"You never even told your Mama?" the magistrate said.

"Because of the neighbors and what they might think." Pink wept uncontrollably until the divorce was granted. The magistrate proved to be one more bald gentlemen who wanted a fistful of her pink dress and she made a vow to herself that she would one day have revenge on him, too, or at least on some other jester in black robes.

She fulfilled her vow seven years later. After she'd acted her way into Blackwell's Asylum, Justice Duffy became the subject of political cartoons and lost his next election. She was to fulfill her vow again in 1890, two years after the strikeout.

Nellie Bly was born to be a correspondent, the world's greatest. She tried once to settle down and be a teacher. She thought she might enjoy a quiet life of circling grammatical errors, but she left college when the trustee swindled her out of the last of her Daddy's estate. It was a blessing. It was fate. Lacking funds, she joined the *Dispatch* in Pittsburgh. She knew that New York was the single destination for a serious correspondent but there was a quota on girl reporters and she took a situation as a Manhattan governess until, she prayed, a female might get married or sacked.

A month of waiting seemed an eon. She hated mind-numbing hours with children, but she used the time to think and think. One day she lost her purse and her last ten dollars at the playground in Central Park. That gave her the pluck to leave the children in a sandbox and to barge into Joseph Pulitzer's office unannounced. She told him that she wanted to infiltrate the asylum and report on its conditions.

Mr. Pulitzer said she'd never pull it off. "Your chronic smile prevents you from deceiving a soul." However, he told her that if she happened to succeed on her own, "I will personally rescue you from the white-capped nurses."

"If I succeed will you also sack one of your girls to make room for me on your reporting staff?"

Mr. Pulitzer agreed and, to this day, her heart beats high in her chest to recall her steps into Blackwell's. Her heart won't pound like that again until the day she steps into Casey's mansion.

It was the Hungarian publisher Pulitzer who gave her the pen name after a Stephen Foster song.

> *"Nelly Bly! Nelly Bly! Bring the broom along,*
> *We'll sweep the kitchen clean, my dear,*
> *And have a little song.*
> *Poke the wood, my lady love*
> *And make the fire burn,*
> *And while I take the banjo down,*
> *Just give the mush a turn."*

She detests the lyrics—and therefore the *nom de plume*—but no girl identifies herself in print and stays above reproach. She changed Nelly to Nellie to make a statement, to let everyone know that she'd never be limited by any man, even a man as flush as Joseph John Pulitzer.

Blackwell's Asylum gained for her instant fame and she wrote the book *Ten Days in a Mad-House* that sells and sells for twenty-five cents a copy in a time of dime novels. A year passes, and she has everything she needs. Thank God, she still has her virtue no matter what's in the public record of Pennsylvania. Any ambitious reporter could find her perjurious testimony about being savaged in a mop closet and atop a piano. But what she fears most is that her true age is also trapped in the county records and could be made public. She prays for a fire. Her twenty-fourth birthday approaches. All girls lop off a year or two if they are pretty enough to get away with it, but it would be a scandal if the nation knew she'd lopped off three.

She need never marry. Book sales have left her well-situated. Love-sick men say they were put on earth to take care of her, but she knows they are truly on earth to deny her fate. She barely has time for reporting, she is invited to speak at banquets everywhere, all the way to San Francisco, from where she travels on April 20th, 1888 to the farmlands of the San Joaquin Valley to attend her first base ball match and to see the barbarian Casey make a fortune playing a game.

She has no idea what to wear to the match. She's been warned that the weather spikes from cold to hot a few miles east of San Francisco. She decides she can't go wrong with a white dress that shows a tint of pink in direct sunlight.

It's the springtime of the year and the springtime of her fame. That is a splendid thing, but she finds herself trapped at a base ball match that goes on and on. It has no end. She learns from her escort that the game has nine endings like a cat has nine lives. By the second ending she's grown bored with the match *and* her escort. She hates escorts, they restrict her freedom. She hates base ball, she has no patience for boys of the pasture, but she has an appreciation for their physiques and their bats, and the sound made when a sturdy Irish boy now and then hits square a ball.

A sound like none other. Like the crack of a cane against a piano. Like the crack that one day awaits her inside Casey's mansion, the crack a cue ball makes on the first shot of billiards. They call that shot *the break*, but she doesn't yet know that it will break her soul.

"Base ball is a man maker."—Al Spalding

March 26,1885
It's a Thursday

CHAPTER THREE

three years before the strikeout

The San Francisco jailhouse mixes its meals together like goulash. Walter Brewster eats little. He dislikes one food touching another and he's famished when he comes before The Judge.

"How to you plea?" The Judge says. Walter never lies. He'd stolen laundry off a lady's line and he says "ninety-nine percent guilty" because nothing's a hundred percent.

"Now, Mr. Brewster, that's just terrific."

The Christian woman he stole from asks The Judge to go easy on Walter. "He's a dodo who exhibits no sign of drunkenness," she says.

The Judge tells Walter that it's in his best interest to apologize to the woman.

"Sorries." His stomach growls.

"You're forgiven," she says.

"Dodos went extinct because they were a-easy to catch," Walter says.

"That's funny," The Judge says. "You're no dodo, but you're surely curious."

"I'm very curious about a few things. I'm not curious at all about most things."

"I hope horse manure interests you. Shovel it up along Market Street for six months to pay your debt to the San Francisco society. Or, Mr. Brewster, you can umpire the Jabbering Seals in the D-league for a season.

D-league umpiring leads to good money if you stick it out. No one sticks it out, that's why it leads to good money."

"I enjoy base ball," Walter says.

"Look at me," The Judge says. Walter thought he already was looking at The Judge, but apparently he's been looking at his own feet. "Every spectator understands he has less skill than the players, but they believe in their hearts that they would make top-notch umpires. Many strikes are ball-like and many balls are strike-like. If Pope Leo were an umpire, he'd catch hell. The umpire is the one man on the yard who can't win."

Walter wavers. No one likes to lose. He's thinking six months of manure might be OK when The Judge says, "On your best days, no one knows you're around, and that's your reward for a job well done."

Walter likes the sound of that. He likes going unnoticed. One Sunday, when he was sixteen—years after Papa left—Suzie Jefferson spoke to him out of the blue. "Are you stuck up or something?" she said after church. Walter was so surprised he looked her in the eye. They were the color of redwood bark.

"You never talk at school," she said. "Like you're too good." Her friend whispered in her ear. Walter had good ears. He heard Suzie Jefferson's friend whisper, "Walter Brewster thinks his shit don't stink."

He wanted to tell Suzie Jefferson that he rescued her everyday from the oncoming train, that he was put on earth to keep her safe. Instead he said, "My shit stinks."

The girls pinched their noses with gloved hands and giggled. "Were you raised in a lighthouse?" Suzie Jefferson's friend said and the two skipped off in their church dresses. Walter didn't know what Suzie Jefferson's friend meant, but he now wished The Judge would sentence him to a stint in a lighthouse rather than umpiring or manuring.

"Are you listening to me Mr. Brewster?" The Judge's voice is low and loose like horse hooves on pea gravel. He looks down from the bench. "Hear me," he says because Walter is in a world where engine steam showers Suzie Jefferson's golden hair and hides Walter in its fog. "No father ever lit his pipe, looked his boy in the eye and said, 'I want you to be an umpire.'"

Walter decides right then that umpiring's way better than pitchforking manure.

"Does a crowd of people bother you?"

"In tight spaces," Walter says, "but the ball yard is big."

"Now, Mr. Brewster, that's a hell of a note." Walter doesn't know what that means, but The Judge sounds happy. "I need you to tell me you're doing this on your own volition. I don't want you to be coerced, I won't be cruel, and umpiring is cruel and unusual punishment."

"I want to be an umpire," Walter says. "I want to be a good one."

Walter's stomach growls. The Christian lady gives him two bits for food and whispers a prayer for him.

The base ball season is still a month off. The Judge has connections and gets Walter an apprenticeship at the *San Francisco Chronicle*. Walter takes to typesetting straightaway because it requires memorization and focus. One evening after work, The Judge takes Walter to a sandlot near the *Chronicle*. He makes Walter tote a gunny sack of balls. "It weighs a ton," The Judge says. That's an exaggeration, but it weighs so much that Walter has to drag it behind him.

On the way to the sandlot The Judge says he was born in England but doesn't have an accent because he moved to Hoboken, New Jersey when he was two. He played base ball for a variety of clubs and hit into the National League's first triple play.

"Triple plays are quite rare," Walter says, "How often does a batsman come up with no outs and at least two men on base? You need that for starters."

"Umpires who make it to a second season are more rare," The Judge says. "They're ex-players like me because we think we know the game and we think we know the rules. Most make crummy umpires; it's impossible for most of us to exchange the accolades for the abuse. Most umpires move on to pool halls and bucket shops. Now, Walter, you'll be my grand experiment. You'll be the first umpire who's never played."

"I played one-old-cat with my sister Annie Katharine."

"Don't tell anyone that. Tell them you played in the Cactus League. Tell them you got your odd walk by crashing into another outfielder. Coaches like new umpires, at least for an inning or two. They believe anyone with a pulse is better than the umpire they had yesterday."

The Judge hands Walter a mask. "It cost three dollars, so don't break it." He laughs and says it's a joke. "Dick Higham was the first umpire to wear one."

Walter knows that Dick Higham got kicked out of base ball when they found out that he was paid by the gambling society to cheat for the Detroit Wolverines. "I don't cheat and I don't lie," he says.

"They don't know if Dick Higham cheated, they just think he did," The Judge says. "I'd like to thank him. I'd have a mushed-up nose if it wasn't for Dick Higham strapping on a mask."

Walter tries his on. It belongs, as if it's a thing that's been missing. The Judge pulls a ball from the gunny sack and hurls it into the mask's wiring like he's gone mad. Water sprays Walter's face. The balls are waterlogged, that's why the sack weighs a ton.

"Stop blinking," The Judge hollers. "Pathetic umpires stand ten feet back of the plate and off to the side, but that won't make it in the modern game. Some get in tight alright, but dance to dodge. To call your best zone you have to lock in back there, head still, nose on the ball, eyes tracking. Track this one in." The Judge splats another ball into Walter's mask. "You have to trust catchers, who will fail you. You can't flinch. You'll get hit, sometimes it hurts like the dickens."

"I don't read Dickens, I don't read fiction. I don't read anything from the beginning, I start in the middle."

"The dickens isn't *Charles Dickens*, it's the devil," The Judge says. He splats a faster one into Walter's mask. "Al Spalding invented a rubber protector for the nuts that's inflated with air, but it costs ten bucks and that mask cost three. We'll sacrifice your vegetables to save your handsome puss."

"I'd invest ten bucks if I had it," Walter says. "I hope to have a good woman some day to love and protect."

"Anything's possible," The Judge says. "If you'll believe Dick Higham wasn't a cheater, I'll believe you'll find a woman—and know what to do with her."

"I'll take her to town."

"You're damn funny." The Judge shows Walter how to interlock his hands over the groin. "That slows the pitch some, but doesn't stop many. The cranks call it *ringing the cow bell* when an umpire folds over. They clank cow bells from the bleaching boards. The base ball magnates don't care if you want a family. They encourage cow bells, they encourage anything that gives hearty enjoyment for an entertainment nickel. Thank goodness more and more girls are showing up in the grandstand shade. They don't appreciate saucy humor."

"Pretty girls?"

"You know what."

Walter doesn't know what, so he listens close as The Judge teaches him things he should do on the field and off. The Judge's mentoring never officially ends. In late May, two months after the season begins, The Judge tells Walter never to speculate about what outfit may win today or tomorrow. "Never opine because opinions get misconstrued. We'll always be suspected of fixing. Except for Honest John Gaffney."

In August, The Judge tells Walter to catch morning trains. Ball players stay up half the night and are rarely found before noontime. "Base ball outfits are to be avoided at all costs, players and coaches."

The Judge offers his advice right up to the very day of the strikeout. Walter never forgets a word. He locks in back there and he pays for it with foul tips to the shins, knees, ribs, ears. His biceps get bruised orangeish-yellow-green, and he gets hit in the feet enough with low corkers to peel a toenail away about the time one grows in. He loves every game, every pitch, even when he takes a foul tip to his Adam's apple in July of eighty-seven. He, too, has a low gravelly voice for a spell until he gets hit with one in the nuts that raises his voice back to normal. Still, no pitch makes him the eunuch Casey will soon call him at the start of Season Four.

That godawful eighty-eight season is still a year off when The Judge comes to watch Walter work a game at the Haight Street Grounds between the Cuban Giants and a picked nine of Irish. It's high-level exhibition ball, the best ball Walter's umpired.

The Judge sits in the bleaching boards; Walter doesn't know he's there until the game's over. They go for Chinese and beer and The Judge says, "Now, Walter, you've come a long way. You have great judgment, you make the good calls, but you walk away from players and coaches when they're still talking to you."

"I know," Walter says.

"They don't like that. Annoys them. Even when they're grousing, you have to pretend to listen. Otherwise they get madder."

"I know." Walter says. "I try. Before the game at the plate meeting, I let the coacher of the Irish slap me on the back like we were buddies."

"Never let them do that. They'll turn on you. They're the first to throw a tantrum when a call goes against them, they think you betrayed them like Judas or something."

"I know," Walter says.

"I'm tired of you saying that," The Judge says. "People who know everything can't be taught anything."

"My problem is that I just don't care beans what other people think."

"I suppose not caring is a valuable umpiring quality."

Walter clarifies. He can't lie. "I care, I just don't know what anyone's thinking. I don't read minds."

"Now, Walter, you're the oddest, most honest man I know. The thing you lack is field presence."

"What's that?"

He strokes his whiskers. "A grip on the situation, an aura of command and savvy, you know it when you see it."

The Judge has presence. He employs facial hair for authority in the courtroom and on the yard, he has the dundrearies made fashionable by President Chester Arthur and he looks as ancient. The Judge is thirty-six, twenty years younger, but they could pass as twins if President Arthur hadn't died last year.

The Judge was born breech, "with my head in fifty and my tukhus in fifty-one." He says he slid home feet first, "back assward." He's the opposite of Walter. Friendly and chubby and he always has to pee. Walter never has to pee. The Judge has the prostate and presence of an old statesman.

"How do I get field presence?"

"You're a short duck," The Judge says. "Stand straight, for one thing, especially when a player or coach yells at you."

"Short helps me declare balls and strikes," Walter says. "I bend my knees a little to align my eyes with the front elbow of tall batsmen, the top of the zone. If my eyes move up, it's truly a ball."

"You're accurate as anyone, and you have the endurance of an Indian pony. You see everything."

If there's a leaf stuck to the bottom of a cleat he sees it. If it's stuck there because of duck shit, he smells it. If a girl ever whispered "His shit don't stink," from the grandstand's tenth row, Walter would hear it with the ears of a rabbit.

"I still don't know what field presence is," Walter says.

"Shoulders back. Be certain even when the call is too close to be certain. Umpires who vacillate lose respect."

"Didn't know umpires had any respect to lose," Walter says.

The Judge laughs and laughs. Walter never knows when others will find him witty. When The Judge stops laughing he says, "You just need a bit more dash and vim if you're to have field presence."

When The Judge strikes out a batsman he hollers, "Strike Three, yooooou're out." He hollers loud enough for the coloreds to hear from way down the foul line. If the batsman grouses about the call, The Judge hollers, "That's a strike anywhere on the Pacific slope!" All of that and more is field presence, Walter decides. The Judge isn't perfect like Honest John Gaffney, but field presence goes a long way.

"I'll try to have presence."

"It's theater. Don't fret about it. Protect the game."

Walter likes the sound of that. "I like protecting what's important."

"That's what umpires are for. You're a sophomore. You're twenty-three, but you don't look it, not with those peach cheeks. Grow a mustache. Why do you want to be the only man on the yard without one?"

Walter shrugs. He shaves every morning; he doesn't like change.

"I've taken you to school. You've become a damn good umpire, better than I expected. I'll write base ball minister William Rufus Wheaton and tell him you're ready to move up."

Minister Wheaton must have been a busy man because the eighty-seven season passes, and Walter's still umpiring the Jabbering Seals. He takes The Judge's advice and grows a lame mustache. Like magic, on April 19 1888 at 4:48 in the afternoon, Walter gets that first knock ever at his boarding-house door. It's a telegram from Minister Wheaton. The Judge was beaten by toughs at a game in Santa Cruz. He has games to umpire in the San Joaquin but he can't climb out of bed to take a leak. Walter's to catch the first train. A big-time appointment, biggest of his life, twenty-one dollars for the three-game series.

If The Judge were OK, Walter would be working another crappy D-leaguer in the San Francisco cold, but now he's on his way to the sunny valley to umpire the Mudville Niners. They were never out of first place last season with Casey batting .388. No man has hit with such distance since bat and ball were invented; that's what the sporting writers write.

The Niners would be good enough to cop the pennant in the National League or the American Association, win the World Series. The Niners have the money to commission a fast train, stay in nice hotels, but the players who underpin Casey are all running from the authorities. Casey's about the only Niner who could step onto a platform in Philly or Beantown without being served for passing bad money or fondling tobacco-shop girls against their will.

Umpiring the Niners is a big opportunity. He'd be doing somersets, but hoodlums about killed The Judge. Walter doesn't like that his big break comes at The Judge's expense, but he gathers his gear and rushes to the San Francisco depot on Market Street. He catches the midnight sleeper to Santa Cruz to check in on The Judge before going on to the San Joaquin.

Walter never sleeps on trains. The Judge says that trains rock him like a baby, but all Walter ever does on trains is think. Tonight, he thinks back to when they took Moms to the Marine Hospital that Houses Crazy Seamen. He joined the merchant marines for a spell, then panned for gold in California cricks. He enjoys panning, he's cut out for it, but he couldn't eke out a living from cricks that had been panned out for a decade. He promised himself that he wouldn't be late for the next rush, even if the gold were discovered at the North Pole.

Because he was ten years late panning, he potshot quail to eat before he stole laundry off the line. Potshots on the ground are unsporting. "Got to get them to fly," Papa once said. "Though potshots are OK if your family's hungry."

Before Papa left, he taught Walter to obey the law, but he also said that no law is set in stone. That's why Walter stole those clothes. His own were threadbare, they couldn't make the tail of a kite. He didn't want to be arrested for nakedness and that's why he ended up before The Judge. It's why he ended up umpiring and typesetting and why he's on this train in the middle of the night to Santa Cruz.

Walter thinks about other things. He thinks about fishing with Papa. Sometimes Papa pointed out a trout breaking into sunlight, but Walter would glance up too late. When they weren't biting he studied dark clouds of gnats and listened to grasshoppers slap around plant to plant.

"Fishing's about faith," Papa said. Walter barely heard him, he'd abandoned his pole to push ants into antlion pits with a stick. Beetles roamed and spiders spun, the sandy soil was a-crawl. Near the water, he turned over damp rocks in search of pill bugs. Pill bugs live where it's damp, but not where it's real wet, never near a waterfall. He'd put his cheek down on the ground to get an angle. Pill bugs have long antenna. People call them roly-polies, potato bugs, doodle bugs, armadillo bugs. They have a lot of names but they have only one angle, all they see is the damp brown ground. Even when they're rolled up. They can't jump, not even with eight legs. Nose to ground their whole life.

Compared to pill bugs, Walter's a god with unlimited angles, but he still can't see the future. He knows today's destination is the San Joaquin with a brief stop to see his mentor in Santa Cruz, but he doesn't know his destiny. He doesn't know that he will strike out Casey in sixteen hours.

Papa never scolded Walter for abandoning his pole. When Papa hooked something he let Walter land it and gave him credit when Moms fried it up in butter and set it steaming and pink on the breakfast table.

"It's odd that Walter catches all the fish," Moms would say.

"Is it odd, or is it God?" Papa would answer.

"If a grizzly and a wolf fight, which one wins out?" Walter asked.

"The one with the grit," Papa said then reconsidered. "I don't know. The one who does the right thing, fight or flee."

"What's righter, fighting or fleeing?"

"Takes wisdom to know," Papa said. "Oftentimes you just wait and do nothing, sit tight and let God solve things for Himself."

"Why do they call fishing angling? Are pill bugs afraid to die? Ants are. Kick over a hill and see them panic."

Papa never once scolded Walter for his constant questions. "Maybe they dart about joyful to have a hill to rebuild." Papa was seeing it from a different angle. "Who knows the mind of an ant? Don't know my own mind most the time. All I know is it makes no sense to worry about tomorrow. God is already there."

Walter liked being alone with Papa. That's when Papa listened to Walter real close, when Annie Katharine was home with Moms, crying the colic. "Fishing's more about releasing problems than catching trout," Papa said. "It gets me absorbed in something besides myself. When I whistle my line back and forth, I abandon thoughts about yesterday and tomorrow. That's when God lands in my heart as a fly on the mirror of a lake."

"Do trout ever live in ugly places?"

Papa's eyes smiled. "None I know of. No exception to that rule as far as I know."

"Pill bugs live ugly lives under rocks, right next to beautiful Bean Crick."

Papa, like everyone else, wasn't interested in pill bugs. He noticed the sunset. "Red sky at night, sailors delight."

Walter was exhausted from doing nothing and chilled by the sunburn on his face. He took no delight in the red sky, because Papa didn't let him out of the cleaning. With a white lantern at their backs, Papa cut each trout up the belly, pulled out the guts and handed the hollowed-out fish to Walter. Walter ran his tiny thumbnail up slippery spines to clean out the blood lines and they sent it all downstream in the dark to where Bean Crick fed the Zayante, which fed the San Lorenzo and the Bay of Monterey and the Pacific.

Bean Crick waters eventually run right past the Marine Hospital that Houses Crazy Seamen. People call asylums "bughouses," and they mop the bughouse floors with the gutty water that Walter once fished. They mop those floors more often since Nellie Bly exposed Blackwell's Island Insane Asylum in New York. She sneaked in and now they're putting some elbow grease into Moms floors—all because Nellie Bly broke the law a continent away.

Walter once sent Nellie Bly a letter of gratitude. She never wrote back. The Judge said she gets a mountain of mail.

The train to Santa Cruz slows to take a curve. Walter forgets about Nellie Bly's mail. He prays for Moms and The Judge. And, for Papa and Annie Katharine, wherever they may be. Walter tells God he won't believe in Him if The Judge is hurt real bad. He'll be even angrier at Him, but then he wonders how he can be angry at Someone who doesn't exist. Maybe anger is proof that God does exist. God abandoned The Judge just as Papa abandoned Walter. Walter will never abandon someone he cares about. One day, he'll die keeping someone he loves protected and safe.

The train pulls into Santa Cruz in the wee hours. It's dark, the eastern sky will soon be red. Red sky at morning, sailors take warning. It will be almost dark when Casey strikes out. The western sky will be red.

Maybe God looks out for Walter from the bleaching boards. Maybe His presence keeps Walter from surrendering to the forces of melancholia that took hold of Moms. She's in the weeds, and sometimes she is out of sorts, and sometimes she has a circus in her head. Walter inherited Moms weeds, but he didn't inherit whatever made Papa run.

"One who is curious in observing the labor of bees, will often be stung out of curiosity."—Alexander Pope

April 20, 1888, 3:48 in the morning
It's a Friday

CHAPTER FOUR

fifteen hours before the strikeout

S anta Cruz is a ghost town before dawn. Nobody's about, not a gaslight burning. The surf of the Pacific is the only sound once the train pulls out. Walter hikes to the hotel on Beach Hill with a satchel in his hand and a newspaper baton rolled under his arm. The dirt of the deserted street is chewed so soft by yesterday's hooves that Walter feels he is losing progress, as if he's caught in a riptide of earth.

He pauses outside The Judge's door to prepare for the worst. He takes a deep breath of sea air, puts the newspaper in his satchel and enters without knocking. The room is pitch dark and smells of a dogfight—a cocktail of piss and blood and excrement. The Judge's shit stinks.

"How are you?"

"Terrific, Walter, just terrific."

Walter lights the lamp. The Judge is flat in bed and complains of broken ribs, but says he is pleased for the company. He winces and coughs blood into a handkerchief. "My vegetables hurt, except maybe I can't feel them."

There are dark stains on his sheets below the waist. The Judge looks for a place to vomit, but retching is a painful option, and he changes his mind. "I've been through the mill," The Judge says.

"Pardon? You'd be better off in a receiving hospital."

"The only one's in San Francisco. Doc came and went." The Judge talks at the ceiling. Shallow breathing restricts him to few words at a time. "Gave me morphine. Says I'll probably live."

Walter wants to protect The Judge, but all he can do is tidy up. He picks a blue suit off the floor. The jacket buttons are gone, the trousers caked in dry blood about the crotch and cut off by the doctor with a knife. There's a tin plate of fried eggs on the floor that someone left behind, and Walter tries to shovel a cold bite through The Judge's lips of cracked leather. Walter's prepared to do anything to get him better, but he's helpless.

"Time is all there is to do," The Judge says.

"How much time?"

"Now, Walter, no one knows exactly. I'll be on my ass all season. I'm going to quit. It's anybody's guess why I do it. I'm a justice of the peace for chrissakes. Mayor E.B. Pond doesn't go house to house emptying privy vaults, but I go yard to yard to get hollered at and spit at. Now look at me. The shit-house beast caught me."

The shit-house beast is invisible and lurks about the yard. Any umpire who works long enough gets caught one day, the story goes. Umpires believe it to be fact. Walter never did, but he believes it now. He's yet to be caught. Not on a base ball yard, anyway.

"The shit-house beast is vicious," Walter says.

"No shit, Sir Walter."

Walter moves over by the lamp and pulls the minister's cable from his shirt pocket. "From the Northern California Base Ball Association. Arrived yesterday, 4:48 in the afternoon. My first knock ever." Walter's voice turns apologetic. "William Rufus Wheaton gave me your Niners games. One Friday, two on Saturday."

"What's today?"

"Friday. Can't stay, I'll catch the eight o'clock to the San Joaquin unless you need me here."

"Game's at three-thirty," The Judge says. "Good umpires arrive early. You shouldn't've stopped."

Walter's not here for The Judge, not entirely. He's here to say sorries for taking his mentor's games and he's here for a dose of wisdom to get him through the next two days. Walter needs field presence. He needs confidence and he goes fishing for some.

"The minister's cable says you recommend me as an up-and-comer, never a loafer, drunkard, nor asleep at the switch." Walter knows what asleep at the switch means. He knows about Indians and pill bugs, but he knows the most about trains.

"Doesn't mean we should get married," The Judge says.

"The minister tells me to stay out of trouble."

"Good, sound advice."

"You're the game's best, you and Honest John Gaffney. See where it got you."

"It's the second time the shit-house beast caught me. The last time was in Detroit."

"You never told me about Detroit."

The Judge changes the subject. "The Niners games will be lopsided. Nothing you declare will influence the outcome."

"I know…"

"Now, Walter, I told you to quit saying 'I know.'"

"Let me finish," Walter says. "I'm agreeing with you. A monkey can umpire these three. The Oakland Tribunes are deep in the cellar again."

"They're in back of Podunk."

"Huh?"

"Podunk's an awful make-believe club in a backwater make-believe town. The thing is, it won't matter if you declare every banger, whacker and nip in the Oaklands favor."

Walter wonders if there are make-believe girls in the Podunk grandstand. He's squirmy thinking about that, so he thinks about some numbers. He's good with numbers, he calculates that umpires average two hundred eighty balls and strikes, outs and not-outs a game. He tells that to The Judge.

"We get paid for balls and strikes and two or four decisions a game on the sandbags that are close enough for a disinterested eye," The Judge says. "A jackass can do the rest. Why we do it is anybody's guess. I belong in a bughouse. All umpires do, no offense to your mother."

"None taken."

The Judge umpires to stay humble. That's Walter's hypothesis. Everyone kisses his rear when he puts on the black robes. He puts on a blue suit and takes the abuse to put all of those *yes-yer-honors* in perspective.

Walter umpires because it eases his loneliness, which is odd, the more crowded the bleaching boards, the more alone the umpire is. Umpiring's better than seafaring. Better than panning. Better than typesetting. Time slides by on the yard and time's important, or the railroads never would have established time zones.

He remembers an item he typeset a week ago about Casey for the *Chronicle*. He read it upside down and right to left. He started in the middle. "It said Casey's the driven snow," he tells The Judge. "It said that whenever Casey's tempted to swear he says, 'My gracious.'"

The Judge laughs until he about coughs up a lung. He gets tears of pain in his eyes, but it clears the phlegm from his chest.

"Casey's a scofflaw," The Judge says. "Worse than that Bakersfield shortstop who shot someone, or rustled something, and was captured near the White Sands of the New Mexico territory. There were no trees and that gave him a few hours before they found a telegraph pole to stretch his neck from."

Out of the blue, The Judge tells Walter about his beating. Walter knows what out of the blue means. When Papa left it was out of the blue, that's what the neighbors said.

"Santa Cruz catcher Rube Burns had problems with my zone," The Judge says. "Pitchers and catchers can be a pain in the ultimatum." Walter gives him his canteen. The Judge swishes and spits a bloody mouthful.

"Quit with the water, it makes me have to pee," he says, but it seems to be good on his throat. "It started when I called a simple ball."

Umpires prefer declaring strikes. Without strikes, a base ball game would never end. Walter wishes base ball had a clock like trains and football, though he's got nowhere to go after the game is over except back to his boarding house and his globe. He's never declared an undeserved strike just to hurry a Jabbering Seals game along.

"A simple ball," The Judge repeats. "The catcher Rube Burns was a turd. He swiveled his head back at me and said, 'That was a strike.' I told him, 'Yeah, and neither is the next one.' I'm the rankest umpire he's seen."

"We're all ass-shit." That's sarcasm, Walter's learning to use it.

"Players can't tell a good umpire from bad," The Judge says. "My zone's the same for all clubs, consistency is what matters. Late in the game, two out. Runner on third. The batsman hit one off the handle, a nubber to the Santa Cruz first baseman, who charged, picked it up, tagged the runner six feet in front of the bag."

"Inning's over. Easy money," Walter says.

"So I thought. Ball squirted loose, it's on the ground."

"Oh, he dropped it. Not out." Walter tucks his hands into his armpits because he may be wrong.

"That's what I hollered. *Not out.* I changed my declaration when the ball squirted loose."

"Slow down. Read the play. Get it right. That's what you taught me to do."

"No one's going anywhere until we make the call," The Judge says. "The run scored and Santa Cruz coach Ducky Johnson was in my face. He said the batsman took a dirty swipe at the first baseman's hand and knocked the ball loose when he was being tagged. Ducky was hot. He's usually OK, and I suspected that he was telling the truth."

"You're thinking that Ducky Johnson had a better angle?"

"I got that pit in my stomach," The Judge says.

"I hate that pit," Walter says. "It's the worst part of the job, when I'm unsure and the fanatics maybe have reason to holler for once."

Walter's favorite thing about umpiring is when he makes a razor-close declaration that goes against the home club, one that he's certain about. He likes it when the multitude goes red faced from carping. Walter soaks in the roasting and he thinks, *All you sweet folks kicked the shit out of that one.* He doesn't know why, but he savors the vitriol when he knows he's right. But he gets that pit when he thinks he may be wrong. It's nice to know that The Judge gets that pit, too. Makes Walter feel normal.

"With a runner on third, I was trapped at home and my view got impeded," The Judge says. "I didn't see a dirty swipe. Small Tuesday crowd. Maybe three hundred. But they threw a conniption. I saw the ball on the ground. 'How it got there is anybody's guess,' I told Ducky. Ducky hollered, 'You're the only one guessing.'"

"Can't declare outs we don't see," Walter says.

"Ducky said, 'Make it right.' I told him that I work hard to get all my decisions right and maybe that wasn't my best one ever. I let him go on. But when it went on too long, I told him, 'OK Ducky, you think I kicked it. I'd let your fanatics decide but they no longer allow grandstand voting. Just like they forbid fielders plugging runners for outs. The game's moved on and so, Ducky, must we.'"

"They need two umpires out there," Walter says. "Two would see more angles. Two would've seen how that ball got to the ground."

"There's been a drumbeat for two." The Judge says. "One for balls and strikes and all points near home. Skipped bases are an epidemic."

"Some day we'll work together," Walter says. He'd like that, but The Judge says he's finished umpiring. His eyes were always squinty from years of city soot and yard sun, but now his left is swollen shut. Walter peers into the slit to see if The Judge might have lost an eye. All he sees is a red spot that matches the one in the egg yolk on the floor.

"You may at last be half blind like the fanatics say," Walter says.

"That's funny," The Judge says. "I'd laugh, but I have the gronk."

"The gronk?"

"When your face feels so much like your asshole your bowels don't know which way to move."

Walter figures it's a joke and works up a laugh. "Some day we'll work together," he says again, but The Judge shakes his head no and gets back to his story.

"Ducky retreated to his bench but he had some words for his catcher Rube Burns on his way. The next pitch was down the middle, chest high. Burns made no attempt to get a hand on it. The pitch cracked my collar bone."

"The catcher made no stab at the leather whatsoever?"

"I was locked in, ball went into my collar untouched. Dropped like a dove taken by shotgun. I heard the grandstand gasp. First the sick thud and crack, then gasps of surprise, three hundred at once."

"Let me guess." Walter closes his eyes and imagines the crowd. "The gasps were sincere for a second. Then they changed to delight that you got what was coming."

"That's right, Walter, a whole second of sympathy. My pain and their pleasure made me mad as a hornet. Burns turned and flashed a grin. I was dying."

"And the catcher was a-grinning?" Walter says. "They ought to string them up. Rube Burns and Ducky Johnson both. String them up next to that Bakersfield guy."

"I doubt if even a two-bit fine will come of it. They say they want base ball to be family entertainment, they want spectators who enjoy a game played scientifically, but fines are forgiven or forgotten or paid in full by the clubs. Battered umpires are good for the gate."

"One sick thud's as good as three bell ringings. They don't care, they think we're all cheats like Dick Higham."

"You don't know for sure if Dick Higham cheated," The Judge says.

Walter shrugs. "It's a stunner that they don't set up a turnstile and charge four bits to watch you heave blood here on Beach Hill."

The Judge got back to his story. "I tucked my hands into my armpits and I gave the fanatics the hidden bird. Then I tossed the both of them. Ducky left in peace, but the catcher grabbed me by my mask and pushed me backward. He took his mask off and clocked me with it square. I got on my feet in time to find myself circled by hoodlums. A dozen or more. They said I'm to blame because I missed the dirty swipe. One got in my face, said he's close kin to Rube Burns and Rube Burns built his catcher's legs unloading merchandise at his seed and feed and Rube Burns harms no umpire unless he deserves it plainly."

"I know what happened next just by looking at you."

"One face said I'm a lollygagger. I said a few words back, terrible words that might get me prosecuted by the postmaster if I put them in a letter. Another face said I'm going to hell for words like those and for being in collaboration with the gambling society. That made me crazy. I was boiling mad when I felt a couple of rights to my ear from somewhere. My blindside. I was back on the ground and the mob kicked me in the head. I covered up and they switched to my prick."

"Did you get a look at them?"

"Now, Walter, would you get a look if it was *your* prick? They wore tall hats and bright vests. I remember this pretty woman. She was back a few steps spurring them on. Hers is the only face I remember. She's forever ruined pretty faces for me. The cops came along."

"Someone decent enough to get the law?"

"The gendarmes carried me to this hotel as the horde threw coal at us from a trestle. I'm sure the Santa Cruz club made sure my beating got in every newspaper around. The whole town will be at the next game hoping for a repeat. I'm glad you're not working that game. Check my pockets. I'm owed seven dollars."

Walter picks trousers off the chair. "No pockets left. I guess they trimmed you. All I find is this bloody booklet of rules."

The Judge says he's too crippled to care about the money. Exhaustion takes a grip and he sleeps. Walter leafs through the booklet, but he didn't sleep on the train, and his eyes grow heavy too. He closes them and listens to the rattle of The Judge's morphine snoring.

Walter awakens after a doze. The risen sun pours through the window. He reconsiders the shit-house beast. He's good at dodging it. If he gets nose-to-nose with a coacher or player, he takes a step back to make it clear who's the aggressor. If dirt is kicked at his feet, he backs into the grass. If some coacher or player hollers longer than is merited, he nods and pretends that they have a valid point of view. Walter says to them, "I hear what you're saying," which is his code for "You're effing wrong."

Walter gets polite when others get rude and he gives them the last word no matter how stupid that word is. It keeps things from going round the bend. The more demented the coachers get, the cooler he gets. He's too small for fistfights. He's too slow to run. Someone has to stick around to protect the game, and that's Walter.

The Judge thinks he taught Walter everything, but Walter had thick skin long before they met in the courtroom. After Papa left, the more anger

Walter allowed himself to feel, the more he boiled over. Moms says anger is the devil's cocaine. She's right, Walter was apoplectic the day he broke his hand against a tree. He thought he could knock down a redwood with his fist. Right then, he stopped getting angry altogether. His hand still hurts, it helps to squeeze something, loosens it up. Reminds him not to get angry.

The Judge wakes up recoiling, as if he is reliving boots to the groin. He hollers "Screw Detroit!" then calms down. "Dammit, Walter, are you still here? I thought you had someplace to be."

"Sun's up. Game starts in nine hours, precisely. You need something before I go? Water?"

"That'll make me pee." The Judge's voice is stronger from the sleep. "I want to give you some advice. I want you to listen. This is the Northern California Association, better base ball than you've seen. Two or three outfits are as good as any team back east."

"The Niners are one of them, but a quilting club can drub the Oakland Tribunes. We talked about it. They haven't a single crack player."

"Mouse Mathews."

Walter knows the name from typesetting. Two years ago, Bobby Mouse Mathews was a topnotch pitcher with the Philadelphia Athletics, one of those rare guys who transitioned from underarm to an unrestricted overhand delivery. He was the first to throw a curve and a spitter, an upshoot and a slow rise. He's 5-foot-5, he'll be the shortest hero alive if he can beat Pud Galvin of the Pittsburgh Alleghenys to become the first pitcher with three hundred career wins. Mathews' arm went flimsy a year ago in an April snowball fight and he's gasping to get those four wins he needs. He signed with the Niners last year, pitched two losses before they let him go. He spent eleven months learning to throw with his left.

"Pitchers can't switch arms like crop rotation," Walter says. "The Niners will drub the Oaklands for sure." He pulls the *Chronicle* from his satchel. It's still rolled in a baton and he flattens it out on The Judge's bed. "I found this on the train floor. Says Mouse Mathews has run out of arms and continent, says he's lame. He hasn't a five-in-a-hundred chance of beating the Niners, that's the feeling amongst the gambling society."

"The Niners can't lose," The Judge says. "Except this is base ball. The Oaklands have Old Reliable Jake. His legs are buckshot, he's moved over to first base, but he can still hit. The Oaklands signed some hot-stuff catcher. Nobody knows much about him, he never gets in the newspapers talking Spanish."

"They're thin at the bottom of their order," Walter says. "They bat T.J. McAloon with a withered arm."

"You'll skate, but if Mouse pitches around Casey, keeps the score low…" He coughs and coughs. "I think I've failed you, I haven't prepared you for the unexpected."

"The unexpected's a struggle for me. Worse than field presence."

"Just be ready for a long, hot afternoon," The Judge says.

Walter holds up the dusty newspaper. "See this headline?"

"Hell no, Walter, I'm flat on my back."

Walter reads it aloud.

IS CASEY THE BEST PLAYER EVER?

Better than Cap Anson?
Bring us your votes

The Niners hired Cap Anson as coacher when he quit playing in Chicago two seasons ago. Anson won the flag for the Niners in eighty-seven and the *Chronicle* says he may be both the greatest player and the greatest ever to skipper the game. His pitcher covers the bag when a grounder pulls the first baseman to his right. He employs many new ideas like that. Anson says different positions require men of different temperaments, that a catcher is a man of bravado and wit. An anxious man is best at third base where hit balls arrive before nervous tendencies interfere.

"I wonder what position I'd be best at," Walter says. Never the outfield, not with his gait, or pitcher with his sore hand. He's too short for first base. "Cap Anson's a base ball genius. His brain's worth a dozen wins a season. He wants to put large numbers on jockey silks to let fanatics in distant bleaching boards identify one mustachioed player from another. His idea is to number players in the order that they bat, Casey would be No. 3, Jackleg Preacher No. 4."

"Anson's as much of a racialist as he is a genius," The Judge says. "He'd rather have a sharp stick in the eye than let a Negro play. When he was with the Chicagos he muffed easy plays at first base to lose games for his Negro pitcher. Anson partly owns the Chicago club now and he was behind the gentlemen's agreement to leave coloreds unsigned in the big leagues."

"Californians aren't racialists," Walter says. "They dislike the Chinese is all."

"Anson wouldn't accept the Niners job until the Northern California Base Ball Association left coloreds unsigned and restricted colored fanatics to their own section in the bleaching boards."

Walter reads the newspaper headline to The Judge again, and then asks, "Do you think Cap Anson was a better player than Casey?"

"Batsmen are born, not made, and these two are batsmen from the ground up. I've never worked behind Casey, but blind veterans go to games to listen to him hit. Anson's smarter, uses more head work. He's got pace, he was the first man to circle the sandbags in fourteen seconds, but he retired unloved."

"Everyone loves Casey," Walter says.

"May the record reflect, they adore him. One Californian will trample up the back of another for a chance to die for Casey. He'll get elected best player ever in the *Chronicle*. Casey'd get elected governor if he threw in his hat."

"He wears a cap, not a hat."

"The Sacramento government gave him a hundred country acres on the outskirts of Golden Gate Park and built him his winter mansion. It comes with a four-acre garden, trees of pomegranate, pear, fig and a Chinaman to take care of it."

"I know," Walter says. "I read it typesetting."

"Even in this sour economy, no taxpayer resents Casey's free acreage as long as it keeps him from jumping east. They don't care a lick."

The Judge tries to sit up to tell Walter something. He can't, but he pulls Walter's sore hand to his whiskered cheek. "Get your mind focused," he says. "The San Joaquin isn't San Francisco with its opera houses and roller rinks. Base ball is all there is, base ball and rabbit scourges. They call it Mudville as a joke. It never rains, although their long drought ended this winter."

"You're telling me to stay out of trouble. Just like Minister Wheaton did in his telegram."

The Judge winces and collapses flat to his back. "I'm telling you that feelings among the partisans run high. The Niners believe God sits in their grandstand and Satan wears a blue suit. The cranks are unhappy with anything short of a dynasty. The Niners have won nineteen straight going back to last season when they captured the flag. Two more and they'll tie the record, a sweep of these three gives it to them outright. They'll see you in hell if they lose."

"I'll stay out of trouble, any idiot could."

"Watch out for Anson, he's full of trickery."

"I know," Walter says.

The Judge winces. "When he played for the Chicagos, he often wagered on them to win. Once, when they fell behind in the late innings, he got into an argument with the umpire, told his clubmates to stomp away like brats. The game was declared unfinished, washing all bets."

"Anson's a pain in the ultimatum," Walter says, parroting The Judge.

"When the Chicagos were in Troy one time, he came to my plate conference with his fly undone. I let him know, a gesture of goodwill to spare him embarrassment. He stared me in the eye and said, 'Only a cocksucker would notice.'"

"Did you toss him?"

"You don't toss Anson. You don't toss Casey or Anson at the Home of the Mudville Niners unless you want to wake up dead."

"You don't wake up if you're dead."

"Now, Walter, I did this morning."

Walter rises to his feet; he has a train to catch. "Thanks for the good advice. This is a big break. Never wanted it like this, hope I'm up to it."

"I wanted to see Casey swing from the heels. He never gives umpires shit, that's one thing."

"Never has reason. Always circles those sandbags."

A train whistles. "Get going. You're a bucket-assed kid with a fresh, faint mustache, but you'll do OK. Take that booklet of Northern California rules with you for the train. Rules differ from association to association. Last year the newspapers complained about all the one-to-nil games, said pitchers had the upper hand. They put a thumb on the scale in eighty-seven, gave batsmen a fourth strike, but they're back to three."

"How many balls?"

"Five, down from seven two years ago. They always screw with the rules. They ought to keep them just like the Knickerbocker Club wrote them down."

"I hate change."

"I know," The Judge says.

"People who know everything can't be taught anything," Walter says.

"Some joke." The Judge has more advice, he hurries to get it out. "Cap Anson will test you. On close declarations, he lets out a screech like a rabbit dying. Don't let the noise surprise you. The first time a banger goes against him you'll hear the screech. You'll feel the pressure in your sphincter."

"Not today I won't. They'll be up a dozen runs by the third inning."
Walter moves toward the door. "Got to go. Anything else to know?"

The Judge groans. "You're not ready."

"I know."

"Should've sentenced you to picking up horse manure." His voice is
weak, barely audible, he needs more sleep.

Walter wants to say, "I know," but he gives The Judge the last word
and lets him nod off.

"Baseball is like church. Many attend, few understand."—Leo Durocher

April 20, 1888, 2:28 in the afternoon
It's a Friday

CHAPTER FIVE

four hours, twenty-two minutes before the strikeout

Nellie Bly has never witnessed a base ball match, although she's often invited by suitors in New York. She has no earthly desire to attend this one in the arid air of the San Joaquin, but stardom comes with a price. She has a public to attend to, a book to sell, and she feels obligated to appear wherever an overflow crowd awaits. On a whim, she brings along a pair of eyeglasses in case she wants to see the finer points of the game, though she can't imagine why.

An afternoon of sunshine seems less terrible when she steps through the wooden turnstile into the largest venue imaginable. There's a two-decker grandstand. The sod is mowed short and groomed like the felt of a giant billiards table in *Gulliver's Travels*. She is so in awe of the vast, blurry expanse of green that she almost forgets to lift her petticoats for the climb to her seat.

A banner high overhead cries **HOME OF THE MUDVILLE NINERS**, so large she can easily read it without her glasses, but she puts them on. The venue seems out of place in the San Joaquin, a land of farmers where work comes before play. Barely fifteen thousand live within twenty miles, but a sizable portion abandoned their Friday chores and dipped into rainy-day jars. They've made their ways by foot, saddle or bicycle, by hook or by crook, to form a sea of black bowler hats. Sprinkled in are ladies in hats of feathers. They sit in the grandstand shade, as does she, where there isn't enough breeze for feathers to quiver.

Farmers are in the bleaching-board sun, many with young sons. In the shade, the ladies are outnumbered by gentlemen three dozen to one. That is one reason she was asked to attend, to make base ball respectable to the finer half. Base ball magnates imagine the future populated with young ladies.

She removes her glasses. The worst part of the afternoon is to be her escort. He is some eligible muckety-muck, the son of the California governor or a senator. He's the most handsome man in the lower grandstand. He seems to think so anyway. He is convinced that he is an expert on everything, especially base ball, and his calling is to use his collegiate oratory to explain the inane game to her. Worst of all, his name is Kip. She forgets his last name to keep him humble.

Nellie Bly loathes having to take the arm of any escort. She is modern. She would proudly step through the turnstiles independent, but times aren't changing fast enough. Ladies have long attended amateur contests played by college men but it would be a scandal to watch Irish ruffians spit and scratch and play for money without a male companion along.

She appreciates athletes. She fancied herself a tomboy as a child. She was a better equestrian than any Cochran Mills boy. The Home of the Mudville Niners would be heaven for a full-out run on horseback. She longs to ride astride on this pasture of professional perspiration. She craves the grassy land beneath her horse's feet, not splinters beneath her derrière. The grandstand seats are as hard as a virgin saddle. Thank God and His stars for petticoats.

No one recognizes her. They won't until she's been introduced. They only know that she is important because Kip's her escort. He insisted on arriving an hour early to show her off. Promptness is not a virtue in her eyes, and she's surprised to see people already packed in tight with moods as sunny as the day.

"The Niners haven't lost since last September," Kip says to sound smart. "Everything's going this valley's way. Eleven inches of rain have fallen the last six months and the San Joaquin River runs swollen. Mudville may at long last live up to its name. The first cherries will be ripe a week early."

He speaks as if she were a city girl. Had he done his homework, he'd know that she was reared among plain Pennsylvania people in a country town. Her daddy was a man more athletic than Kip, but Michael Cochran never would have taken base ball seriously.

"The big league season opens today back east, but California base ball is two weeks old."

Nellie Bly puts on her eyeglasses. They make her hot and she fans herself. "It's stuffy for April. Why is that little man wearing a winter jacket?"

Kip laughs. "There are no little men down there, Miss Bly."

She points. "Him. The one in the rumpled blue suit."

"Oh, he's no man. He's the umpire. Never seen a happy one. You do indeed have the observation skills of a correspondent. No one notices the umpire before a game. Girls swoon for the players."

"I prefer books to biceps. Why do they waste this much farm acreage? Are all base ball yards this large?"

"This one's modern. They could stage Buffalo Bill's Wild West show entirely in foul ground. Annie Oakley's the most famous girl in the world, but you're a close second, Miss Bly."

Stupid man, he doesn't even know he blabbered an insult. "Kip, is this match *almost* ready to begin?"

He doesn't get rattled when she uses his first name to put him in his place. He just keeps talking. "They brought in an acoustics expert from the Royal Society to make the fanatics and their cow bells all the louder."

"Cow bells?"

"The base ball writers say that you ladies don't belong at the yard. We Republicans believe that's hogwash."

"Look, Kip, he's already drinking from his canteen."

"Who?"

"The little man."

"Girls are an umpire's best friend," Kip says. "A female presence improves the character of the men, tamps down vulgarity."

"Men care too much about scoring points and winning outcomes. I daresay, such arousal should be found only in religion, or in our nation." She removes her glasses and peers into Kip's eyes. "Or, in the right woman."

"Forget the umpire, Miss...buh...lie," he says. She enjoys his stammer. "Ignore him, Miss Bly, at least until he messes up. That will be soon enough. Just wait until Casey comes out of the clubhouse. You'll hear this place roar like a circus lion. He's a man's man. You'll hear arousal in the voices of the ladies."

"Why are those seats empty?" She points to the blurry bleaching boards in the distance.

"The Negro section. They stayed home. They like Casey, but they don't like Cap Anson."

"Cap who?"

"Captain A.C. Anson. That's him down there in coat and tie. The man in charge of the Niners club. Like Joseph Pulitzer's in charge of you and *The New York World.*"

Another insult. No man is in charge of her. And the nerve, comparing base ball to the nation's most powerful newspaper. The readers of one of her columns would fill these seats fifty times over.

She pays more attention to the umpire because Kip is against it. She puts on her glasses to watch him perform yeoman service, going through a certain ritual. He paces to the outfield fence with an unusual stride, like a horse with the tickle of a thorn in its hoof. She has yet to get a good look at his face.

"Four hundred thirty-two feet to dead center," Kip says, as if the number has mythological meaning.

Beyond the fence is the War Monument surrounded by azaleas in bloom. The sod no longer resembles felt. Her eyeglasses turn it thick and ankle deep and it appears as if the umpire is stepping uphill, though the resplendent pasture remains as level as a billiard table. Billiards is another game women have recently begun to watch men play. These are upending times. Smoke and slang, no thank you.

"They even have a kid to write the score on a blackboard," Kips says. "In California, we think of everything."

"What's this chicken netting for?" Nellie Bly says. "It interferes with my view."

"The backstop. We've thought to protect ladies from scorching foul balls. We have ideal seats, no pillars." Kip forces her attention to the brown dirt. "That's the diamond," he says.

"The blandest part? Why name it the diamond?"

"Home plate is marble from Italy."

"It reflects the sun into my eyes." She removes her glasses.

Kip starts to explain the purpose of the three sandbags. Thank the Lord, a gentleman with a megaphone interrupts to introduce someone named Clarence. Three cheers erupt for a boy leading the Niners onto the pasture. She puts on her glasses. He must be about twelve, less than five feet tall, black as a seven-dollar ton of coal and dressed in a suit with brass buttons. He gives the audience quite an exhibition of dancing and feats of baton tossing.

"Mascots entertain fanatics between innings, divert attention from home-team errors, spur the crowd on during rallies, and taunt opponents.

They're kept for as long as they bring luck and sacked amidst losing streaks. Clarence has California's safest job."

Errors, rallies, streaks and endings. Nellie Bly ignores half of Kip's words. "Who's the gentleman with the megaphone?"

"The tally-keeper. He's been instructed to introduce you. Be ready to wave."

"I do not need to be told when to wave, Kip."

Behind Clarence marches a brass band and behind the music is a god of a man with a shock of red hair. He has to be Casey. Behind him are eleven more ball players, general roustabouts, the kind who deflower factory girls in every town. At least, that's what Nellie Bly imagines. They are as opportunistic as the doctors in Blackwell's Asylum. They doff their caps to the slides of trombones and the percussion of applause. Their every sin forgiven because they excel in base ball matches.

The game is scheduled for three-thirty, but when the band finishes "When Johnny Comes Marching Home," the tally-keeper hollers through the megaphone that the Oakland train is running late and the game won't start until four-thirty.

That spoils what's left of Nellie Bly's mood. Time is unimportant to her, she's dreadful at newspaper deadlines. But she has a suspicion that the game will never end once it starts. She removes her glasses and fastens boredom to her face.

"We can slip away as soon as the Niners put things out of reach," Kip says. "We'll get out ahead of the traffic."

"If there is no risk in the outcome, why then are all these people here?"

"This is a picnic more than a game," Kip says.

"What on earth will we do until play starts?"

"Watch the Niners fungo," he says. "See, they catch whatever comes on the fly or on the bound. Admire their new Spalding & Brothers uniforms?"

She puts on her glasses. White knickers, *MUD VILLE NINERS* hand-stitched across jockey silks of goldenrod, polka-dot neckties to match polka-dot stockings. "It is a bit over the top," Nellie Bly says.

"Like something out of the Beer and Whisky League," Kip says. "Don't worry, Miss Bly. They don't serve spirits here, they're prohibitionists in the San Joaquin."

"I know men. They have smuggled in their own flasks."

"No Sabbath ball, they'll play two tomorrow on Saturday to keep Sunday holy."

"Who sits through two?" Nellie Bly says.

"Girls haven't the stamina." Kip marches on through her expression of annoyance. "Last season the Niners wore different color uniforms for each position. Al Spalding's a friend of my father's. Spalding can sell anything to anyone."

Nellie Bly is interested in business, but she doesn't respond to remain feminine. She decides to make the best of things and puts a smile back on her face. "Look, they have already stopped playing their fungus." The players stand about in threes and fours. "They have nothing left to do."

The tally-keeper introduces an old sergeant in the grandstand who was shot four times in 1863, but never dropped the Confederate flag.

"Californians supported the Union, but these San Joaquin folks were Confederates—Democrats just like Joseph Pulitzer and your newspaper." She detects a tone of superiority in Kip's voice. "We Republicans, we objected to Cap Anson's ban on Negroes in Chicago. Now he's importing racialism to these parts of California."

Nellie Bly would side with Kip's sentiment, if only his words were coming out of any other mouth. "Look," she says. "Casey's stepping across the dirt."

"The diamond."

The sun strays in and out of white clouds and flashes off his steel-plated athletic shoes. They've been polished black as Clarence, probably by Clarence himself. They are size twelve or thirteen, but they kick up less dust than the skirt of a strolling lady.

"Casey's a grandstander," Kip says.

"He grins at the ladies. Have they no pride? Why do they wave handkerchiefs at him?"

"Look, he's smiling straight up at you. Someone must've pointed out where we're sitting."

Kip waves both hands at Casey like a child, but Nellie Bly examines her nails. She has scruples and deportment. She's dressed in white, a hat with white feathers, and he stares as if she were cat's milk and wants to lap her up. He at last gives up on her and waves to other ladies who wave back. They are attractive for farm women, few are frumps and schoolmarms. They have faces of virtue—except when they're swooning for Casey.

Near Casey is the umpire, and she would have at last gotten a good look at his face had she not been defending against Casey's leers. All she notices is that the umpire has a wisp of a mustache that can't compete with the coarse whiskers of the other players. He stares at her with an odd expression of longing, as if she were an oil painting, not flesh and blood.

He turns his face the instant he sees her looking back and performs another duty. He may be handsome, but she's unsure, she barely got a glimpse. He's a head shorter than Casey and content to hide in Casey's red-headed radiance.

"I was invited to Casey's mansion once," Kip the name-dropper says. "He lives alone on the edge of Golden Gate Park. It was cold and smoke was rising from three chimneys. It got late, the streetcar closed, and I was invited to spend the night. In the early morning, I saw a girl, not quite a woman, in evening attire come out of Casey's bedroom. No one showed her to the door except a sheepdog. She left without a coat in the direction of the McAllister and Haight Street lines."

"Surely his niece."

Kip laughs. "She did have reddish hair."

"Casey's hair looks like a pelt and covers half of his forehead."

"You don't find him handsome? Other girls do. There's a lot to admire. He hit like a grown man before he was twelve."

"So fascinating." She prays that base ball will be less boring than talk of it.

"Every big league club back east wants Casey, they beg him to come play, but he's loyal. The papers say he's the driven snow."

"California Republican papers, no doubt. He's skipped a haircut or two. He must have fair Irish skin, but he's forever in the sun. It is not yet May and he has a tan the shade of an old bridle."

"Girls fret about freckles," Kip says. "My advice is to never let faces fool you."

"Thank you, Kip," Nellie Bly says. "His face does not fool me. Casey's the only clean-shaven player out there."

Atop Casey's shock of curly red is his cap in a balance. She refuses to gawk at him like a simpleton and finds the umpire again. His back is to the grandstand; he goes about his duties in an official way, tries to look busy while waiting for the tardy Oakland boys. She never longed more for a train to arrive.

The crowd gives Clarence three more cheers as he climbs atop a pole, opens an umbrella, and jumps thirty feet to earth. Like Barnum & Bailey. He rolls three times until the umbrella is bent and ruined but the Negro child is unharmed as if his upper and lower body were made of clay from the Kiski riverbed back home.

The players stage a long-ball throwing contest from home plate. Nellie Bly finds it to be entertaining. The rules are clear and Jackleg Preacher wins at 125 yards, 11 inches. Casey plays no part, but once the contest ends, he heaves one from first base an impossible distance across the diamond and in the direction of a fancy man who is parking his rig outside the yard.

Sitting next to the man in the rig is a small dog with curly, white hair and Casey's thrown ball hits the beast in the ear. The dog has time for a yip and a fall to the ground before it is run over beneath the rig's wheels. The fancy man leaps to the dirt to embrace the beast. She catches her breath and the crowd murmurs, but Casey restores the picnic mood with a doff of his cap. Photographers beg him to freeze in his throwing motion to preserve the moment. The flashes hurt her eyes.

"That's a thing you won't see twice in a lifetime." Kip points to the flap of the pennant. "He threw that against the breeze."

More people stream in through the turnstile as a distant fanatic plays "Turkey in the Straw" on a squeezebox. The tally-keeper announces Mayor Lodowick U. Shippee is in attendance. The mayor is four rows down, directly behind the marble plate and chicken netting. Kip pouts that the mayor has better seats. Two other functionaries take bows. They are saving her introduction—the best for last. She removes her glasses in preparation.

The blurry-blue umpire seems to have a nervous urge to keep moving. She puts her glasses on, hoping at last for a better look. She has no idea why. Probably because everyone else ignores him. With his wire mask under his arm, he paces off the distance from the plate to something her escort calls the *pitching box*. The front line of the pitching box is sixteen strides from the plate, the back line two strides deeper.

Nellie Bly is the only one watching, all other eyes follow Casey across the way where base ball writers trail him a polite distance like quail chicks. He steps into the player's outhouse. The yard goes boneyard quiet to hear his water or worse. The writers crane their necks as if they long to see through the slit of moon on the wooden door. Casey exits after a minute and roars erupt. As if being employed in the labors of the toilet is a heroic feat only Casey performs.

When the roars die, the tally-keeper introduces her. She, too, is staring at Casey's outhouse exit, and the announcement of her name catches her completely off guard. She almost loses the gum she has forgotten beneath her tongue. She is given no chance to pinch her cheeks to give them color. She is given no chance to remove her glasses. She stands and smiles and waves bespectacled. The audience erupts. Her heart swells to be reminded that her name is known to distant cherry orchards.

She remains standing, and the crowd applauds on and on until Casey appears to become envious. He advances to the plate and blows a kiss through the chicken netting. The crowd yearns for her to return the favor but she disappoints them. She sits down; it's an awkward circumstance until the tally-keeper saves the day.

"The train has arrived and the Oakland outfit will be here soon," shouts his voice through the megaphone.

More cheers and applause. The tally-keeper hollers that every seat is sold, even though there remain stretches of empty bleaching boards in the Negro section.

"Positively, no more money will be taken today," he shouts, "but there will be two more games tomorrow at one o'clock." Jeers erupt from the long line outside the turnstile. Casey appropriates the megaphone from the tally-keeper.

"C'mon in. All comers. You can stand on the Negro boards if you don't want to sit on them." His minions pore in. Men and sons annex the seats. It takes some time. With megaphone in hand, Casey stages a mock newspaper interview of himself.

"Mighty Casey, how do you stay in such athletic shape?" he says in a town-crier holler from the first-base side of the plate. He steps to the third-base side, turns and hollers through the megaphone, "I play billiards."

Base ball writers scribble away. Casey steps back to the first-base side. His spikes flash like a windmill at sunrise. "How do you know when a pitch is a strike?" He steps back across. "I don't swing at strikes, I swing at balls that look big. I swing to win the smiles of the bonny lasses."

He steps again to the laughter and the waves of lace handkerchiefs. "Casey, what's the hardest part about base ball?" He steps amidst chuckles. "They throw you a round ball and give you a round bat and tell you to hit it square. Same ole, same ole. I can hear the breeze on the seams, I can hear the viz."

He turns and lowers his voice. "What does viz sound like?"

"Like *viz*, dummy, quiet like the footfall of a pussycat."

"Mighty Casey, what's the secret of the long ball?"

He strokes his clean-shaven chin and pauses in thought at his own question. He draws a pocket watch from his knickers to create suspense. He lowers the megaphone and speaks softly so that only the base ball writers can hear. Nellie Bly knows he is saying something off-color, she sees the imp in his eyes. And indeed, the reporters snigger and stop their scribbles.

The grandstand delights in Casey's mime, the ladies smile dumb and wave their lace.

"He's a skunk," Nellie Bly says to Kip.

"I've yet read a word in *Spalding's Base Ball Guide* about Casey being anything but a saint."

"I know the character of men better than *Spalding's Base Ball Guide*," she says, and Kip laughs like she's told a joke, as if he's already forgotten the shame-faced girl who exited Casey's mansion in evening wear with Casey's dog panting. There must be something about base ball prowess that induces amnesia among its partisans.

Boos, hisses and groans erupt from the crowd and Nellie Bly wonders if the breeze and modern acoustics have lifted Casey's jockstrap lexicon into the throng, but then she sees the Oakland Tribunes stepping off a horsecar. Boos grow louder as ten men walk onto the yard in their road grays of twilled flannel. In contrast to the goldenrod jockey silks, the Oaklands' tatters make them appear as if they reside in a rescue mission. The Niners have dozens of bats, but a total of three rest upon Oakland shoulders.

Eight of the ten Oaklands are shorter than the shortest Niner. One is shorter than the umpire. "That's Mouse Mathews," Kip says. "The biggest one's Old Reliable Jake and that tall, thin, dark one has to be the Mexican backstop no one knows a thing about."

"I thought this chicken netting was the backstop."

"Catchers are backstops, too," the know-it-all says.

The Mexican stands out like old copper among the sunburnt Irish. He sits on the pasture grass and pulls from a gunny sack a pair of shoddy spikes. The tally-keeper hollers that it is ten-cent Boy's Day and that the same train has carried two hundred San Francisco orphans to the game.

"Casey paid their fares," the tally-keeper announces to cheers.

The sad boys have dirt-stained faces and no place to sit. Some find their ways up faraway poles to get a vantage over the outfield fence, or they sit in trees like August peaches until branches sag to the ground. The place is to the gills.

"Andrew Carnegie wouldn't get in, for all his millions," Kip says.

Some boys shinny up the War Monument beyond the fence in dead center, and a gray-haired veteran a few seats away shakes his one fist and curses the disrespect. His empty sleeve causes Nellie Bly to recall her stepfather. She hates the memory of Jack Ford and his footless limp.

The umpire has no limp, but he does have that odd stride. He seems oblivious to life's distractions and Cap Anson startles him from behind.

The Niners boss smirks, the ambush seems to have been premeditated. The umpire's back is to the grandstand. Nellie Bly still craves a good, long look at his face. Cap Anson's blue eyes are set deep. A handle-bar mustache is waxed to a pointed curl below a nose too large for the face. His lips belong on a fish. He shakes the umpire's hand like he is pumping well water, as if he's running for office.

The umpire isn't a glad-hander and the two stand silent until Cap Anson barks at his mascot. "Clarence, go find out who's running the Oaklands and tell him to join us at the plate sometime today."

"Yes sah, Cap'n."

Old Reliable Jake meanders over. "The big man from Oakland has shovels for hands," she says.

"That's why he's first baseman," Kip says. "He's forty-two. Maybe forty-three. He's also the coach, the seventh coach in two years, the Oaklands are in the cellar again."

The umpire digs a shiny coin from his pocket but he doesn't flip it. The umpire, Cap Anson, and Old Reliable Jake talk some more. Then fisticuffs almost break out between Cap Anson and Old Reliable Jake. The umpire steps between the coaches, though the two are much taller. Old Jake has a ruddy complexion. His neck turns red and his acne scars turn redder. Cap Anson gives him a long stare.

"Do baseballers customarily greet each other with such brotherhood?"

"I've never seen such evil before the first pitch," Kip says. "Jake's ready to take a swipe. He won't though. Cap Anson's an all-timer, he was part of Chicago's Stone Wall infield, earned a record salary."

"Everything you say starts with base ball and circles back to money. Is that all West Coast men think about?"

"On the contrary. Casey prefers a modest salary, says it keeps him close to the people, but he gets a quarter of the gate."

"Oh. That is why he welcomed those latecomers to stand in the Negro section."

"Clubs back east don't cotton to Casey's portion, sets a dangerous precedent. Al Spalding made it big in business, but Casey is the first player to get wealthy off the game itself. Casey's rich, soon to be stinking rich, but Cap Anson takes pleasure in being the smartest base-ball man on the planet."

"Smarter than you, Kip?"

The umpire borrows the tally-keeper's megaphone and hollers the official start time is four fifty-seven. "Precisely." He is at last facing Nellie

Bly long enough for her to get a good look, but the megaphone hides his face. He hollers that the hometown Niners elect to bat first and the crowd grumbles as if that's unexpected. The umpire says the Oakland battery is Mouse Mathews and Grasshopper Nova.

Eight Oaklands run out onto the dirt, three of them continue on for a distance into the pasture. The tall, skinny Grasshopper Nova squats behind the marble and catches balls barehanded from the figurine pitcher.

"The backstop's hands look like gnarled driftwood," Nellie Bly says.

"Ball players are a gritty bunch. Players back east are experimenting with buckskin gloves, but Californians will forever play bare-fisted. You've probably noticed that California men aren't as dainty as New Yorkers."

"I have noticed quite a lot."

"Mouse Mathews doesn't throw hard like he once did. He's a southpaw now, the dummy hurt his right arm throwing snowballs in Baltimore."

Clarence brings around the house broom and sweeps the marble like it's a kitchen floor. The Niners truly do think of everything. The umpire turns his cap backward and puts on his wire mask. The Mexican does the same. A Niner player named Barrows comes to the fresh-swept marble with a bat over his shoulder like a rifle and the umpire points at the pitcher and says, "Play ball."

It's all very serious for an event that Kip describes as a picnic. She's seen enough. She removes her glasses, praying for the Friday afternoon to pass in a bleary blur.

"When you come to a fork in the road, take it."—Yogi Berra

May 1, 1888, 11:37 in the morning
It's a Tuesday

CHAPTER SIX

ten days, seventeen hours after the strikeout

The second knock ever at Walter Brewster's boarding-house door is a fist that vibrates the moose antlers. Walter ignores it, he gives the visitor a chance to change his mind. When the knock's repeated, he hollers for patience.

"Hold your horses!"

He snatches his trousers from a hook. The base ball is still in his sore hand after endless sleep. He shoves it into a pocket and throws open his life. He's expecting nighttime, but a blush of bright hits him, warm for a foggy day. He's lost track of time, something he never does. He's been asleep for hours and hours, maybe days and days.

"You're the umpire. Been looking for you all over town, it's like you don't exist."

"Sure, I exist," Walter says. His eyes adapt to the elephant-gray day. He sees a white shirt, black tie, a trimmed mustache beneath a reporter's nose. The visitor's about thirty. His mustache thick and manly, his pencil gnawed and gnawed.

"Other papers quit looking for you, only me now. I'm stubborn, persistent like a river cuts a canyon."

"That takes eons."

"Funny," he says. "An umpire needs a sense of humor. Only way to survive that line." He talks matter-of-fact and fast. "Why are you hibernating in the dark on a glorious day?"

The reporter's arms hang relaxed, but there's a swirl of excitement in an undercurrent of monotone, as if he's discovered a lost treasure. He tilts his brim to block the fog-smothered sun and peers past Walter into his tumbledown room. "Too nice a day to be cooped up. Air's snug and woolly like grandmother used to knit. Umpires aren't vampires, are they?"

Walter must deny his identity soon, or silence will make it true. He doesn't flat-out lie. "Maybe you knocked at the wrong door, mister." He alters his squint into an expression of confusion. "Woke me. What time you got?"

"Not noon. Not quite."

"What time you got, precisely?"

The reporter takes out his watch. "Eleven thirty-nine. Queer time of day for shuteye. Have you been reading the papers? Blames are on you. Cap Anson says he's seen hundreds of umpires. You're the blindest. Blind or crooked or both."

Walter pulls the base ball from his pocket and hides it behind his back. He squeezes it to take the edge off his voice. "Who'd you say you were?"

"Charles Wood Dryden in print. Wood in a friendly conversation." He pushes up the brim of his hat to reveal more of his face. "With the *Examiner*. You've heard of me. I shot that grizzly in the Tehachapi Mountains to prove they aren't extinct in California. That was the last one, God willing. Tossed myself over the side of an Oakland ferry to prove local authorities are incapable of timely rescues."

"Seconds matter when a man's drowning."

"Got that right. Just like you got strike one and strike two right."

If Walter were in open air, he'd walk away. He does it all the time, The Judge calls it *French leave* because the French leave parties without saying so long to the hostess. The Judge says Walter has turned French leave into artistry.

"Give our kid publisher Willie Hearst some credit, he got the *Examiner* from his Daddy as a birthday present a year ago, turned the sickly sheet around." Wood Dryden's lips move like a horse eating oats. "The *Examiner*'s as influential as the *Chronicle* all of a sudden. San Francisco's got a newspaper war like they do in New York. I'm Willie's headline magician. Just back from London where I trailed Jack the Ripper through the slums of Whitechapel. Guess that qualifies me to find an umpire. I've trailed you here to…"

Wood Dryden flips through his notes. "What are you, a ghost?"

"No."

"Funny. Nobody knows a thing about you. Court records say you stole some worthless clothes. I had to cash in a few favors to find you here at…four thirty-one Broadway."

"Wood Dryden?"

The reporter sticks out his hand. "That's my name. Didn't catch yours."

The stall has paid off. Wood Dryden's uncertain that he's found the umpire. He has no more than a hunch. Dryden withdraws his hand to flip back in his notebook. "I've been doing some research, tying up loose ends."

"Loose ends?"

"They blame you." He stops flipping. "Here it is. Here's what Casey told me. Quote: 'Blake did his part, Blake tore the cover off the ball. Blake's swell. Let's remember the first pitch to me was in the dirt, the second out of human reach. Couldn't be hit with a wagon tongue. Nope. I always take responsibility, I always take ownership, it's the way we orphans been raised. But everyone saw, the snippet Ump saw it hisself. Two balls that he declared strikes. C'mon, he was out to get me. With two strikes I had to protect. Swung at a high one. No choice, no choice at all, I had to protect, and don't forget the blinding sun was setting in my eyes.'"

Wood Dryden lowers his notebook. "Unquote." He waits for a response. Walter looks at his feet, squeezes the ball behind his back.

"Casey's a man of Christian charity right before he blames you and the Almighty in the same breath. I took a trip the day before yesterday to the Niners' yard. The noon train. No one there, they don't play in the San Joaquin on the Sabbath, but I saw the layout. The sun sets behind the plate, couldn't have been in Casey's eyes that time of day. Square at his back. The Almighty's not to blame. Neither are you."

"Maybe an umpire lives a few doors down," Walter says. It's a lie, so he adds, "I don't think so."

"Sun wasn't in your eyes either. The pitcher Mouse Mathews was blinded, but Casey could see forever, all the way home to Golden Gate Park."

"I'm never home." That's true. "Never in the daytime, except lately."

"Relax buddy. I'm here to get your side. Always two sides." Wood Dryden removes his hat and the smell of oil drifts in through the door. "See my hair. I part it down the middle, exactly down the middle, same as my reporting."

"Enough oil to fry chicken."

"You're a riot. I like umpires. Colleagues at the *Examiner* got their backs up when I told them umpires are same as reporters, job to do. You and me, we tell the truth about what we see, damn the consequences. Let me guess. Sometimes fanatics come down after games to clap you on the back like you're the greatest thing since the soda fountain. They treat me like that, too, when they like the words that I write. They treat me differently when they don't."

Walter feels Wood Dryden's stare. The Judge says toe-watching makes a man seem guilty so he looks at Dryden's belt buckle.

"I write honest, disagreeable words, you make an honest, disagreeable call. Then we're Satan himself. Takes courage to do the honest thing."

"*Cojones.*"

"What?"

"Balls. Takes balls."

"God, you're funny." He peers past Walter again. The room is small and monkish and he's embarrassed to have another human scan it.

"Doesn't matter what you call," Dryden says. "Doesn't matter what I write. Lots of people will like it and lots of people won't. Casey's no saint. Not like they think. He's the one man I know who struts sitting down. I wrote that, but Willie Hearst trimmed it out. We have to write pleasantries about Casey. People who love Casey buy papers to love him more. Those Casey-kissers want to hang you by your whatnots."

"*Cojones.*"

"You're an uproar. You should be on stage."

"I want to stay low."

"Tell me your side. Casey's a windbag. Course, I can't write that, but I can write that you were doing your job and maybe you missed one pitch and you're sorry. The minister fixed things for you, he let the Niners win. Did you really think the catcher Fleetwood Walker was Grasshopper Nova? Did you really think he was Mexican? Willie Hearst wants me to expose you as a member of the gambling society. Like Dick Higham in Detroit. Expose you so Casey can be perfect again. That's wrong. I can't turn you into Honest John Gaffney, but I can make your life go easier if you open up."

Walter tries to shut the door. Wood Dryden stops it with his foot. "Casey's one regret in life is that he can't sit in the grandstand and watch himself swing. Say, is that a base ball behind your back? How'd you get that nasty cut on your head?"

Walter had forgotten about both. "Forgot."

"I've been authorized to pay you. Willie Hearst says to give you nine bucks anytime you talk to me and never the *Chronicle.*"

Walter pushes the door against Wood Dryden's foot. "That's more than for a long day of umpiring," Dryden says. "Nine dollars just to flap your gums for a minute. Say something funny about the strikeout. Never known an umpire to be cheeky like you."

"Never said I was the umpire."

"Some umpires are assholes, think they're God's gift. Not you. I can tell that you're a humble man." Wood Dryden pokes his beaver-chewed pencil into Walter's shoulder. "Casey called you a snippet. An odd snippet. It's time you evened the score."

"I've got nothing in that regard. You've knocked on the wrong door."

"Really?" Dryden says it like he's an easterner who believes no one. "Tell me why you let Fleetwood Walker stay in the game when he's no more Mexican than Frederick Douglass. Thank God the minister fixed your mistake, gave the win to the Niners. Does that bug you? Tell me about Old Reliable Jake spearing you into the Mudville dirt. That's how you got the cut on your head, an inning before the strikeout."

Walter gives another push on the door. "We'll print something with or without your cooperation. I'll tell my readers that you're off your rocker. You give me no choice. Hearst will print it, I guarantee he will."

Wood Dryden keeps his foot in the door; he won't give up. "You better tell me why you called those two balls strikes. I'll sort all of this out, you know I will. I thrive on shoe-leather reporting. Nellie Bly's story about Casey's strikeout got New Yorkers—the whole country—interested in you. But there's no shoe-leather reporting she can do in New York. This story's all mine."

The mention of her name stops Walter's pushing on the door. "I love Nellie Bly."

"Get in line buddy. Do you know where the catcher Fleet Walker is? He's disappeared, too. Cap Anson and Casey told you who he was, but you'd been thrown on your head by then." Wood Dryden points his pencil at Walter's forehead. "You were in a daze. I can write that, I can blame Old Reliable Jake for your mistakes. I'll say he gave you a concussion. Do you know where the Negro catcher is? Are the two of you in cahoots?"

Walter resumes pushing on the door. Wood Dryden fists a ding out of his hat to get ready to leave. He claps it on his head and pulls his foot away. "Best give your side. Look me square in the eye and tell me the truth. I'll print it just like you tell it. Word for word."

"What did Nellie Bly write?"

"To hell with Nellie Bly, pardon my French. Tell me and nine dollars—ten dollars—is yours."

Walter closes the door and hollers through it. "I don't make up stuff for money. I'm no Dick Higham."

Wood Dryden hollers back. "You're no Honest John Gaffney neither. You're odd. A weirdie. Take care of that cut funny man."

Walter flops back in bed and stares at the ceiling to let his eyes and mind readjust to the dark and quiet. As a typesetter at the *Chronicle*, he'd been around enough reporters to know Dryden is the stubborn type who will knock on doors for months. Fortunately, editors have no patience. Their job is to fill white space and they will tell Wood Dryden to quit wasting precious time, that no reader ever cared beans about an umpire. They'll tell Wood Dryden to move on.

Walter will stay in hiding. Days. Stay low. Weeks maybe. It doesn't matter. He tosses the base ball up over the musty moose antlers and catches it. Over and over. He counts. Four hundred thirty-two times. He naps. He tosses the ball and catches it four hundred thirty-two times again. He repeats the whole sequence four hundred and thirty-two times. That's 186,624 ball tosses until it's days, maybe weeks, after Wood Dryden's knock.

He makes a half-baked plan to go to New York to tell his story to Nellie Bly. Then, maybe, he'll go on to the North Pole. He pays a last visit to Moms at the Marine Hospital that Houses Crazy Seamen. Moms won't miss his absence, she sleeps and sleeps and is alert only in the afternoons. He arrives at three o'clock. She sits and smiles among the dull seamen. For a long time, she doesn't have any recollection of Walter, but before he leaves she says, "You weren't a fussy baby like your sister Annie Katharine. You cried some at nap time, but I tricked you, I laid you on your back. You hated that. I let you fuss a minute or two and when I turned you on your belly you were in heaven."

Walter kisses Moms' cheek. He's never kissed another cheek except Moms' and Annie Katharine's. He wishes he'd kissed Papa's.

"That's what the Good Lord does," Moms says. "He puts us on our backs for a spell. We all get stuck on our backs from time to time. That story is repeated over and over in the Bible. Do you still have Papa's Book?"

Walter nods, but Moms slips into delirium and he leaves. On the way back to his boarding house, he thinks about Papa and where they fished Bean Crick near Mount Hermon, where the water feeds the thirsty roots of redwoods before it feeds the Zayante and, eventually, the Pacific. The

Bean Crick redwoods are so thick that sunbeams strive to find the ground. Walter thinks about how Papa and he peed side by side and straight into the Bean Crick ripple. They'd take aim, their eyes forward, fathers and sons never look each other in the eye when peeing. Walter never looked into Papa's eyes most any time. He wishes he had, but Walter looked at redwood cones on the ground. How odd that the biggest trees in the world have tiny cones.

The Judge is like a father to Walter, now. Without The Judge, Walter would be almost an orphan. The Judge taught him that an umpire moves his feet to get the best angles. Walter remembers the last time when he and The Judge met for Chinese and beer. The Judge was off to the outhouse. Walter decided he was sick of staring at the painting of the Indian Wars in Montana. Walter switched seats to see things from the Judge's angle. The Judge had a view of Filbert Street falling steeply to San Francisco Bay. Not a painting of the Bay, the real Bay that could anchor the navies of the world. Walter remembers looking out from The Judge's seat to where the sweep of the sea ended at the horizon and Walter imagined that his pee mingled with Papa's halfway to China.

Walter has an affection for China. The Transcontinental Railroad was built by Chinamen.

Walter decides for certain that it's time to move his feet and go to New York. Then he changes his mind. Walter doesn't change his mind often, not when he's certain, but he changes his mind about telling his story to Nellie Bly because she has never answered his letter.

Forty-four days after the strikeout, he's still in his room at *El Coraje* boarding house. He tosses the base ball in the air over and over, four hundred thirty-two times, then he goes out and buys the *Examiner*. The date on the newspaper is June 3rd. The strikeout was April 20th. It's a Sunday, Walter can tell by the newspaper's girth, two fat sections, sixteen pages. He reads all the items from the middle down, he reads an item about a two-foot bride who took her vows standing on a chair, another about sailors who have seen sea monsters but won't come forward because they fear public ridicule. The items come with illustrations. There's an item about San Francisco lawyers employing girls to type. They're paid a fortune, eighty dollars a month. Not for their proficiency on Remington contraptions, but for "exquisite figures, languishing brown eyes and other qualities of personal attraction."

Buried at the bottom of Page Four is a tiny headline, barely a headline at all.

CASEY AT THE BAT

A Ballad of the Republic, Sung in the Year 1888

The headline is but one font larger than the poem below. Newspaper poems are an afterthought, something to fill white space. Walter reads it, he starts in the middle, he figures Casey won't strikeout in verse, he'll hit a homer over the War Monument and win the game. Newspaper poetry always ends on a good note.

Not this time. This ballad is truthful, Casey strikes out no matter how many times Walter reads it. *"Kill him! Kill the umpire!" shouted someone on the stand.* The poem is signed Phin; the poet is too proud to put his name to it. He would get angry mail for portraying Casey in a negative light.

The next Sunday, June 10th, 1888, Page One of the *Examiner* has a giant headline and a six-column epic by Charles Wood Dryden.

EXCLUSIVE ENCOUNTER WITH CASEY'S UMPIRE

The Scoundrel's Name is Walter Brewster Lets His Mama Rot Among Toothless Seamen

Wood Dryden describes his knock at Walter's boarding-house door six weeks ago. Dryden writes that he had hoped to leave the umpire in peace because Walter Brewster is quite odd and suffered a concussion. But the poem has reignited public interest, he writes, and the truth about Brewster must at long last be revealed.

The story is wrapped masterfully around an illustration of Walter. The scar above his eye is exaggerated. He looks like Frankenstein's monster. He reads from the sketch down.

> Brewster is an unfriendly man, short enough to stand beneath Casey's chin. He squints on foggy days as if into a bald sun, which makes him seem blind indeed.

His friend is Judge Gold, who no one has seen since his Santa Cruz beating. The men of San Francisco County will decide The Judge's fate when he stands for reelection come November 6th. The Judge will be defeated once the voters learn that he taught Brewster to call balls and strikes. Correction: The Judge taught Brewster to call only strikes.

The umpire has a melancholic mother. I visited Rebecca Brewster at the Marine Hospital that Houses Crazy Seamen. She was pleasant, though the winds of life had taken their toll. She had no recollection of her scoundrel son, and I believe her to be telling the honest truth.

Mrs. Brewster asked me to keep an eye out for her sweet husband, whoever he may be. She is a woman starved of social intercourse and destined for an unmarked grave.

I offered Walter Brewster opportunity after opportunity to give his version of affairs. He declined. I cannot blame him. Five thousand eye witnesses are ready and willing to refute all but the absolute truth.

Casey told me he forgives and forgets, but he says Brewster must be banned from base ball in the name of fair play.

"My gracious, imagine him umping somewheres else," Casey said. "C'mon, rooting him out is best for the national game."

———

Try KO KO TU LU flavored Chewing Gum

Walter pulls clothes off nails and stuffs them into his satchel. He shaves his wispy mustache. He salutes goodbye to his moose antlers; he takes nothing else except his base ball. He's aboard the first train east.

The song of the rail and the mountains of the Sierra Nevada range would cause any atheist to reconsider. Nevada is what hell is like. No life except jackrabbits and Indians dressed in red blankets near the stations. Somewhere near Winnemucca, or Elko he decides on his new name, Claude Ponsonby. Annie Katharine often had tea with Queen Victoria; she pretended to be Princess Claudia Ponsonby. Walter never played make believe, just like he doesn't read fiction, and he lets his distant memories of Annie Katharine assign to him his new identity.

Claude Ponsonby plans to go on to New York to find Nellie Bly, but he disembarks at Promontory, Utah to see where the Golden Spike of the Transcontinental Railroad was driven in 1869. May 10th, precisely, when Walter was almost six. Papa had already left. The Golden Spike is in a later time zone, it's an hour earlier back home in San Francisco. Two hours later in New York.

Ponsonby hasn't the fare to board the next train. There's no newspaper published in Promontory and he hikes a couple of days into Salt Lake City. Charles Penrose, editor of the *Evening Deseret News,* says he can't hire Ponsonby because he's odd and not Mormon, but Ponsonby convinces him with a presentation of his typesetting capabilities.

The key to typesetting is focus and memorization, something Moms said are Walter's gifts from God. All the letters of the alphabet are in a tray known as a case. The capital letters are in the upper part of the case, and the small letters in the lower part. The upper-case letters are arranged alphabetically except J and U because the alphabet back when the printing press was invented had no sounds for J and U. Those letters were later added out of order in the 25th and 26th place in the tray.

The lower case is what confuses apprentices. The letter e is most common, so it has the largest compartment closest to the typesetter's right hand. The letters t, a, i, n, o and s are also near the right hand. Most distant is the letter q. It seems helter-skelter but it's all set up scientifically for speed and accuracy.

There are also compartments in the case for $, &, and for thin spaces that are used to justify the lines, and leading, which widen or narrow the lines to make a short item longer or a long item shorter. When the *Examiner* printed the Casey poem, there was no leading. The headline was small to be shoehorned into a tight space. Even so, the words of the poem were squished. Squished words are said to be *huddling.*

Once an edition is printed, the typesetter's letters have to be cleaned with a brush and put back in the case. Letters can get mixed up. The lower-case p's and the q's especially. Moms used to say, "Mind your *p's* and *q's*" when neighbors were visiting. When she had the melancholia she said she was "out of sorts." Typesetters are out of sorts when they run out of a letter that they need.

Speed is important but not at the expense of accuracy, just as distance is important in umpiring, but not at the expense of angle. Typesetters learn to read upside down and right to left. They're not allowed to talk. Concentration of the mind is essential, as it is with umpiring. A chattering man in the composing room is a nuisance, and Charles Penrose hires his first gentile employee when Claude Ponsonby promises not to talk on and on about pill bugs and other things of interest.

New York typesetters are the best in the world, and Ponsonby plans to get good enough to typeset for the *New York World*.

Charles Penrose is a bit of an oddity himself, a Latter-Day Saint with an English accent, about fifty. He spends his free time writing lyrics for hymns, and he blames the completion of the railroad for polluting the Utah territory with those from outside the faith.

For months, Ponsonby typesets the news of Salt Lake City. Some is sad. A pre-dawn fire kills a family with eleven children on East Temple Street. A bucket brigade is of little help and the item ends with a mention of the alarm clock found in the ashes and set to go off minutes after the fire began. That's an example of irony.

Here's another, maybe. One day in the summer, Charles Penrose dispatches Ponsonby to a mountain drowning. All the reporters are out on assignment, as are the newspaper's four horses. Ponsonby's in pink condition and he hikes seven rocky miles to a waterfall. Five boys have been pulled out by rope and they leave muleback to the morgue. One boy remains, alive and weeping. Ponsonby sits next to him like Walter sat next to Moms, feeling helpless now as he did then.

The rising mist smells of moss and timberline snowpack and renders Ponsonby's pencil useless. No muskrat has ever been wetter, their clothes are soaked from waterfall mist and their bodies shake as they watch water plummet into the churn of the pool. The boy says that his best friends, more friends than Ponsonby believes is possible, drowned one by one jumping in to rescue each other.

Ponsonby drapes his soggy jacket around the boy's shoulders and leads him from the roar, as Walter never can with Moms. They sit in the sun on a rock warmed by July, their backs to the last cascade of a hard Wasatch winter. Ponsonby squeezes the base ball, his hands are too cold to feel the heartbeat.

"I tried to rescue them by reaching in with a tree snag," the boy says. He's seventeen, Ponsonby just turned twenty-five. The boy peels orange lichen from the rock with his fingernails. Ponsonby forces himself to find the boy's eyes. They are red, dancing with grief and starting to deaden with shame. Like Papa's were. Ponsonby can't think of an intelligent question a reporter might ask and he sits there dumb.

"I screamed for them to stop jumping in." The boy's telling the truth about screaming, his voice is almost gone. "The color drained from each face. They grew tired; I saw each go under." He finds Claude Ponsonby's eyes. "Have you ever seen someone you love give up and die?"

Ponsonby nods his head yes. It doesn't feel like a lie, although he doesn't know for sure if Papa is dead or alive. Ponsonby remembers that he's the reporter and hurries to come up with a question. "Were your friends strong swimmers?"

"Each and every one. So am I, but here I am."

"I swim like a one-legged frog," Ponsonby says.

"I saw them swallow mouthfuls of water, I saw them struggle to live." As the boy goes on, Ponsonby cries involuntarily, without sound or expression. He might not know that he's crying, except tears splatter the base ball already soaked in mist. Base balls weigh a lot when soaked, a sack of them weigh a ton. Ponsonby cries because he can't drag the soaked boy from the roar. The boy will always hear that roar.

"I saw each give way," the boy says. "Their best not good enough."

"You were smart not to jump in," Ponsonby says.

"I don't feel smart. I'm the lucky one, but I don't feel that way."

Ponsonby writes his first and only newspaper item about the boy who was wiser than his friends. He writes that there is a brand of courage in not jumping in, accepting things for what they are. He writes about how survivors feel guilt and shame, and how he made better time hiking down a mountain but it was more painful than walking up. He typesets his own upside-down item. There is an inch or two of white space that he can't fill with leading. Charles Penrose tells him to write a few more lines. Ponsonby has nothing more to say and this is what he writes with the letters in his tray.

Jays are queer birds, they find life unbearable unless they can hear other jays. Jays are also called camp robbers. Camp robbers that live where they cannot hear the caw-caw of other camp robbers go mad.

> Friends and family are respectfully requested to attend funeral services of our lamented children.

Charles Penrose reads Ponsonby's item from the proof. He tells Ponsonby, "You had sand to stop off at the morgue to stare into…" he reads directly… "lifeless doll's eyes…white, wrinkled fists with strands of hair pulled from the heads of others…"

Charles Penrose peers over the top of his eyeglasses. "My God, Claude, this is grisly, like Edgar Allan Poe."

"Poe used the same words over and over, words like nevermore," Claude Ponsonby says. "He's buried in Baltimore at Westminster Presbyterian. I try not to use the same word too many times or I get out of sorts."

There are p's and q's to mind. Ponsonby cleans them with a brush and puts them back in the case. He doesn't last as a reporter. He can't write another word, except for a second letter to Nellie Bly, a letter of gratitude when he learns that The Great Asylum for the Insane broke ground in Agnews, California. He's happy for Moms but he can no longer hear himself think through the colic of that waterfall and the silence of the jays. He focuses evermore on his typesetting—he gets better and better at it.

One day he's laying down a story upside down and right to left. It's about Albert Spalding, the Chicago business magnate. He's bringing a base ball tour to Salt Lake City on October 31st before traveling on to San Francisco, the Sandwich Islands and Australia. They will barnstorm in five continents and complete a 30,000-mile journey by the April start of the 1889 season.

Among those along are Niner coach, Cap Anson, his Negro mascot Clarence Duval, and an angry Casey, who did little but strikeout over and over again throughout the 1888 season. The exhibition will be played near The Mormon Temple, under construction. It casts an afternoon shadow over the yard that serves as the community's ice skating rink in the long winter. There's no home run fence. There's a hill beyond the outfield that becomes a toboggan run. The hill gives an elevated view of the diamond and it is there that Ponsonby plans to sit when Casey comes to bat.

As the tour makes its way westward from Des Moines and Omaha, an Indian summer in Salt Lake turns dreary. Nighttime rain puddles the yard on October 30th, but it doesn't dampen Utah's desire to witness the best ball players in the land. Twenty-five hundred are in attendance when Ponsonby sits on the toboggan hill among the wet coughs of those who arrived aboard a train from a mining town. The town of Helper sits in the mountains and it takes two engines, including a helper engine, to climb to the top. A helper engine pushes from the back, a double-header has two engines in the front.

By the third inning, the citizens of Helper shiver and cough as though suffering from the ague. They're curious about Clarence; they've never seen a black-faced man who has never set foot in a coal mine. He wears a new mascot outfit, but Ponsonby's curious about the workings of the umpire. Ponsonby maneuvers closer, until he's standing behind the chicken wire in back of the plate.

The Judge didn't quit after all. He isn't moving well, but he is off the crutch and has field presence. "Strike Three, Salt Lake City, the garden spot of the Rockies!" he hollers.

Ponsonby plans to get The Judge's attention once the game is over. They'll get Chinese and beer. There are Chinese in Utah; they built the railroad. Clouds grow dark over the Wasatch Range as the fourth inning begins. It sprinkles and Ponsonby fears the game will be washed out.

Billy Sunday's at the bat and that's when Clarence starts hollering through the chicken wiring. "That there's Casey's umpire! That there's Casey's umpire!"

The Judge's face turns happy. Cap Anson's face turns sinister as if he's been bombed with poop from a gull and it's just then that rain pours thick and cold. The crowd runs toward the Mormon Temple for shelter. Walter's carried along with them, his feet in no control of his direction. He's smushed like huddled letters; he can't lift his arms in a mob that moves as one like a slow, human avalanche.

The crowd is too thick for Casey to penetrate in pursuit. It's raining enormous drops. Walter hears in the distance Cap Anson's scream like a dying rabbit. Walter looks back to see an infield of mud. Water cascades down the toboggan hill into an outfield that could be fished. The Judge waves from a liquid yard.

Casey's farther away each second. Like a man caught in the ocean riptide and on his way to China. He'll soon be long gone to play ball beneath the Sphinx in Egypt. It never rains in Egypt. Beneath all the rocks of Egypt, Casey will never find a pill bug.

These are the saddest of possible words:
'Tinker to Evers to Chance.'"—Franklin Pierce Adams

April 20, 1888, 4:06 p.m.
It's a Friday

CHAPTER SEVEN

two hours and forty-four minutes before the strikeout

The tally-keeper introduces her. I had no earthly idea Nellie Bly was in attendance, and the hair stands up on my arms. She's dressed in white, more aura than flesh. I can't help but stare. A goddess, bright among men in the charcoal of grandstand shade. She smiles to the cheers and waves in white gloves, but the moment's spoiled when Casey advances toward the backstop and blows her a kiss.

She ignores him, which makes me appreciate her all the more. I've been in love dozens of times with girls I've never met, but never in love like this.

"I thought she'd have bigger bubs," Casey says to a base ball writer.

I want to protect her honor, but umpires aren't given that luxury. Rural Cemetery's the place I'll be buried were I to take a swipe at Casey. Just then, more cheers erupt when the tally-keeper announces that the Oakland outfit has arrived at the train station.

Casey muscles away possession of the megaphone, says, "Afternoon," and gets around to doing a mock newspaper interview of himself. The fanatics laugh at his every joke, but I don't enjoy clownish humor. The Judge says my funny bone's in an unorthodox place.

"Casey, what's the secret of the long ball?" Casey asks himself. He draws a pocket watch because the passage of time creates suspense. Timing's important in humor. He lowers the megaphone to his hip and speaks softly so that only the base ball writers can hear. I hear, too. He tells a joke that's off-color. Off-color means risqué.

My eyes are squinty. They're unaccustomed to the desert sun and the bright uniforms the Niners don. I prefer the coolness of the color blue, but the Niners scream hot. Casey's big and loud and hot and off-color. He tells another joke, only me and the writers hear.

"What's the difference between a fastball and a mother-effer fastball?" He rounds the plate and puts an index finger to his lips. "Shhh, I must be discreet." Writers lean in. "The fastball is a blur. C'mon, the fastball is smoke, no man gets around on the mother-effer fastball. Nope. Except a pocket pool champ like me."

I don't get the joke. Boos and groans erupt in the crowd. I wonder if the breeze lifted Casey's foul words foul into the packed grandstand and into Nellie Bly's sweet ears, but then I see the Oakland Tribunes stepping from a horsecar. Most visiting ball clubs parade in uniform to the yard to promote the game. The Oaklands are way too late for that. Their outfits are gray and their shoes are polished with stove blacking. They're too ragtag for a parade and, anyway, the last thing the Niners need is one more soul wanting in. Folks stand packed with their toes on my foul lines and orphan boys have climbed the War Monument.

One of the Oaklands carries a gunny sack to his bench. He's tall and athletic. He must be the catcher nobody knows about, the Mexican. I've seen him play somewhere before and I'm trying to remember when Cap Anson startles me from behind. I startle easily because I have a one-track mind. A one-track mind plows forward, it doesn't change directions or it derails.

Cap Anson smirks and shakes my hand like he's on some ballot. I maintain eye contact for a second, but that's all I can muster.

"You're the best umpire I've seen all day," Cap Anson says.

"I'm the only umpire you've seen today."

"That's the point, *dummy.*" His fly is at half mast. The Judge warned me, so I don't fall for it. I look at his mouth but not as high as his eyes. His smile drains away when I don't warn him to button up.

"What time is it?" Cap Anson's mouth says from beneath a waxed mustache.

I have a pocket watch, but I use the sun to estimate. "Four-thirty, maybe."

"Best we get after it."

"The railway's to blame," I say. "We'll give the Oaklands a minute to get limber."

Cap Anson shifts weight, he doesn't like me acting in charge. He barks at his mascot. "Clarence, go find out who's running the Oaklands and tell him to join us at the plate sometime today."

"Yes, sah, Cap'n."

"That darkey is a no-account illiterate." Cap Anson's making conversation like people do when they're stuck with someone unorthodox and quiet. "Clarence knows dice games, but he can't read or write his name at age fifteen."

"He looks twelve," I say.

"If we ever lose two straight I'm sacking him."

"That might be a season or two." I kick myself for opining about the outcome. I don't really kick myself, that's an expression.

"You're right," Anson says. "I hope that's not the last thing you get right today."

"That's sarcasm," I say.

Old Reliable Jake of the Oaklands meanders over. I shake a hand that engulfs mine. "I'm player *and* coacher and that saves the *Oakland Daily Tribune* six bits," he says.

"Welcome to God's three acres," Cap Anson says. "Aren't you Oakland's eighth coacher in two years?"

"This is the nicest yard I've seen," Old Reliable Jake says. "Ours sits on an Indian burial grounds."

"The Ohlone Indians," I say. I know about Indians, but not as much as I know about trains and pill bugs.

"It's why my club's forever cursed," Old Jake says.

"I read about your rickety stand collapse last season," Anson says. "Wiped out half of your fanatics." He chuckles.

"Nineteen hundred at that game, just nineteen died," Old Jake says.

"One percent," I say.

Anson spits. "When have the Oaklands ever had nineteen hundred at a game?"

I introduce myself. Neither man hears my name; coachers never do. I dig a coin out of my pocket for the flip. I plan to flip it high and flashy for Nellie Bly but Cap Anson says, "Put the damn coin away. The Niners choose to bat first."

Anson studies me and Old Jake for a reaction. We don't react, we don't give him the pleasure, but it's queer that he wants his club to bat first. Maybe he wants to hit before the ball gets mushy. A mushy ball is an equalizer for weak outfits like Oakland, but balls don't get pulped until the later innings, so there's no real advantage. I figure that Cap Anson's move is about salesmanship more than base ball strategy. If the Niners bat first they will bat in the ninth inning even if they're ahead by a hundred runs. That'll give Casey one more at-bat to send the fanatics home satisfied they got their dime's worth.

I understand, but Old Jake is insulted. Jake thinks Anson's up to something. Jake shuffles his feet and I say, "If your club wants to bat first, we'll have a flip."

"Oh, no we won't," Cap Anson says. He thinks I'll do whatever he says.

"We'll bat last," Old Jake says. It's the smart move, but he's unhappy. The Oaklands will lose no matter who bats when. I hate to opine, but it's a foregone conclusion.

Old Jake tells me his list of batsmen and I write them down with a stump of a pencil. Then, Anson tells me his list of batsmen. Another surprise. Barrows and Cooney always bat first and second ahead of Casey and Jackleg Preacher. I've seen the box scores in the papers. They call that *setting the table*. But today, the Niners' two crummiest benchwarmers will bat near the top of the order. Barrows is leading off as always, but Cooney's batting dead last. Jackleg Preacher is sitting this one out entirely in a display of disrespect for the Oaklands.

Anson spits. "I'd rest Casey, too, but the folks pay to see him. They'd dismantle this new yard board by board."

Gentlemen from back east can see their way past a snub, but Old Jake's from Visalia and he's not thrilled to see crummy Flynn bat in the two spot and Blake, up from the Copper League, bat third in front of Casey.

Cap Anson takes another dig at Old Jake. "Flynn's usual position is chasing away juveniles, who peep at the games through knotholes. Blake's fat and runs like Grover Cleveland. He's good for selling scorecards and cigars. Neither Flynn nor Blake bats his weight. That's a buck-twenty for the whippersnapper."

"Why don't you release them?" Old Jake says.

"They play for meal money."

"I see," Old Jake says. "That lets the Niners fatten Casey's Wells Fargo account. No player should get rich. It's ruining a good game."

Cap Anson stares ugly at Jake. Old Jake says, "Your fly's open."

Cap Anson stares and stares. I know what he's going to say, I just wonder when. "Takes a cocksucker to notice," he says finally.

I ask Cap Anson to double check his list of batsmen to make sure there's been no mistake, but he'd rather get into a staring match with Old Jake over the top of my head. A fistfight before the first pitch won't sit well with the minister William Rufus Wheaton. Won't be the best thing for my future. Cap Anson takes another dig; he says he's uncertain if Blake's first name is Jimmy or Johnnie because Blake is some sap he found in the cherry orchards this very morning. Old Jake has a ruddy complexion. His neck turns red and his acne scars turn redder. Jake's ready to take a swipe, but Cap Anson knows he won't, and he smirks and shifts weight, takes pleasure in being the smartest base ball brain on the planet.

Old Jake grumbles an aside. "We're a soft mark, but you're the cocksucker. No doubt."

"Don't get your back up," Cap Anson says. That's an expression too, cats and dogs do it when they're mad. It makes more sense than falling from rain clouds.

The coachers are on edge but I don't expect anyone to raise sand before the first pitch. "You two take a breath," I say. "Count to ten."

I wonder if Nellie Bly notices my field presence. Maybe I still don't have any, and I do everything I can to keep her from seeing my face. I look down my foul lines. Men have their toes on the lime, and other men are standing three rows deep. They're restrained by a rope and self discipline. That concerns me some. Fanatics are known to squeeze the yard a step smaller when an out-of-town fielder is running out of room chasing down a pop fly.

I can't worry about things that haven't happened yet though. The best thing is to get the game underway. I put my notebook and pencil stump in my pocket. I ask for the megaphone, and I holler the official start time is four fifty-seven, precisely. I'm feeling out of sorts, we should be in the sixth or seventh inning by now. I tell myself I've nowhere to be, I tell myself to relax and focus.

I holler that the Niners have elected to bat first and the Oakland battery is Mouse Mathews and Grasshopper Nova, and that's when I remember where I've seen the Mexican. He was with the Cuban Giants when they barnstormed through San Francisco last year.

Grasshopper Nova was a Cuban then, I can't say why he's a Mexican now. All I know is that he's the color of weak coffee and the best catcher I've worked behind. On the Haight Street Grounds, he was devoid of fear. I remember that he can outrun an antelope on the bases, and I don't know why it took me this long to place him. Nerves, I suppose, and that distraction sitting all in white behind me.

I take a deep breath as Grasshopper receives warm-ups from the southpaw into bare, gnarled hands. Clarence brings around the house broom and sweeps the marble. I turn my cap backward and put on my wire mask. The catcher does the same. I never look at people, but I take a glance up at her. She's looking back, I swear. My insides are mussed up. No girl ever looks my way. No girl ever looks any umpire's way, nobody does, not until there's some controversy to holler about.

Maybe she's admiring my blue suit, it's a cool color amidst the hot colors of the Niners. I take a breath, I ignore my nerves, I think of The Judge flat in a Santa Cruz bed. "Now, Walter," I say to calm myself. "All there is to do is to stay out of trouble."

Barrows steps in and I point at Mouse and say "Play."

Mouse is a challenge to umpire, his pitches slow halfway to the plate, he has them on a string. There's no rotation to the stitches whatsoever and when the breeze kicks in at my back, the ball dances like a marionette.

The first fastballs from the Niner ace, Squawks Clarke, are the opposite. They surprise me with a mosquito's hum. They explode in my face like nothing in the D-league. Before each delivery, Squawks turns his body around to face second base, winding his watch-spring skeleton. Then he skips sideways toward the front of the box. Each pitch nicks, or nearly nicks, one edge of the plate or the other. I adjust to his speed. I adjust to his accuracy. I trace each pitch back along its comet's tail, and I holler "Striker" if any stitch of the ball crosses any sliver of the marble.

Mouse's pitches barely get there at all. The Niner batsmen think any girl can hammer him and frustration already carves at their faces by the second inning. The fanatics hiss and boo Mouse and me when Casey walks on five consecutive balls, but Casey steals second, takes third on a deep air ball, and comes home on a punk hit off the end of someone's bat. Casey slides in feet high. No play is made at the plate, but Casey throws the Mexican catcher a mouthful of spikes.

"*Pendejo, cabrón*," Grasshopper Nova says.

Casey gets in close to the catcher's face. "Shut your yap, beaner." Then he doffs his cap and gives Nellie Bly an electric smile, swats at his ass as if dusty knickers is the worst injustice of his orphaned life. Grasshopper doesn't take a sock at Casey, that's good luck. All I want is for the Niner victory to unfold, work two more games tomorrow, collect twenty-one dollars, prove to the minister that I can handle a top-tier brand of ball.

The fanatics are loud. The noise nags at me, but the Oakland Tribunes quiet things in the bottom of the second inning on a baser by Cannonball MacKenna and a smack into the gap by Ham Adams. The sod is thick, but the ball keeps rolling and finds a hole in the fence. Adams circles for a four-bagger. The two-to-one Oakland lead sours the mood and out comes Cap Anson to kick and spit juice and complain about who knows what.

"A hole's in the fence," he says.

I shrug. "It's your brand-new fence."

"That's ass-shit."

"Something to fix before tomorrow."

"You're new to this association. You don't have the slightest inkling."

I hear no question and say nothing. *Don't answer anything but questions*, that's what The Judge says.

"Your zone's in the shithouse."

No question.

"Do you have a personality?"

"I flunked umpire charm school."

"That's ass-shit."

I give him the last word. The Judge calls it my specialty, but now I wonder if Nellie Bly thinks me weak. I can't stop thinking about her; I have a one-track mind. The Judge and Nellie Bly are the two most important people in my life. The Judge saved me. Nellie Bly saved my Moms. I'm in love with Nellie Bly, always will be, though I will never see her again.

The Niners tie it two-all on an Oakland blunder, a two-out pop-up by Blake with Barrows on third. It's a skyscraper. Up and up it goes. Down, down it comes fair near the plate. The catcher has the easiest play on the ball, but Mouse calls out for first baseman Old Reliable Jake to take it because the Mexican is at risk of misunderstanding his own name.

Balls spin backward when they're hit straight up and the spin can carry them forward ten feet. Pill bugs are terrestrial isopods. That's how slow Old Jake is, but he hustles enough to run a little past it. He finds a way to muff the spinning ball, drops it, and turns mad as all get-out. He throws his cap at the ball on the ground and the fanatics holler remarks about his partial baldheadedness.

Later on, the Niners are pitched twenty-one straight balls but don't score a run. Barrows takes his base on five straight. Mouse throws two more balls to Flynn. Barrows is thrown out stealing on ball three, I suspect the Mexican deciphered Anson's private code of signals. Flynn walks on two more, and then Mouse's dancer pitch goes amok, and he throws four more balls to Blake. That's fourteen straight. The next pitch hovers in chin high and I'm ready to tell Blake to take his base, but he's thinking no pitcher throws another ball with Casey warming up on deck with three bats. Maybe Blake's afraid to be sent back to the Copper League for being a ne'er-do-well. Out to prove something, he squeezes the bat with nicotine-yellowed fingers, swings like a dope and bounces a bug bruiser to Old Jake at first for the second out.

Cap Anson hollers, not at me, but at Blake for swinging at ball five and for moving Flynn to second, which leaves first base wide open for the Oaklands to walk Casey. Mouse throws three balls at him, but Casey says, "Folks pay to see me hit," rearranges his feet and takes a swing at a high one. Casey whips rapid wrists, strikes it straightforward in the face and off it journeys deep to left.

The world slows for Casey like it slows for me when there are close bangers and whackers at first, except it slows enough for Casey to plot and commit murder. His stance is like a coiled rattler, his swing a hiss. But Mouse has a queer advantage. His pitches drift impossibly slow and Casey pulls a high and outside pitch way left. Clearly foul, it is certain to roll on a hundred miles before it climbs a draw and stops in a snow drift among cannibalized skeletons on Donner Pass. That's an exaggeration. Some of it is.

What most surprises me about a base ball hit by Casey is the sound, or the lack thereof, like one of those knockout punches everyone suspects is phantom until some boxer wakes up in the morgue. There's no sting in Casey's hands when he hits one out of creation.

After precisely seven seconds in the air, the ball lands foul and over the outstretched reach of two kids on a telegraph pole, bounds forty feet over the hands of ten more on a hill, and disappears into thick weeds. A hundred boys risk poison oak and nettles on a fox hunt for the sphere. Young boys are usually efficient with their leather chasing, but we stand around to learn that the ball vanished into some delinquent's pocket.

Clarence trots on out. "Some cranks deputized themselves to hunt the kid down," the mascot says to me, handing Casey a canteen.

Clarence hoists Casey's lumber from the ground and encourages him to straighten out the next one. Things take forever. Enough time passes for Grasshopper Nova to mumble an impatient "*andale*," and for me to remember more about him, the Cuban catcher who's now a Mexican.

I remember reading an item last year in the *Chronicle* about Levi Goldschmidt, the Jewish owner and manager of the Cuban Giants. His daddy is a rich Los Angeles banker, and Goldschmidt spent the first thirty years of his life in the misery of wealth, leisure and a perfect climate. He started the ball club to keep from hanging himself, and he did it with players who were going unsigned in the big leagues. It was a brilliant scheme, Goldschmidt made twenty-seven thousand dollars last season, the Chronicle said, because the whole world loves to watch a team of happy dark players beaten by a team of angry freckled Irish. I don't know if there were any real Cubans on the team, maybe one or two. The rest were Negroes pretending to be Cuban. Plus this catcher, now with the Oaklands, who's suddenly Mexican.

Like me, Goldschmidt has a funny bone in an unorthodox place, and he handed out Cuban names to his colored Giants. They played exhibitions and they never won. They jumped to an early lead, but the Irish boys staged a comeback every time, even if it took some terrible errors by the Giants. With the outcome always in doubt, nobody left early, the hawkers sold out of cheap cigars and caramel candy and the Cuban Giants got invited to play on down the road, two towns in a day.

Last year when I worked their game on the Haight Street Grounds I found seven or nine cents about the plate. The Irish were staging their late rally and each time I looked down I saw another Indian head in the dirt. I kept looking after each inning. When I was picking one up, I glanced from my stoop to see Goldschmidt, Grasshopper, and two or three players as black as Clarence sniggering at me from their bench and nudging elbows into each other.

They were in jeopardy of losing another game, yet having fun, which bothered me because it was at my expense. I didn't know at the time that The Judge was watching me from the bleaching boards or it would have bothered me more. Later, over Chinese and beer, The Judge said he saw Goldschmidt seeding those pennies between innings. The Judge didn't know why except that Goldschmidt probably thought it was damn funny.

Grasshopper Nova was digging an elbow into Goldschmidt at that exhibition game last year as if he had some command of English. That's my point. I never get to my point as fast as I'd like. I can go on and on, but here's my point: He knew English then but he knows only Spanish now. Today, Grasshopper shows no sign of recognizing a word of English, or of recognizing me; I doubt if he's taken the time to see a face behind my mask. Hardly any pitches skipped by him on the Haight Street Grounds and none get by him today even as the breeze at our backs blows Mouse's pitches around until the Niners are swinging at duck down.

The Mexican is what The Judge calls an *umpire's catcher*. He gets low on his haunches to give me a full view of the plate and he gets his feet narrow to block dirt balls without exception. He circus catches wild pitches one-handed with a long reach. I lose all worries about taking one in the ear or the nuts and that does miracles for my zone, helps me focus, though I'm still distracted by loveliness on my back. If Casey blows her another kiss, I'll take a sock at him, I swear.

The ball Casey hit into the poison oak and nettles is still missing. In Boston, they kick in a second ball to prevent delays like this. In this association, even a ball ripped open to the core is irreplaceable until the inning is over. I read that rule on the train over in The Judge's bloody booklet. I appreciate frugality as much as anybody; I'll stoop for any Indian head Levi Goldschmidt chums at me. But if I were a club magnate, I'd kick in a buck twenty-five for a second ball to keep things moving.

At last the delinquent coughs it up, and the Niner inning crawls on. Casey's foul to Timbuktu convinces Mouse to throw ball three, four and five, except Casey rearranges his feet once more and swings to steal ball five from the cosmos.

The Judge hates it when base ball reporters lie about the bat's breeze. He says he has never felt a breeze from any bat in all his years and that base ball writers are mugwumps, fuds, and ligners for saying so. But Casey's uppercut sucks my cap off my head from beneath my mask. It steals air from my lungs. His swing is late, and his bat snatches the ball an inch from the catcher's gnarled hands. He slugs it alright, but Salty O'Reilly, playing deep in center, runs to the spot and takes it over his shoulder at the fence.

Base ball writers say Casey has a mischievous twinkle, but when I pick my cap off the dirt and look at him, all I see are the dark eyes of an orphan's slight. Casey lofted what should have been the twenty-first consecutive ball for the third out.

Time's a remarkable thing. The game marches on at a clip; it's almost over before I know it. The Niners take to the field in the bottom of the eighth and I think of The Judge in a Santa Cruz room that smells of a horse with glanders. Once he heals and makes his way back to the grogshop, I'll have a story to cheer him. He will laugh and laugh about those twenty-one balls. I'll laugh, too, but The Judge will laugh until he has to pee and leave me staring at that Montana crick bubbling into the painting's infinity.

Time has digested all but three outs for the Niners, six for the Oaklands. I know the score, but I look at the blackboard because I don't believe it. The Niners only have two runs when they anticipated a dozen.

The Oaklands also have two, two more than they ever dreamed they'd a-score, and they're advancing to the bat in quest of one more.

My sole mission remains to stay out of trouble, avoid the shit-house beast that caught The Judge. I'm an inning and a half away, but the score is 2-to-2.

I don't care beans who wins. I never opine, but it would be nice if the Oaklands won one for all the misfits of the world. All the *retards* and *spastics, imbeciles* and *pea-brains* and *village idiots*.

Best for my health though, if it were the Niners.

*Hey now, you're an all-star, get your game
on, go play."—Smash Mouth*

Nov. 10, 1889, 3:11 p.m.
It's a Sunday

CHAPTER EIGHT

one year and two hundred four days after the strikeout

Joseph J. Pulitzer's secretary lacks the resolve to stop Nellie Bly from barging past. She finds Mr. Pulitzer shouting through a speaking tube. If he's not on the telephone cajoling with a Vanderbilt, he's hollering through voice-pipes to a floor below. Growling is his way of life. When he passes away, which may be sooner than later, she suspects that he'll growl his guttural Hungarian accent via a speaking tube up from the grave.

He's half insane, but it took an insane man to turn the hapless *World* into a juggernaut and the penniless Elizabeth Jane Cochrane into Nellie Bly. He likes her—and not in a lecherous way. He likes her because she is his invention.

"Eh, who left out today's temperature in zee forecast?" he shouts into the tube. He signals her to sit in a chair of red leather. Guests sink deep so that Mr. Pulitzer gains a head in height. She knows the ploy and remains standing. It drives powerful men batty when girls do the opposite of what they're told.

He's forty-two but seems eighty, the age her dead daddy would've been had he survived his crippling malady. That was eighteen years ago when Pink was seven. Mr. Pulitzer's teeth are the color of the yellowed piano keys she played back then.

He hollers into the pipe. "New Yorkers are entitled to know how cold it is."

The magnate at last stands to fulfill his duties as a gentleman. He tries to intimidate her in the manner of a starved pirate, little more than an

Adam's apple on stilts. His face, rumored to be exceptionally ugly, is hidden behind a beard. A thick head of red hair, flat to his head the last time she saw him, has grown wild. It makes him taller, but he's unwell. He's absent weeks at a time. There are rumors that he rents an entire floor at a Paris hotel and sits in the dark. He has a nervous affliction that might land him in Blackwell's if he weren't stinking rich.

"Readers blame us when it's cold or hot, as if we cause the weather, as if I'm the Almighty," he says.

Nellie Bly quips. "Threaten them with a flood, that will give circulation a bounce."

He seldom laughs; he mourns his daughter, who died of pneumonia five years ago when she was shy of her second birthday. Nellie Bly prays the girl has gone to heaven, but that's unlikely. Mr. Pulitzer's a Jew and a secular one at that.

He and his wife Kate live uptown on 73rd and summer in Bar Harbor. They're dear hearts, everyone agrees, even though he leaves the theater alone, annoyed at rustling programs. Trinity Church bells irritate him, he jumps if a hinge squeaks. He built the eighteen-story Golden Dome to put distance between himself and the tremor of the presses. His office has leather-lined walls to make quiet quieter. He wouldn't survive an ending at the Home of the Mudville Niners.

Electric lights illuminate the dome's exterior at night, New York's tallest, 309 feet to surpass the spire of Trinity Church. It will be featured on the cover of the upcoming World Almanac. Mr. Pulitzer paid $2 million to build it. All in cash.

"What's so urgent, eh Miss Bly, that you had to push in on a Sunday?"

She generally gets what she wants from men, but Mr. Pulitzer presents a challenge. She lets him marinate in cranky impatience and makes him stand as she walks to a window overlooking the city. The largest window in America. Squeeze a dollar a day of profit from each one of a thousand employees, that's all one needs to be rich. At least his fortune wasn't given to him; he's not a spoiled heir like William Randolph Hearst in California.

Mr. Pulitzer pays his right-hand, John Cockerill, twice the salary of a U.S. Senator. Colonel Cockerill's fully in charge when Mr. Pulitzer disappears to Paris or Bar Harbor. Mr. Pulitzer drove one editor to drink, one to suicide and a third and a fourth to insanity. Colonel Cockerill has an advantage. He *arrived* insane. He shot a man in St. Louis and escaped prosecution due to the *Dispatch's* influence. He drinks too much; he was engaged to be married until the evening he made water into the grand piano of his future in-laws.

Other reporters take urgent concerns to Colonel Cockerill. Nellie Bly takes hers straight to Mr. Pulitzer. She wears her glasses when she visits the dome's top. She's severely near-sighted without them, and the view runs from Long Island to Governor Island and to the forest in the distant north. The towers of the Brooklyn Bridge seem close enough to touch. How farcical that New York's highest overlook is wasted on a man who'd be content placing telephone calls from an outhouse throne.

"The dizziness of American freedom," she says at the vastness.

Mr. Pulitzer bought the *World* six years ago from propagandists who used it to inflate the price of stocks. The newspaper seized influence when it explained away Grover Cleveland's illegitimate child in 1884. If six hundred New York men had voted another way, the state and the presidency would have gone to James Blaine.

The *World's* Circulation ballooned from 17,000 to 250,000, surpassing all comers. There are a lot of comers. The city's 1.5 million are served by fifty dailies that sell three million copies. She's proud to be a part of it, but she's discontent. She's come to Mr. Pulitzer's dome today to extend her wingspan.

"Why are you here, Miss Bly?"

Reporters at competing papers criticize the *World* as lowbrow and edited for the working masses. They accuse it of covering only crime and corruption. Last summer's heat wave killed four hundred children in the ghetto. Mr. Pulitzer wrote the Page One headline *How Babies are Baked*. Shocking, but he'll build another skyscraper before he's done, he wants to build above the God he doesn't believe in.

The trades attribute soaring circulation to sensationalism, two-cent copies and free copies given to hotel guests. Her colleagues wallow in poor esteem. She wonders why. The trades deride the *World,* but readers love it.

"Are you here for the scenery?" Mr. Pulitzer says. "Speak, Miss Bly, I've work to do."

She takes a deep breath. The odor of his office is of sweet cigars, richer than the cigarette smoke that clouds the newsroom. Two washings are required to remove an afternoon's work from her hair. She feels his bullfrog eyes on her back as she stares out at the Statue of Liberty. He sighs impatience. She looks up to stretch her neck. The ceiling is frescoed but no one ever notices, no one notices anything save this view.

"Why do you suppose the French designed Lady Liberty to be unattractive?" she says.

Mr. Pulitzer's rare laugh turns into a serious cough until he can't answer.

"They hid her figure beneath an unflattering bronze gown," Nellie Bly says. "Do you suppose it was meant as an insult to American women because we have morals? Even so, I trust the French more than the Brits."

"I don't trust the French, the Brits, or you, Miss Bly," Mr. Pulitzer says. "Charles Dana at the *Sun* is right. If we let women vote it will introduce a spitefulness into politics that is peculiarly feminine."

"Be that as it may." She twirls to catch his watering eyes weakly staring at her through pince-nez spectacles. He's more blind than she is—but not as blind as he lets on.

He raised the funds for Lady Liberty's pedestal, but no amount of philanthropy immunizes him from the sign on his desk. ACCURACY IS TO A NEWSPAPER WHAT VIRTUE IS TO A WOMAN. It's so large she could read it without her glasses. She suspects he displays it to annoy her.

"The trades say that girl reporters are less accurate," Nellie Bly says.

"They over-exaggerate. That's a known fact."

"Who? Girls or the trades?"

"Both. Newspapers run on tobacco, but girl reporters gripe about spittoons. Girls keep men hobbled inside a jacket."

"I daresay, you need never wear a jacket for me."

"Of course, I will. You're my treasure. You make men clumsy, get them to say stupid things for print. Never seen anything like it."

Mr. Pulitzer treats newsboys well, pays them a fifty-fifty split, a cent for every copy. The sad orphans love him as a father and she suspects that he loves her as a daughter. That's why she forgives him, but she continues to stand, even she doesn't know why. Probably to punish him for the precious words that yesterday were trimmed from her work to make room for an advertisement for men's long underwear now that frost has arrived.

"Girls ruined this business, but I'll wear a jacket as long as you manipulate your smile. Please sit."

Male correspondents are always competing for conspicuous play. Her life is different. She leaves evenings at seven o'clock to dine with sources at the Baldwin Hotel. Her items are *always* Page One with her name in the headline, but she stands to punish Mr. Pulitzer for his failure to give her an assignment as meaningful as the one that made her famous. Her infiltration of Blackwell's Asylum was two years ago. Those clippings will soon yellow in the morgue.

"The trades are saying I'm a one-trick pony."

She loves reading her name in other newspapers. The *San Francisco Chronicle* gave her credit when The Great Asylum for the Insane broke ground in Agnews, California. That prompted a second letter of gratitude scribbled in the hand of a gentleman with poor penmanship. His first letter arrived two years ago from San Francisco. The second letter arrived more recently from Salt Lake City. The gentleman's mother is housed at The Marine Hospital that Houses Crazy Seamen, a firetrap that will be abandoned when The Great Asylum opens.

Both letters touched Nellie Bly for their brevity and honesty. Letters from women go on and on about nothing. Letters from other gentlemen are flirtatious. But these two letters said only that she'd saved his mother's life. They were written in the same hand, but the signatures were different. The first letter was signed by a Mr. B-something, and the second letter by a Mr. P-something. Both signatures were illegible. The sender was apparently ashamed that his mother was in a madhouse for hysteria.

She loves the letters above all others. She saves them in their envelopes and uses them as a bookmark, the San Francisco and Salt Lake City postmarks rising above the pages of *Ben Hur* or *Gulliver's Travels*.

"You're not a one-trick pony," Mr. Pulitzer says. "Everyone remembers the story you wrote about Casey's strikeout."

She's not proud of it, but no girl had ever reported a sporting item, and hers went into syndication. It made gentlemen laugh and laugh and turned the nation more base ball crazy than ever. Female attendance is through the roof, although Negro attendance has fallen sharply due to the banishment of base ball's last colored player, the catcher Fleetwood Walker.

"You could join the hunt for Walter Brewster," Mr. Pulitzer says.

The missing umpire went ignored by the eastern press. The disinterest ended when the little-known actor, DeWolf Hopper, memorized the fifty-two lines of the *Casey at the Bat* ballad in one hour and recited them at the Wallack Theater in New York. That was in August 1888, four months after the strikeout. By happenstance, there was a club of base ball players in attendance and they stood on their seats and cheered like hooligans. DeWolf Hopper repeats the ballad night after night to theaters packed with two thousand and more. The poem's made Hopper rich and famous and has caused New Yorkers to take a keen interest in Walter Brewster's whereabouts.

"I will never attend another base ball match," Nellie Bly says. "I pray never to write another base ball item again."

Wood Dryden, a reporter at the *San Francisco Examiner,* has been on the story since Day One. He accuses the umpire of driving the Northern California Base Ball Association minister to the grave. William Rufus Wheaton was seventy-four, but spry before the strikeout. He became the subject of cartoons and died more or less of public criticism, for assigning an inexperienced and inept umpire to a critical game.

Mr. Dryden owns the umpire story. *The Journalist* trade publication declared him the first correspondent outside of New York to rank among the best. Nellie Bly remains the only female correspondent so honored. The madhouse story was her idea, and at last she's come up with another. She's as slim as a child, but she'll need to have the presence of a fat opera singer to convince Mr. Pulitzer of her scheme. It's perfect. But Mr. Pulitzer will never agree to it—because he loves her as a daughter.

"I will soon move to London," she says to the window. "I was offered a situation with *Vanity Fair.*"

Mr. Pulitzer coughs again, this time to stall. She knows he can't let her go. "*Vanity Fair* is a society magazine for people of privilege," he says.

"Nevertheless, it behooves me to leave."

"Tommyrot. What can I do to change your mind? Eh? A bonus."

"I deserve one," she says. "My salary is enough to make a common cow cry."

"You'll have your bonus. The long economic depression is at last over."

"There has never been a depression for newspapers," she says. "The funds for this view were collected penny by penny from my efforts. Girls make livings while men make fortunes."

"I want to make you happy."

She turns. "All the money of the Vanderbilts will not make me happy. I am weary of being famous for being famous. I am done wasting time going through bags of mail. I never escape the tyranny of the letter opener. I need to write something of consequence again."

"Please sit."

She sits on his desk, which makes her a head taller. "I have an idea for a story. A series of stories. Three months of stories, if all goes well."

"Meritorious," Mr. Pulitzer says. "Please take a chair, like a lady."

She smooths her dress and eases into the deep leather. "You will not approve of my idea, congressman."

He dislikes being called congressman, which is why she employs it. He was elected four years ago, but found it impossible to work among corrupt politicians while operating newspapers devoted to weeding them out. He resigned after a few months.

"You will not approve," she says.

"I approve ideas that sell copies."

"You are familiar with the novel *Around the World in Eighty Days*?"

"By the Frenchman."

"It is pure fiction—at least it was when first published fifteen years ago. Mankind has never seen such progress."

"The Frenchman Jules Verne."

She takes a tattered copy of the book from her satchel and hands it to Mr. Pulitzer. "I've never had the time to read it," he says.

"It is not lengthy. To the point," Nellie Bly says. "I read it four times. Now, I intend to circle the globe in eighty days."

Mr. Pulitzer at last sits, grimacing on his way down. "You have never once been at sea, eh?"

"I have ridden down riverbanks so steep that my stirrups were near the horse's ears. A girl who can do that can get her sea legs."

"When was the last time, sweetheart, you opened a door for yourself?"

"Just now, when I entered this crow's nest."

"These are indeed days of great advancement, skyscrapers and Linotype," he says. "It may be possible to circumvent the world in eighty days. For a bloody man. A girl could never do it, not one as thin as a poplar. Look at your tiny feet. Eh? What size are they?"

Her lips grow taught. "My strides are longer than yours, congressman."

"That chair swallows you whole. You'd be eaten by lions."

"I have no intention of passing through Africa."

"Heathens everywhere in China. Every man a hoodlum, every other girl a whore. Congress passed a ban on Chinese immigration eight years ago, but that won't protect you abroad. Yellow rapists escape punishment."

She scoffs. "Your Colonel Cockerill escaped punishment in St. Louis due entirely to your influence."

"A girl needs a mountain of baggage for an eighty-day trip. You couldn't carry it all."

"If you say no, I will move my belongings to London."

His legs and arms seem drugged with heaviness. There is a twitch in his fingers holding the book, more noticeable than before. His reddish hair grows more disheveled in front of her eyes. "I may have an idea." He hollers down through the speaking tube. "Colonel Cockerill, find Claude Ponsonby and send him to my office. Eh."

Nellie Bly knows the name. She's never met Mr. Ponsonby but he's a rising star in the building, a new typesetter from Utah who is impossibly fast and accurate. Most typesetters are Irish, but Mr. Ponsonby's said to be odd. Maybe a Mormon. Know one knows anything about him. The oddest of men, who says little unless he gets started on a prolonged diatribe about points and picas.

He's yet to be blamed for a single typo. She cannot count the times Irishmen's typos blemished her good name. She has excellent penmanship, but if she happened to scribble the word typo in her copy, it would surely be printed in the newspaper as *tyqo*. Readers believe that reporters are responsible for headlines and misspellings. If Mr. Ponsonby makes her seem smart, then God bless the Mormon's soul.

Mr. Pulitzer pulls a handkerchief from his breast pocket and blows his nose. He removes his eyewear and dabs his weepy eyes with the same snotty rag. "I lost a bet to Ponsonby," he says. "I wagered he couldn't do the typesetting of two men. He did the typesetting of three."

Mr. Ponsonby arrives in a jiffy. He's breathing hard; he didn't take the elevator. Mr. Pulitzer stands for his entrance where he remained seated for hers. The typesetter is short, but more handsome than she expects, even in his work apron with a pocketful of composing reels and tying-up string. Typesetters wear short sleeves to keep their shirts from being ruined with the printer's ink that forever stains their fingertips. No matter how handsome, Mr. Ponsonby's doomed to marry a plain factory girl.

He's nervous in her presence. His blackened fingers pull a base ball from his apron's pocket. He's clean-shaven and vaguely familiar, but they've never met. She would have remembered that scar on his forehead. Perhaps she ignored him once or twice in the elevator, though the composing room's on the second floor above the din of the presses, and the men in short sleeves are expected to hike the stairs. Nellie Bly never goes down; she's never toured the presses. Where some people fear heights, she fears being trapped in the banging bowels below.

"Ponsonby, meet Miss Nellie Bly."

Men are often fumbling and speechless when they meet her, but Mr. Ponsonby can't breathe. Other men are in awe, but his reaction is beyond that, like a man who seems happy for the first time in his life, a curmudgeon who is suddenly inclined to do handsprings in Central Park. For all her marriage proposals, she's never seen a man faint at the sight of her. Mr. Ponsonby might be the first.

"Ponsonby will be your escort around the world," Mr. Pulitzer says.

It's her turn to faint, not from delight but from outrage. She nearly loses control of the gum under her tongue. "I will not," is all she can muster. She's on the verge of an embarrassing meltdown, one of those tantrums gentlemen reporters have when their items get spiked to make way for hers.

"Ponsonby, remember our wager? What did I promise you if you were to typeset at the speed of two? Eh?"

"A holiday, sir. A week off and a train ride to Bar Harbor."

"You've hit the lotto, Ponsonby. Any man who can do the work of three deserves a holiday for a king. You're getting a trip around the world. I have a simple question. Is it possible to complete it in eighty days?"

Mr. Ponsonby responds quickly. "I've long plotted it on a globe. I believe it is possible with the completion of the Samut Prakan to Bangkok railway. At the mouth of the Chao Phraya River."

Mr. Pulitzer laughs and coughs. "Mr. Ponsonby is an almanac, eh?"

Nellie Bly rolls her eyes in an exaggerated way so that they are sure to be seen behind her glasses. "Mr. Ponsonby seems to be one part almanac, one part cobbler interested in my shoes."

"Size three," Mr. Ponsonby says.

"Do you also work in a carnival?"

"You're the world's best correspondent. I admire you more than anyone in the world."

Nellie Bly is touched. "Thank you, Mr. Ponsonby. You seem genuine and sincere and honest, I owe you honesty in return. I will travel alone. It has nothing to do with you. I despise all escorts. I have yet to meet one I can stomach for three hours, much less three months."

Mr. Ponsonby takes no offense but Mr. Pulitzer does. "This is not negotiable, eh. You will obey my demand. Girls don't travel the world alone." He points to the insulting sign on his desk. "I will protect your virtue as I protect this newspaper's accuracy."

"Let me assure you, congressman, my virtue needs no protection."

"I will not have Nellie Bly walking about unescorted. Even Annie Oakley travels with western men to protect her. And she shoots straighter than any man."

"Does Mr. Ponsonby even know how to box as a gentleman? He may be from the west, but he does not appear to be a man of derring-do. Annie Oakley has more courage."

"I have *cojones*," Mr. Ponsonby says. "I have a sister named Annie."

"He speaks in gibberish," Nellie Bly says. "I will be leaving for *Vanity Fair*. This is the straw that broke the camel's back."

"Huh?" Mr. Ponsonby says.

"He's odd," Mr. Pulitzer says. "All typesetters are odd. We're all odd. Ponsonby and I are in the same camp. He's loyal. I know his character; we've played chess. He sees things from a unique perspective."

"Angle," Mr. Ponsonby says.

"I vouch for his honor," Mr. Pulitzer says. "I trust him as a son. He's almost biblical in his servitude. He never drinks; he'll never be three sheets to the wind."

Mr. Ponsonby gets a confused look on his face as if the entire discussion is in French. Nellie Bly gives the room her smile of a dancer with blistering feet. "What you say, congressman, does not matter two straws."

"Three sheets? Two straws?" Mr. Ponsonby says.

"Miss Bly, you are no longer to behave as a child," Mr. Pulitzer says. "The pluck and sand that brought you to fame is gristmill for gossip. Imagine if I make no attempt to keep you from harm's way? What will readers say if something happens to you? I will be roasted and deservedly so."

"I waive you of all responsibility; it will be my fault whatever happens. A loving God will not let me be ravaged by a yellow man."

"Maybe I shouldn't have saved you from the white-capped nurses. Maybe you belong on Blackwell's Island."

"You belong there, congressman. You and your quirky chess mate can live out your days together."

"I'm making a huge sacrifice, giving Ponsonby up when Christmas advertising will push the *World* to twelve pages."

"Twelve pages times 250,000 copies equals three million," Ponsonby says.

"Keep him," Nellie Bly says. "He is prideful and horrid, showing off his calculations. Eighty *seconds* with him is too many."

"You give me a protesting stomach," Mr. Pulitzer says. "I've yet to shoot a woman. Neither have I understood one. The earth is filled with opium dens, joss houses, peep shows, vice and squalor. Every man a hoodlum…"

"…Every girl a whore. Asia is no less safe than Manhattan," Nellie Bly says.

"Four hundred New York girls arrested for soliciting last year, up from one-sixty in eighty-seven," Mr. Ponsonby says, squeezing his base ball. "I read it upside down and right to left."

"It's because of the crackdown," Mr. Pulitzer says. "Any young lady unescorted late at night is arrested."

"Women deserve freedom." Nellie Bly says. "If men can't behave, they are the ones who should be sequestered."

"You'll warm to Mr. Ponsonby. He's an acquired taste."

She removes her glasses for emphasis. "I stepped inside the lunatic asylum alone."

"That was different. Then, you were a penny-poor governess. If things had gone south, no one would have noticed. Ponsonby will not only protect you. He'll protect me as the owner of this institution. Like it or not, you're the *New York World's* most priceless asset."

"A slave it seems."

"An investment. My fiduciary duty."

"Then I'll be on my way to *Vanity Fair*."

"You're talent is too big and rambunctious for anywhere except New York."

Mr. Pulitzer is right about that. "If you insist on Mr. Ponsonby going on my detail, I will cross the street to the *Sun*. Charles Dana will gladly finance my voyage. My readers will cross the street with me. Imagine the circulation of this miserable little sheet the day I resign."

She's right about that. "We'll send a man to race against you, eh."

"I will race whatever horrid man you choose to put up."

Mr. Pulitzer slams the novel on his desk. "Our hand-picked man will set sail tomorrow. He'll be in England while you're still negotiating with Charles Dana. You'll be stuffing your bags with girl things when our man gets to Paris."

She stares at Mr. Ponsonby. "I will not have my readers believe that it was this curmudgeon who circumnavigated the world and let me tag along. Readers will think I am this typesetter's stenographer."

"We'll tell readers you're going it alone. Nothing sells papers like a girl at risk."

Mr. Pulitzer is making sense, now. Her expression must thaw because he slaps Mr. Ponsonby on the back in victory. "Maybe we'll kill two birds."

"Beg pardon?" Mr. Ponsonby backs away as if he dislikes being touched.

"Maybe you and Miss Bly will find the umpire in Timbuktu, eh. The *San Francisco Examiner* is still writing about Walter Brewster. Nobody's seen him since he escaped through a downpour into the Mormon Temple.

Mr. Ponsonby, without invitation, recites a stanza from the middle of the ballad.

"From the benches, black with people, there went up a muffled roar,
like the beating of the storm-waves on a stern and distant shore.
'Kill him! Kill the umpire!' shouted someone on the stand;
and it's likely they'd a-killed him had not Casey raised his hand."

"I wish Willie Hearst never had published that poem," Mr. Pulitzer says. "The entire nation wonders what has become of WalterdamnBrewster."

"I am happy he struck out Casey," Nellie Bly says. "The endless match might still be going to this day. Thank my stars, Casey struck out and there were no additional endings. I wanted to get out ahead of the traffic, but the score remained close. When the umpire was speared head first into the ground by Oakland's Old Reliable Jake, my escort begged to stay."

"Casey's still crazed," Mr. Pulitzer says. "He abandoned his participation in the five-continent base ball journey with Al Spalding's team. He won't rest until he finds the umpire. He's obsessed."

"Red-haired men are all obsessed," Nellie Bly says. "All men of all hair colors are obsessed, even bald men."

"Willie Hearst and Wood Dryden won't rest, either, until Brewster's found."

"Newspapers outside of New York are published with scissors and a paste pot." She folds her arms. "I won't slow to look for Walter Brewster in Timbuktu or anywhere. My journey is a race to make history."

"Agreed," Mr. Pulitzer says. "You will suck the air out of the umpire story. Talk of him will dry up the minute you set sail. We're way behind on Walter Brewster, so let's put him in the shade."

She puts on her glasses. Mr. Ponsonby's squeezing his base ball and mumbling another stanza and staring at her feet again. Then he looks up and square into her eyes as if she were the blessed French nun Anne-Marie Javouhey. Nellie Bly can't imagine eighty days with a man who worships her in such an unconventional way. He's like a loyal dog, except a dog would provide more engaging conversation. If she falls overboard at sea, this milquetoast man will dive in to drown in her company.

"Speed is of the utmost, Mr. Ponsonby, far more so than my safety," she says.

"Don't listen to her," Mr. Pulitzer says. "Protect her. That's your one job. They'd lynch me if anything unsavory happened to NelliedamnBly."

A headline cries out the next day in *The New York World*:

NELLIE BLY TO CIRCLE GLOBE IN EIGHTY DAYS

——————

Jules Verne's Fiction to Become Fact
Our Sweetheart Nellie Promises to Perish at Sea
Rather than Face Abject Humiliation

——————

Daring Attempt by Our Unescorted Beauty

The item has one quotation from Nellie Bly. "I would rather complete my journey dead and successful than alive and behind time. Wish me God-speed."

Much of New York City swarms Hoboken Pier to wave to their heroine. Claude Ponsonby steps aboard the Augusta Victoria unnoticed. He's never noticed.

Unless something disastrous happens.

"Let me root, root, root for the home team,
If they don't win, it's a shame."—Jack Norworth

April 20, 1888, 6:12 p.m.
It's a Friday

CHAPTER NINE

thirty-eight minutes before the strikeout

The Judge had warned me about Cap Anson's screech but it catches me by surprise anyway. It comes as the shortstop's throw smacks into the first baseman's hands and I declare the Niner runner out. It's a dying-rabbit screech to grab the attention of coyotes on over to Calaveras County. The fanatics agree with Cap Anson's opinion, and they remind me of my incompetence.

"Only horses sleep standing up," one hollers, which is a falsehood. Elephants do too. Flamingos.

Cap Anson follows up his screech with a second visit. He approaches me, fly still undone. He walks slowly, makes the crowd wait. I rise from my crouch, remove my mask and take a deep breath of my favorite time of day. Games are usually over by now. The men who stand in the Negro section remain in the sun as do those restrained by ropes down the foul lines, but the grandstand is prepared to lay down a blanket of late afternoon shade that'll swallow me from behind.

For now, the yard remains in sunshine, a blur of oils on a canvas, brown soil across the bottom, brilliant grass in the middle, sky blue on top. Rather than find Cap Anson's eyes, I find the white-capped mountains a hundred miles off in foul ground left of third base. Anson likes to be a card at the Home of the Mudville Niners, and he hands me a pair of eyeglasses. The audience roars with laughter.

"You missed that one," Cap Anson says, but he's wrong. Partisanship deceives eyes. I heard the snap of the ball then the thud of the runner's foot at first base. If the foot had arrived ahead of the ball I'd have heard a thud-snap. I'm on my game, I'm seeing balls and strikes, bangers and whackers like Papa saw trout rise from waters beneath the willows. The sun is low and warm at my back like his lantern was when we cleaned our catch. Nothing interferes with my eyesight and judgment, I haven't missed one all day.

I hand the glasses to the Niner mascot. In good fun, Clarence puts them on, stands behind the plate, and pretends to declare strikes. He gets laughs, but fewer than I expect. There's tension about. The merriment of the early innings has gone sour. From the sea of bowler hats rises a quiet of discontent. The men were expecting a done deal by now, a dozen runs or more. They were expecting Niners pitcher Squawks Clarke to have switched to an underhand delivery to rest his arm for two games tomorrow. He can't rest. It's a duel; the score's two-all in the bottom of the eighth. The picnic is over; the game far from it.

The fanatics decide they've been overly civil and it's high time they give me a roasting about my zone. They say I'm inept in general and if I got one declaration right it must've been when they were on the crapper. They chirp that my judgment has gone south. "If you had one more eye, you'd be a cyclops."

I've heard such remarks before. I've heard them in a half dozen languages at Jabbering Seals games. "We know you're blind. We've seen your wife."

I ignore it like The Judge taught me. The fanatics pay for the privilege, he says. But they have no imagination. The next time I meet up with him for Chinese and beer, we'll think of some fresh aspersions for them to cast. That's assuming there is a next time for The Judge. I think of him in a hotel bed on Beach Hill and I shiver. Not for him, but for my own vulnerability.

A voice behind me cuts to the bone. "If the Niners streak ends today, it's on you ump." It comes from a few rows up, from the direction of Nellie Bly's fancy-man.

"Finish strong." That voice is from inside myself. My toes curl under to regain focus.

Squawks Clarke can't save his arm for tomorrow. His pitches sing soprano. Mouse Mathews is at the bat and he has a half tick to gauge the path of Clarke's pitches before making a decision to swing or not. It's pitcher vs. pitcher. Squawks hasn't allowed a base runner since the ball rolled under the fence, but Mouse biffs a baser. It skips five or seven times like a flat stone on a pond, gaining speed over the top of second base.

T.J. McAloon is next and, with that withered right arm, lays down a bunt with his left. Flynn pegs it to first but it sails into the mob behind the ropes and the Oaklands, like that, have runners on second and third, nobody out.

I hate to see games booted away unscientifically. On the other hand, I can't be blamed for throws into the mob, and if the Niners lose, Flynn will be the goat. I'll be let off the hook, which is where I long to be. I look about the crowd. Anguish is on every face, as if the farmlands have been devoured by locusts. Nellie Bly's is the lone smile. She is especially pretty without her glasses. Her fancy man is in hell, but she seems to enjoy his being there.

Grasshopper Nova is at the bat and Squawks whistles the next pitch behind his head. I have to believe the Niners have it in for him. That's the most dangerous pitch there is; batters instinctively duck into it, but the Mexican stands like a statue. The ball travels an inch behind his skull, clips his cocked bat, hits me hard in the mask, and I holler "Foul."

"*Órale*," the Mexican says and the fanatics cheer.

"Time," I holler, and I walk halfway to the pitching box. I stop short because I'm headachy from the blow. "No glory in being a man-hitter," I tell Squawks Clarke, but he doesn't care two cents about Grasshopper Nova or me. He spits juice and digs a trench with his spikes. "Throw at a batsman again, and I'll toss you," I say. "Nobody gets killed on my yard, not with but an inning left to play."

The Judge would be proud of my command, my presence. I step over to the Niner bench and tell Cap Anson his pitcher's been cautioned, and I make sure Old Reliable Jake hears it coaching at third. I'm being courteous to all parties, but all parties reward my courtesy with ugly stares and spits.

I'm a bit shaken—that pitch would've killed me without my mask—but I get back behind the bat and holler "Play," which is a queer word for all-out war.

Grasshopper Nova is a better catcher than a hitter. He nubs the next pitch toward Blake, who fields it with ease. Blake takes a look at Mouse on third to discourage an attempt to score, and then throws to first.

The Mexican has pace. Thud-snap. "Not out," I holler and I'm damn certain of it.

Another rabbit screech. "You made that declaration from Nevada."

I don't want a hollering match across the diamond, so I walk through a mudslide of boos to the Niner bench. I look Cap Anson in the chin and I say that I try to get as close to first base as I can, but I'm stuck near the plate with Mouse a threat to score.

"You want me closer to first or for the declaration at home?" I say.

"I want a real umpire. You're ass-shit."

I hear no question, and I give Cap Anson the last word. Old Reliable Jake steps to the bat with the bases drunk and nobody out. The bases aren't really drunk; there's a runner aboard each. But they wobble due to my headache. Old Jake crowds tight, his toes on the marble, his elbows hang in the strike zone. He wants Squawks to stone him, he'll go to the grave to push across a run. All joy's been beaten from Old Jake. He gets blamed in the *Tribune* each time the Oaklands lose and the Oaklands lose each time.

Five pitches later, I declare striker three. It's a pitch inside enough to spin a cap, but Old Jake's tight, a strike no doubt. Friendly cheers come from the crowd, but Old Jake says I'm a pissant.

Salty O'Reilly calls me a pissant, too, when he takes a third strike at the kneecaps for the second out. That stirs more loud cheers of kindness from the Niner crowd. Friendly cow bells clank, the Niner fanatics are thinking my zone's pretty righteous after all; I'm only half blind. Old Reliable Jake arrives from the Oakland bench with a second opinion.

"You're a cave cricket."

He's hot, his acne scars aglitter with pus. I remove my wire mask and put it under my arm. I give him two seconds of eye-to-eye respect before my gaze darts away. I'm not interested in faces; I'll know if a man's fly is unbuttoned before I'll know the tilt of his brow. I'm unobservant about lots of things, which lets me be overly observant about the *right* things.

"Get in the game arsehole," Old Jake says. "You're the rankest umpire ever set foot on a diamond. You struck me out on a pitch that about put me in the hospital. Salty's was in the effing dirt."

I let him exaggerate all complected. Umpires who defend themselves make things worse. Old Jake's vitriol wears on me some, but the Niner fanatics get behind me with boos for him. A breeze kicks up a coolness on my sweaty neck. The tintinnabulation of bells are on my behalf. Old Jake sees me looking at the ground in comfort and assumes I'm unimpressed with his words. He figures hollering louder will grab my attention.

I long to remind him that I had nothing to do with the pop-up he fumbled that let a Niners' run score, or that he crowds the plate way too tight. I want to say that he's lucky because the Niners couldn't score on twenty-one straight balls. I want to say that the Oaklands lose all the time to podunk teams far worse than the Niners, and today they have their chance. But I say nothing. I don't opine. I keep my yap shut and let the catcalls encourage him to sit down his butt.

"If you're going to screw me, at least kiss me first," Old Jake says. I take a glance up at Nellie Bly to see if she's offended. She seems to be enjoying things.

Old Jake retreats but takes a detour past the Niners' bench. He tells Cap Anson the Oaklands are being home-towned. Anson farts and says the Oaklands are alive only because one rolled under the blessed fence.

I fear them taking socks at each other, but Old Jake keeps walking to his bench. The fanatics feel the need to rub salt in Old Jake's wounds and they holler in unison "left, right, left, right, left, right," with his each step. Jake picks up three bats, every bat the Oaklands own, and hurls them out onto the diamond. He has crossed a line and deserves a tossing, but I figure an ejectment might signal that I've lost control of things and cause William Rufus Wheaton to rethink my future appointments. I recall that Cap Anson called Old Jake a cocksucker before the first pitch and I figure things are even.

I'm seven outs away from getting out of here intact, and I let the lumber scatter harmless. Nobody's hurt. Old Jake detects weakness though, and he's back in my face spewing sewage breath and The Judge's voice is in my head telling me to hold my own or things will go round the bend. Round the bend means the same thing as haywire. I don't know what it means when things have gone haywire, but I know things are going south.

"You're a stiff," Old Jake hollers at me. "An effing stiff."

I want to say that I'm the one disinterested party at the yard, but I hear no question.

"You're at heart a Niners man and everyone knows it." Old Jake puts the bill of his cap an inch from the top of my head. He sprays like a tomcat and I turn the bill of my cap around to the front to ward off spittle into my eyeballs. He tries to get his bill under mine to beak me on the forehead, but I'm too short. He uses his foot to drag a pile of dirt on my shoes. I'm looking at my feet when they begin a slow retreat, exploring for grass.

"Sit down, Pop," a fanatic hollers at Jake.

Old Jake is still hot about his own strikeout. He points to the pitcher's box where Squawks tosses the leather up and down. "He tried to plug me. Didn't he?"

A question, so I respond. "You were crowding, toes on the marble. It was a strike for sure."

Old Jake plows another dirt furrow over my shoes. "Blind as a cricket." Maybe his breath smells less like sewage, more like tin. "You're missing a good game."

I can't help myself. "Yeah, I know," I say. "Where is it?" It's a good joke but Old Jake doesn't laugh. "You're blind as a cave cricket, an effing cave cricket."

"Sit down you old buggy horse," a fanatic hollers at Jake.

"Horses don't sit," I mumble, but Old Jake doesn't like me defending him.

"You're an embarrassment to Honest John Gaffney," he says to me.

"Honest John Gaffney's a tall tale, a fish story." I kick myself for responding, for encouraging more conversation.

"That's bull," Jake says.

"A decision's been made. We'll live with it."

He stoops and makes another failed attempt to beak me with his bill. "You must be in collaboration with the gambling society, like that umpire Dick Higham in Detroit."

I back farther into the sod as Old Jake gets hotter. "I'm doing my best to keep you in the game," I say. "Accusing me of skulduggery makes that a challenge. Go back to your bench."

"What if I don't?"

"Then we'll find another way."

Old Jake tries to kick dirt into my shins but we're in the grass. No sandstorm rattles off my trousers, and Jake gets aggravated all the more. He raises both arms in the air and bumps me with his torso. Then he blames *me* for the bumping.

"Touch me again and I'll knock your nose foul," he says.

"I meant to toss you."

"Go ahead. Toss me." He throws his cap and the fanatics renew their remarks about his baldheadedness.

"Go home, hairy," one hollers. "Go home to Oakland, old man, and worry about your bowel movements."

Cap Anson smirks from the Niner bench in his coat and tie and trousers with an undone fly. Squawks Clarke flips the ball up and down in the box. Old Jake bumps me again and says, "I warned you never to bump me." He retrieves his cap and bumps me once more. I don't make a big show of it, I point to the turnstile and say, "Time for you to go."

"What?"

"Catch the early train."

"What?" He raises his hands to the air like it's a big surprise. "You're jacking me?"

"Yeah, you're gone." I look him straight in the eyes so there's no misunderstanding. "An ejectment from the grounds."

My eyes can't keep ahold of his. I find a cord in his ruddy neck that stands out. Then I look at his hands. His fingers extend into clam rakes, then clinch into freckled boulders. A cry rattles in his throat, his body shakes head to toe like a dog shitting chicken bones.

"You're jacking me?"

"One of us has to leave The Home of the Mudville Niners and it can't be me."

Old Jake gathers up the scattered bats, and he heaves all three toward the pitcher's box. Squawks stops tossing the ball in case he has to dodge, but the willows tumble short. Squawks smirks. Cap Anson smirks. Clarence leans on the broom and smirks. Jake hollers that I'm a shit-ass two or three times as he gathers the bats into a fresh bundle and heaves them in my direction. I side-step one that bounds by end over end.

"Don't call me a cocksucker," he says.

He's gone irrational, hearing things, forgetting who bumped who and who said what. "I never called you nothing," I say.

I'm losing my presence. I'm feeling like I did that time I slugged a redwood tree. I make a fist with my sore hand. I need to be alone for a second, so I turn my back on him and walk toward second. Jake trails after me, chaffing. We walk first toward Mouse on the bag at third, then toward Grasshopper on first, back toward McAloon. I walk in a zigzag and he zigzags to follow. Old Jake is on my heels like a duckling who quacks one language. "Don't call me a cocksucker. You're the ass-shit cocksucker. You're the shit-ass."

His old legs are buckshot. I out-maneuver him with my odd gait, but he anticipates one of my zigs near second and zags to appear in my face. "You're umpiring this game for one reason."

I stop. "What's that, Jake?"

"To fleece us."

"You need to leave," I say.

"You're here for one reason," Old Jake says.

"To do a job. A square job."

I hear a fanatic holler in my support, "Where's your cane, Grandpa?"

Old Jake stays in my face. "You're a loafer."

I have the hide of a rhino but it bothers me that Nellie Bly has to hear him call me a loafer. I turn my back to him again. Old Jake pulls second base from the ground and hurls the sandbag at me. It goes high of my head and thirty feet into center field. I aim my steps for home plate because the wheels have fallen off and, unlike Papa, home is where I need to be.

Old Jake follows. He grabs the broom from Clarence and swings it at me. I duck a couple of slow swipes and he throws the broom away. He lies down on the plate in histrionics, blubbering like a colicky baby. I'm tempted to do the same to disrespect him, but I turn my back on Old Jake and ignore him. He gets up behind me and his tinny breath is a furnace on my neck. He grabs me by the shoulders and turns me with those clam rakes. I'm ready to duck a sock when he seizes me two-fisted by the collar. Rather than a stand-up fight, he yanks me in one motion by my bow tie and off my feet.

I hear squeals from beneath feathered hats as Old Reliable Jake spears me face first into the dirt. I'm a penknife in a game of mumblety-peg. It happens too fast to feel pain, it happens so fast that it does not occur to me anything extraordinary is happening. By the time I know that I've been caught back assward by the shit-house beast, I'm back on my feet. Blood pours from above my eye and drips warm from my chin to my mask wedged under my arm.

"I'll pack your mud with that broom handle," Old Jake says.

"Is that why they call this dry town Mudville?"

He doesn't answer my question. He shoves me back to the ground, straddles me, pries open my jaw and spits juice down my throat. That inspires strength. I push him off and I'm up coughing and retching and there's too much blood running into my eyes to see Casey coming. He's there all at once between us, his back to me and his saving hands held high to Old Jake.

"C'mon, coacher," Casey says.

The Niners run from all positions and Jackleg Preacher's up from the bench because that's what an outfit managed by Cap Anson does to protect a player worth all the gold that's left in California. The other bench empties, too, but if one Oakland player takes a swipe at Casey, a hundred toughs will pour in from behind the foul-line ropes.

I want to assume command, but the oil paints of the yard go black, and *I'm a small boy examining a pill bug.*

"Are you OK ump?" It's Casey's voice from beneath the rock.

"Something's tugging at Papa's fly rod," I say.

A fighter's on the other end, Papa says. Try to land it, never fear losing a fish—or you will.

"Hey, Ump, wake up."

"Home is where I need to be," I say.

Back home, Annie Katharine screams with the colic. Papa puts a stale biscuit in her tiny fist. She quiets for a second to examine it, teethes it, but her crying resumes.

"Ump, you OK?"

"When you're up to your neck in shit it doesn't hurt to piss your pants."

"You're funny," Casey says. He hoists me up from the tar pit of the painting. My knees buckle in the oil and Casey sits me down. He tugs my cap low over the cut to dam the blood and I sink back into tar. Daylight turns to pitch.

"Abe Lincoln was lonesome. Newton, too, beneath an apple tree when gravity hit him square. Emily Dickinson was scared to come out of her room for her father's funeral."

"He's gone mad, Captain, he's talking poetry. Hey, Ump, how many fingers am I holding up?"

Moms' fingers are purple. She's come out from the dark of her melancholia to make my birthday supper. The front door is open to cool the house from the June stove, and to welcome Papa—if he ever comes home. The food is eaten, only purple lips and a purple dish where blackberry cobbler once steamed.

"Clarence, go get the smelling salts. The Ump's up a creek."

The fragrance of chopped walnuts sweeps about with Moms but she is distant and tired. The boy takes care of her and Annie Katharine. Annie Katharine's easy to care for, she soon outgrows the colic, but the boy doesn't know what to do about Moms.

"He's muddled, Captain," Casey says.

The boy finds Moms half alive in the attic. She's been missing for two days.

"He needs a doc," Casey says.

"I see this all the time," the doctor says. "Another woman suffering hysteria and the general paralysis of isolation and it's too bad they never have the money to build The Great Asylum for the Insane over by the Lick paper mill in Agnews. Your Mama will be its first resident if it gets built. Until then she'll have to live at the Marine Hospital for Crazy Seamen."

"He's muddled. That's a fact."

Cap Anson spits juice. "He's an umpire ain't he?"

"Pray," Annie Katharine says.

"I do. To God. I've tried praying to Jesus. I can't connect with anyone human."

My eyes open wide to the stench of salts. My head aches, my cap's two sizes too small. Casey hoists me to my feet for a third time. I look past him into the grandstand. A straggling few are up to leave. One is Nellie Bly, but her fancy-man begs her to stay. He wants to see Old Reliable Jake maim me more, but a legend stands in Jake's way.

"C'mon, coacher, the ump's had enough. You've given the devil his due."

A couple of my teeth wiggle at the touch of my tongue and drops of warm blood splash about my feet. The mob behind the ropes is itching to break through. Casey holds up his hand to quiet them. He takes the megaphone from the tally-keeper and hollers, "By some miracle no one's been hurt."

"That's just terrific," I say, echoing The Judge's voice in my throbbing head.

Clarence brings me my canteen and washes blood from my eyes. The mascot's brass buttons sparkle in the sun.

Old Jake points at me. "This is between me and him."

Casey placates Jake. "The snippet's full of gall. Makes shit up out of whole cloth. He was odd from the start. He sees even worse because you threw him on his noggin. He's optical delusional."

"He's a cocksucker," Old Jake says.

"Watch your mouth, there's ladies," Casey says. He looks into the grandstand and smiles at my Nellie, all in white and I'm sure that she doesn't smile back or Casey's face would've lit up. "Take a breath, coacher. C'mon, the Ump ain't worth a hangnail."

Old Jake decides there's no path to me and heads for the clubhouse. I know how fast he's walking because I hear "left, right, left, right, left, right," with each step.

"You OK Ump?" Casey says. A drop of blood falls from my mask. Casey takes a step back to keep it from splashing on his spikes. "You're lost at sea."

"There's no sea this far inland."

"You OK to finish this game out?"

"Snug as a bug." I tell Cannonball MacKenna to step up and finish Oakland's at-bats while it's eighteen sixty-something.

"It's 1888," Casey says.

I'm woozy, and I take a step back to save my balance and look out past the game. Shade consumes the audience, their color has gone gray, but sunshine still floods the green of the yard and a red fire fills the western sky. There's a pound, pound, pound at my temples.

I wiggle my teeth with my tongue. I see the blackboard and I try to recall how the Oakland Tribunes took a four-to-two lead. A miracle of some sort. Why Papa left I'll never know. I couldn't protect Moms from the shadows. Annie Katharine got better. Moms didn't.

Casey smiles up into the grandstand again. I glance at her, but I'm embarrassed for being man-handled. She puts on her glasses and I face away. I'll never look at her again. I long to take French leave, but that's a luxury umpires can't afford.

"What time is it?" I say.

"Nearing sunset," Casey says.

"What time is it, precisely?"

"Blazes, Ump, I don't know. Nope, I don't. This has turned into the biggest game of the century and you don't know up from down."

CHAPTER TEN

one year two and hundred-eight days after the strikeout

The Augusta Victoria is the first liner with twin propellers and the world's fastest. Nevertheless, it tosses on the sea like a lobster pot. Nellie Bly is delighted to dine with Captain Barends the first evening of her trip around the world, only to urp the motion of the sea into her napkin. She excuses herself to find Mr. Ponsonby waiting outside the captain's door. He's a smudge of gloom, but at least he has put on a gray worsted suit. He never touches anyone, but he takes her arm and assists her to her stateroom. Her hair is cut short according to style and he holds the loose strands back from her face as she vomits into a thunder mug.

"I crave land under my feet," she says.

Mr. Ponsonby goes to the galley and returns with ginger root and green apples to settle her stomach. By the time the steamer arrives in England, she's herself enough to grant an interview to *The Times of London*. The awful male correspondent asks for her impressions of Annie Oakley, who will be arriving to London in a week.

"I face more danger than any girl of the Wild West Show," Nellie Bly says to the reporter, who wants to start a hen fight between the world's best-known females.

She decides to give it to him. "I have been advised to pack a revolver in my valise," she says as he scribbles, "but it behooves me to come down on the side of sophistication. Good girls are seldom sharpshooters or know the mechanics of a gun. What reason do I have to arm myself against a world that embraces me at each port? I am bound for Arabia and Penang. A parasol for shade is a greater weapon in such climes."

Mr. Ponsonby carries no firearm, either, and after the interview she worries that he can't protect her and is along only for a holiday. She rarely treats him well but her rebukes don't seem to bother him. He appears joyed to board each and every train, even an all-night mail carrier. Passenger trains are crammed with snobbish Englishmen who believe her American accent is an invitation to take liberties. Stepping aboard requires a leap of faith, but Mr. Ponsonby warns hooligans to "mind your *p*'s and *q*'s." They respect his tone if not his fist, which is forever squeezing that base ball with ink-stained fingers.

She tries from time to time to converse. "Tell me about yourself. I know little of you except that Mr. Pulitzer has a grand affection."

Mr. Ponsonby, as always, is stingy with his words. He mumbles an inaudible answer.

"I am unsure how you plan to defend me," she says.

"I will."

"For the life of me, I do not know how a typesetter made Joseph J. Pulitzer a confidante. A chess mate. It gives you a measure of power that has put you in over your head. I noticed your scar, it gives you the air of courage. When and where did you acquire such a cut?"

He looks at his pocket watch. "We're ahead of schedule," he says.

That's true, until the next day when Mr. Pulitzer cables an order to pay a visit to the home of author Jules Verne in Amiens, France. His house is made of brick and stone. Nellie Bly holds a white rose in her gloved hand as she enters through a winter garden enclosed in glasswork. A shaggy dog bounds out to greet her. She yearns to turn the beast over to scratch its belly, to determine if it is male or female. The dog prefers an ear-scratching from Mr. Ponsonby, whom she introduces as an American correspondent in Paris and her escort for the evening.

The author's wife is attractive for her years and doesn't seem jealous, but Nellie Bly puts on her glasses out of courtesy. After supper, Honorine Verne excuses herself with the English she knows and takes up her knitting, entrusting the world's most famous daughter to its most celebrated fictionist. Mr. Verne guides her and Mr. Ponsonby on a house tour. Nellie Bly teases Mr. Verne that she intends to let her readers in on each nook and cranny.

When the marble stairway turns narrow, three people become a crowd. She convinces Mr. Ponsonby to return to keep Mrs. Verne company. Jules Verne's English is little better than his wife's, and there are awkward pauses at hallway bends where he lights gas lamps with a candle. The tour ends at his study. A leather armchair, a tidy desk with only a penholder, a bottle of ink and a globe. This is where he creates wonder with the scratch of his pen by the flutter of candlelight. She shows off her pluck. She sinks deep into his desk chair where he invents novels that will be read on stormy nights for centuries to come. His globe was long ago traced with a blue line for his imaginary journey. She is flattered that he has started a pink line for her actual one, which so far goes from New York to France.

She promises her readers never to keep anything from them, and she confesses that she blushed to see a warm fire burning in a Franklin stove and an iron bed near the far wall. "My mischievousness often plays havoc with my dignity," she writes, "but Mr. Verne is a man older than sixty with heavy, white brows. I am a tall and slender girl of twenty-four, five-foot-five, 112 pounds, who loathes May-December relationships."

The only lies are about her age, and that she loathes older men. She has warmth for those who remind her of her long-deceased father.

After the story is published, Mr. Pulitzer cables that bags of mail have landed on her desk. She knows what the letters say, and she scribbles a Page One item in defense of her honor.

"I refuse to answer insinuation and exaggerations. Let me be frank. There was wine offered and his bright eyes beamed with interest as the fire crackled. Flashes of flame greedily caught fresh wood but I departed so as not to get behind time. Mr. Verne's bed is for afternoon naps and I preserved it that way."

She is thankful for Mr. Ponsonby's company on Christmas. They visit a Chinese village where lepers are permitted to marry and bring diseased babies into cursed existence even as her colleagues in New York sit snug by stoves on Newspaper Row and are sent home early with Mr. Pulitzer's complementary turkeys under arm.

On Boxing Day, she happens upon execution grounds where Orientals have been disemboweled on red-colored earth. Twelve men had been slaughtered on Christmas Eve, not in her presence, but she tips a guard to see a fresh head.

"The ancient Mayans played a sport," Mr. Ponsonby says. "The team that won sacrificed their captain with a decapitation."

"Heavens," Nellie Bly says. "Why the winning captain?"

"The object of the game was to become worthy to be sacrificed."

Mr. Ponsonby acts as if that makes sense, as if he wished he were the worthy captain. He never seems homesick, not even for Christmas tidings. He is by her side as if she is his family. Like it or not, he is always near.

Late in her journey she insists that Mr. Pulitzer cable her at dollars a word to let her know when her reports had appeared in print. He replies that one item, then another, were held until the next day to make space for Fleetwood Walker, the Negro catcher who she saw that 1888 day at The Home of the Mudville Niners. He, of all people, had committed murder in New York, of all places, Mr. Pulitzer explained.

Mr. Ponsonby knows nothing about Fleet Walker except to spout a litany of numbers. "One big-league season with Toledo. Forty-two games in 1884, batted .263."

"Stop with the base ball jargon and jabberwocky," she says. "I am stuck in China while Mr. Walker is putting my voyage in the shade."

"Negroes went unsigned after the 1884 season."

"Yes, I know why Mr. Walker pretended to be the Mexican Grasshopper Nova. I was there; he was the backstop. Yes, I know there are two meanings to backstop. Men think girls know nothing of base ball and fungus and extra endings. I saw Mr. Walker catch the final fluttering strike."

"I know." Mr. Ponsonby stammers before saying, "Your item was published everywhere, in the *Evening Deseret News*."

"Millions claim to have been among the five thousand at the game. I am happy you are honest enough not to be one of them."

At her first opportunity, she sends a cable of costly length complaining that her items are getting short shrift. She threatens to end her progress on the spot and live out her days among sad natives. Mr. Pulitzer cables back to admit that nothing is more important than her race around the globe—not even the trial of the century.

Train after train is crowded with yellow men, but she misses trains once she is aboard a stagnant liner across the Pacific with never an island in sight to distract her thoughts. After weeks of constant traveling, she has an urgent desire to get home to her own bed, to the trial, but Yokohama to San Francisco is a horrid two weeks against headwinds blowing half a gale. The steamship Oceanic seldom exceeds nine knots. Sometimes she feels as if she is blown backward. Mr. Ponsonby assures her that she is closing in and will arrive well ahead of her eighty-day goal.

The ocean frightens her, a flat surface for as far as the eye can see. She fears it more than she fears being trapped in the Golden Dome's bowels with the banging presses. The sea hides unimaginable depths where creatures roam weightless. A storm might leave her on the bottom with other treasures that have been swallowed and forgotten.

The Oceanic stops nowhere except for coaling. Steering passengers are heathens and godless, and so she imprisons herself in her stateroom. Mr. Ponsonby is one door down. She knows that he is listening for her faintest whimper. She sobs one evening to see if he will knock. He does, but of course she doesn't answer.

More than the ocean's depths, she fears that the world's newspapers are no longer tracking her every inch of progress, but her fears are eased when she alights in San Francisco to the flashes of photographers.

Starved to see her name again in headlines, she buys the *San Francisco Examiner* from a newsboy. She is certain her arrival will be splashed across Page One with the Fleet Walker trial below the fold. Her lips grow taut to see a third item given the most conspicuous play.

EXAMINER OFFERS MISSING UMPIRE $3,000 FOR REPEAT CLASH

Come Out Walter Brewster and Umpire Casey for One More At-Bat

---

Eye Examination Included at No Charge

She shoves the headline in Mr. Ponsonby's face. "Yesterday, it was a murder by a Negro. Today it is bunkum about the umpire."

"The headline's forty-eight point. A point is .013837th of an inch."

She throws the paper at Mr. Ponsonby to demonstrate disgust for his lack of concern and his compulsion to show off his calculations in every conversation. She grabs the paper from out of his hands. Why the ballad *CASEY AT THE BAT* still causes a stir is beyond comprehension, and she is about to throw the paper to the floor when she sees that Wood Dryden has inserted her name into his item.

She reads aloud: "Perhaps the stunt girl Nellie Bly has captured the blind, coward umpire Walter Brewster along the Adriatic and is towing him to the Pacific slope for a second go at Casey."

She hates being called a stunt girl, more than Mr. Pulitzer hates being called a congressman, more than the umpire Walter Brewster must hate being called a blind coward. He wasn't a coward, she saw him declare pitch after pitch without concern for his well being. He stood right behind Fleet Walker, the murderer-to-be.

"Wood Dryden will never appear in one of my items," she says, but if the sycophant feels the need to build himself up by putting her down, then she will read further. The *Examiner's* offer is $3,000 to the missing umpire and $3,000 to Casey for one at bat. The *World* wants the rematch to occur at the opening of Manhattan's new Brotherhood Park, but Casey prefers the *Examiner's* counter offer at the Haight Street Grounds, a ten-minute ride from his mansion. She reads on and is surprised to learn that her own *New York World* started the bidding a week ago at $2,000 each.

"The whole scheme has been cooked up by Mr. Pulitzer, while I was risking my neck. Listen to what Casey says." She reads aloud to Mr. Ponsonby: "'I'll go anywhere, I'll go to the moon,' Casey said. 'The dough's not important. Nope. I'll give a thousand bucks to the Mount St. Joseph orphanage if the coward ump shows his mug. C'mon, if I strike out, I'll give my orphans Willie Hearst's three thousand and chip in three thousand from my own pocket.'"

"That's a fortune," Mr. Ponsonby says.

"That *is* not the point. I have risked my life and wasted my youth on the rocky seas."

She bites down on her chewing gum to arrest an urge to scream, to slap Mr. Ponsonby in the face with the *Examiner*, to change him into something lovable. At least Mr. Pulitzer has commissioned an engine attached to a single Pullman car to bring her the last leg across America. The people of San Francisco wish her Godspeed on her final leg across the continent. She is soon the fastest, most weightless, freight in rail history. She waves at blurs of worshippers lining the tracks.

Mr. Ponsonby ignores the crowds. He reads other pages in the newspaper. "Looky here," he says. "There's another item about you. It says infants are christened Nellie Bly McElfresh in Waggoner, Illinois and Nellie Bly Thomas in Fisherville, Virginia."

Nellie Bly retrieves her smile. "There must be tiny Nellies suckling at mothers in hamlets everywhere."

Mr. Ponsonby reads her the item, then reads the newspaper aloud, middle to end. There's an advertisement for instantaneous photographs on

Larkin Street, another for a miracle cure for barren women who desire to be in a family way.

"William Randolph Hearst published a large illustration of a flag hoisted with its latest circulation number—52,628. Mr. Dryden may be reporting for the largest newspaper in California, but he has one-fifth your readership."

Her mood lifts. Mr. Ponsonby seems almost adorable. He reads aloud the local brevities column, the fire record and the names of the gentlemen arrivals at The Palace Hotel. Once he finishes reading every inch, he counts telegraph poles from the swift train and calculates their speed with his pocket watch. Sixty miles an hour. Then he calculates how far they've traveled only to go around in a circle. "You can't go any farther on earth than back to the same place," he says.

She wants to sleep, but insomnia has been a permanent affliction since she recovered from seasickness on her first day. She needs a holiday to shop the Ladies Mile, to order a dress at Ghormley, lunch amidst gentlemen diners at Delmonico's, some sun bathing when spring comes to Coney Island. But mostly she craves to see her work in print, to see her name in headlines large enough to be read from across the street without her glasses, smell the Page One ink and to have her sixty-point life rub off on her hands.

The ink stains on Mr. Ponsonby's fingers have worn away. She's feeling better, thanks in small ways to him. She feels an affection. She opens her book. Her place in *Ben Hur* is marked with the letters from the anonymous gentleman with poor penmanship, the one whose mother is at The Marine Hospital that Houses Crazy Seamen. The letters are succinct; she has them memorized, she rarely takes either out of the envelope. She closes her eyes and lets the words of the letters and the hundreds of nursing baby Nellies bring her peace. She falls asleep to the sound of the abbreviated train traveling a mile a minute through the green plain of the San Joaquin.

She opens her eyes. In the distance, shines the ball yard where she saw Casey strike out. The stadium's empty. Californians who line the tracks and wave must be the same thousands who witnessed Casey's ridiculous failure. Despite the rate of speed, Mr. Ponsonby spots a small boy wearing an umpire's mask. Mr. Ponsonby says the boy must have found it back along the tracks in the weeds.

"Californians have fallen more in love with me than they did with their clumsy Casey," Nellie Bly says.

Mr. Ponsonby squeezes his base ball like it's his last possession. She closes her eyes and bowls her admirers by. The ride through the valley is velvet, the tracks without curve, a flagman at every switch to give her the right of way home. At this speed, the wind is left behind.

A Rockies snow blockade had stopped continental travel all week, but it's cleared just in time. Soon she waves to a cornet band in Hutchison, then on through prairies of the Middle West with stands of cottonwoods every thirty miles and women waving from clotheslines. Children are on fences and flapping American flags. Then prairie dogs. Grass stirrup high. The train clatters by dead rows of Illinois corn and stockyards and into a haze of Chicago greeters at Polk Street Station where she learns from Mayor Cregier, a political buddy of Mr. Pulitzer's, that she is on pace to cross America in one hundred hours.

"Ninety-nine," Mr. Ponsonby says. "That beats the record by twenty-four hours."

She jumps to the Jersey City platform on January 25th, 1890, at 3:51 p.m. Mr. Ponsonby records her official around-the-world time at "precisely" seventy-two days, six hours, eleven minutes, fourteen seconds—important only to her escort and the reader who won "Your Nellie Bly Guessing Match" and a voyage to Europe.

Cannons boom eight miles off at Fort Greene, loud enough for Mr. Ponsonby to step in to shield her. She pushes him aside, tells him his job is over. A band plays an overture on the pavilion followed by Scotch pipers and riders from cycling clubs. Roman candles burst the stench of sulfur into daylight overhead. Spalding's World Base Ball Tour is still out there somewhere, long forgotten in the freezing rain of Dublin or Egypt's dust.

She puts on her glasses. Saturday afternoon well-wishers in bundles are endless and crane for a glimpse at her; children sit aboard their fathers' shoulders a half mile in the distance. A woman hands her a newborn named Nellie Bly-something. Photographers flash pictures, but Baby Bly cries at her touch. Mr. Ponsonby covers his ears and she returns the little dear to begin her speech.

"As a gleeful child, I discarded my shoes and stockings to run about the banks of the Kiski River in a pink frock and sunbonnet." She concentrates on hiding her western Pennsylvania accent. "Lake Erie and the Atlantic are much closer and more convenient, but the Kiski's waters wind down to the Mississippi and into the Gulf of Mexico. I am like the Kiski; I had more logical places to end up, but I was pulled along by His grace and your gratitude to this platform where, at twenty-four years of age, I stand."

She pauses to let the audience roar, but her words have vanished into open air with the cannon sulfur and the odor of the tides. There's no applause beyond the first few rows and she intends to demand Page One publication of her speech when she arrives at the Golden Dome.

Mr. Pulitzer, of course, is on his telephone when she enters. He hangs up immediately, stands, and pumps Mr. Ponsonby's hand. A year ago, she saw Mr. Pulitzer explode in rage when a tailor made his trousers too tight. Now, his trousers are about to fall in a heap about his ankles. He kisses her cheek. He may be dying, but he finds the energy to slap Mr. Ponsonby on the back as if they are brothers, embrace him, tell him to pull a chair around.

"Welcome home," Mr. Pulitzer says. "How was your journey?"

"Tortuous and torturous." Nellie Bly says.

"The wear and tear of the road, eh."

"I am lucky I did not wind up twenty thousand leagues under the sea." Neither man understands her joke. Neither reads fiction; they are on the same page.

She remains standing, forcing Mr. Pulitzer to do the same. Mr. Ponsonby sits as he was told. Out the giant window, ships arrive in the distance and she imagines the first thing immigrants know of America is her tiny silhouette in the skyline beyond the Statue of Liberty. She lingers at the window to punish Mr. Pulitzer for giving conspicuous play to the Negro killer and the missing umpire. If it were in her power, she'd make all men forever stand, especially those who flip past her work in barbershops to read about mindless sporting matches. Mr. Pulitzer stays standing, Mr. Ponsonby collapsed in his chair. She forgives Mr. Ponsonby. It wasn't easy keeping pace with a woman of her glide.

"I apologize for the absence of champagne," Mr. Pulitzer says. "This is to be a celebration, but you can circumnavigate the globe ahead of schedule and my secretary is late with the bottle."

"I daresay, there is no reason to toast me for doing my job."

"Tommyrot," Mr. Pulitzer says. "You will have your toast. And your bonus."

"I prefer a holiday to a bonus. President Harrison has invited me to the White House, I feel obligated to accept."

Mr. Pulitzer wheezes at the mention of the Republican. "Go in the spring. I need you on an urgent detail."

"The Fleetwood Walker trial?" Nellie Bly says crossing her legs.

"Eh, we have five good men on that, we need you on an excursion."

"An excursion! I have not slept in my own bed for a million nights."

"That's 2,740 years," Mr. Ponsonby says.

"And you have been my shadow for each minute."

"You're late." Mr. Pulitzer's bark is at his somewhat pretty secretary entering with a bottle and three glasses.

Nellie Bly sips champagne with arms crossed. Mr. Pulitzer blows his nose and his fingers twitch in his wet handkerchief. Mr. Ponsonby doesn't touch his glass; he leaves it sit while he fidgets with his awful base ball.

"San Francisco loves you, Miss Bly," Mr. Pulitzer says. "The city will welcome you back."

"San Francisco? I was there a hundred hours ago. I will travel to Washington and no farther. After my White House visit, I will never board another train if I live to be old."

"I would have kept you in San Francisco when you alighted from Japan, but you had to complete your journey," Mr. Pulitzer says. "You must return. You are perfect for this detail."

"Detail?"

"The umpire detail. The only story people will be interested in now that your journey is complete. Except the Negro's trial."

"The umpire is a California infatuation," Nellie Bly says. "I would call him a hoax, an hallucination, if I had not seen him with my own eyes. He merits no mention in *our* pages. If he does, he belongs in the sporting news among other matters of snot and perspiration."

"Our sporting reporters are dead weight, they've been unable to keep up. Willie Hearst published that damn ballad in the summer of 1888. Here it is, 1890, and Wood Dryden has been writing items the whole time. The *Examiner* has passed the *Chronicle* in San Francisco on the umpire's back."

"The umpire is a long-ago thing of the past, not the morrow," Nellie Bly says. "Why waste a second of my time?"

"Eh, the story never dies. Last month, the *Times* said *Casey at The Bat* rivals *Now I Lay Me Down to Sleep* as the bedtime verse children most request. The *Cosmopolitan* dispatched a reporter to a York, Pennsylvania schoolyard to ask children to recite both the ballad and the Gettysburg Address. The ballad, twice as long, was recited with more accuracy. That spawned items about the state of American education and the demise of patriotism, alarm over social ills of all kinds, and ineffective legislation from Albany to Harrisburg. The poem is lore, a part of our culture. I'm tired of getting beat by everyone, I'm tired of getting beat by the kid, Willie Hearst. His daddy, George, parlayed a four-hundred-dollar claim into the Comstock Lode. The Hearst's are lucky."

"What sort of man is the umpire?" Nellie Bly says. "What sort of man will not come forward for three thousand dollars?"

"He sees misfortune in fame," Mr. Ponsonby says.

"When is fame *ever* a misfortune?" She turns to Mr. Pulitzer. "Put me on the Negro's trial or put me on holiday."

"You witnessed Casey's strikeout," Mr. Pulitzer says. "You're up to speed. Casey refuses to speak to Wood Dryden. But he'll open his mansion wide to you. This story is an evergreen. No one tires of it. Base ball is the very hallmark of nineteenth-century America. Its drive and struggle."

"I have no desire to visit any man's mansion. I want to be in the courtroom. What does the Negro say in his defense?"

"He has none. Only his wife sitting behind with three darling children. Beautiful woman, Arabella Walker. She's as lovely as—you Miss Bly."

"Be that as it may."

"Almost, and almost as white."

"Fleet Walker's wife is white? I daresay."

"Almost. They're estranged, but her tears well up from hazel eyes all the same. Fleet Walker came to New York, killed a white bricklayer. New Yorkers can't get enough of it, but the trial goes to jury in a day or two. A conviction an hour later. After that, the one story will be the missing umpire, the biggest news in the land. It's high time we were at flank speed."

Mr. Pulitzer hands Mr. Ponsonby two tickets. "Your train back to San Francisco leaves in two hours. Readers never tire of Nellie Bly, they will devour each observation she has of base ball—with your help."

"I have never once needed this typesetter's help?"

"You've seen but one stinking base ball game."

"The one match that matters."

"Ponsonby knows everything about the game."

"He knows the numbers, little more. I will not spend another second with an escort now that I am back in America. I look in my pocketbook, and there he is."

Pulitzer slams his open hand on his desk. "San Francisco's Chinatown is as unsafe as Asia. The Barbary Coast is worse. I need you both on this detail. I need my team. Willie Hearst has been shopping for a newspaper in New York. He's a vulgar adolescent who thinks I'm aging and ailing and blind for the kill. The megalomaniac hasn't done anything except inherit silver; he's a spoiled brat who steals my ideas and deposits them in his bank account. He steals my nuggets and prints them in San Francisco. Now, he plots piracy in my backyard."

"I see. This is no simple search for the umpire," Nellie Bly says.

"A preemptive attack. While Hearst is newspaper shopping, I'm going to steal the umpire detail out from under him. A shot across his bow."

Nellie Bly tries to sound offended. "And I am the cannon fodder you intend to employ?"

"Accept it as a compliment. Nothing better for circulation than finding Walter Brewster. Nothing short of a war. If you don't find him, I'll have to start one."

"Get me into the jailhouse to interview Fleet Walker," Nellie Bly says. "I saw him squat in front of the umpire for two hours. They had a report. He will know something of Mr. Brewster's whereabouts."

Mr. Pulitzer claps his hands. "I'll arrange a meeting if it will get you on the train west."

Mr. Pulitzer stands up before Nellie Bly can change her mind and shoves a fist into the air. He coughs once more and pushes down his wild hair with both hands. "I'll plaster your fetching face on newsstand posters throughout New York. *Nellie Bly to Find the Umpire in Eighty Days.*"

She sighs. "I suppose we in the Golden Dome must always think of the morrow. I own no newspapers except for the copies I buy; I require a salary that reflects my standing."

"Agreed," Mr. Pulitzer says. "You'll have your salary. You and Mr. Ponsonby will head for the jailhouse, then run for the train."

Mr. Pulitzer claps Mr. Ponsonby by the shoulders. "Your job's the same. Protect her."

"You don't want me at her side when she interviews Fleet Walker," Mr. Ponsonby says.

"Of course I do. Jailhouses are unsafe." Mr. Pulitzer turns to Nellie Bly. "The nation's most beloved girl inside the cell of its most famous villain. We'll say that you're alone with a murdering Negro who has nothing to lose. Miss Bly, you'll have more courage than any girl alive, more courage than Annie Oakley."

"I like the sound of that."

"Find the umpire. If you don't find him, I'll start a war and send NelliedamnBly."

"War in no way frightens me. I wish to be the first girl to file from the front."

"With Mr. Ponsonby at your side to keep the shells from chipping your nails. Mr. Ponsonby is biblical in his servitude, eh. Mr. Ponsonby will never let you down."

"A life is not important except in the impact it has on other lives."—Jackie Robinson

October 7, 1856, the wee hours
It's a Tuesday

CHAPTER ELEVEN

thirty-one years before the strikeout

Moses Fleetwood Walker is born in Steubenville, fifteen miles west of the Ohio River, *God's River,* because only it and the Quakers stand between his family and the slave market of Wheeling. His mother is a midwife, his father a Baptist preacher and the first Negro doctor in Ohio.

Jefferson County has no dentist. Fleet's father seizes the opportunity and extracts teeth with bullet molds. That rains prosperity, and Fleet grows up in one of the town's largest homes on its wealthiest street with the undertaker, sexton, chocolate merchant and barber as neighbors. All are Negroes except for the chocolate merchant, who has an endless Quaker family.

Fleet runs in an out of the Quaker home, gathering enough youngsters to play one-old-cat. He's nine when Lincoln is shot, and the chocolate family weeps with the coloreds in the street.

Scientific journals are a staple in Fleet's home. One says Negroes are headed the way of the Great Auk unless they stop breaking miscegenation laws that prohibit breeding among the races. A consensus of scientists believe mulattoes to be as mules and can't reproduce, but Fleet's mother delivers babies of all shades. His own skin is lighter than his parents; he's buckskin bay enough to pass as *mestizo.*

Fleet attends amalgamated schools and takes plane geometry, physics, mechanics, ancient history and the science of government even before he takes his place among Oberlin College's Class of 1882. Negroes at Oberlin obey the same rules as the whites; they are forbidden to drink liquor and

119

pray mornings and evenings at the chapel. Fleet prays for base ball season to begin until his third year when 17-year-old Arabella Taylor steps on campus. Then he prays to get her alone.

Arabella comes from Cincinnati's octoroon aristocracy, the Taylor family with the calm and manners of those free before Emancipation. The Taylors sit up front at Trinity Episcopal with the white widows. If Fleet Walker is lighter than his parents, Arabella Taylor is two shades lighter than Fleet. She can stay in hotels.

Fleet and Arabella skip chapel one evening to sit in the bleaching boards of the Oberlin base ball field as she reads aloud from Alexander Pope's *Essay on Man.*

"Hope springs eternal in the human breast; Man never Is, but always To be blest."

Hopeless describes the love Fleet falls into as he listens to her voice and watches the evening dew turn home plate slippery. He takes Arabella by the hand and strolls her around the bases as the sun disappears even before it goes down.

"I can't wait to see you play at the game you love," Arabella says.

"Until you came along, I never loved anything more."

Darkness creeps until home plate and Arabella are the only things white enough to see. He buffs the marble with her backside. Neither finish college. Seven years before the strikeout, Arabella Taylor gives birth to Cleodolinda. The wedding's a year later at Trinity Episcopal where a new altar is donated in memory of her grandparents. Trinity has a pipe organ and all the money it needs.

Fleet wants his daddy to perform the wedding ceremony.

"No Ironside Baptists," she says. "Half the people at our wedding will be white."

"Bella, Trinity allows coloreds in their pews but none are buried in their cemetery."

She laughs. "Things will change long before we need a cemetery."

He makes another plea for his daddy, and she at last agrees. "If you promise no fraying to and fro, no knocking over the pews. Tell him that we don't want some jackleg preacher."

Fleet plays one big league season. The next is the season of 1885. Negroes are never banned outright, but the owners agree not to sign any. And so Fleet uproots his family from Toledo to California where he plays for the Cuban Giants and is signed by Oakland before the 1888 season.

Arabella resents Fleet for taking her from Ohio. She hates that he pretends to be a Mexican and she promises never to attend another game.

One Friday morning, Cleodolinda's asleep. Fleet picks up four-year-old Thomas, and kisses his face and neck until he giggles. Fleet wants to be early to the train bound for the San Joaquin and the Home of the Mudville Niners where the Oaklands are certain to lose. Arabella refuses to let him kiss her cheek. "I saw you packing your revolver into that gunny sack," she says.

"Bella, the San Joaquin is known for its racialists."

"There've been no lynchings. Give me the gun."

"What will you have me do if hoodlums come down after me? Hide in the shed behind the lime and grass seed?"

"What will I have you do? Stop pretending to be a dumb Mexican for one thing. You're an embarrassment to your children."

"Bella, come to the Oakland yard next week. Bring the kids. I'd like them to see me play. I'd like *you* to see me one last time before they figure out who I am."

"If I bring the kids, we'll have to sit in the colored section. Those rickety stands collapsed last year."

"Then come alone. You can sit anywhere."

"I won't. Not so long as you wear those cheap grays of Oakland flannel. Not so long as you're Cricket Nova."

"Grasshopper," Fleet says. "Bella, I'm Mexican by choice. I could play in Pittsburgh with my brother, they need me to make a Negro league viable, but we'd starve on what the Pittsburghs pay."

"Then quit. You can be lawyering by next week." Arabella's father has a position awaiting Fleet in Cincinnati.

"*I'm* the leader of this family. Bring Thomas and Cleodolinda to the yard to see the best catcher in the game. Bring them next week or I'll give you a slap."

"Go ahead," she says with hands on hips, "but I may be pregnant."

"Pregnant? You won't even cuddle with me."

"We did during the off-season. Now begins another summer."

Fleet gathers his gear. The way to stop arguments is to head for the station. "You've overstayed your welcome in base ball," Arabella says.

"I'll play for as long as I'm forbidden."

Arabella starts crying. "What has happened to us? We once fit in. We still fit in better with whites than with Negroes of a different stamp. The blue-blacks stir the trouble that sets people against us all."

"The blackest children admired me the most in Toledo. The darker they are, the more they look up to me."

Arabella sniffles. "I suppose we have a duty to set an example, to show the blackest children that they, too, can reach a high plane of living. The poorest are downright tragic. They dislike me for no reason except that I remind them that their Carolina mamas were once raped by white *gennulmen befoe gawd's own eyes.*"

She clutches her purse tight to mock. She doesn't care a lick that Thomas soaks it in. Arabella points at him. "I worry what will happen once he's no longer adorable."

"President Abe Lincoln changed things," Thomas says.

"Nothing changes," Fleet says. "Cap Anson came to chase Negro players out of California just like he did in Chicago. Anson's a hater. God played a wicked trick when he made base ball's greatest player its biggest racialist."

"Cap Anson's a powerful man," Arabella says. "He has more important things on his plate than chasing you out of anywhere."

"That is the *only* thing on his plate."

"Negro ball players are partly responsible for the color bar. They got greedy and wanted more than two players per team."

"Toledo never had three, and we pretended to be sick the day they took the team photograph," Fleet says. "I study racialists. I watch them do this and that. Anson tells reporters that base ball yards are the same as swimming holes. The reporters smile and nod and print anything that comes out of the bigot's mouth."

"Negroes dislike splashing about in the same water as much as whites do," Arabella says. "Let's not argue, Fleet. It's all so dreary. You enjoy the suffering, or else you'd be lawyering."

"If I start lawyering, my first case will be to fight Cap Anson to the Supreme Court."

Arabella puts hands on hips. "Won't that be a waste of your talent for rhetorical exercise. You *like* to lose. It's why you played for the Cuban Giants. It's why you play for the cursed Oaklands."

Fleet sees Thomas examining his own dark skin. Anger takes over Fleet so fast that he can't control it. Anger's been his life-long sin; it comes from nowhere. He knows he should walk out the door and head for the station, but instead he makes kindling of a chair. She smiles whenever he loses his temper in front of Thomas, as if she's teaching the boy something. A month ago, Thomas got tears in his eyes, but now that he's four he no longer does.

Fleet gets control of himself by thinking about the game ahead. He rubs his son's head. "Life is like bad umpiring. Cope, son, figure out a way to win despite the obstacles."

"Thomas, honey, life's bigger than a ball diamond," Arabella says.

"Why do you insist on taking me down a peg when I'm trying to make him a man?"

Arabella speaks to Thomas. "I studied French at Oberlin. I believe umpire is from the old French *nomper*."

"Mama, what does *nomper* mean?"

"One who is unequal," Arabella says.

Thomas laughs. "Like sad Negroes?"

Arabella kisses Thomas on the cheek. "Count your blessings. Boys woke up this morning on mattresses that smell like pee."

"Bed-wetting Negroes are better than umpires," Thomas says.

Fleet laughs. "You're right about that. Nobody respects them. I remember the time Levi Goldschmidt dropped pennies in the dirt just to watch a dumb umpire pick them up. That umpire was almost as dumb as the one who got beaten like a plow horse in Santa Cruz this week." Fleet shakes his head. "He was a justice of the peace."

"All umpires are *nomper*," Thomas says.

Arabella laughs, and the argument ends with everyone in agreement. Cleodolinda rises in time to give her daddy a sleepyhead kiss on the cheek, and Fleet heads for the station.

"There you go," Arabella Walker calls out to him.

"There I go where?"

"To hell if you don't change your ways. Stay clear of the Irish boulevard trash. Your johnson and your temper; what's in your trousers and what's in your gunny sack is what will get you hanged by the neck."

After the strikeout Moses Fleetwood Walker is banned from base ball coast to coast. The pregnant Arabella moves to Cincinnati with Thomas and Cleodolinda. Fleet moves to New York where he works as a railway clerk. He handles registered letters on runs to Syracuse.

On a late December night, nineteen months after the strikeout, there's a street stabbing outside O'Brien's saloon. Fleet still doesn't know why he becomes so blinded by anger from time to time. He runs until he's exhausted, then circles back. He hides up a fire escape, wiping bloody hands on his gunny sack. The moon has yet to rise; stars sparkle a foot beyond Fleet's reach. A heavyset reporter arrives at the scene. O'Brien's is two miles from the Golden Dome. It's near deadline and the trolley is closed until morning. The reporter is sweating despite the cold.

Fleet watches from above, blending in with the shadows. He knows he's guilty, but it feels like someone else did it. The dead man is face up beneath a street lamp. Blood fills his mouth, a deep knife wound begins left of the groin and travels upward.

The reporter looks up and down the street, a cop and a lamplighter the only men in sight. The cop is young, barely eighteen. He acts annoyed with the fat reporter, but cops like the *World*; it's the newspaper their friends and families read.

"My shift's ended," the cop says to the reporter, "but I'll be here freezing my ass until the undertaker's wagon comes. What's taking so long? Priest left a half hour ago."

"Who did this, Jack the Ripper?"

It's a joke, but the cop rolls his eyes. "The Ripper kills London whores. That's why we've been arresting unescorted girls at night. We want no copycats."

A stray cat hurries past Fleet's feet and down the stairs of the fire escape. Belly low to the ground, the cat stops, rubs against the cop's boots, purrs, laps blood from the corpse's open mouth. The cop curses the nickel's worth of chow mein he ate hours ago. He slaps his nightstick against his boots and it echoes into the quiet, into Fleet's elevated shadows. The cat does not frighten, it laps on with relish, its bent tail slashing back and forth. The cop kicks the cat away. Too late. The cop vomits on the stab wound before he has time to turn his head. He heaves a second course in the gutter, a third on the wooden sidewalk.

The reporter laughs a mouthful of gallows humor. "You must be new." He speaks aloud as he scribbles in his notebook. "Victim's about forty, five-foot-eight, one-sixty. Covered in cop vomit." He laughs again. "Rock in his hand, a laborer's hand."

The reporter has a disappointed expression. He stops scribbling. "He's insignificant, not important enough to bump a Nellie Bly story from the Orient. They'll hold this for a day, maybe spike it altogether."

The undertaker's wagon arrives. Fleet uses the noise to hop from the fire escape and hotfoot it to Coogan's Hollow along the Harlem River. The cop hears him, makes chase, but an antelope can't catch Fleet. He runs to the new Polo Grounds and hides in a shed of lime and grass seed. Fleet's trapped and caught and the machinery of the law is set into motion. Three hours after he's force-marched to jail, the cop shows him the *World's* headline through the bars.

Prayer-less Doom

———————

**Screams for Mercy
How the Craven Fleet Walker Slashed a
Bricklayer to Death
Base Ball's Last Negro
Destined for the Chair**

"That's right," the cop says. "You'll make history, the first man to be shocked to death. Let's see you outrun electricity."

The cop lets Fleet read the story. The victim is Patrick Murphy, they call him Curly, has a wife. The story's Page One because the culprit is Moses Fleetwood Walker, the last Negro to play big league ball, the catcher who pretended to be a Mexican when Casey struck out. Joseph Pulitzer seems determined to try Fleet Walker in the *World's* pages. The bricklayer Murray was no angel, served three years in Alabama for burglary. Witnesses say he threw a stone at Walker. Murray was intoxicated, but so was Walker, he had a general dozy look. Killed a married man with steady work.

What's Fleet Walker's defense? The bricklayer came at him. Walker could've run, but he stabbed Murray with a knife hidden in a gunny sack. Murray saw nothing coming through burlap. Some witnesses say Murray was stabbed after he busted Walker in the chops, others say Walker chased Murray down the street. A foot race. No contest.

Walker's got more education than his lawyer Hoyt Harrison. Five character witnesses are coming to New York from Steubenville, Ohio. They're neighbors of Walker's where he was raised, but the Quakers won't be able to explain why a fortunate Negro slices a hard-working man from the stones up.

Arabella Walker is on her way from Cincinnati. They're estranged, but she'll sit behind him at trial with their children. Cleodolinda's eight, Thomas is six, and the baby George is not yet walking. Three darlings. Arabella's a beautiful woman, almost white, tears will well up from hazel eyes. A bonanza for the defense. A treasure trove for the New York press if he's found guilty and fried, a treasure trove if he's not. The trial of the century.

Nellie Bly makes it around the world in seventy-two days. Hours later, the world's most beloved girl enters the cell of its most infamous black man. Fleet recognizes both her and her escort, the umpire with courage, the *nomper* with *cojones*. But Nellie Bly introduces him as Claude Ponsonby. Fleet sticks out a hand that shakes with the jitters. He needs a beer. He wonders why the umpire hasn't come forward for $3,000. The escort stares at the ground until Fleet withdraws the greeting. The umpire wants to stay incognito? Fleet respects the wish. Walter Brewster stood up for Fleet that day Casey struck out. No other umpire, no other man, would've done that.

"I must be big news, or Nellie Bly wouldn't be here," Fleet says.

"Each edition about you is published in record time," she says. "Each minute costs the *World* seven hundred sales and the one thing Joseph Pulitzer hates more than losing two cents it's contributing three to Charles Dana at the *Sun*. Mr. Pulitzer assigned five good men to the story, I will be leaving town soon. You have this one chance to tell me the truth before I am off to California."

Fleet looks at the escort. "People who know me know I couldn't murder anyone."

"Be that as it may," Nellie Bly says. "It will serve you well to tell me each detail if I am to convince the public. I daresay, the evidence against you is compelling. The policeman retched on the crime scene, that is the only thing in your favor."

"I don't deny killing the bricklayer. Self defense."

"A hidden knife indicates forethought." Nellie Bly puts on her glasses. "You had a pistol in that gunny sack as well?"

"To scare away bigots."

"If you are electrocuted, Mr. Ponsonby will be there to pray for your soul. They will never let a girl reporter be a witness."

"You don't pussy-foot around do you?" Fleet remembers why he resents white women. He's attracted to them, of course, even the Irish boulevard trash, but they're all the same.

The escort tosses Fleet a base ball. "The leather calms me," the escort says. "Maybe it will calm you, too."

"Never once have I seen that ball leave your hand," Nellie Bly says. "Even when you are asleep on a train. I thought I might have to hire a surgeon to remove it like a tumor."

Fleet squeezes the ball. It's like new, the one pitch old. It helps him tell the truth about the stabbing. "The saloon keeper recognized me, saw me play in eighty-four. Said the Toledos lost to the Metropolitans that day. He invited me inside."

"Was Curly Murray in there?" Nellie Bly says.

"No. He and his friends were outside when I was leaving. I had three beers. Wasn't drunk. One of his friends shouts, 'You're putting on a good many airs for a damn Negro.' He didn't use the word Negro. He used the word *coon*. I told him that I had as much right as any Irish loafer. I said Irish, I didn't say *mick* or *paddy*. That's when a rock hit me in the head from behind. Look. Cut through my hat and raised this."

"I see no lump," Nellie Bly says.

"It was the size of a half dollar but the swelling's down. My lawyer Hoyt Harrison has my derby to wave around in court. The rock cut through the band and felt. I was hunting for a stone to throw back when someone says, 'Kick the coon's head off.' That's when I gave Curly the stab he won't forget."

"The citizenry is against you," Nellie Bly says. "Even the leaders of the Negro society say it is killers like you who are responsible for the racialism they're always working to tamp down."

"You sound like Bella." Fleet feels that rage welling up. He squeezes the ball; he wants to throw it at her pretty head. "I'm innocent."

"Be that as it may."

"Do you intend to convict me in the newspaper?"

"Trust me. I am on your side. Why are you jumpy? I know horses and I know when one is skittish."

"I'll go to Sing-Sing no doubt." He addresses the escort. "Maybe I want to test that new chair. No matter what, I'll be better off than Mouse Mathews."

"Mouse Mathews?" Nellie Bly says. "I know that name."

"The pitcher," the escort says to his feet. "Struck out Casey. Three pitches."

"I know. I was there, Mr. Ponsonby. Everyone says they were, but I truly was. As was Mr. Walker. I have attended one base ball match in all my life and I was there for the moment that defines the game."

"How nice for you," Fleet says.

"I believed you to be a Mexican. Everyone did. What was your *nom de plume?*" She tosses French words around like Arabella, too.

"Grasshopper Nova," the escort says.

"Mouse is penniless in Baltimore," Fleet says to the escort. "Syphilis and mental deterioration. He can't recall that game or any other."

"Athletes certainly do roll the dice with the lifestyles they lead," Nellie Bly says.

"The umpire Brewster might not remember the game, either," Fleet says. "You saw Old Reliable Jake throw him head first into the dirt." Fleet tosses the ball back to the escort. It seems like a shorter toss, as if the cell is shrinking. "Getting that last strike past Casey was like sneaking sunrise past a rooster."

"Beg pardon?" the escort says.

"Do you know where the umpire is now?" Nellie Bly says.

"I might," Fleet says. "I knew that Mouse Mathews is in Baltimore, didn't I? But Mouse was my bunkmate. Pitchers and catchers always bunk together. I have an affection for Mouse. Can't help you with Brewster. No one has an affection for umps. Don't know him from Adam."

"It appears I have wasted my time. I need to file a story soon. I will write a Page One item about Strike Three from your point of view. I will make you seem human to the public. You must tell the truth though. Remember, I was seated behind you. I will know if you fabricate a single detail. It will behoove you to be honest."

"I get amnesia when I go this long without a drink."

The escort tosses back the ball. "This will have to do."

Fleet squeezes his shaky memory from it. "Ten thousand eyes were on Casey. He stood stern, his muscles knotted. The sneer went out of his lip. I wouldn't let him focus. I called him a *pendejo* as loud as I could. '*Chinga tu madre,*' I hollered."

"I did not hear you shout Spanish obscenities," Nellie Bly says. "It was so loud though. No thunder clap has ever been as deafening as those red-faced farmers."

"Casey pounded his bat on the plate in front of my squat. The vibrations rose from my spikes, but I heard nothing in the roar. The sun was finally down, Mouse was no longer blinded, but he left the brim of his cap pulled low to hide the excruciation in his eyes. His arm was limp, worthless.

His fastest stuff floated into Casey on a ferry. The breeze died, the yard was suffocated in noise and stillness. From the back of the box, my bunkmate switched the ball from one hand to the other, his final pitch to be delivered with his right."

"He switched arms?" Nellie Bly says. "Is that legal?"

"To his original right that won so many games," Fleet says.

"Two hundred and ninety-six career games," the escort says.

"His right had just enough strength to grind the ball into his hip."

"Did Casey notice the switch?" Nellie Bly says.

"The only thing Casey sees is Casey," Fleet says. "He pounded again and again without sound. Three mourning doves flew lost and low overhead in search of a roost. Casey raised his bat in circles above his head and the doves swerved in unison, their wings cut through the yard's noise with a whistling beat."

"I do not remember any of this. You paint base ball like a picture. A work of art."

"Mouse began his approach. From the back of the box he took a deep breath, a small step, then a hop and a skip toward the plate. His original right arm creaky over top."

Fleet holds the ball over his head to simulate the trajectory of the pitch. "The new ball floated in white. A sea breeze kicked in from the west, my neck cooled. Friction caught these seams, there was no rotation on these catgut stitches as Mouse's butterfly pitch floated in high, so high that Casey's monstrous hands relaxed. He had decided not to swing."

"But he did swing," Nellie Bly says.

"The pitch was certain to be ball one," Fleet says. "The pitch began tracking to cross him at the eyes." Fleet holds the ball at his own eyes. "Casey's hands tightened when the pitch dropped another inch. Earth defeated heaven, the ball drew near, without spin, more slowly than physics allow. Casey has ears that can hear grass grow, he can hear the wind on the seams of the ball."

"Viz," the escort says.

"He has the eyes and reflexes of a hawk," Fleet says. "He can catch a leaping salmon by the tail. His strength doubles at game time and increases with each inning."

"I know little about base ball," Nellie Bly says, "but I know about men. Manhood cannot be measured with a tape around the biceps."

"Children are told never to go into Casey's mansion, or they'll be eaten," Fleet says.

She rolls her eyes and puts down her notebook. "You are teasing me, treating me like a schoolgirl. Did he extract his bat from a stone like Excalibur?"

"This is no tall tale," Fleet says.

"Casey is a skunk." She removes her glasses and smiles like white girls do when confronting a smart aleck.

"He says 'My gracious,' when he's tempted to swear," the escort says. "I read that while typesetting."

"He's a snake in the grass, who is loved and respected," Fleet says. "The most dangerous snake of all." He continues on with his tale. "No longer at Casey's eyes, the ball tracked to his nose, his chin, his throat."

Fleet lowers the ball to his Adam's apple. "When it reached the plate, it fell like wet snow, moved sideways at a tangent, disappeared, reappeared."

"I do admire your imagination, Mr. Walker."

"I swear it's true. Mouse calls it his *puzzler pitch*. Casey's mass stayed back, electricity flowed from his hips, through his arms to ignite his wrists. He had to swing, he knew the umpire might call Striker Three. Casey knew Walter Brewster had the *cojones* to do it. The bat lashed at this white sphere that stood still at the top of the zone. There was an odor, as if pent-up vapors were escaping the grounds. I don't know why. We were in the San Joaquin and all of those Indians are buried under the Oakland yard."

"The Ohlone Indians," the escort says.

"Then mysterious groans from Casey, or from his bat, or from the bowels of the earth. All went quiet. I blinked, I listened for the crack, waited for five thousand hearts to be tenderized by bat on ball. I heard nothing except the thump of a heart behind me."

Nellie Bly plays along. She puts her white-gloved hands to her breast. "An Edgar Allan Poe heart thump?"

"Walter Brewster's heart thump."

The escort looks for the first time into Fleet's eyes. "The shit-house beast was there," Fleet says. "I felt breeze, but it smelled like shit."

"The stench of God's mischief," the escort says.

"Utter quiet," Fleet says, "and I wondered if Casey had hit one to kingdom come, sucked the noise with the ball over the War Monument."

"I know," the escort says.

"How?" says Nellie Bly.

"I know the feeling," the escort says. "A fast train sucks away noise when you stand a bat's length away from the tracks."

"Then gasps, thousands at once," Fleet says. "The ball wasn't landing four hundred thirty-two feet feet in the distance. The ball wasn't over the War Monument. The ball was in my cracked hands. The ball was *here*." Fleet shows the ball to the escort. "I never felt it hit my hands. It was something, *cabrón*, really something."

The escort looks at his watch. "The time is two fifty-seven. Train to catch. San Francisco."

"Are you certain you do not know where the umpire is?" Nellie Bly says.

"He'd look different without a blue suit and mask. He'd still be odd, but he'd look almost human."

"Help me find him, and I will help you. I have a million readers and I can persuade them to see your situation in a better light. I will order up an illustration of your lovely wife and three darling children."

"He was behind the bat with me. That means something. A man gets to know another man behind the bat. The catcher and the umpire are the only two facing out at the yard."

"They see things from the same angle," the escort says.

"Be that as it may."

"You're not interested in my best interests, Miss Bly. That umpire and me, we'll always be brothers. There's not another white man I'd say that about. We'll never see each other again, but we'll always be two drunken Indians riding a single pony."

"Sorry to see you in here," the escort says. "You've had some sorrowful luck."

"Don't waste your sorries. I'm innocent, it's obvious."

"I daresay, a good family man is dead and you did it. Perhaps you do not deserve the chair, but perhaps you belong in Sing Sing."

"Perhaps we all belong in there," Fleet says. "You can strip a man of his life with your pen without losing sleep."

The escort raises his voice to defend her. "Everyone loves Nellie Bly, all of New York bathes in her every word."

"I see, you're in her camp," Fleet Walker says. "You can't protect her. The shit-house beast lurks wherever someone tries to succeed where they don't belong."

"Nellie Bly will succeed, she'll find Walter Brewster," the escort says.

"Maybe," Fleet says. "But the shit-house beast will one day catch her too." He holds up the ball. "I wish the fattest part of Casey's bat had caught this sphere. I wish he'd hit the shit out of it. I wish the Oaklands had lost. Hope springs eternal, but here I am without any."

"I bet Walter Brewster will come out of hiding and testify on your behalf," the escort says. "It would mean something to a jury."

"What would it mean?" Fleet asks.

"The umpire won't come out even for three thousand dollars. If he comes out to swear to your character, a jury will be swayed."

"Swayed by what?"

"By the umpire's honesty. By the umpire's *cojones.*"

"You're a dunderhead and a dunce."

"A jury might see the case differently," the escort says.

Fleet replies with sarcasm. "You mean from a different angle? Everyone hates the umpire. Everyone hates him except me and his mama. That's a shit-ass idea."

Fleet hands the ball back to the escort. The cell seems too tiny to toss it anymore. "The umpire best keep his yap shut. They want to fry Walter Brewster more than they want to fry me."

"Yesterday's home runs don't win today's games."—Babe Ruth

January 28, 1890, 6:27 a.m.
It's a Tuesday

CHAPTER TWELVE

six hundred eighteen days after the strikeout

The pillow Nellie Bly pulls over her head fails to blunt the commotion of steam and machinery, much less muffle the snores of the male passengers. One man wakes himself with his own snort. American sleeper cars are no more than bunk houses that rock and creak and are packed with bald men that creak at the joints as well.

To avoid rising, she thinks back on the past few days. She and Mr. Ponsonby didn't go straight to the train station after their visit to Fleetwood Walker's jail cell. First, she interviewed De Wolf Hopper in New York and wrote an unflattering exposé about the two-bit actor. They next traveled to Worcester to interview Earnest Thayer. He hadn't even witnessed the strikeout. He scribbled *Casey at the Bat, a Ballad of the Republic, Sung in the Year 1888* on a whim and said he didn't mind that Hopper was getting rich reciting it on stage. Neither knew anything of the umpire's whereabouts, but Mr. Thayer gave her a letter he had received months ago from William Thompson, owner of the Wolverines Base Ball Club in Detroit. It concerned the dirty umpire Dick Higham, and she suspected that the letter was a piece of the puzzle.

Her next stop was Baltimore to go searching for the pitcher Mouse Mathews. Mr. Ponsonby had seen illustrations of Mr. Mathews in the *Sporting News* and spotted him freezing near Charles Street Union Station. The little man was crazed with syphilis, as Fleet Walker had warned, crazed into utter oblivion. He stared at Mr. Ponsonby and hollered "Kill him! Kill him!" over and over until a policeman asked them to leave to calm the man down.

Nellie Bly wishes she had made a last demand of Mr. Pulitzer before agreeing to chug back to San Francisco to find the umpire. She wishes she'd forced the old Jew to acquisition the same one-car train that had whisked her east in record time. Instead, she is imprisoned in a dreary ten-section Pullman that has been in ceaseless service for a decade, her berth shielded by a curtain of threadbare silk and whatever decency God bestows upon the men aboard.

She clamps the pillow tighter to her head, wishing she were visiting President Harrison. In Baltimore, she was but two hours away from the White House, but for some ungodly reason she obeyed Mr. Pulitzer's orders and stepped aboard this train and headed west. She stopped yesterday in Chicago to interview Cap Anson. By some miracle, her escort left her alone before they arrived at Mr. Anson's stoop. Mr. Ponsonby said he had neglected his primary duty and excused himself to cable Mr. Pulitzer to assure him that the *World's* most valuable asset was safe and sound.

"I cannot believe that a man who knows every trivial tidbit about base ball will skip a chance to meet one of the game's greatest participants."

Mr. Ponsonby scurried off with his odd stride. She was happy to have an hour without her barnacle attached, but Mr. Anson was all about unpleasantries and one of those men immune to a pretty girl's flirt. He had just returned from Spalding's World Base Ball Tour, a five-month stunt that he considered greater than her fete of seventy-two days.

"Try doing what you did east-to-west, while stopping for games in every port," Mr. Anson said. He had a condescending smirk, his fly was unbuttoned, and he took great pleasure in his attempts to shock her. "Girls of the Sandwich Islands perform the hula. Australian girls serve beer. The girls of Ceylon have soft, black eyes, which they use to some advantage. Boys at sea get coltish."

"Be that as it may."

"We took the time to throw Clarence overboard."

"Your loyal mascot? Why?"

"Over the S.S. Alameda, to lure sharks that we shot with revolvers. Sharks didn't like the taste of him. It's a scientific fact, they didn't even nibble, so we fished Clarence out coughing and alive."

Mr. Anson never shut up about his voyage. "In Egypt the boys rode camels to the game. We threw base balls at the Sphinx, and Fogarty, the Philadelphia outfielder, struck it in the eye. Casey would've knocked its digit off, but he never rejoined the tour after chasing Walter Brewster into the Mormon Temple. We had an extra spot and Al Spalding got Judge Gold to come along and umpire. Gold trained that some-bitch Brewster, but we never gave him grief about it. Not once all the way around the world. I told The Judge I wished he'd umpired that afternoon in Mudville. Things would've been different. No poem. History changed."

"Do you know where Mr. Brewster is now?"

"No. I forgave him, but Casey never will. Hasn't hit a lick since the strikeout." Cap Anson chortles. "The *San Francisco Chronicle* doesn't write stories about who's the best anymore. Everyone knows it's me now. I hope some reporter finds the umpire before Casey does. Wood Dryden will find him. He came to Chicago last week, the *San Francisco Examiner* paid his way."

"Mr. Dryden did not attend the match. I did." It was high time Nellie Bly got Mr. Anson's goat. "I happen to believe Mr. Brewster umpired satisfactorily."

"Like hell." Mr. Anson buttons up right in front of her.

"I understand it is an unpopular opinion. Nevertheless."

"Maybe his strike zone was better than we thought at the time. But he let Moses effing Fleetwood Walker play on. Even after he knew he wasn't a Mex-can. Brewster shouldn't've been there and neither should've Fleet Walker and neither should've you. I've nothing against girls or coloreds, but neither belong at the yard. Everything I do is for the good of the game. *My* game."

"Take pity on Mr. Walker," Nellie Bly said. "He may be the first man electrocuted."

"He won't suffer. Just like the illiterate Clarence didn't suffer amidst sharks. Walter Brewster will suffer if Casey catches up to him. He would've caught him in Salt Lake, but it was raining to beat the band."

That dreadful interview with Mr. Anson is now hundreds of miles down the tracks. Nellie Bly squeezes her pillow to her ears and does her best to erase it from memory. Thinking about the bigoted girl hater and his unbuttoned unmentionables puts her in a mood even before the sun has risen. She rolls to her side and looks out the frosty window to estimate the time. Mercifully, the night is ending, the snow gray in the pre-dawn.

Claude Ponsonby always knows the time precisely. He's a clock with feet. She smiles. She'd never confess it, but she's grown attached to her escort as Mr. Pulitzer had predicted. Mr. Ponsonby has now been with her for weeks and weeks, twenty-four hours a day, more hours than any man in her lifetime except her dear dead daddy and Jack Ford, the limping animal her mother divorced.

She has grown attached, though Mr. Ponsonby has many faults. Too many to count. He never understands a joke. He never understands an idiom—such as raining to beat the band—and yet he unleashes a cutting wit from time to time. He never lets one food touch another on his plate. Sometimes he eats fast and waits on her to finish. At other times he chews so slowly that she waits on him. Never once does he finish at her pace. After all this time, he can't get himself synchronized. He's lost in another world, but when she captures his attention he's absorbed in her words like no man she's known.

He says he likes the confines of his berth. Her berth makes her antsy, it causes her to recall the broom closet and straw hamper of Pennsylvania. She considers telling Mr. Ponsonby about Jack Ford. That's how much she trusts him with a secret; she has never trusted anyone more. Dear Lord, she even considers telling him her actual age.

"I once went a year without speaking, a year without saying a word," he said before turning in last night.

She laughed, certain it was a joke. But he was telling the truth, because he never lies, not even to protect her feelings. His infrequent words are at times complimentary, then at any instant spatter as hot grease.

He's gone unshaven for days as if he's hiding his dimples from whatever looms up the tracks. He has eyes as blue as Cap Anson's, a face girls fuss over. A face that should not be carpeted over with a beard. He is interested in her, but he's too shy to let any girl know.

She told him that Cap Anson had been inappropriate, hoping to make him jealous. Instead, he felt guilty for not being there. He wanted to steer the train around and give the greatest player his greatest sock. Mr. Ponsonby protects her, not because she's Joseph Pulitzer's asset, but because she's special to him.

She rolls to her back and pulls the pillow to her face. Ahead looms a barbaric morning. She must face it, but she procrastinates, she slips into a recollection of past marriage proposals. Her latest came two weeks ago in the middle of the Pacific when Mr. Ponsonby was fetching her a ginger beer. A Virginia tobacco magnate said he must betroth a woman who can travel with scant luggage. It was a joke, but had she jokingly agreed, they'd be honeymooning at Niagara Falls this instant. Her newspaper days over.

It's getting light outside. Mr. Ponsonby is reclined inches above her. She knows he's awake and in need of the privy, but he plays the martyr to let her sleep. Sometimes she feels it's her duty to keep *him* safe. Safe from a world that's unkind to odd men. His mission is clear and simple. Were she to fall down a deep well, all he need do is rescue her or die trying. Protecting Mr. Ponsonby is more complicated. He has some sort of mental disorder that traps him deep in a well of his own making. He is both hard as nails and fragile.

She scolds herself for feeling sorry for him. He needs his satchel stored beneath her berth and she stays in bed to punish him for his crimes. He is aloof and incapable of pleasure, as if he were captured in a Jane Austen plot. He's stubborn. The Good Lord knows. Once he sets his mind to something, he does not let go, and he has set his mind on protecting each hair on her head. He's a typesetter, as poor as the tobacco magnate was rich. Yet, her affection is the only thing that makes the journey tolerable. Her affection will remain sisterly. He will never try to be romantic with her. He's incapable.

She settles into memories of Booker Stevens and the suicidal Gunner and so many other proposals. A nearby snort brings her out of a half dream. She finds her glasses and unbuttons her curtain a slit to see an early riser dressing in the aisle and without regard to her sensibilities. Men with decency sleep in their clothes when aboard trains, removing only their shoes, but this one wears a union suit that is snug around an erection. He probably had a salacious dream about her.

What is it about American trains? By some convention, men and women share the same car. Nowhere else on earth are ladies subjected to such degradation, and she must soon parade in her modest nightie to the dressing room in view of creation. In China, where the Christmastime earth is red from disemboweled Orientals, ladies have more privacy than they do aboard a west-bound Union Pacific.

Out the curtain slit are two more men up and out of bed. She sees them in a way their wives rarely do. She has no choice but to stay in her berth all day or rise and let them gawk. In a fit of pique, she hustles to the lavatory with dress in arms, valise over shoulder, eyes straight ahead, passing through the unspeakable.

The days of train robberies ceased eight years ago when Robert Ford, a distant relative of the animal Jack Ford, shot Jesse James in the back of the head. That hasn't stopped shameful salesmen from wanting to steal kisses in dark tunnels. Some aboard would be capable of worse if tunnels were longer. The porter named George is the only one with the decency to turn his back to her. The railroad hires anonymous spotters to make sure Negroes in their employ never stare at white women.

The train car is more barbarous than Blackwell's asylum. Madhouses condemn girls to a life of bedbugs and bastard babies, but at least the commodes open to something other than thunderous tracks and the sweet reek of man pee.

No girl ever longed more for a mirror, though not the mirror of honesty Mr. Ponsonby reflects back at her. She needs a *true* glass mirror. She finds one at the washstand and does everything possible to make herself human. She's alone and she lets her dress fall to her ankles. She examines every inch, even her bare bottom. There are still no freckles as Booker Stevens had insisted. She has clear skin and full lips, the two things men of all lands value as much as a figure of her proportions. A waist of twenty-five inches, hips and breasts nine inches more. Men in some lands prefer women plump, but they all gravitate to the same ratio. She is fetching for all she has been through, but her face shows the stains of travel. Her hair is tossed and starting to grow too long to be fashionable.

She wonders why Mr. Ponsonby shows no interest in faces. A proper face overcomes a lot, her mother used to say, the same mother who let Jack Ford chase her into the hamper. Nellie Bly pumps water into the basin and does her utmost. She spits out the gum that's been beneath her tongue all night, replaces it with a fresh piece.

Upon her return, the porter George is at the ready to help Mr. Ponsonby climb down the ladder from his berth. He needs no help. Mr. Ponsonby's not one of those muscle-bound men who tosses medicine balls, but he's in better physical shape than a typesetter ought be. George can be fired if he touches her without permission. She stands in close, but Mr. Ponsonby is the most nervous of the two men. He finds his satchel and leaves for the washroom to straighten up. He is either too embarrassed or too preoccupied with himself to acknowledge her. The most accomplished man in America at typesetting can't string together seven letters to say "morning."

He returns in his worsted suit, his growth a day thicker. "It might behoove you to shave," she says. He says nothing, and she remembers that he responds best to questions. "Are you sprouting a disguise?"

"Yes. Men of the West don't shave. I'll look like Buffalo Bill Cody when we reach the Rockies."

She laughs. "You should employ your sense of humor more often."

"You can be Annie Oakley."

She purses her lips at the insult. "There is that hurtful wit I warned you about. I will seek the conductor. I will tell him who I am and he will escort you to the immigrant car or throw you off into the elements."

Their seats face each other. Mr. Ponsonby takes the side traveling backward. A gentlemen never takes that seat, especially in summer when sparks fly through open windows. It's winter, but the windows on this ancient Pullman no longer close snugly. She examines her lap. She sees no fine ash settling on her dress and she decides not to make a fuss about it. She leaves her glasses on for protection against an errant spark.

"Sometimes you are a considerate, kind man. Other times you believe you're the measure of all things."

"Typesetters measure many things, but no one can measure all things."

"Everyone is prideful about something," Nellie Bly says. "Some people are proud that they are not proud. You fall into that camp."

The porter George is busy with other berths, and Mr. Ponsonby leaves to find her a bun and a cup of steaming coffee. She feels the stares of men the moment he's gone. She thumbs through her *Atlantic Monthly* and turns her attention to the two other women in her car. They boarded in Chicago. They are lovely and she was unable to ascertain before going to bed the prettiest of the two. Sunshine settles things. One is a decade older, wears a wedding ring, and has but a few precious years left to be attractive. She probably goes to bed at home with inch-thick cold cream and this morning she woke up chapped. She's humming to herself with eyes closed.

The other is a blonde and reminds her of Leonara Barner, the smutty actress once courted by Mr. Pulitzer's right hand, Colonel Cockerill. Miss Barner and Colonel Cockerill were engaged until he made water into her parents' piano. This traveler's younger than Miss Barner, almost too young for womanhood at all. She dares to wear finery inappropriate for a girl whose breasts clearly need the patience of another year to fill a blouse.

Nellie Bly suddenly feels old, almost ancient. She will be turning twenty-six in May, although everyone believes she is two or three years younger. She wishes she were home at last. She longs to sleep in a batter of cold cream.

The married woman opens her eyes and Nellie Bly smiles at her over the *Atlantic Monthly*. They'd enjoy a conversation, but Nellie Bly rarely tells other women who she is because they try to lure her into gossip. They expect her to give unflattering opinions of her famous acquaintances. If the men knew who she was, they'd line up to ask about her unchaperoned journeys through lands of savagery. Men crave more than conversation. They crave smiles and eye contact, but this morning they're craving it from the blonde.

Nellie Bly wishes the blonde were an ugly suffragist. Nellie Bly is modern, never one to settle on a life of labor pains and recipe exchange, but she has no idea why suffragists neglect their appearance merely because they are intellectually inclined. Why be as a man, when dress and beauty are arrows absent in a man's quiver?

She makes certain she isn't cow-chewing her gum; it's the little things that keep a girl ageless. The smutty girl-hussy has dimples and curls, golden from a dime's worth of peroxide of hydrogen and a nickel's worth of ammonia. At second glance, the hussy's hair appears genuine, not streaked or greenish like those who bleach in a bowl. She is fair-complexioned, but her feet are probably two sizes too large. Nellie Bly takes a quick scan about at the gentlemen. Half of them are looking at the child over their newspapers. Gentlemen are such disgusting creatures of the eye.

Mr. Ponsonby returns with refreshments and Nellie Bly's never been more happy to see anyone. He gets nervous when she examines his kind eyes, and so she stares at him in the window's reflection. His whiskers have altered his appearance. The combination of the beard and the scar on his forehead do indeed make him appear western. Even taller.

"January is the most cheerless month for scenery," she says. "Sad birds frozen to fence wires. The congressman will never be forgiven for sending me on this detail. Do you know the time?"

"Eight fifty-seven."

She stretches and smiles. "As it turns out, I am glad for your company, it breaks up the day."

He takes that as an invitation to launch into a monologue about how the Panama Railway cost six thousand lives for fifty miles of track. Reporters know a little bit about everything. Mr. Ponsonby knows everything about a few things. He'd rather read the train schedule than a great work of fiction. She'll never rescue him from the odd world he inhabits.

"Tell me how you got your scar." She touches her own face above the right brow and pouts her lips.

He hesitates. "Fly fishing. My father was unaware of me behind him. I was looking at a pill bug when he hooked me with a back-cast. Cut the barb out with his penknife."

He never lies, except by omission, and he modifies his story. "I was a small child, I healed cleanly, I got no scar from that."

As a game, she tries to lure him into an untruth about something else. "Do you approve of women who grow fat?"

He shrugs and pretends to have no opinion.

"Wives must remain coquettes without double chins if they want husbands interested and guessing," she says. He shrugs again, and she sighs. "Are you a Mormon?"

"No."

"Mormons know all about wives. They have several, it's why your Utah will never achieve statehood. Mormons will never go to heaven. Neither will Mr. Pulitzer, sadly." She watches scenery for a mile and says, "Mr. Ponsonby, what do you think of me? A penny for your thoughts."

She expects another shrug but his face lights up brighter than she's seen. "Your words have changed the world."

She practices humility. "A few babies christened Nellie Bly here and there. I cannot believe I am being dragged into the Casey tarpit. The match itself was quite a spectacle. You should have seen it."

"I like ball yards. I like the game, except it's not timed. You never know how long it will last. You owe me a penny. For my thoughts."

"It is an expression."

"You don't have to pay me. You've changed bughouses from coast to coast. My Moms will soon move into the new Great Asylum for the Insane."

Nellie Bly is stunned at this level of honesty. Family secrets of a delicate nature are kept in mop closets because of the neighbors and what they think.

"You're the reason the Great Asylum is being built," Mr. Ponsonby says. "Near the Lick paper mill, a day's ride from where this train's going. You've changed Moms' life. You've changed the world."

She's flattered beyond belief and she takes a slow breath to enjoy it. Then, something begins to nag at her. "Thank you, Mr. Ponsonby, but the story of your mother belongs deep in a novel, not in the open air. Perhaps you will take the time to visit her."

"Only if I can leave you in safe hands. I'll never strand you with another ball player like Cap Anson." Mr. Ponsonby squeezes his base ball as if it's weapon enough to save her from dragons.

"I can take care of myself. I am a woman of pluck; you should know that about me by now. There is only one thing in life that I fear."

She's about to disclose that fear when the train slows into St. Louis and she finds herself starved for the latest news and in search of a newsboy selling copies of the *Dispatch*. She is stunned by the banner headline.

"There was no verdict in the Fleetwood Walker case," she says. "The jury ended in disagreement." She digests the item and stops here and there to give Mr. Ponsonby the highlights. "Arabella Walker embraced her husband. Two of his children cried and clung to his legs as he walked free. Reporters hollered after him. 'Are you guilty?' Mr. Walker shouted, 'Of one or two beers.'"

"I like Fleet Walker," Mr. Ponsonby says.

Nellie Bly glares up from the newspaper. "You barely met him. He's an awful, brooding man. You see only the good in people."

"I could never be a reporter. I tried once at the *Deseret News* and failed miserably."

"Mr. Pulitzer should have assigned me to the trial of the century, not this wild goose chase."

"Huh?"

"The missing umpire is of human interest, but it could have waited."

"Your timing is perfect. The trial's over."

"You are right. It will fade into memory soon after we alight in San Francisco. My readers crave something new. They always do. I must not let them down. I fear I will. The umpire has been seen only once in two years." She removes her glasses. "The one thing I fear, Mr. Ponsonby, is failure. I feared I might fail at sneaking into Blackwell's. I feared I might fail to get around the world in eighty days. Today, I fear I will never find the umpire. He is a needle in a haystack."

"Beg pardon?"

"When we went around the world, at least we knew where we were going and the speed we had to maintain."

"You won't fail."

"Failure is the one thing from which you cannot save me, no matter how much courage you muster."

"I'll save you from anything," Mr. Ponsonby says.

She leans across to kiss him on the cheek. It's innocent with barely a hint of the devil, but men shift their stares from the blonde.

"You can do anything," the red-faced Mr. Ponsonby says. "You could be put in charge of armies."

Nellie Bly's heart melts at the sound of that. "A woman to end all war?"

"War won't end, but soldiers won't desert you. They will find death easier to accept than the disappointment in your face."

His words both soften and encourage her heart. "I will not fail. Be careful, Mr. Ponsonby, I will throw you on these tracks to succeed."

"I'll gladly be run over. You saved my Moms."

She shushes him. "Keep family secrets close to the vest."

"Huh?"

She puts on her glasses and picks up *Ben Hur*. She removes the envelopes that serve as bookmarks. She recalls the letters inside the envelopes from the anonymous San Francisco and Salt Lake City gentleman whose mother resides at…where? She opens one envelope. The mother mentioned in the letter resides at the Marine Hospital that Houses Crazy Seamen.

"What are the odds?" she says.

"The odds of what?"

Could the letter writer and Mr. Ponsonby be the same man? Impossible. She thinks back, she can't remember ever seeing Mr. Ponsonby's handwriting. She has nothing with which to compare.

"The odds of what?" he repeats. "I am expert at calculations."

Nellie Bly convinces herself that it's all happenstance. Next, she convinces herself it is not. How many men from Salt Lake have mothers in the same California madhouse? Men who play billiards call an impossible shot a *fluke*. This is more than a fluke. No shot made in billiards, no matter the impossible angle, has ever been this unlikely.

Were Mr. Ponsonby a normal man, she would have put two and two together long ago. He has kept her off balance with his quirkiness. She glances up from her novel. Mr. Ponsonby's eyes are cast down as always, but not trained on her tiny feet. They instead are trained upon the poor penmanship scribbled on the envelopes. His fingertips are dug into his base ball. His glance into her eyes falls away.

She snap closes the book over the envelopes and he flinches. This is not the time to confront him and, anyway, her mission is to find the umpire. She can't let a typesetter from Salt Lake detract from that. Could he be a stalker? She's dealt with her share of them but never one clever enough to convince Mr. Pulitzer to hire on as her escort. Stalkers are also odd but Mr. Ponsonby is incapable of that *modus operandi*. It's all some crazy coincidence. Stalkers are dangerous. Mr. Ponsonby is the very picture of safe.

Mr. Ponsonby puts his hand to his beard. "How will you find Walter Brewster?"

"How do I accomplish anything? With effort and energy rightly applied. What a squall it will cause."

"A woman capable of leading armies must have a plan of attack. Will we visit Casey's mansion?"

"In due time. First, we will visit the man named Judge Gold. He was the umpire who trained Mr. Brewster. He was supposed to have been the arbiter at the Home of the Mudville Niners on that spring day, but he was beaten in Santa Cruz. Mr. Brewster took his place. Judge Gold is Mr. Brewster's friend. His mentor."

"He won't tell you anything."

"Why not? I have a way with judges. I received a valuable tip about Judge Gold."

"A tip? From whom?"

"A letter from the owner of the Wolverines Base Ball Club in Detroit. I receive many letters, as you can imagine. This letter concerns Judge Gold and the dirty umpire Dick Higham. It was passed along to me by way of the newspaper poet Earnest Thayer? It is quite interesting, not to me, but to those who crave endless afternoons of base ball like an addict craves morphine."

"What does it say?"

"I will use it to pry the information I need from Judge Gold. If he does not steer us to Walter Brewster, I will write a lengthy item exposing The Judge. I will tell the public who he really is."

"Who is he, really?"

"Next we will knock suddenly at Casey's door. Catch him by surprise. If Judge Gold does not pan out."

"I know what pan out means because I once panned for gold."

She turns to the scenery out the window. She half expects to pass the umpire aboard a slow freight train, a hobo wearing a wire mask, carrying a bindle and huddled between flatcars of logs. There is nothing human out there, not a sod house, only endless falling snow streaming by parallel with the smoke and steam of the locomotive. She is cold from a draft of outside air slipping through the window's weathered crack.

"Perhaps Walter Brewster was found and murdered and buried by Niner fanatics. Perhaps he was murdered by Casey himself and is buried beneath the Temple in Salt Lake. Perhaps Casey buried him beneath the Home of the Mudville Niners or Golden Gate Park."

"You think he is dead?"

"Quite likely, though his body will never be found. I am happy that I was not assigned to the murder trial. The umpire detail will turn out to be the story that seals my legacy. The story that convinces everyone that I am no stunt girl, the one that legitimizes my other successes."

The old train creaks on. The nights are marked by the vibrato of the locomotive, the warble of the carriage, the heaving and straining of the soot-spewing monster. Calamitous mornings of men in union suits are replaced by afternoons of magazine articles and snippets of odd, honest conversation with Mr. Ponsonby until sagebrush pokes through the snow. Late one night, they share intimate stories about their mothers. She feels she knows all there is to know about Mr. Ponsonby and he knows far more about her than anyone should. Still, it nags at her that he is her letter writer. It nags at her that there may be more to his mystery.

On a bright afternoon, the train climbs into the foothills of the Sierra Nevada. She knows that the sunlight reflects from the snow, makes her face blanch and sets off her eyes. She removes her glasses. She feels the stares of gentlemen shifting from the blonde, and she keeps her head cocked toward the window. Mr. Ponsonby travels across from her, moving backward and winding upward and westward and awkward.

She is at the worse possible angle at this point in time. A coal spark from the train's smokestack threads its way through the window crack and finds her eye.

"Yet another fluke. What are the odds?" It's the absolute worst pain she's experienced.

Mr. Ponsonby attempts a rescue, and she blames him for stealing her proper seat from the start. She pushes him away and finds a pin in her handbag, wraps the head in the corner of her lace handkerchief, and sweeps it around beneath the eyelid. The cinder remains lodged as tears run down her cheeks. She pulls down on her lower eyelid and fails again to wipe the cinder away.

"Go and convince the conductor to stop at the next station house. Tell them who I am."

Mr. Ponsonby takes the pin from her hand. "Trust me. I'll keep you from harm, I promise."

He removes the cinder with a typesetter's hand. She looks up with tear-washed eyes, blinks a number of times, and kisses her dear escort's cheek. Throats clear all about, and Mr. Ponsonby is adorably embarrassed.

That evening, Nellie Bly confides in Mr. Ponsonby as she has never confided in a man. She tells him about the mop closet. She reveals her age. Mr. Ponsonby is the first gentleman since her father who believes she can lead armies. He has faith in her success.

She decides to trust Mr. Ponsonby completely. The dear man will never let her down.

"Do they still play the blues in Chicago When baseball season rolls around?
When the snow melts away, do the Cubbies still play
In their ivy-covered burial ground?"—Steve Goodman

May 21, 2017
It's a Sunday

CHAPTER THIRTEEN

one hundred twenty-nine years after the strikeout

Harold Higham dies at his home in Tallman, N.Y. denying that the brother of his great-grandfather, the only umpire ever banned from baseball, wagered on games.

Harold Higham practiced maritime law and spent his free time exploring baseball archives of the 1880s. Umpire applicants to the National League were voted on by team owners. The twenty-four with the most votes were hired. Dick Higham, who had played every position except pitcher, placed third in the 1881 voting. He was assigned to Providence, moved to Detroit, then to Troy, and finished the season back in Detroit.

He was so admired that a testimonial game was held in his honor at the end of the 1881 season where the Detroit Medical Center now stands. He finished atop the owner voting before the 1882 season. No other returning umpires were selected. Owners considered newcomers superior to those with proven incompetencies.

But things turned sour for Higham in 1882 when William Thompson, a meat wholesaler, alderman, and owner of the Detroit Wolverines, became suspicious of Higham's calls. When his team surrendered twenty-three runs on July 14, Thompson hired a private detective who unearthed letters between Higham and the young shister, Soapy Smith. Higham wrote "buy all the lumber you can" when Soapy Smith was to bet on a Detroit win, according to the detective. The letters were never produced, although some say one found its way into the hands of Earnest Thayer after he wrote

Casey at the Bat, a Ballad of the Republic, Sung in the Year 1888. Others say that same letter found its way into the possession of *New York World* reporter Nellie Bly, but Harold Higham researched the newspaper archives and Nellie Bly never wrote a word about it.

When owners met to discuss the allegations, only one Wolverine was batting above .269, making Higham's strike zone suspect. No other reason was given in the minutes for his banishment.

"It can be stated clearly that Dick Higham never confessed to any wrongdoing and denied accusations," Harold Higham wrote in the *Society for American Baseball Research.*

Soapy Smith moved to Skagway to con prospectors during the 1898 Klondike gold rush. The *Detroit Free Press* said that Dick Higham became a bookie and a race track lout, but Harold Higham found no evidence of that. He determined that his great-granduncle changed his name and moved to San Francisco to resume umpiring and to become a justice of the peace named Goldman, but known simply as The Judge, or Judge Gold. He was reelected time after time.

"Only Honest John Gaffney was considered to be a better umpire at the dawn of professional baseball," Harold Higham wrote.

After his beating in Santa Cruz, The Judge umpired Al Spalding's World Tour before retiring from baseball. He never married. He moved to New York and lived to be 104, long enough to hear Jackie Robinson play against the New York Giants, 570 on the radio dial.

Moses Fleetwood Walker was the last African-American to play in the Major Leagues until Robinson. Walker died in 1924 at 67. He is buried at Union Cemetery in Steubenville, Ohio next to his estranged wife Arabella, who died of cancer at 32 in 1895. The couple is surrounded by white people, including the famous sports commentator and Las Vegas bookmaker Jimmy "The Greek" Snyder.

Snyder was born in Steubenville in 1918. He was five when Fleet Walker died. He bet $10,000 on the 1948 election between Thomas Dewey and Harry S. Truman, getting 17-to-1 odds. He knew Truman was going to win because women didn't trust a man with a mustache.

CBS fired Snyder as a commentator in 1988 for saying: "The black is a better athlete to begin with, because he's been bred to be that way. Because of his high thighs and big thighs that goes up into his back. And they can jump higher and run faster because of their bigger thighs. And he's bred to be the better athlete because this goes back all the way to the Civil War, when, during the slave trading, the slave owner would breed his big black to his big woman so that he could have uh big black kid, see. That's where it all started."

"It is dangerous to spring to obvious conclusions.
Baseball is not an obvious game."—Roger Kahn

February 5, 1890, 3:15 p.m.
It's a Wednesday

CHAPTER FOURTEEN

six hundred twenty-six days after the strikeout

Nellie Bly is one of the two most famous girls on earth, but the first thing Judge Gold notices when he answers the knock at his chambers is Walter Brewster at her side. The Judge hasn't seen his protégé in fifteen months, not since he ran into a Salt Lake City downpour. The Judge's heart leaps. He wants to embrace him like a son, but Walter looks at his base ball.

Nellie Bly introduces Claude Ponsonby as her escort.

"Claude who?" The Judge asks, barely containing glee behind his dundrearies and black robes.

The Judge plays along. He turns his attention to the lovely girl, who needs no introduction. He makes chitchat by asking about her trip around the world. Nellie Bly says that it was completed with effort and energy rightly applied.

"I know you were on Al Spalding's World Tour, but I have no patience for it," she says and steers the conversation to Walter Brewster's whereabouts.

"You were among the last to see him that day in Salt Lake," she says.

"I saw little but Walter's backside. He was a bucket-assed kid as he ran from the storm, up the hill and into the Temple. Casey never stood a chance to catch him."

"I must find Mr. Brewster. It is urgent."

"He seems to be popular these days. Wood Dryden of the *Examiner* is hunting him, too. I've seen neither Walter nor Casey, though Casey lives a few miles from here. He rarely comes out of his mansion. Not since the eighty-nine season. Not in daylight, anyway."

"I am not here about Casey," Nellie Bly says. I am weary of him. Casey this, Casey that. Will Casey ever hit again? Will Casey retire? Is Casey headed for the madhouse? Is Casey getting fat? Will Casey have a Second Coming?"

"California remains in mourning," The Judge says. "The pride of the Niners hasn't hit his weight since the strikeout."

"He batted .125 in 1889," Walter says. "Less than most any adult's weight—except Miss Bly's."

The Judge laughs. Walter hasn't changed a bit, except for that lame beard. A disguise of some sort. His funny bone is still in an unorthodox place; half of what bubbles from his mouth remains comical, truthful, nonsense.

"I daresay, Mr. Ponsonby, do you intend to tell Judge Gold my age, too?" Nellie Bly says.

"Please have a seat, Miss Bly," The Judge says to rescue Walter from a loutish answer.

She doesn't know Walter is Walter, but she seems to know that he will blurt out her age if she doesn't tell it first. "I have been sitting for three solid months. I turned twenty-five sitting. Now, tell me Mr. Brewster's whereabouts. You must exchange letters with your apprentice now and then."

"Walter isn't a letter writer."

"The sooner you steer me in the right direction, the sooner you get me out of your hair."

"Huh?"

"I enjoy your company, Miss Bly, but your quest is as urgent as you say. That Wood Dryden's a step ahead of you."

"I would not wager on that, were you a wagering man." Nellie Bly, for no apparent reason, discharges a sarcastic smile.

"Wood Dryden's been by to see me more than once. You're right, he's no closer to Brewster than you are. Indeed, I believe you are very close."

Walter laughs at the inside joke. Nellie Bly deserves to be the butt of it. She has some nerve, implying that an umpire, any umpire, is a wagering man. But Walter's laugh doesn't phase her. Nellie Bly seems to have learned to accept that he responds unnaturally in inappropriate places.

"I taught Walter Brewster to umpire. I taught him to trust the inner voice that is a man's judgment. I taught him to stay a step ahead of the shit-house beast."

"That is the second time I have heard that awful colloquialism in the past days," Nellie Bly says. "Mr. Ponsonby never swears, but he said it in the jailhouse cell of Fleetwood Walker."

Walter mumbles at his feet. "The beast lurks invisible about the yard."

"So the story goes," The Judge says. "The story is true. I'm proof of that, and so is the missing Walter Brewster. I'm happy to tell you my impressions of him. I'm sure, Miss Bly, that you write the facts. I'm certain, unlike Dryden, you let readers form their own opinions. Wood Dryden bloviates and exaggerates. He's a *putz*, a *schmuck*."

"Do you pretend to be Jewish?"

"My name is Goldman, but the name Gold wins me votes on Election Day." He hopes that exposing a vulnerability will soften her inquisition. "We all pretend to be something." The Judge laughs. "Everyone except Walter Brewster. He's incapable of being anything except himself."

Walter squeezes the base ball. He's shamefaced knowing that The Judge is aware of his ongoing deception, but Nellie Bly pays no attention.

"I am here to help your Mr. Brewster," Nellie Bly says. "He is a despised man but I have the power to persuade people to believe otherwise."

"Then you do use your talents to deceive," The Judge says. "You try to form public opinion. That leads me to distrust you. No one ever helps Walter."

"You did," she says.

"I made a solid umpire out of a petty thief. I turned a boy into a *mensch*. You'll let him down, I would wager on that, Miss Bly."

"Were you a wagering man." Her sarcastic smile flashes again. She knows more than she lets on and The Judge's heart sinks. He longs for his chair, but she remains on her tiny feet. Her smile makes him feel insecure. He feels his presence draining away. She doesn't know she's feet away from Walter, but she's smart about something else. She knows about The Judge's past.

"I will never wager against you, Miss Bly."

"Be that as it may. I was in the San Joaquin when you were bedridden in Santa Cruz. While you were flat on your back for saying a base ball player was safe, for making an errant declaration, I was at the Home of the Mudville Niners in my white dress and hat, admiring Mr. Brewster's blue suit and professionalism. I was there for the strikeout. You were not. Casey's swing was a blur, I felt the bat's breeze." Nellie Bly puts her gloved hands above her breasts. "Casey's swing pulled the very air from my lungs."

The Judge fears what she knows. He lashes out at her before he can stop himself. "Reporters are mugwumps, fuds, and ligners. They fan their own fumes."

"Be that as it may," she repeats. "I feel I know Mr. Brewster. I sat there for four hours, two hours before the match ever started. I sat there ending after ending. For the life of me, I never got a clear look at his face but I have a sisterly affection. In the last ending, they wanted him killed. Everyone except for me. Mr. Brewster needs my protection."

"Walter needs to be left alone," Judge Gold says. His throat is dry, his voice sounds like he swallowed sand. "We all do."

"He judged balls and strikes to the best of his ability, just as you judge the guilt or innocence of pickpockets."

At last a kind word. The Judge wants to warm to her, but he knows better. "Please sit, Miss Bly."

She remains standing. "I felt sorry for Mr. Brewster. I still do, for all umpires. Why in heaven's name do you do it, Judge Gold? Not for the money. You are a man well-situated."

"Now, Miss Bly, when I put on a blue suit, that's when I'm a man of integrity. More so than when I wear these robes. It's impossible to explain to anyone except another umpire, just as the conditions of war are impossible to explain to a civilian. As a service to my country, I make sure the national game is played honorably."

The sarcastic smile returns to her mouth.

"Nellie Bly will one day be put in charge of armies," Walter says.

The Judge doesn't understand Walter's compulsion to promote a girl so pompous, so irritatingly grand—so eager to expose him. Both of them, himself and Walter. Given a chance, she'll expose The Judge's dark secrets. She'll drag Walter through the mud. She'll drag the two of them in tandem.

"Life is unjust. Your reward for serving your country, Judge Gold, was that beating in Santa Cruz." Nellie Bly walks to the chamber window. "If you must umpire, why do you do it in this climate? San Francisco is as awful as London. Full of fog, full of obfuscation. Just like war. Some days the weather here is worse than—in Michigan."

The mention of Michigan puts The Judge deeper in a mood. He recalls his two beatings. One physical in Santa Cruz, one emotional in Detroit. He recalls the testimonial game they played in his honor at the end of the 1881 season. He recalls the pretty Santa Cruz woman a few steps back spurring on the men in tall hats and bright vests. That girl has forever ruined pretty faces for him. "I never dreamed that Nellie Bly was such a pain in the ultimatum," he says.

Walter pipes up in her defense. "Everyone loves Nellie Bly."

The Judge laughs. "What was your name again?" He knows that Walter is incapable of a lie.

"Claude Ponsonby," Nellie Bly says annoyed at the diversion. Shame returns to Walter's face but she goes on as if he's not there. "The missing umpire, Mr. Brewster, has been demonized for no reason, and we are the only two in America who want to set the record straight. If I do not find him, I can be of no help. Though I never got a good look at him, I know that he is nothing like Frankenstein's monster as the *Examiner's* illustrations suggest."

"You don't know Walter and you don't know me."

"I will make it safe for him to return to society. Just as you have resurfaced here in San Francisco."

"You want to sell three more copies of Joseph Pulitzer's sheet."

"I will make Mr. Brewster rich off of Mr. Pulitzer's money," Nellie Bly says. "Three thousand dollars awaits him for a repeat clash with Casey."

"Be that as it may," The Judge mocks her with her own words. "Apparently, money is not enough."

Walter stares out the window, escaping the conflict. He points to the *Chronicle's* new ten-story building, made of brick and stone façade. There's a clock at the top. "Three twenty-seven. Precisely." He turns his notice to an oil painting on the chambers' wall. It is of a massive snow-covered mountain. Not snow-capped, but white, peak to valley. Tumbling in the foreground is a river with a rocky shore. The river is iced over but it appears to be moving.

"The Yukon's Denali," The Judge says and Walter smiles knowingly.

"It will be awful if Wood Dryden finds him." Nellie Bly softens her tone. "If you want to protect Mr. Brewster, tell me where he is."

The Judge watches Walter stare into the painting. "He's in his own world. That's where to look."

"Well, then." Nellie Bly's eyes turn cold and hard. "You leave me no choice but to come after you, Judge Gold. I know who you are. Who you *really* are. I received a tip in a letter. It was passed along to me by the reluctant poet Earnest Thayer. The perfect tip. The letter was sent to Mr. Thayer from a Mr. Thompson, a Detroit alderman and owner of the Wolverines Base Ball Club."

The Judge swallows the sand in his throat.

"You are the third stupid judge I have snookered."

"He isn't stupid." Walter changes sides to defend The Judge. "He's the opposite."

"You know about trains and typesetting. You would not know a cheat. If someone told you to buy all the lumber, you would return with a wagon of pine." She addresses The Judge. "Tell me where Walter Brewster is hiding. Tell me now, or *The New York World* will publish a never-ending exposé that will haunt you until the November election."

"Anything you write will be more kicks to my prick. Nothing more."

She pretends to be insulted. She turns to Walter. "Mr. Ponsonby, The Judge here is Dick Higham. The cheating umpire banned from base ball."

"No he's not," Walter says.

The Judge feels bad that Walter is learning about this now. He *is* Dick Higham. Even though the wagering part is untrue, Walter should have heard it long ago over Chinese and beer. The last thing The Judge wanted was for Walter to be hurt by a man who he trusts; hurt by the father figure who has looked out for his welfare. Hurt by his only friend.

"You are not," Walter repeats. There are tears in his eyes.

The Judge confesses. "It's true. It's true that I'm Dick Higham, but the rest is flat-out false."

"That is only the half of it," Nellie Bly says. "Dick Higham and Honest John Gaffney are one in the same."

"They're not," Walter says. "That's preposterous. They are opposites."

The Judge wants to embrace his friend; to squeeze the hurt from Walter's eyes. His arms extend beneath his robe. "People are not what they seem," he says. "I've learned that on the bench and I've learned it on the yard. I'm more than one person. We all are."

"I intend to publish my story unless Judge Goldman or Mr. Gaffney or Mr. Higham—whoever you pretend to be—tells me where to find Walter Brewster. Tell me and the men of San Francisco County will reelect you come November."

"If I tell you, Casey will kill him—and get away with it."

"Like Fleet Walker got away with it," Walter says. "Fleet's more than one person, too."

"Casey wouldn't even stand trial," The Judge says. "Casey's a state treasure. All of California will protect him, at least the memory of him. I alone must protect Walter. He's like a child. He's like a son."

"I am America's daughter. I will save Mr. Brewster and I will save you too. I will save both of your reputations just as I saved Fleet Walker from the electric chair. Where is Walter Brewster? That is all I demand to know. I am starting to believe that he is walking about in plain sight."

"How'd you know," Walter says.

"Know what, Mr. Ponsonby?" Nellie Bly says, annoyed at his interruptions.

"That I'm Brewster."

Nellie Bly laughs in disbelief. The Judge believes the confession is ill-timed. But Walter says it with presence, which makes The Judge proud.

"Sometimes an umpire can have his nose on a play, be so close, that he loses his angle," Walter says. "Reporters, too, can get too close to see what's happening."

She kisses Walter's cheek. "You feel a need to protect everyone. Even a cheat like Judge Gold."

"I'm Brewster," Walter repeats.

"How farfetched," Nellie Bly says.

"It's all in the Bible that Papa left behind."

"You're as curious as many in the Bible, that's for sure," The Judge says. He addresses Nellie Bly. "Mr. Ponsonby is a special man, I can see, but he's not Brewster."

"Of course, he is not." Nellie Bly faces Walter square. "I know who you really are."

"I'm Walter Brewster. I'm a descendent of William Brewster, a pilgrim on the Mayflower. He named his daughters Fear and Patience and his sons Love and Wrestling. Papa named me Walter, thank goodness. Love Brewster wouldn't last an inning."

"You are that letter writer from California—and from Utah. I figured it out. I am a trained correspondent. How long did you think you could pull the wool over my eyes?"

"Huh?"

"He is deaf to figures of speech," Nellie Bly tells The Judge. She faces down her escort. "You are the man who scribbles in poor penmanship," she says. "Your dear mother is housed a half-day's ride from here at The Marine Hospital that Houses Crazy Seamen."

"Yes, I know. I told you that. I'm Brewster."

"Mr. Brewster is not a letter writer. You heard The Judge say so. You, Mr. Ponsonby, are my letter writer. I love your two letters. I have received thousands but I love yours the most." She kisses his cheek again. "I never wanted you along. I thank Mr. Pulitzer for insisting."

She turns to The Judge. "Stop this charade, this misdirection. Tell me where Mr. Brewster is. In exchange, I will let you go on living as Judge Gold. I will tell a half truth. The better half. I will tell my readers that you are Honest John Gaffney. I will not tell them that you are also the cheat Dick Higham. You will win every election. California's next governor in a landslide."

"You're as blind as any umpire who has ever set foot on a dirt diamond. Go ahead and write about me, Miss Bly. Leave Walter Brewster alone."

"Everyone's alone," Walter says.

"Have a heart," The Judge says to Nellie Bly.

"Everyone has a heart," Walter says. "Sometimes my own pulse fungos back at me from this base ball."

"I daresay, Mr. Ponsonby, this judge, this gambling cheat, has no heart."

"He has a tremendous heart. Everyone has a heart," Walter repeats. "More than one because we're all more than one person. We all see things differently because we all see them from different angles."

"Where have you gone, Joe DiMaggio?
Our nation turns its lonely eyes to you
Woo, woo, woo."—Paul Simon

April 20,1888, 6:32 p.m.
It's a Friday

CHAPTER FIFTEEN

eighteen minutes before the strikeout

The squeezebox polka goes silent. As the ninth inning begins, no one dares leave. The fanatics are stuck like flies in the sticky oils of the painting. They could leave but they stay to suffer together.

The only movement is the kid erasing the blackboard to put the Niners two runs to the bad. I remove my mask. It's 4-to-2, all in favor of the Oaklands. I pull my cap over the cut to slow the bleeding. The Judge's gravelly voice is in my ears telling me to find my way, to find my sea legs. *Now, Walter, stay consistent. Focus on everything. Except the outcome. Let the outcome be what it will.*

Cooney digs in for the Niners. He bats second behind Barrows except for today and it's a stroke of Cap Anson genius that a time-tested hitter is leading off the ninth inning from the ninth spot in the order with Barrows on deck. However, it's an Anson blunder that crummy Flynn and the inept Blake follow Barrows. They are sure outs. Casey's due up fifth. If Cooney and Barrows don't make their way on base, Casey won't get his chance.

The pitches of Mouse Mathews float to the plate in the backlight. I'm half conscious, my decisions fall into a hypnotic rhythm. Ball, strike, ball, ball, ball, strike, foul. Cooney swings again at the eighth one and the audience bewails a nubber off the bat's end for the first out. Barrows suckers at the first pitch and chops one high enough to give the fanatics a moment, but T.J. McAloon short-hops it with his one hand. Like that, there are two outs and the yard's as silent as an October snowfall.

I thirst. I crave a night's rest, a month off. I put my mask under my arm. I remove my blood-soaked cap and wipe my face with it. A few fanatics escape the gummy flypaper and head for the gate. Casey's not up, he's not on the deck. He's in the hold. The gambling society would give the Niners an even chance if Casey were advancing to the plate, but Flynn and Blake stand in the way of a miracle. Flynn is capable of a scratch hit once in a blue moon, Blake a bleeder at best.

Flynn is thin, a mustache on a head of bone. I sink low to align my eyes with his front elbow, he takes the pitch, I declare a strike. The throng has given up and their disapproval is half-hearted.

"Hey ump, even a blind squirrel finds a nut once in a while," I hear. "Somebody nail the plate down, it's all over the place."

Flynn takes the next pitch, it paints the edge, I declare striker two, the throng boos, but not at me, it's at Flynn to swing the thing. It's at the Niners for losing to a gaggle of Oakland mishaps.

Flynn swivels his head like an owl, looks back at me. "Th-th-th-that's t-two mah-mah more you mah-mah missed," he says.

My concussion leaves two Flynns standing there stuttering. "Best get the bat off your shoulders," I say. "If you go down looking, we'll both need a deputy's escort to the train station."

Flynn's face swivels forward toward the pitcher. His freckled hands squeeze the bat handle. The Mexican catcher holds his hands wide of the strike zone for an outside sucker pitch, but Mouse is tired and in pain, he wants it over as much as I do, and the pitch arrives fat and flat. Flynn swivels from the hips and laces a daisy cutter up the middle. There are no daisies, it's a figure of speech, but Flynn's on first nevertheless.

Cheers erupt, then quiet whispers of prayer for Blake. Casey's on deck, he's off the bench, he has time to lift three bats to his shoulder when Blake pulls back an inch with flabby hands, wills himself patience. The pitch floats six inches high of a strike and he hits it on the nose. It might be a four-bagger except it's hit so hard that the cover peels from the ball like an orange rind. The cover lands at Mouse's feet, but the guts whistle on into the gap. Flynn almost trips on the unwinding yarn as he rounds second and pulls into third. Blake's slow, they call it *dragging a piano*. He cuts first base a step, chugs toward second. A close play develops. My feet are under their own power like a Ouija board planchette. I run out onto the diamond, get my angle and ready myself motionless for a hard slide. At the last instant I take a half step left, sacrifice my angle a bit to remove my shadow and to put the play in the sun.

Two Blakes and two balls arrive at once. Time slows in a dust halo. I have an hour to make the call, so it seems, and I declare in favor of Blake. He's not out by a coat of paint. Maybe I'm wrong, but Honest John Gaffney never made a more popular declaration. The audience cheers as I walk back to the plate. I'm no longer the goat. The Judge has been bedridden by the shit-house beast, and here I am taking his accolades at The Home of the Mudville Niners. Here I am, the one-eyed king in the kingdom of the blind.

I find myself wishing Papa were here to witness the grandeur. I want to give him the credit for my applause just as he once gave it to me when I landed the trout that he hooked and Moms cooked. I want Papa to hear the crowd thundering loud enough to drown out a million babies with the colic.

Mudville joy flutters down on magic carpets of ladies' handkerchiefs. Casey stands relaxed in the falling lace. Accolades are workaday to him, but this is a roar no man gets used to and he gorges on it. Blake stands on second like he's there every day. Flynn wobbles atop the sandbag at third, I wobble at the plate, me and the stuttering Flynn balance on opposite ends of a row boat. Me and Flynn try not to capsize in the noise.

The multitude advances step by step with Casey: the cry of farmers, the bay of tired war veterans, the last hurrah of broken prospectors. Poles and micks with nothing in common holler like their barns are afire. They have one reason for living and it resides in the speed of Casey's hands and in the grain of his bat. He advances with the whole of the San Joaquin shoehorned with him into size twelve steel-plated spikes.

Fanatics and hoodlums lean over foul lines and orphaned boys sway in trees. Each small voice contributes to the bedlam, each face is the color of the blood that soaks my tie and splashes about my shoes. The hearts of five thousand throb as one in my aching head. I'm about to declare the most important pitches of my life and if any man accuses me of double-sighted half-blindedness, he will be altogether right.

Casey smiles a canyon and says, "C'mon Ump, you're not up to snuff. Forget about declaring strikes, I'll be swinging for the fence."

The deafening yard captures his words and buries them into its blurry oils and beyond. The low sun at my back sparkles off the white-capped Sierra Nevada a hundred miles away in foul ground. Casey stands splendid. He was born for this, born for adoration. He drops two of his three bats for the Negro mascot to retrieve.

I belong in a bed next to The Judge, but I'll get past this last batter one way or another. I bite my tongue to keep from retching, I stay upright and alone and nothing exists in the roar except for Casey, the timber in his hands and the coverless ball in Mouse's left that Casey expects to unravel on out to Donner Pass.

Casey hollers at the pitcher. "Ready when you are Mouse, you low-down bunghole." He cozies into his stance, no hint of a crouch, his feet the width of his shoulders, muscles flow rather than bulge. His willow waves skyward in small and haughty circles.

The catcher Grasshopper Nova takes a peek back over his shoulder to see if I'm on my feet. I am, but my hand finds him for balance. I focus on the left hand of Mouse from where I will track the pitch. He's about to deliver when Cap Anson hollers, "Time!"

As he rises from his bench, the mascot Clarence hands him a new base ball as white as Casey's knickers were before he slid spikes high into the Mexican in the first inning. Cap Anson approaches with a friendly expression.

"That ball's done," the Niner coach says. Anson extends the new ball toward me as if he's Saint Nicholas. "Here's one fresh from the box."

"The game ball's shoddy, I'll give you that," I say. "They always are by the ninth, but we play on with what we got."

"The yarn's half unraveled."

"Worse than most, I'll agree, but we can't introduce a new ball when it's Casey's turn at the bat. That wouldn't be fair play."

"It makes no difference who's at the bat. The ball's cooked," Anson says. "New box arrived yesterday; we spent twelve bucks a dozen. J.D. Shibe in Philly makes the best, double lockstitched."

"Rules," I say. "Magnates disallow new balls to save a nickel. It seems unfair to the Oaklands to let one in now. I'll give Clarence a minute to get the leather tacked on best he can."

"Your job isn't to save us a nickel with a shoddy ball."

"Ensure square play, that's my job. You want to win square, don't you?"

"The first rule is to do what's in the best interest of the audience," Anson says. "None of us get paid except when crowds like this show up."

"You had no concern for the audience when that juvenile delinquent stuffed Casey's foul ball in his pocket. Remember? Back when Mouse Mathews pitched twenty-one straight balls, and you didn't score? We waited around forever for that foul. Why didn't you introduce a fresh ball then?"

Anson extends the white ball to me again. I refuse to take it and a high note enters his voice. "The Boston Beaneaters use two."

"They alternate to avoid undue delays, not to gain the advantage. This association's rules say no extra ball unless we lose one up there in the eaves." I point above the grandstand and the fanatics boo because they think I'm paying them some attention. "The Oaklands just scored two with the mushy ball. Guess you'll have to do the same."

Anson tosses the new ball at the catcher, but Grasshopper Nova makes no attempt to catch it, he lets it splat white into the soft dirt like albino tobacco juice.

"This is ass-shit," Anson says. "Your eye's filled with blood. Maybe you should sit down and we'll find us a volunteer to finish out."

"I need to vomit, but we'll finish out square."

My head aches, but the wheels are turning in Anson's. "A new ball's fair at the start of the ninth inning," he says. "The Oaklands will get equal chances in the bottom if we tie or go ahead. See? It's square."

That makes just enough sense for me to pause, and for Anson to get that smirk. "Remember? I elected first bats. I do things for a reason. New inning, new ball."

I'm this close to yielding to his argument, ready to take the path of least resistance to get the game over.

"We already have two outs," Anson says. "The Oaklands will get the new ball for three outs if we catch them. If any outfit gets the advantage it's them."

My answer surprises me. "No." My change of mind surprises me more. "OK I'll allow it."

I bend over and pick up the new ball at Grasshopper's feet and he says, "*Chinga*."

"I'll allow this new ball and a dozen more," I say, "but each will be introduced in fair rotation. For as long as one ball stays in the yard that's the one the pitcher throws. If Casey fouls the squishy ball into the crowd, this new ball comes in. Just like in Boston. A new ball is introduced if a gull flies off with it, or a gopher snake swallows it whole."

"*Bueno*," Grasshopper says.

I now see why newspaper cartoonists depict Cap Anson as a bawling baby. His face turns red like he's taking a silent poop. His voice moves toward a screech. "That's not how we do it at the Home of the Mudville Niners. This ain't Beantown. We demand a new ball. Now!"

"Your yard. Your gate. My game. Sun's low. We can stand here ad nauseam or we can get back to it and give your fanatics their four bits worth." Anson searches for the sun behind me as if he realizes for the first time that it sets once a day. We're in no imminent danger of running out of daylight. Casey needs a half minute to succeed or fail. If he succeeds, Squawks Clarke can get the Oaklands out in the bottom of the ninth. My main concern is if Casey bats home Flynn and Blake to tie things. We have time for a tenth inning, an eleventh at the outside, if I can stay conscious.

"A tie ends the Niners' win streak same as a loss," I say. "If Casey ties things, you'll be wishing for another inning before the sun goes down."

"C'mon Captain," Casey says. "Let's play, The Ump has a frigging bug up his butt. I'll hit anything pitched my way."

I've studied a lot of pill bugs, but one has never found its way up my butt. Anson makes another inspection of the sun and retreats, because the one thing he likes better than getting his way is winning twenty straight. Clarence busies himself at mending the ball and that's when it dawns on me that it's suppertime. I'm not hungry, but my stomach's full of empty and it clears my vision some. I squeeze the new ball for more clarity, put it in my coat pocket.

Casey studies his giant hands around the bat handle, hands that connect to wrists as one solid piece of anvil. "A man has to have goals," he says to no one. "My goal is to have people say, 'There goes Casey, the greatest hitter who ever lived.'"

He twists the handle and sawdust floats off in the breeze toward Mouse. It's a breeze in Casey's favor out to the War Monument. Satisfied with his grip, satisfied with meteorology, Casey glares out at the Oaklands, first to taunt Mouse, then to taunt the seven, then he turns around and belches an oyster smell at the catcher and me.

The outward breeze doesn't stop the invasion. I turn for fresh air. That's when I see the sandbag open at first. I failed to notice it before, and The Judge is in my head scolding me, it's my job to know the circumstances. Any sane outfit will feed Casey five balls and trot him on down. That will choke the bases, but it's the obvious strategy. Anson doesn't seem so smart now.

Mouse might even hurl one at Casey to take advantage of the new rule that awards first base to batsmen struck with a pitch. The rule's meant to protect them, but Casey might get one in the ear. That's an example of irony. But if Mouse plugs Casey, the Niner bench will pour onto the yard and the cranks might pull Mouse's two bad arms off like a daddy long-leg's. They might yank off the withered arm of T. J. McAloon for good measure. I might suffer collateral damage. The wiser play is to serve up five balls.

I study Mouse to see if he's rational enough to do the wise thing, but he's not looking our way. His line of sight tracks into the Negro section where a big man stands in a dull uniform of second-quality flannel. Sure enough, it's Old Reliable Jake. He's made his way without changing, and he's among the Niner cranks. He's easy to pick out in his road grays and a face as ruddy red as aging venison.

The cranks enjoy him, they have adopted him as one of theirs. Any man who spears an umpire face first is OK, and they slap him on the back and egg him on to order Mouse to pitch to Casey. They yearn for Casey to deliver the sockdolager, or start a riot. Win or lose, one way or another, they'll have their fun.

Old Reliable Jake stands on the Negro bleaching boards and makes a pitching motion. Every crank within two rows of him mimics him. Then, Old Jake hollers down, "Pitch to the S.O.B."

Casey doffs his cap. The doff is subtle, a flash of red hair to the girls. To Nellie Bly. Base ball etiquette forbids doffs in advance of an accomplishment, it's an unwritten rule of sporting contests and violates all standards of modesty. But Casey's a popinjay, and the insult gets the Oaklands mad as hell. I've never seen such sour faces, the faces of persistent loss, faces now willing to roll the dice no matter the odds. Casey's doff puts a hole in the soul of Mouse. He will do what Old Jake orders. He'll pitch to Casey, or maybe plug one in Casey's ear after all.

I holler, "Time!"

I ask Clarence for the broom, and I round the plate to sweep. I make eye contact with no one, I remove my wire mask and talk loud enough for Casey to hear over the noise. "Best leave your cap on your head until you do something of merit."

"Best you mind your ass-shit business you shit-ass," Casey says.

I'm feeling I did the wrong thing, saying words to Casey because he doffed his cap at Nellie Bly. Saying something out of jealousy. To even things up, my next words are for the catcher. "Don't get ideas. If the pitch comes in at Casey's head, if I suspect man-hitting, I'll toss you. You and Mouse will be squeezing in next to Old Jake. Go tell your pitcher he's been warned."

The catcher doesn't budge, he stares ahead like I'm speaking Chinese. I don't care, I'm all in favor of getting back to it. I hate to admit it, but I'm in favor of Casey making good so I can get out of here in one piece.

"They're dead if he plugs me," Casey says. He points at Grasshopper, then at Mouse. "Him and him, dead and deader," then he grabs a fistful of dirt and rubs up his hands until Grasshopper and I are in a dust cloud. He drops dirt on the marble that I just whisked clean and wipes a smear across the NINERS stitched on his jockey silks.

"You're uppity," Casey says at me. He points his bat at Grasshopper. "You're as uppity as this black beaner; uppity for an Ump who owes me his life. I'm done protecting you. If the fanatics make their charge, you're on your lonesome. I'm going to hit one out. If I don't, Mr. Beaner eats half the ball and Mr. Ump eats the other half hisself."

"*Cabrón,*" Grasshopper says.

"Shut your yap and watch me hit the wobbly piece of shit over the War Monument to Antietam."

"Baseball has always been a reflection of life.
It adjusts. It survives everything."—Willie Stargell

CHAPTER SIXTEEN

the tenth anniversary of the strikeout is tomorrow

The reporter's knock at Walter Brewster's door sounds like it did ten years ago. Fleet Walker is probably asleep in his room, but he wouldn't answer anyway. He refuses to play butler to two white guys.

Knocks are a rarity at this house at 432 Lake Laberge Boulevard in The Bronx. Neighborhood children keep their distance from the infamous killer, the Negro who got away with it. The Judge scares kids with his dundrearies and limp. They'd love a chat with Walter though, the umpire made famous by the poem, but he rambles on about trains and jerry couplers without looking anyone in the eye.

Even broom salesmen pass this house by, which makes this knock a rarity just as the knock was ten years ago at *El Coraje* boarding house in San Francisco. Walter listens from the kitchen. "He's gone fishing. Adirondacks," The Judge tells a lie at the screen door. His voice is more gravelly in the morning, difficult for Walter to hear from another room.

"When do you expect him?" asks the visitor.

"Walter stays away weeks at a time. Been gone nine days, since Easter Sunday."

"Can you give him a message?"

"Can, but won't," The Judge says. "For one, I can never find pencil and paper. You best shove along."

Walter hears the door shut in the man's face. The Judge limps into the kitchen for a third cup of coffee, so much coffee he will have to pee soon.

"Easter Sunday's redundant." Walter squeezes his base ball. "Easter's always on a Sunday. Was that a reporter?"

"*Tribune.*"

"One hasn't been by for five years, precisely. Not since the fifth anniversary."

A voice echoes from the hallway. "They'll keep coming until you tell your side."

The knock woke the widower Fleet. He moved in when Arabella died of cancer three years ago at thirty-two. They never reconciled and the court ruled him too dicey to raise their three children. His kids went to live with her parents in Cincinnati. He's bitter, he talks about loading ships with Negroes and moving them back to Africa. He's serious about it, he's raising money, his plans are exhaustive.

"I can't believe it's been ten years," Walter says. "Easter fell on April Fool's Day in eighty-eight."

"Now, Walter, that was a Sunday."

Women shy away from Fleet because he's dangerous. Others are attracted to him for the same reason, but he mourns Arabella and misses his kids too much to pay them any mind. None of the three roommates mentions women, it's been a complicated subject for The Judge ever since he got his privates kicked to mush in Santa Cruz.

Walter likes girls, he liked them ten years ago and he likes them now, he likes them a lot, but he never talks to any. He thinks about Nellie Bly every day. He hasn't seen her since February 9, 1890. The day he failed her miserably. A Sunday.

She caught the first train from San Francisco back to New York by her lonesome and quit journalism on the spot. No one ever reported that The Judge, Honest John Gaffney, and Dick Higham were all the same. The Judge could have gone on winning elections, but he moved from San Francisco and in with Walter here on Lake Laberge Boulevard in The Bronx.

With Nellie Bly retired, Wood Dryden became the most famous journalist in the land until Spain sank the USS Maine two months ago with the *New York Journal*'s Jayson Kelley aboard. Kelley drowned in Havana Harbor. He was already famous, but his drowning made him a renowned celebrity.

Nellie Bly Seaman remains a legend. She employs her fame and fortune to raise money for newsboys and other orphans, she's always in the society columns. Four years ago, she was on Page One of all the papers when she got engaged to the old man millionaire Robert Seaman and she was on Page One again ten months later when they married. She's thirty-two, so say the papers. Robert Seaman's seventy-five.

She's never again set foot outside of New York, not since she returned alone from San Francisco eight years ago. Walter hopes to bump into her, to apologize, to find out what happened to her, but they don't travel in the same circles. Walter rarely circles beyond the front yard.

The Judge is in the bathroom. He sits to pee. "Now, Walter, I've finally decided," he hollers.

"Call me Avocado Jones," Walter shouts back. He changed his name, he doesn't like people thinking he's Brewster, the poem's umpire, but his roommates call him Walter anyway. "Decided what?"

The Judge doesn't answer until he's back in the kitchen, his fly unbuttoned Anson-style. "To go with you to the Yukon," he says. "You said you wanted to go. We need an adventure. To find some gold before it's gone. I'm too old to join the Rough Riders and fight the Spanish."

"Count me out," Fleet says. "The Yukon's whiter than base ball."

The Judge and Walter "Avocado Jones" Brewster leave a month later to spend a year hiking arctic trails with secret tales. They witness the shooting of Dan McGrew by the lady known as Lou, but they never find much gold. Avocado Jones spends most days mining his mind. He thinks about Nellie Bly and how he let her down. He thinks about that day Papa walked out of his life in the middle of Annie Katharine's screaming fit of colic. Mama was visiting neighbors. Little Walter didn't want to go with her, neighbors made him antsy. Papa stayed home with him and the baby.

Avocado Jones is panning Bonanza Crick one day. After thinking about Nellie Bly, he remembers the many times Papa and he went fishing Bean Crick in the redwoods of California. Moms always had supper ready, they'd say grace and Moms would glance up from folded hands like she was thankful for little Walter. Her smile soothed his sunburn. He was happiest at the table. Annie Katharine spoiled it. She started in with the colic. She bawled every evening once supper was ending and she kept it up until bedtime.

All evening, Moms and Papa took turns walking her in their arms. Papa was always first to lose patience. He'd go outside with his *King James* and a lantern. It would grow dark. Five-year-old Walter sat next to him, their lantern shadows cast long over Bean Crick's ripple. When Annie Katharine at last fell asleep, there was a silence that was swallowed by the ripple and frogs and a million crickets.

Before going to bed, Walter would look at Annie Katharine asleep in her crib. Her tight fists had opened into tiny pink blooms of palm. The world was never more at peace when Annie Katharine opened her hands from fists bunched in pain.

A few days after Papa left, she stopped crying. It was as if her colic had chased after him out the door. That was Walter's first encounter with irony. As Annie Katharine grew older, she followed Walter around. She did what her big brother did. Walter never cried, and so neither did she. She did, however, let one food touch another on her plate.

Moms' melancholia set in as Papa stayed missing. She was too lost in her distance to demand chores. Annie Katharine grew old enough to play one-old-cat. The bay stump and a boulder were well-spaced for safe havens. Walter preferred Indian War games, he boosted her into the pepper tree to gather ammunition, and they blew it through reeds at each other and argued about who shot who first. They skipped flat stones sidearm across Bean Crick, scattered fish from their holes, five skips, sometimes seven, the last too short and rapid to count. They waded the crick until the bottom fell away. She went under pretending to drown. She frightened him every time she did that and she'd giggle when he pulled her up by the hair. She floated without effort, her wrinkled toes in the air above the water, her open palms magnified below. Walter swam like a one-legged frog but he always saved her.

Autumns gave way to rainy winters and to springs of sweet loquats from the tree. When June came again, they dug a pit, put sharp sticks at the bottom, laid bay branches over the top and waited to trap the cannibals that never came.

Men from Mount Hermon visited from time to time. They told Walter nice things about Papa. They said he had a genuine way around others, a hand clasp that won friends. Papa looked at everyone with kindness in his eyes. They were stumped about Walter, stupefied. They didn't know why Papa's qualities passed Walter by so completely.

Walter looked for Papa in the cannibal pit. He looked for him among the five thousand at The Home of the Mudville Niners. When Walter went around the world with Nellie Bly, he looked for Papa in Brindisi, Penang, and Singapore on the Malay Peninsula. He looked for him where Jules Verne's marble stairway turned narrow.

Walter last saw Moms the day he last saw Nellie Bly: February 9, 1890, a Sunday almost two years after the strikeout. Moms was still in The Marine Hospital that Houses Crazy Seamen, now she's in the Great Asylum for the Insane. That's a continent away from The Bronx. She wouldn't know him anyway. She recognized him only for a brief minute when he last saw her. She looked up from her praying hands and smiled at him like he was five.

"You never had the colic," she said. "You were a good baby, although you were easy to startle. You pumped your little arms and legs at the sizzle of bacon." Then Moms repeated and old story. "I laid you on your back. You hated that. I let you fuss a minute or two and when I turned you on your belly you were in heaven."

Nellie Bly was gone when Walter returned to The Palace Hotel. He had no idea what had happened but he knew he had failed her miserably.

Moms never blamed Annie Katharine for Papa's disappearance. And out in the tundra of the Yukon, while squeezing his base ball and panning for flecks of truth, Avocado Jones stops blaming his sister, too. He realizes that Papa had to put up with more than Annie Katharine's colic. He had to put up with a son who would never grow out of his odd gait and into normality.

Papa shook Annie Katharine the day he left, the day Moms was off visiting with neighbors. Her colic got on Papa's nerves so much that he started to shake her into a scramble before placing her gently on the floor and walking out the door. Walter thought it was her screaming that drove Papa away. But in the Yukon, Avocado Jones realizes that Annie Katharine's screaming was what they call *the straw that broke the camel's back*. Tiny Walter had loaded the other straws.

Walter doesn't blame himself for being odd as much as he blames himself for visiting Moms instead of escorting Nellie Bly to Casey's mansion on February 9, 1890.

As Avocado Jones, he pans and pans most of 1898 until the flecks of his guilt outweigh the Yukon's largest nugget. He rarely thinks about the strikeout. When he does, he doesn't think about strike two or Strike Three. He only remembers strike one. He remembers everything about that first strike on April 20th, 1888. A Friday. The sun was moving low at his back.

"Every strike brings me closer to the next home run."—Babe Ruth

April 20,1888, 6:39 p.m.
It's a Friday, a minute before strike one

CHAPTER SEVENTEEN

eleven minutes before the strikeout

C asey points fifty-four ounces of second-growth ash in the direction of center field, his left-handed reach seems halfway to the War Monument. The fanatics cheer, Casey scratches his crotch with his right hand and they cheer the more.

The breeze picks up and cools my back. I'm taking some comfort in it when I see a small boy fall from a telegraph pole in the distance. One second he's celebrating Casey with arms in the air, the next second he's falling thirty feet. My head hurts all the more to see him land, but there are no gasps, all eyes are trained on the center ring. I listen for the dull thud of the boy's landing, but instead I hear a fart. Casey smiles when the breeze fails to beat it back.

The catcher takes off his wire mask. "*Culo.*"

Casey musters another.

"*Joto.*" Blood oozes from the catcher's split palms as he makes fists and rises. He's nose to nose with Casey, the catcher's about to take a sock. The cranks hiss and haloo when I wedge myself between them. Casey has the clear advantage, he has the Mexican by forty pounds, but I put my back to the batsman and the boos turn to cheers that I've identified the catcher as the instigator.

"Back away or I'll toss you," I say to Grasshopper Nova.

His face fills with a sense of injustice. He motions with his mask at Casey.

"The batsman deserves it," I say, "but if I toss him we'll have half of California paying us a visit. If someone has to be sacrificed I'm afraid it's to be you. Step back. Now."

"*Pendejo*," he says over the top of me, then obeys me in surrender.

"Same *olé*, same *olé*," Casey says.

There's chaffing from the fanatics; they feel I've cheated them of bare knuckles, but it changes to a happy roar when Mouse Mathews pulls the bill of his cap down to a thick mustache and readies himself. He's about to pitch to Casey with the game's outcome on the line. The fanatics go quiet. Casey's minions know that he can hear the breeze on the ball. They go quiet so that Casey can hear the viz.

I ready my eyes. All I see of the pitcher's face is his chin in the last cry of sun. Casey's bat circles high above his hands. His smile curls to a sneer. Mouse starts farther back in the box. He takes a hop and a skip and overruns the rules. He steps his right foot beyond the box, he doesn't toe the line, but I ignore the infraction. We're brothers in misery, we both want this over.

Mouse lets go of the ball. I stop my breath midway into my exhale to still my aching head. The ball waltzes toward the middle at eye level, then flutters. It swings back and forth and drops to cross the plate, exhausted at the knees. Casey has all week to study it. The sun's behind us, the perfect backlight. The circle of his bat above his head comes to a stop. He takes a six-inch step forward with his left. His hands and wrists move as one. He has too much time, enough time for second thoughts. His hands stop as they reach the middle of his chest. The executioner does not throw the switch.

"That ain't—"

"—STEEERIKER—"

"—my style—"

"—ONE"

We say.

I don't realize that the angry roar is directed at me. I'm lightheaded again, all but passed out on my feet. The yard's loud but distant, it no longer surrounds me. It surges from beneath, carries me to the mountains.

"Kill him!"

The roar continues. I look out into the painting's oils. Fanatics stomp and holler. The ground shakes. Time slows.

Baby Annie Katharine sits on the floor and screams and wails and bawls and her colic is the one noise on earth the roar can't drown.

I thirst. The sun's going down. I touch my forehead. My fingers are covered in blood as bright red as the sky. I look up into five thousand angry faces. I need to pee. I thirst.

Annie Katharine's face cries over Moms' left shoulder. It cries over Moms' right shoulder. She cries when Moms carries her face down on her belly and she cries when suckling oatmeal from Moms' fingers. Papa and the boy Walter are busy shelling walnuts at the table. Moms bounces Annie Katharine, "to get the gas moving." The baby wails to the rhythm of the bounce, to the drum of Papa's hammer. Moms walks Annie Katharine outside, points to cows lowing across the crick. Moms gives up, comes back in where Papa and the boy are shelling and she sets Annie Katharine on the floor.

"Let her cry it out," Papa says striking a nut, but Moms is back to pick her up. Annie Katharine wants to stop, she buries her face in the fat of Moms' arm. She cries, muffled for a spell, and at last falls asleep. Papa stops with the hammer so as not to wake her. Moms smells Annie Katharine's head and kisses it and says, "Poor baby, you'll out-grow it soon."

Moms leaves the next evening to take a welcome pie to new neighbors. She says the family can tag along, but the boy wants to stay home. Listening to Annie Katharine is better than listening to neighbors tell him to come out of his shell. Neighbors like Papa and his handshakes, Papa has presence, but he stays behind with Annie Katharine and the boy. Annie Katharine's fussy, but Moms won't be at the neighbors for long.

It's late; the sun's angling.

Angling through the open door. Annie Katharine starts with the bawling. "Where's Moms?" Papa says. He gives Annie Katharine a stale biscuit to teethe. He lifts her above his head to take her mind off things, walks her on the porch, shows her the sunset, says it's God's way of tucking us in. Annie Katharine cries on, "Where's Moms? It's getting late." The boy plays on the floor, he pretends his rusty rail spikes are cowboys. The spent shotgun shells are Indians. He's happy by his lonesome, he drowns out the bawling with his play. Papa paces, he wants out of his skin.

The roar of the yard drowns out everything. I startle when someone hollers, "Kill the umpire!"

The boy startles when Papa hollers "Shut up!" at Annie Katharine. The boy looks Papa in the eye. He sees frustration.

Anger and frustration from every face of the oily roar.

Annie Katharine bawls and wails. A daddy long-leg crawls over the boy's rusty rail spike. The boy captures it and pulls off a leg.

Jimmy's safe at second and Flynn's a-hugging third. The pitch arrives. I see a piece of the ball catch the top of Casey's knees. It ain't his style.

Papa shakes the baby.

I declare "STEEERIKER ONE." The grounds shake in disagreement.

Papa shakes her a second time. The boy pulls off another leg. Papa's about to shake her a third time.

What happened to the boy who fell from the telegraph pole? No one notices; no one seems to care.

The biscuit falls from her open hand to the floor. She's quiet, she's limp. Her tight fists open into tiny pink blooms of palm.

Casey has second thoughts, his hands stop at his chest, sawdust sifts from the bat handle. The lifeless, spinless, ball catches knees. Casey does not throw the switch.

Neither does Papa.

"That ain't my style," Casey says.

"This ain't me," Papa says.

"STEEERIKER ONE."

Papa's face goes ashen. He hugs Annie Katharine's quiet, limp body to his chest. Precisely where Casey stops his hands.

Papa's eyes are moist. He sets her on the floor belly down, he stands looking as the outside turns to dusk. He has lifeless doll's eyes. He stands there forever. At last, he gives the boy a hug, the wet of Papa's eyes spread to the boy's cheeks. "The family will be better off," he whispers, then he turns and walks out the door.

Flynn's a-hugging third. He's a hang-dog, skin on skeleton, the evening sun pours through his flesh.

Annie Katharine is quiet, belly down in Papa's sunset shadow for one, two, three long slow steps. Papa walks out the door without looking back. She lifts her head, whimpers softly at first, then with deep gasps. The boy runs to the door. "Papa!"

"That ain't my style."

"Papa! She's OK Papa," the boy hollers out the door. A jay caw-caws the last caw-caw of the day.

"STEEERIKER ONE." My body shakes in the roar.

Casey turns. "Oh, I highly question that, Ump. C'mon, you got a train to catch?"

The boy hollers out the door again and again, he hollers himself hoarse into the dark. Then, he doesn't speak for a year.

"Kill him."

I look to the crowd; there are five thousand trapped in the oils like flies or they'd a-be down to pluck my limbs one by one. I exhale until all my breath is gone and I take up as little space as possible behind the bat.

"Kill him. Kill the umpire!" the town of Mudville hollers, and it's likely they'd a-killed me had not Casey raised his hand.

"Fair is foul, foul is fair."—William Shakespeare

CHAPTER EIGHTEEN

nine minutes before the strikeout

The umpire breathing down the catcher's neck has backbone, or he's loony, one or the other. Grasshopper Nova is prepared for ball one when he hears "STEERIKER TWO!" in his left ear. Who knows if the call comes from courage or stupidity? The umpire might be correct, it's probably a strike, but he's *loco* no doubt and Grasshopper says, "*¡Ay, caramba!*"

"Fraud," cry the thousands. "Ride him on a rail."

The umpire has no friends in this county, and the cranks might soon be down to murder him. He's already dead on his feet from the beating he took from Old Reliable Jake last inning. The umpire started the day with a funny walk. Now he labors to take any stride at all.

This strike two pitch floated about aimless, maybe it missed the zone, maybe it grazed, it was one of those that goes either way. At first it rowed toward the plate's middle, but it rowed so slowly that Grasshopper was surprised it didn't bounce. Casey was cocked and set to swing from the heels. He seemed committed, too far along into his stride to stop. And then the ball caught air like a pine cone and swerved up. Grasshopper had never seen such a thing; a swerve from the knees to the shoulders. He didn't believe such a swerve was possible.

The racialist Cap Anson may be the greatest overall player in the long, twenty-five-year history of the game, but Casey's a batsman from the ground up. The ball rose and fell and, at last, swerved upward so much the final foot of its flight that Grasshopper had to spear it one-handed near Casey's chin. Casey's wrists reversed a runaway train. When he stopped his swing in time, the fanatics were certain it was a mile high, but it shaved the top of the strike zone with a stain of tobacco juice. It would have missed by the thickness of the ball's cover because Blake on second base had torn off the cover, but the mascot Clarence had somehow managed to tack it back on.

Grasshopper studied mythology at Oberlin College. He studied the Bible and he knew the umpire had to be tempted to say ball one even if strike two was the honest, righteous call. It would've been so easy to say ball one. It would've been the path of least resistance. Were Grasshopper placed under oath and asked if the pitch had caught the zone, all he would say is "Anyone's guess," except he can't say a word in English, and if he does, he'll never play base ball again.

Mouse Mathews and Grasshopper bunked together ten days ago in Sacramento the way pitchers and catchers do. William Dargie owns the Oakland Tribunes Base Ball Club and he put the players in a hotel for a couple of days so they could train for another long, losing, hopeless season.

Grasshopper likes Mouse, even though the pitcher took the longer bed. Mouse is nine inches shorter, but he said that Grasshopper likes to sleep curled up in his squat because he's a Mexican. Mouse didn't think Grasshopper understood. Grasshopper was offended but he couldn't show it.

The pitcher treats him better than other ball players. Mouse treats him as a friend when they're alone. Mouse is a man who likes to hear himself talk. He talked and talked pitching strategy as if he were being understood. "Some batsmen are never ready to hit the first ball pitched, so I put a strike flat over the middle. Others are antsy and I work them wide. You can't work the same batter in the same way. Sometimes I cross them by pitching the sphere exactly where they want it most."

Mouse sat on his elongated bed and dug his fingernails into the leather of a ball. His ears were big and so thin that light from the lamp filtered through them. "Let me show you a pitch I learned from Toad Ramsey of the Louisvilles."

Grasshopper smiled dumb.

"I've perfected it. I call it my butterfly pitch. I can throw it with my right or my left, but my left is sore now, too."

Grasshopper nodded. "*Mariposa* peech."

"*Si, si*," Mouse said. "My puzzler pitch, I'll be throwing it for *el strikos*. The out-curve and in-shoot are what the best pitchers work with today, but this is better. I can't say why it works—not scientifically—but it works best with a breeze in my face. Batsmen know the butterfly is coming because it crawls in slow, but it does them no good. The butterfly is best when a batsman is worked up and mad as a horsewhipped slave."

Grasshopper's jaw clenched at the remark. He had read a journal article last time he was visiting his parents in Steubenville. Scientists performed autopsies on soldiers in the war. On average, white brains are bigger than black ones. Another article said it's impossible for a base ball to curve. Scientists are pea-brain retards.

Mouse says Grasshopper's easy to talk to, says he listens better than someone who "*parlez vouzes*" American. "I know you'll hate catching my butterfly, but what else am I to throw to Casey? Getting one past him is like sneaking sunrise past a rooster."

That one-sided conversation in Sacramento seems a lifetime ago. It's nearing sunset. Blake's the tying run on second, he's a *gordo* and Casey will have to hit it in the face to score him. Grasshopper turns his attention to Flynn, the miracle on third. Flynn barely has a face, a mustache on a warped skull. Ice tongs must have grabbed ahold of him at birth. He celebrates off the bag, does the dance of a man who gets as far as third base once or twice in a lifetime.

Most catchers stand a few steps back of the plate unless there are two strikes. Grasshopper gets in tight, as if every pitch is a dropped-third situation. That lets umpires get in tight, too. Lo and behold they declare a more accurate zone. His clubmates laugh, they say he squats lazy-like.

Grasshopper misses Thomas and Cleodolinda. He will forget the fight he had with Arabella by the time the train heads back to Oakland Saturday night. He'll want to go to church with the kids in the morning, but Arabella will be afraid someone will think she's married to a Mexican. She's spoiled, she's used to sitting up front with the white widows.

She doesn't realize that she's married to the best catcher in base ball. Few pitches ever escape his hands. He's relaxed, but Casey's jaw is in a clench, and his forearms ripple like snakes swallowing desert rats. He has two strikes, but he won't swing at the next pitch unless he's in love with it.

Grasshopper studies umpires; he knows how they do this and that, and the next pitch will be declared a ball if it wades in square down the middle. All umpires are odd or they wouldn't be umpires. This is the oddest one yet, but no umpire's odd enough to declare a third strike on Casey at the Home of the Mudville Niners with a nineteen-game streak in jeopardy. Smart money is wagered on the next pitch being ball one.

Maybe not. This umpire's not himself. Two hours have passed, and the game started two hours late due to the train delay. In the seventh inning, the umpire was on his game, his face was pink with springtime sunburn, now it's caked dark in blood thanks to Old Jake. The umpire got strike two on Casey right, probably, but it was by guesswork. He's nowhere near Planet Earth. He's unpredictable, but in the end he will save his white ass. He will call the next pitch a ball. The price of living is sometimes a piece of soul, something Arabella teaches little Thomas.

Grasshopper loves base ball. It lets him forget things. He's almost forgotten the fight he had with his wife. She calls herself one part African queen. She straightens her hair, her lips are thin. She checks into hotels in her lavender dresses and hazel eyes and sophistication as he sneaks up the fire ladder. If he takes her arm in public she pulls away.

"Your grandparents were slaves, same as mine," Grasshopper tells her.

"House servants, never field hands," she says.

Grasshopper steps onto each yard, hoping to forget his arguments with Arabella; hoping for an umpire with devotion and consistency. Clubs never get an umpire made to order unless they get Honest John Gaffney. Gaffney came along at a good time, he was working that same season Dick Higham got banned in Detroit. The game needs an Honest John. But Gaffney would have called at least one ball on Casey by now. To save his skin.

This umpire's doing no dirty piece of business. By some miracle, the Oaklands are one pitch from a Page One win, but when Grasshopper looks out at the faces on his eight clubmates, it's difficult to detect an iota of joy.

They telegraph their fear of Casey, their fear of losing, and the audience adds something dark. Thousands want Casey to win it, but a hundred or more are prepared for the umpire to declare Strike Three so they can dismantle the yard board by board. Grasshopper's familiar with that dark something, it consumes him when Arabella tells Thomas to kowtow.

Flynn's still way off the bag at third. There's never been a lulu more ripe for the picking. Flynn's head wouldn't look like that if Grasshopper's mother had delivered him. She never uses ice tongs as a midwife. Grasshopper can imagine ice-tonged Flynn apologizing to Cap Anson, "Sah-sah-sorry kah-kah-captain, the mah-mah-Mexican threw the bah-bah-bah-ball," but Grasshopper doesn't throw to third because this umpire is nuts enough to declare Flynn out on a razor-close play. The game would end with Casey scratching his nuts, and the fanatics would pour down like ants to sweetmeats. Grasshopper doesn't attempt to pick Flynn off, doesn't even make a faint.

Grasshopper does some reconnaissance just in case the umpire's suicidal. He sizes up the cranks standing down the third base line. A rope and a hundred feet separate them from home plate. He's been called Fleet since he beat the fastest Quaker kid in a foot race. He'll reach his gunny sack in time. But Arabella's right. If he brandishes the pistol, the fanatics will lynch him by his johnson.

"And, please stop introducing me as Mrs. Walker," Arabella always says. "That's your mama."

Mouse is stalling. He stares in like he's taking a sign. His arm is lame; he's hoping to squeeze one more pitch out of it. This game may never end. The sun low at Grasshopper's back gives him a bright view of the azaleas and beyond to where rain clouds are building around the snow-capped mountains. Mouse is less fortunate. The bill of his cap is pulled to his chin to block the ball of fire he must pitch into. He probably can't see anything above Casey's polka-dot stockings. If Casey blasts one back into Mouse's nose, Mouse will be thanking the umpire for leaving the mushy ball in the game.

The umpire's odd but he doesn't rest on his oars. Grasshopper knows that he has worked with him once before; he recognized him from the word go, but he can't remember where. The umpire knows little things. When foul pops are hit near the chicken netting, most umpires follow the ball's path off the bat. This one ignores the ball and finds the catcher's eyes. That's the only time he looks into a man's eyes. It lets him matador out of the way so Grasshopper can give chase, and the umpire gets an angle to see if it's a catch or a trap against the backstop.

The humane thing is for Casey to end it, win it or lose it. The cruelest thing is to hit home Flynn and Blake and cause Mouse to pitch extra innings. His arm is hanging by a strip of bark. The harder he throws, the slower he gets, and the smartest thing all along was to feed Casey five balls with first base open. But Old Jake gave him orders from the Negro bleaching boards: "Pitch to the S.O.B."

Even with two strikes on Casey, Mouse could ignore Old Jake and feed five balls. Grasshopper wants to call time and convince his pitcher to do just that, to ignore orders, but he can't let anyone know that he speaks English. He stays in his squat. He hollers "ándale" to encourage Mouse to get things over and that's when Cap Anson rises to his feet, takes a long drink from his canteen, and calls time.

"Oh, Lord, not again," the umpire says under his breath.

The yard goes silent as Anson takes another drink. Dark anticipation builds, then it turns to jubilation as Anson begins his walk to the plate.

He barks at the umpire before he's halfway there. "You're blind."

For some reason, Anson catches a glimpse of Grasshopper in the eye. The catcher looks down the way Mexicans do, and Anson addresses the umpire again. "You're blind."

The umpire says nothing. Grasshopper wants to chime in, he wants to quip that no umpire has ever heard an insult as original as "You're blind." Grasshopper says nothing.

"Where was that damn pitch?" Anson says.

The umpire puts his wire mask under arm. "Caught the plate alright," he says.

"Hell, it was a mile high."

"Two miles," Casey says. He straightens his polka-dot necktie. He raises his hand above his head to exaggerate where the pitch crossed, then scratches his armpit through his jockey silks. The crowd cheers as if scratching his pit is a colossal event, as if a pit-scratching is an heroic feat only Casey performs.

"That's where the pitch crossed," the umpire says. "Where Casey's itching. The armpits are at the top of the zone this season, *your* rulebook says."

Anson points at Casey's head with his canteen, and splashes of water vanish into the dust. "Up in his eyes, that's where the pitch was. High and way outside." The umpire says nothing until Anson asks, "Wasn't it?"

"Caught a piece of the corner, or I'd have said ball one."

"A mile outside," Anson says.

"Two, Captain," Casey says. "I toldya." He flips his bat one-handed and uses the handle end to draw a line in the dirt a foot off the plate. "I got two strikes when it's two balls. C'mon, Ump, the first one about bounced. Get one right, wouldya."

The umpire ignores Casey, looks at Anson in the vicinity of his nose. Speaks to Anson's waxy mustache. "Two close pitches, I'll give you that," he says. "Not the easiest strikes ever called, but they're coming in slow. I'm seeing them like they're phosphorescent."

Anson's fish lips turn taut. Casey kicks dirt, and Anson's voice rises a notch. "You're a self-satisfied some-bitch. Who you trying to hornswoggle?"

"I've got a lot to work on," the umpire says. "Humility's on my list, though if I claim humility then I'm boasting and no longer humble. That's what they call a paradox. If Casey fails to reach slow strikes with forty-two inches of bat, that's a paradox he'll have to work on."

"My cock can't reach that pitch," Casey says. "Nope."

The last thing Grasshopper expects is for Anson to address him. "Where did you catch it? Where was that pitch?"

Grasshopper shrugs Mexican-like.

"Where did you catch it?" Anson says louder.

The catcher extends both arms in the international gesture of puzzlement and Anson hollers as if the whole world would understand English if only it were loud enough. "Show me where you caught the pitch."

Grasshopper smiles and nods. "*Mariposa* peech."

Mouse steps halfway to the plate. He thinks that bunking with Grasshopper gives him a gift for translation. "*¿Donde esta* was the peech?"

The catcher raises his sore palms again. "San Joaquin."

"No, dummy," Mouse says. "I'm not asking what valley we're playing in." Mouse bursts out laughing. "A bullfrog speaks more American than Grasshopper Nova. I don't understand his Mexican base ball signs. He just barehands whatever I throw. The pitch was a strike, I saw that much from the box. The umpire calls too many strikes for your pitcher Squawks Clarke, but he gets mine mostly right."

Anson muscles Grasshopper aside and replaces him behind the plate. The fanatics cheer as he hollers at Mouse, "Give me the ball."

The pitcher underarms it and Anson catches it with his left hand. He positions himself as if he's receiving a pitch. He squats awkward because he was a first baseman. He extends his left hand high as he can reach, and he leans on his canteen with his right. He spreads his knees. He wouldn't look like the greatest ball player ever even if his fly were buttoned.

"Is this a goddamn strike?" he says. "Way up here?"

Boos and hisses fall from the atmosphere.

The pitch may have been a strike, may have been a ball, but all Grasshopper knows is Anson is dead right about the umpire being smug. "My little sister hits these pitches," he says like he longs to be speared back into the dirt.

Then the loony umpire asks Clarence for the house broom and circles the plate into fair territory to face the squatting Anson. The umpire mumbles "give me presence," like he's praying to Jesus. Grasshopper wonders what will come out of his mouth next. The umpire brooms dust off the marble. "I won't be made small of," he says to no one in particular. He says it work-a-day as he brooms. "This is my game."

Casey calls the umpire a low-down bunghole and a rat-turd and makes a fist like he's going to take a sock. The audience chants dark noise in support of Casey, but Anson holds up his hand from his awkward squat to make Casey wait. Anson glares until the umpire's brooming is done. The dust settles on Anson's blond hair and sticks to his mustache like pollen to a bee's legs. Anson empties his canteen on the plate and holds it there for the last drops to fall and splash.

"I'm giving the plate a washing. Maybe you'll see it better now," Anson says as the crowd goes into a berserk frenzy.

Anson stands upright. That makes him seem athletic again. He takes a step sideways to let Casey join him, and the umpire has two Adam's apples in his face. Tendons stand out in necks above goldenrod jockey silks. The umpire is about to get a simultaneous licking from the two juggernauts of the game. That's something that will make it into Nellie Bly's New York newspaper.

With the side of his foot, Anson drags dirt over the wet plate. Casey laughs, relaxes his fist. Grasshopper listens for fear in the umpire's voice, but his tone stays steady. "I can toss you for that," he says. "I'd rather get back to it."

"Play will resume when I say so," Anson says. "This is my game. Not yours."

Five thousand cheer when the legend holds the mushy ball high in the air. The umpire makes no effort to reach it. He shifts his mask from under his left arm to his right, switches the broom from right hand to left, turns his blood-caked face to see out at the throng where empty flasks glitter. His eyes scan the most distant bleaching boards. "These last two outs have taken a long time. So far."

That causes Anson to find the low sun. Anson glares at Grasshopper as if Mexicans are to blame for nightfall.

"We're leaving the grounds," Anson says. "We're walking off, all thirteen of us, the whole kit and caboodle. Unless you toss him."

"Toss who?" the umpire says.

"Him." Anson stares at Grasshopper with eyes of cold turquoise.

"Who?" the umpire says.

"Moses F. Fleetwood effing Walker."

Grasshopper wants to hide in the shed with the lime and grass seed, but he plays dumb. The umpire pulls out his pencil stub and notebook with the list of batsmen. "No Moses F. Fleetwood effing Walker listed."

Anson points at the top of the notebook. "Him. Grasshopper Nova. His real name is Fleet Walker, the last of the coloreds. Played with the Blue Stockings in the Beer-Ball League."

The umpire looks Grasshopper over. Neither wants eye contact. "Toss him for what? Stopping pitches and keeping his mug shut? I've received more than my share of bruises today, mostly from Old Jake. I got two when I was behind your catcher. I've tossed Jake. I'll toss everyone else before I work my way around to the one man who has worked to keep me safe."

"You've no choice. He's Fleet Walker." Anson turns congenial. "You're in a daze, I understand. Old Jake hurt you bad, you're not up to snuff."

The umpire leans on the broom and says nothing.

"He's *colored*," Casey says. "He only pretends to be a greaseball."

"Never knew a colored Mexican," the umpire says.

"Are you blind *and* deaf?" Anson says.

"You aren't the first to think so."

"He played with the Cuban Giants last year, we met them on the Fourth of July."

"My birthday," Casey says. "I started the comeback and we blew out their candles."

"The gate was lucrative, but we'll never play that outfit again. They say they're Cuban, but they're mostly colored. Fleet Walker was the lightest among them. That's him alright, hiding behind the mask and mustache and Mex-can talk."

The umpire studies the catcher. Everything except his eyes. "Soil's loam about the plate, makes a catcher's face dirty, makes your own Irishman backstop appear colored this late in the day."

"You can tell he's a Negro, he has that high-hat attitude," Casey says.

Anson raises his voice as if it's the umpire who doesn't understand English. "He's a jackanapes, college makes him no less colored than the illiterate Clarence there. Nothing against Negroes. Some are good enough to be in the big leagues in spring, but they all wilt come summertime."

"Never knew a Negro who speaks Spanish," the umpire says.

"Cuban Negroes," Casey says.

"Is Fleet Walker Cuban?"

"Ohio," Cap Anson says.

"He pretends to speak Mexican to flout the rules," Casey says.

"What rules?" the umpire says.

A screech rises from Anson's voice. "Rule Number One, idiot. Coloreds play no base ball in California this year except on colored teams. Same rule as everywhere."

"I read the rules on the train over, no rule mentions Negroes."

"No writ-down rule, dumb shit," Casey says. "You're a fish out of water. You haven't a leg to stand on."

The umpire looks at his legs. "Got any other unwritten rules I need to know?"

"Yep," Casey says. "No speaking Mexican on the yard."

"*No me chingues*," the catcher says.

"That's what I mean," Casey says. "He takes unfair advantage. You need to stop him, or what are umps for?"

"He sounds Mexican," the umpire says.

"You're pig-headed," Anson says. "I think I'll let Casey take a sock at you."

"That'd be swell," Casey says.

"The association clears players on the rosters," the umpire says. "Once they're on the roster it's out of my hands. I've got enough declaring balls and strikes, enforcing the rules they write down. I'll use my judgment on outs and not outs, but not on complexions. What's too dark?"

"The one-drop rule," Anson says.

"Every chump ump knows that one," Casey says.

"Grasshopper Nova's on the Oakland roster?" the umpire says.

"That's right," Anson says. "But he's Fleet Walker. Ever seen a Mexican this tall?"

The umpire addresses the catcher. "What's your name?" The catcher extends his arms trying to look confused.

"I bunk with him," Mouse Mathews says from Casey's long shadow. "You think I'd bunk down with a colored?"

The umpire addresses Anson. "If he's an illegal player, take it up with the Minister Wheaton once the game ends. That's in about thirty seconds if we get back to it."

"We ain't getting back to it. We're walking off." Anson glares at the catcher again. "In the interest of this Negro's own safety."

"Can't force anyone to play a game, but the written-down rules address it," the umpire says. "If you walk off the yard it will be declared a forfeit—"

"C'mon, that's bull," Casey says.

"—and the Niners lose nine-to-nil. The Niners get fined five hundred dollars, the Northern California Base Ball Association rules say, but that part's up to William Rufus Wheaton."

Anson throws his cap to the dirt. "That's shit-ass. You're letting him squat here and take a shit on the national game."

"We recognized him the second he stepped from the horsecar," Casey says. "Why else would I come home spikes high, back in the second inning? That's why Squawks Clarke threw behind his head in the eighth."

Casey steps up to the catcher's face. Casey has the advantage of a few dozen pounds and fifty-four ounces of white ash. "Why do you act Mexican, anyway? You get pussy speaking the *ol' espanyoley*?"

The catcher searches for a Spanish insult to throw back but the umpire intervenes on his behalf, "Quit your taunting."

Casey makes two fists. "Don't scold me, Ump. I've never been scolded, not even in the orphanage."

Anson steps in front of Casey to stop him from committing murder. "Negroes need to come out of the game for their own protection," Anson says. "Safety and fairness. That's all I'm asking."

"You knew about this two hours ago and said nothing?" the umpire says. "We talk this stuff out *before* the game, we don't wait for the last inning, the last pitch to bring up—chickenshit."

The umpire faces the catcher. He gives Grasshopper a split second of eye contact. "I was in San Francisco last season. I called a Cuban Giants game against a picked nine of Irish. I worked behind the best catcher I've seen. He looked like you. He caught like you. Best confess now or the Oaklands will forfeit later."

The catcher at last knows where he's seen the umpire before. On the Haight Street Grounds when the Giants dropped down from Cloverdale. This umpire picks up pennies like they are nuggets at Sutter's Mill. It was funny, almost as funny as the time Six-Squaws Apodaca put peanut shells under his foreskin and ran naked around the clubhouse blaming gonorrhea.

The catcher smiles at the recollection. A Negro smile doesn't sit well with Cap Anson. "Colored players are fragile. Toss him for his own welfare."

The catcher knows this will be his last game, he's run out of continent and it's best for him and his family if he leaves now to catch a train to Cincinnati to become a lawyer. Fleet will be thankful for the head start, but he also wants to be behind the bat if Casey strikes out. Even if it means bunking forever in Rural Cemetery with the umpire. Grasshopper raises cracked palms to the sky as if everyone's talking Martian.

The umpire turns to Anson. "There's a million people moved to California; everybody resembles somebody. I can't toss a man on a guess. I can never give the answer everyone wants. We'll play on."

"Oh, no we won't," Anson says. "We'll pay the five hundred dollars to protect the national game."

The umpire peers out at the blackboard where the Niners are two runs to the bad. "Free country. Tomorrow's papers will roast you, say the Niners walked off, afraid of losing square."

"That's ass-shit," Casey says.

"That's how it will be in the papers, that's all I'm saying. It'll be splashed in headlines all the way to New York. Don't forget who's sitting lovely in the grandstand."

Some bored fanatics holler to play ball, but Anson wins them back by closing to within an inch of the umpire. "You've never worked one of my games before. Won't charge you a nickel for some advice. I'm a natural-born kicker, bent upon making trouble. Few days pass that I don't get into a scrape. I never yield, never give in. I'm stubborn as a pine knot."

"Job to do," the umpire says. "Nothing personal."

Cap Anson nods toward the hoodlums restrained by a rope. "Seventy-five determined men are out there with horsewhips. They have nothing against Negroes, but they'll protect the game. All I have to do is scratch my ass, that's the signal. I scratch my ass and they'll come. They won't be the gentleman I am. I scratch my ass and they swarm in like locusts. Nobody wants that. Safety's the concern, this is about fairness and safety and decency and the integrity of the game."

The umpire addresses the catcher. "If you want to step aside for your safety, I will allow another player to take your place."

Anson, Casey, the umpire and Mouse stare at the catcher. He stares ahead, he thinks about Lincoln taking a bullet as the theater audience laughed at a funny line, he thinks about Thomas and Cleodolinda and putting his kids on a boat to Africa.

"You best leave," Casey says. "You best do it." The last slice of sun disappears as Casey tugs at the catcher's gray sleeve like on the reins of a sleeping horse. The catcher doesn't budge.

Anson won't budge, either. He sucks his teeth. "Almost nighttime. We'll stand here fifteen minutes until it ain't safe to play on. Save us five hundred dollars to stand here until daylight fails."

"That's one way to go," the umpire says. "Course, if we stand and brood, the score reverts to what it was after eight innings."

Anson screeches. "That's the same score as now."

"Last completed inning," the umpire says. "Four-to-two, all in the Oaklands favor. You elected to bat first, remember? Be different if we got hit by a severe storm, but the sky's clear except for way off around the mountains. If any club wants to stand around and wait for dark it's the Oaklands."

"That's shit-ass," Anson says. "You wasted precious time before the game to let the tardy Oaklands get limber. You wasted more insisting that Clarence tack the leather back on the spent ball."

"The San Francisco papers will say Casey was scared with two strikes. So will *The New York World*."

"C'mon Captain." Casey's nostrils quiver. "The ump's shoddy, he has a frigging bug up his butt. Let me settle this, wouldya? Let me adios one. I'll hit the bejesus out of it."

Anson hollers at the umpire. "If a fraction of your decisions are right, we win this game long ago. Oakland can't win on merit. Remember that one that rolled under the fence?"

"Get that fixed for tomorrow's two."

"The ump's dead if he K's me," Casey says. "So's the Negro. These two bungholes squat to pee. They're dead if this effing eunuch calls a third one. Fleet Walker may be the fastest coon ever, but he'll be chased down by crippled vets and hoodoos in feathered hats. Let me hit, Captain. I'll knock the gleet out of it."

Resignation settles in Anson's eyes. "I've given you chance after chance to do what's right. You'll never umpire another game in California, never anywhere."

"He's a flat failure, Captain, the world admits to that," Casey says. "Old Jake called him a pissant, ain't it the truth. He's a rat-turd, I should've let Old Jake polish him off."

Anson shows off an arm that can compete in any long-ball contest. He heaves the mushy sphere high into the grandstand. It bounces off the eaves and Nellie Bly's escort catches it in front of her nose. He tries to give it to her, but she won't touch it as if it's cow dung. He pockets it as a keepsake souvenir. The crowd boos the theft, then cheers when the umpire pulls a fresh ball from his pocket. Anson retreats to his bench feeling smug, feeling smart that he entered a lively ball for the last pitch to Casey.

When Fleet gets home, he'll tell Thomas that what makes a good umpire and a good man are one in the same. They have to do what's right when it's most difficult. This *nomper* is *loco* no doubt, but he's got *cojones*.

This *nomper* brooms the pile of dirt from the plate as Casey takes practice swings into the accolades. The brooming does only so much, the plate remains painted in thin mud. This *nomper* shouts through the din at Fleet Walker as if they were on the opposite sides of a waterfall.

"When you're up to your neck in shit it doesn't hurt to piss your pants."

"It ain't over 'til it's over."—Yogi Berra

February 8, 1890, 3:39 p.m.
It's a Saturday, two months before the season opener

CHAPTER NINETEEN

one year and two hundred ninety-four days after the strikeout

Casey hates February and March, and he dreads the approach of April. The eighty-nine season was worse than eighty-eight. If Casey let a strike slide by, the cranks on the first-base side hollered in unison, "That ain't his style." The cranks on the third-base side responded, "'Strike one!' the umpire said." They had the whole ditty memorized word for word.

Maybe it was funny once, but the prank was repeated game after game, home and away, same ole, same ole, until the anger of fire ants crawled through Casey's veins. This season he'll put an end to it. He'll climb into the box seats. He'll sock a fancy man down to his suspenders. He wants teeth stuck in his fists; he wants a fancy man's girl to weep for mercy.

Fourteen seasons have come and gone since Casey left the orphanage on Mount St. Joseph. He hit cloud-scrapers at twelve. At thirteen, the orphans were put to work clearing fresh land and the base ball lot was moved to save on broken windows at Charles Robinson Hall.

Casey's in his prime, he'll soon be thirty-two. No one knows the precise date he was born and the Mudville Niners assigned him the Fourth of July. On his 29th birthday, the nation's 101st, he hit a rope that may have yet to come down. The ball left his bat a foot off the ground. It was torpedo low and through the legs of the Lawton Haverlys shortstop Kirk Fleming without a bounce. It would've been a daisy cutter off another man's bat, but it gained gradual altitude, enough to clear the fence by an inch. It was

193

still low and still climbing when it went out of sight. One sporting writer said it hooked left like a golf shot and blasted a crater in the Sierra Nevada a hundred miles off. Another said it climbed high enough to clear them.

That was Casey's most perfect swing, but his worst is the one everyone remembers. Before Strike Three, big league clubs begged him to come play for the Browns in St. Louis or the Brooklyn Bridegrooms, but he's been loyal. Now he regrets ever accepting these acres; Sacramento politicians all but forced him to swallow his mansion at gunpoint. He hates San Francisco's damp, wooden sidewalks. He hates the San Joaquin heat and farmers happy to see dark rain clouds at ball games. California's a jumping off place to nowhere.

After the strikeout, Casey was in bed for a month at a seaside chapel. He's never recovered, and the *Daily Tribune* in Oakland has a contest to let readers predict the day, hour and minute when he will strikeout for the 432nd time since April 20th, 1888, one strikeout for every foot to the War Monument.

Reporters won't leave him alone; they are under every damp rock. The *Daily Telegraph* in London sent a cricket reporter, but Casey told him that cricket is a chump sport, and he steamed home with an empty notebook. Casey talked to Wood Dryden once to say he'd go to the moon for another at-bat with the blind Ump behind the plate. He'd give the $3,000 to the orphanage, he'd chip in another $3,000 from his own pocket for a chance to crush the ball, then he'd crush The Ump's skull.

The Ump stays in hiding; The Ump doesn't care about the dough. Casey's anger percolates. Nothing stops Dryden from fabricating lies and squeezing them off one by one like a sniper. In this morning's column, Dryden writes that Casey has gained thirty pounds in the hot-stove off-season. Casey's as fat as a Cliff House seal. Dryden writes shit like that every day. He writes that Casey trains on late hours and alcohol, smokes three cigars a day, boycotts Mass at Old Saint Mary's.

Last October, Dryden wrote that Casey lit a bonfire in Golden Gate Park and burned his bats. The truth is, Casey set fire to *one* bat, but it didn't catch. It smoldered and he threw it into the Bay. He expected it to float, but it sank like a stone. His mansion is littered, hundreds of bats are placed about, too many to remember all their names. The one on the seafloor is Rex Gallagher. He named it after his own prick, it's the bat he used that awful April day.

Dryden writes that Casey's a dipsomaniac, a rumdum. Dryden writes lies, lies and more lies. There is the rustling of leaves in Casey's ears, uneasiness about his loins, a loss of confidence, night sweats, clamminess around the collar. Casey changes shirts three times a day, writes Dryden, "Casey's stark raving mad."

Dr. J.F. Gibbon found dark spots under Casey's eyes, which explains why they are no longer keen. *Phthisis*, the doc says. *Dyspepsia*. The doc's a quack and Casey sent away for the Electro-Galvanic Body Belt advertised in the *Sporting News*, a cure-all for trembling, sexual exhaustion, wasting of the body, and diseases pertaining to genital organs. The belt cures none of those things, but it does wonders for memory. Each day Casey remembers those seconds in the strikeout's aftermath with clarity. He was on one knee. The rooters went quiet and the Oaklands heaped atop the pitcher. Mouse Mathews was a rat turd. He threw like a girl, nothing close to the plate.

Casey wants revenge, revenge, and more revenge. He wishes he'd bloodied his timber on The Ump's skull, but The Ump and the Negro catcher ran lily-livered into the clubhouse. Casey started after them, but a hoodlum stole his cap from behind. He wanted to chase the hoodlum into the bleaching boards, or The Ump into the clubhouse, but he stood there capless and impotent. He stood there at the gates of hell.

The doc told Casey to quit taking poppy syrup or he'd acquire an addiction like he has to laudanum. Casey has no addictions, but Wood Dryden prints shit anyway. Dryden ambushes Casey's mind day and night. Dryden will one day write that Casey named his member. God knows how he'll find out about Rex Gallagher.

Casey's reading the *Examiner*, trying to take a shit, immersed in his own smell. He needs two or three meaningful shits to get his bat working again, but he's strained for months and months and produced nothing larger than a deer dropping. Dryden's column is about how the second best base ball player in the land was never Casey. The best was Cap Anson, of course, and the second best was Jim Creighton of the Excelsior Club of Brooklyn. Creighton played in the sixties when Casey was still a lad in the orphanage. No one got openly paid back then. Creighton loved the game for the game itself. He killed himself swinging too hard. Dryden says in the last line of his column that Casey is a base ball mercenary, who will never love the game enough to twist himself into the grave.

Casey farts into the pot. That's all he can muster. Nothing else is making its way through the python of his bowels.

Five weeks ago, during the rainy winter, Wood Dryden had the gall to slide into an empty bar stool next to constipated Casey. The groggery was crowded, Dryden never said hello, he pulled off his soaked hat and said, "I have reason to doubt you were orphaned." His rain-wet hair was perfectly parted.

"C'mon."

"Your daddy left the house one evening by horse and buggy, turned around two hours later thinking he'd catch your mama yoked up with the neighbor."

Casey's eyes stabbed at the bubbles in his beer. "Mummy died in childbirth, every idiot knows. My father died a hero at Bull Run, stepped into the downhill recoil of the thirteenth gun positioned in a line at the crest of Henry House Hill. He's beneath the green hills of Virginia."

"Your mama awoke from a deep sleep to see a figure climbing through the bedroom window. She blew your daddy's head off with a 12-gauge, sawn-off scattergun. A mistake by all accounts."

"Where do reporters get this shit?"

"Records. Trusted sources. Your mama's finger pulled the trigger."

"Mummy's fingers turned the pages of the Holy Bible. That's what the brothers at the orphanage say."

"Your mama shot him square in the face." Dryden chortles. "The way you hit a base ball back in eighty-seven. Your daddy was mean and more stubborn than you, wouldn't quit, stayed headless on his feet long enough to kill your mama. Double murder. The sheriff found a six-year-old out back with his daddy's pocket watch and penknife. Found a red-headed boy carving his own palms."

"C'mon." Casey's sphincter tightened. "Wouldya ever print something except lies? Fairies placed me in the orphanage crib, go ask the brothers."

"Let me see your hands."

They stayed around his beer mug. "They're scarred, everyone knows. From swinging fifty-four ounces of second-growth ash."

"Cap Anson doesn't have hands like that. Nor King Kelly. Jim Creighton never did. You're the only player who sandpapers a bat handle smooth."

Casey socked Dryden to the sawdust and hopped a train to Washington to take the President up on his White House invitation. Harrison's handshake was fat and soft and the first thing he told Casey was that he couldn't wait for Nellie Bly to finish her journey around the world so that he could have her down from New York. The second thing was that he wished he had grandchildren. He had the *Casey at the Bat* ballad memorized and he wanted to recite it to tots at bedtime. He recited it to Casey.

"The outlook wasn't brilliant for the Mudville Nine that day.
The score stood four to two, with but one inning more to play."

Casey couldn't sock the president in the puss, so he said, "That's swell," stormed out, made yellow snow on the White House lawn, and checked into Arlington Hotel for some fun. Wood Dryden was one train behind Casey to Washington and checked in two rooms down.

The sniper wrote that Casey partook of Capitol Hill poker games and harlots. He wrote a long column about a girl of the D.C. burlesque who goes by the moniker *Swinging Casey*. He wrote that Casey paid his respects to Swinging Casey instead of taking a day trip to the hallowed battlefield where his father rests. He wrote that the Niners want to sell Casey to Washington, but the Nationals finished dead last in eighty-nine and, like the government, are on the verge of financial collapse.

"Too bad," Dryden wrote, "A ten-thousand-dollar player belongs in a town with a billion-dollar congress."

This morning the *Examiner* reports that Nellie Bly's back in San Francisco. She was seen entering Judge Gold's chambers. No one knows the reason, she was here just days ago on the last leg of her journey.

Casey's on the pot hoping for success. No dice. "The Judge is a good umpire," he says to his dog, Hope. "If The Judge hadn't been beaten in Santa Cruz, Brewster wouldn't've set foot in The Home of The Mudville Niners. If The Judge, or any chowderhead, had been behind the bat, I would've knocked the gleet out of it."

Casey throws the *Examiner* splat against the wall. He curses the pain that rips his shoulder. Hope scrambles and slips on the redwood floor as if the paper's splat is dynamite. Rage fills Casey's fists. He'll saddle up Alexander and storm into the *Examiner*. A sugar magnate shot newspaperman M.H. de Young four or five years ago, claimed temporary insanity. Casey will get off scot-free, too. They'll never lock him up. Maybe they will if his drought doesn't end.

And now the pitcher holds the ball, and now he lets it go,
And now the air is shattered by the force of Casey's blow.

The Ump's to blame, but Dryden is a close second on Casey's roster of ass-shits, and so is the poet Earnest Thayer and the two-bit actor DeWolf Hopper, who recites the thirteen stanzas on stage night after night. The muscles under Casey's left eye spasms when he thinks of the stages decorated in red, white and blue bunting and all the laughing people who deserve a sock, too.

*Ten thousand eyes were on him as he
rubbed his hands with dirt;*

The muscles spasm again. His batting eye.

*Five thousand tongues applauded when
he wiped them on his shirt.*

His sphincter spasms.

Each time Casey strikes out he feels the pressure in his bunghole, but he dare not tell the doc or it will find its way into the *Examiner*. The whole world will have a big laugh. Dryden is funny when he writes shit about other players. Catchers have started strapping protectors to their chests and maybe the sissies will put on buckskin gloves to protect their sissy little hands. Maybe they'll wear lightning rods in thunderstorms.

Dryden writes those things in good fun, but the sniper turns vicious when he writes about Casey. "Casey caught a disease from the smiles of Tenderloin girls," he writes. "Too bad Casey can't hit a pitch that smiles at him."

Casey gets off the pot. He's tired of trying. He recalls the catch he made last August. He wasn't hitting, so he figured he'd rob another man of a double. He dove under a team of horses and made the greatest snag in the history of the game. He leapt up in glory with the leather in hand. Dryden wrote that Casey would've dropped the ball except for his scars and "maybe their ought to be rules against chiseling your own hands."

Terrible thoughts grind at Casey's gut into the late afternoon. He wants to jump his contract and get the hell out of California. He'd hit the bejesus out of them every day at the Polo Grounds.

He rarely leaves his mansion before dark, but he harnesses Alexander to the carriage and rides through the countryside and into San Francisco's bright houses of yellow, red and orange. He says, "Hello" over and over to all who recognize him. They're polite, but he knows what they're thinking.

Wood Dryden deserves a visit. No jury will convict, but the foghorns in the Bay soften Casey's anger, and he steers Alexander toward Market Street. He decides to snag a girl. Factory girls don't give a shit about Casey's drought. Poem or no poem, they swoon as if he never struck out. They complain about his palms on their soft teats, but their own hands are dry from sewing and rough on his nob. The smutty nymphs come in all shapes and sizes. He likes his oozing with lascivious ooze, plump and blonde and starved for Casey's brand of love.

During the season, it was simple. The rat cheese waited outside the clubhouse, home and away. He took his time making his selection. He studied them until the boys got jumpy. Blake and Flynn are grandstanders. The citizens buy them beers for being the heroes of the poem. Flynn and Blake have heads as fat as blue-ribbon pumpkins but Casey still got first pick. He took his sweet time until the stuttering Flynn said, "Geh-geh-geh get on with it, wah-wah we don't have all nah-night."

Blake lost humility when he tore that two-bagger before the strikeout. He hit for a better average than Casey in eighty-nine, good enough to get the twitch Edna to marry him. Casey dicks with Blake. Casey says, "When you come to the yard tomorrow, bring my spikes. I left them under your bed." Blake's a toady; he laughs at the joke time after time. He has to, or Casey would've ridden Alexander over to the butterfinger's house months ago and played a little fungo with the twitch.

Blake and Flynn can't pick up the slack. The Niners lose half of their games with Casey in his drought. Talk of a Niner dynasty evaporated. Attendance has dried up, except for cranks who recite the poem and give him shit.

Hoodoos are like butterflies. Collecting them in winter is troublesome, it requires lifting a finger; it requires harnessing Alexander to the carriage and steering into the busy part of town. At least it's a Saturday evening. Factory girls are off after six days, tired of cocooning around boarding-house stoves night after night with steam rising from their underthings, tired of kneeling at Old Saint Mary's to keep themselves out of the taverns.

Casey will make one lucky tonight, give her something to say in confession tomorrow. Market Street's busy with wagons, people on foot slip between each gap to cross in thick traffic. It's noisy—though not noisy enough. "Extra, extra," a newsboy hollers. "Nellie Bly's back in town."

It bothers him that the famous girl was in the grandstand for his embarrassing moment. It bothers him that she didn't blow a kiss before the game. It bothers him more that she wrote on and on about the strikeout. She's pretty, but he hates proper brown-haired girls; flat-chested nymphs with their dimples and curls.

Casey whispers into the horse's ear. "Who knows, Alexander, maybe we'll stumble upon the perfect lollipop this evening. One who resembles Claudia, or sweet Sibyl."

Claudia was Casey's regular before she got cut in half by a farm implement, a queer accident a mile from the nearest farm. Dryden writes that Claudia's shapely ghost haunts Casey's mansion. Detectives still haven't gotten to the bottom of it.

Sibyl Sanderson sang soprano at the opera and was Casey's real girl. They ate at the finer restaurants, The Poodle Dog when Sibyl wanted to put on the feedbag for French cuisine. She had a heart that danced through her eyes. They skated at the rink in Golden Gate Park and went on carousel rides. Dryden wrote that Miss Sanderson's not the kind to marry though; she's the kind with a figure well made, who flirts and reads novels on Sundays. Sibyl got tired of Dryden writing shit about her and she left to sing in Paris.

The hoodoo Casey spies on Market Street tonight is nothing like Claudia or Sibyl, nothing like any smutty thing Alexander ever trots home. She's not Casey's type, and the horse intends to pass her by when Casey pulls at the reins. This hoodoo resembles Nellie Bly.

Casey whispers. "Brown hair, pretty, no meat on the bones. It's not her. Nope." Alexander flicks a tail and, without effort, drops four or five plops to make Casey envious.

Casey ties Alexander to a post and steps around to where the hoodoo awaits a streetcar. The sun sets at five-thirty this time of year. It's nearly dark, but she recognizes him. "Gawd above, 'tis the ball player who fills the pages of the papers," she says Irish-like. She's younger than he thought and talks like it. "Jesus, Mary and Joseph, too utterly utter, just too, too."

Her voice is intentionally loud to attract attention. She introduces herself, but Casey doesn't remember names. "Your perfume's as thick as your accent."

The crowd giggles, they always do when he doffs his hat and so he reminds himself again to stop doing it. "Have you been to the new phoonograph parlor?" the hoodoo says in a voice heard on out to Alcatraz. "'Tis for music, but you can hear a record of DeWolf Hopper recitin' your ballad. Spiffin'. Utterly too, too."

"Any schoolyard tyke memorizes a stupid poem."

He doesn't like her, but she wants to get jumped; he knows when they do. She says she is just off work and needs an hour, more because her boarding house is in the Tenderloin. She's too skinny. Shit, if she fell from a ferry she would make the splash of a spirit. If a whale happened by, she would slip through its baleen. But maybe she'll change his luck. Maybe that's been his problem all along. Buxom gals like Claudia are unlucky. Thighs of brick-oven dough have been his downfall. Same ole, same ole.

Casey waits for her in a groggery and drinks beer from Germany to kill time. Another and another, he drinks enough to regret missing out on Al Spalding's World Tour. Casey could've spent last winter playing ball in New Zealand and the Holy Land. He could've surprised Sibyl Sanderson in France, but he abandoned the boys in Salt Lake, running after The Ump into a crowded deluge.

Cap Anson wrote Casey a letter about rickshaw racing through the streets of Colombo and about the day at sea when the boys threw Clarence overboard. The mascot made good chum and good fun before they hauled him in wide-eyed and half drowned. The boys rode camels to the game beneath the Sphinx and afterward they hurled base balls at the monster's eye. "We sampled exotic nomadic twat in the nighttime desert sand," Cap Anson wrote. "P.S. I hope you caught that some-bitch ump."

Defiance gleamed in Casey's eye,
a sneer curled Casey's lip.

Casey tires of waiting for the skinny, smutty hoodoo. He has time to find one with udders. He orders a last beer, he's sozzled, and he wonders if Joseph Pulitzer chases Nellie Bly around, jumps her to the vibrations of the presses. Pulitzer has more dough than God. He's old and ugly, but rich guys jump any girl they want. Pulitzer deserves his dough, he hatches good ideas, he had the best idea yet to flush out The Ump, but Brewster's a chickenshit. He stays a fugitive and trims Casey of $3,000. Casey would knock the stuffing out of the first ball pitched in New York's Brotherhood Park, pop the yard's cherry, then he'd knock The Ump's nose foul.

Another German beer lands in front of Casey, compliments of a couple of boys who followed him in from the street. They wave from across the tavern, blow foam off their mugs and give Casey three cheers. Sometimes he's in the mood to be noticed, but these boys hold up Allen & Ginter cigarette cards with his picture, the cards Wood Dryden says influence young boys to smoke before their age. Casey ignores the bungholes and orders his own beer.

He's tried to get back on San Francisco's good side. Archbishop Riordan had a dumb idea. He asked Casey to throw dead chickens as far as he could to raise dough for the orphanage. It attracted quite a generous crowd and he overheard the archbishop tell Dryden that Casey is a man of such Christian works that he has a secure spot in heaven.

Dryden didn't write what Archbishop Riordan said. He wrote: "There was an audible pop from Casey's shoulder that sounded like the snap of a chicken's neck. He can't raise a hand high enough to doff his cap, which is fortunate timing now that he never has reason."

Casey steps outside for a beery piss. Pain screams in his shoulder as he wrestles Rex Gallagher out his fly. He needs the sulfur baths at Skaggs Springs. He can't lift his arm high enough to whack his nob. His palms are too rough, anyway, he's never been able to satisfy himself. He's never had to, not since he left the orphanage.

He wants to quit playing and coach a club, but Dryden writes that no club is desperate enough, what with the opera that plays between Casey's ears.

A different kind of pain screams from Rex Gallagher, a burning scream. Casey shifts his stance to maneuver his nob back into his pants left-handed. He changes his stance each game. He gets closer to the plate, or farther. He concentrates more, he concentrates less, tries to hit blurry-eyed after lushing all night, he tries hitting half sober. Dryden writes that Casey's jowl jiggles when he swings, his playing days are over, and he couldn't coach Sausalito out of the D-league cellar.

Sometimes the poem fills Casey's head until he's down at the phonograph parlor to suffocate on DeWolf Hopper's deep and claustrophobic voice.

> Oh, somewhere in this favored land
> the sun is shining bright;

They won't let him into the parlor anymore, not after he used his bat to pulverize a phonograph.

Casey steps back inside the groggery, back from his painful piss, back on his barstool. The last two inches disappear from his beer. The hoodoo is out of time but he's too drunk to leave. He picks a newspaper up from the bar because Wood Dryden doesn't write for the *Evening Post*. Page One is all about Fleet Walker. The trial of the century has ended. Some on the Yank jury voted the Negro innocent. Casey boils. Only in New York. The strikeout was two years ago, and the backstopper and the coon-loving Ump haven't suffered a wit. Cap Anson's a racialist, but Casey wasn't until the strikeout. He detests Fleet Walker; he detests that the backstopper is off scot-free. Casey sinks scarred palms into his eyes, there's no brand of justice on any coast.

> *The sneer is gone from Casey's lip, his*
> *teeth are clinched in hate;*

Last month that booger-eater Flynn tried to give Casey a hitting lesson. He said, "You hold the bah-bah-bat rah-rah-wrong," but when Casey gave the toady a left-handed sock it was a gift to Dryden; he wrote Casey's larrup is too lame to knock the stutter from Flynn's lip.

Casey picks up the beer that the boys bought him. They give three cheers as he drinks it in three swallows. It's gone so flat he doesn't belch. He staggers for the exit. Just then, the hoodoo waltzes through the door.

"Wouldya get in the carriage," Casey says.

"I'm no ol' hoor. I 'twouldn't go home with a stranger."

"Casey's a stranger to no one, Joy Spot. C'mon, a stroll about my garden is all."

The garden is four acres, bigger than a ball yard, with trees of pomegranate, pear, apple, fig, olive and lemon. "It's like a heaven for the Greek gods of Rome," she says.

"I'll have you back in the autumn, after the season. We'll pick fat grapes in the vineyard and crush them with your skinny butt as we reconnoiter."

She punches Casey in the chest. "I don't know what that word means."

"Means I need to take one more beery leak before we go inside."

The ferns make her skirt wet about the ankles. When he returns from the bushes, she shivers on cue beneath a Monterey pine and complains the clay is ruining her Cromwell shoes. It's a girl lie; the garden path is sandy this near the sea. Casey warns there are snakes near the fountain of Italian marble. He drinks from it and says the water's magic, makes his bat spew fireworks. She slugs him in the chest again.

"Wouldya like to tour the first mansion ever built with bat and ball?"

"I promise to go no farther than the veranda," and when she steps inside it's "to keep from freezin' to death among serpents," and she accepts a drink "to worm me feet."

"You're like a character out of Oscar Wilde," Casey says, handing her a spiked ginger ale. He's never read a word of Oscar Wilde, but every hoodoo is pleased to be told. Every girl gets gushy over Hope. The sheepdog has been gushed over so many times that she no longer wags her tail at the touch of chapped factory hands.

Skinny girls can't hold their liquor; this hoodoo's pixilated after one drink. She giggles without a smile. He gets her walking toward the stairs. She hikes the damp above her ankles to climb.

"I love your red hair," she says. "Do you think your children will be red-heads?"

"Nope."

"Do you like red-headed girls?"

"They buck like goats." She socks him in his sore shoulder.

Casey imagines himself a dragon out of some kind of book. He can spit fire and his mansion is a secret cave where he guards stuff and captures virgins. He's a dragon of exact habit. That's why he goes after the hoodoos at the exact place, never at the foot of the grandfather clock or on the billiard table. Hope lifts a quizzical ear and follows with exactness, the she-dog works her way a step behind, sour face low to the ground or the girls will stray.

Casey takes all hoodoos by their hand the last two steps up the stairs. He longs for one to resist, to let the glass fall and shatter, but they cling to their excuse. Maybe this skinny Joy Spot will yank her chapped hand from his and flee. Where? Only bedrooms are on the second floor. Each has a skylight and he imagines a grandstand of society prudes outside, a chorus of floating angels as he polishes each hoodoo off in a bed of carved walnut. His size twelve spikes flash in the moonlight.

Two steps from the top, Casey leverages his weight until her knees buckle. The glass falls and shatters on the redwood stairs. Maybe skinny hoodoos are different, maybe she will change his luck. Hope laps ginger ale among the shards and, at last, wags her tail.

There was Johnnie safe at second
and Flynn a-hugging third.

"You're hoortin' me," and he spreads his weight until she is crushed beneath a fallen horse, unable to speak, unable to breathe.

"Time to go to town," Casey says. He likes and hates her silence as he strokes brown hair, inhales the scent she can't afford, and whispers "Mighty Casey, mighty, mighty Casey."

Once she passes out under his weight, he picks her up limp from the hardwood and sets her on feathers. He's no scofflaw, he's a man who shakes hands with presidents and wins blessings from archbishops. He never crosses the line. Like a gentleman, he lights a fire, takes off his shirt and Electro-Galvanic Body Belt, his new tan shoes to remove his trousers. Naked, he puts on his spikes without stockings. He takes his time, gives her a minute to awaken. Gives her every opportunity to run, but she undresses. Her willingness drains him of arousal.

"Flynn has bigger teats," he says and he flips her face down in bed as if she's a sawmill board. He compliments her ass, slaps it twice. His teeth clinch, a third slap with the body belt penetrates the spiked ginger ale and she yelps "Jesus, Mary and Joseph" into the pillow, but it does him no good.

Casey laughs a malicious laugh, climbs off, crosses the room, adds scratches to the floor. He snuffs the candle, but the room's no darker. The waxing moon's all but full through the skylight. The fire reflects off Hope's eyes and the hoodoo's red-spanked cheeks. He climbs back on, lowers his expectations, reaches around for what she has. Small-busted girls are sensitive and she says Mary and Joseph again.

"Mighty, mighty Casey," he says. "Mighty, mighty Casey," and he longs for 1887 when he satisfied three or four kittens in one night and woke up piss proud to pee a rainbow. "Mighty, mighty Casey," and he imagines he is yoking up with Blake's twitch Edna. "I need bigger boobies to prime my pump," he whispers, but the hoodoo acts the queen bee.

"Maybe you should run off with Miss Chesty of the circus, seventy inches round is what the *Chroonicle* says."

The band is playing somewhere, and
somewhere hearts are light,

"God, I hate the *Chronicle.* I hate newspapers. Time for you to go."

"The wee hours, 'tis dark outside," and in two seconds she's snoring. He tugs off his spikes, puts on his trousers, heads downstairs. He barely feels the glass shards cutting his feet. Hope lopes behind. Hope hopes for something to eat.

Casey pours a brandy pick-me-up, strikes a match that throws his shadow on the wall. The flame draws into an all-night cigar as the she-dog circles three times before coming to a rest. The pendulum swings on the grandfather clock, Casey winds his pocket watch, thinks about his Mummy, his headless father, and synchronizes the time piece when the clock chimes three.

Bats lean in every corner in all seventeen rooms. He wonders about Rex Gallagher on the seafloor. He wants it back to lean against the grandfather clock. Casey paid a lot for the clock, he paid a lot for his piano and billiard table, twice as much to have them shipped from New York. He gave up billiards after Cap Anson whipped him in a friendly game, and nobody's played three notes on the piano except Sybil Sanderson. Dough means nothing to him since she left, neither do his chandeliers, his Chippendale furnishings, his ass-shit Victorian bric-a-brac, his oversized bathtub with its yellow ring of nicotine, and the broker who makes him more dough with investments in theater and vineyards and Comstock silver. Casey's bursting with money and heartburn; he's rich from cornering the wheat market and yet he feels like one of the down and outs.

Last month, the broker invited him to supper at The Palace to discuss building a track for trotting. Casey wants a sporting goods empire like Al Spalding's, but the broker suggests a secret formula for bottled ginger beer.

The sheepdog stretches ass up, comes over and rubs against Casey's hand. Casey runs fingers into her winter coat. Hope licks the bloody souls of Casey's feet. He lowers his glass, and Hope comes round to lap at the brandy. Casey pulls the glass away and the dog's eyes follow it. Casey winces, damn he hates dead chickens, the pain in his shoulder sings as he works the glass to his lips.

He thinks about Earnest Thayer and DeWolf Hopper.

He thinks about Wood Dryden.

He thinks about the coon backstopper Fleet Walker.

He always thinks about The Ump.

He thinks about the wringing of their chickenshit necks. A hungry man is an angry man and he gets himself some leftover meat from the icebox. He thinks about Nellie Bly and how she refused to blow him a kiss that day before the game ever began. He imagines her visiting his mansion. She'd sashay about as if she owned the place. Her skirts would sweep with the aroma of the melted chocolate they serve at The Poodle Dog. Nellie Bly doesn't have Sibyl's curves, but she has untamed pluck.

Casey spits out a piece of gristle and feeds it to Hope from his hand. The she-dog swallows it without chewing. Casey takes a swig of poppy syrup, hoping for shuteye. Ten minutes pass. Hope pukes the gristle, then laps it back up with zest. She curls up. Her eyes are heavy with brandy and she falls asleep.

Casey farts. He's never sleepy. He's windy no matter what. He never poops; it's been so long that he wishes he had the squirts. He swigs more poppy syrup. His cigar glows and fades and glows.

The hoodoo snores upstairs. Hope, snoring downstairs, wakes and comes over to lick Casey's feet again. Casey draws on his cigar. Smoke swirls in his open mouth. He pulls out his watch, looks at the grandfather clock. The tick-tock of life swings on. He goes outside in the dark and picks lemons from his tree. His shoulder burns with each reach. His hands remain strong though, and he comes inside and squeezes juice into a bowl. His grip is angry, his hands pulverize the rind until the bowl is half full of runny marmalade.

He starts to sweat from the squeezing and he takes off his shirt. He squeezes bare-fisted and bare-chested until yellow lemon rind oozes through his fingers like snake crap. The squeezing hurts his hemorrhoids.

He stilled the rising tumult; he bade the game go on.

Casey finishes squeezing. He sits, drops his cigar butt into the cocktail of brandy and dog drool. It sizzles. He rewards Hope with more laps, takes a mindless sip for himself. The grandfather clock at last puts him to sleep, each pendulum swing takes him further and further inside the zone. Casey and Hope snore and the hoodoo upstairs completes the drunken trio. Casey dreams of the fanatic who stole his cap from behind. He ignores the thief. He chases endlessly after The Ump. He chases him out of the yard, up railroad tracks and into tunnels and tabernacles. It's a recurring dream. Casey never catches him.

"STEERIKER ONE!" The Ump hollers and it echoes in the tunnel.

And somewhere men are laughing,
and somewhere children shout,

"STEERIKER TWO!" echoes off the rounded ceiling of the tabernacle.

But there is no joy in Mudville—
mighty Casey has struck out.

"The worst of madmen is a saint run mad."—Alexander Pope

February 9, 1890, 8:57 a.m.
It's a Sunday

CHAPTER TWENTY

one year and two hundred ninety-five days after the strikeout

C asey awakens in sweats, his neck is torture, his back stiff from sleeping in a chair, a rustling in his ears. He wrestles on his shirt. He winces at the pain in his shoulder. It's barely daylight, but the grandfather clock says it's almost nine o'clock, his watch tells the same.

"Damn the fog."

He remembers the hoodoo. The bitch probably tiptoed out, absconded with two or three of his bats. Casey takes the stairs two at a time. Hope follows on his heels. The smutty nymph sits on the bed naked from the waist up, brushing her hair.

"Sweet Jesus." She hides her bubs behind her hands.

"Time to go."

"What's hell, 'tis the house ablaze?"

"Nope." He thinks of a lie. "Visitors coming."

Her face has a vertical sleep line from spending the night ass up. The line zig-zags up her cheek, stops at her eye, and resumes above on her forehead.

"Don't they teach ball players common courtesy?" She has good reflexes; she catches the dress Casey throws at her. He winces again. She puts the dress aside and grabs her bubs. "Mother o' gawd. I'm about to boorst. Where's the necessary?"

"Use the chamber pot."

Her nose scrunches. "I hate thoonder mugs. I hate being rushed. You rushed your performance last night." She smiles at his loins. "No meat round here on the weekend."

His jaw pulls tight. "You have shortstop hands. Or, maybe they just look big on your teensy udders."

She returns fire. "You're getting podgy."

"C'mon. Wouldya get out. Company coming. You don't want a reputation."

"I can see the headline now." One hand rises to the air and moves across the skylight as if she's reading a signboard. "Mighty Casey has strook out. Again." She laughs until her bad teeth show, teeth that seemed white and straight last night. She's just a kid, too young to have a mouthful of yellow.

His scratchy hands stuff into his trouser pockets to keep from busting her on the sleep line; to keep from giving her free dental work. They find fistfuls of change and he tosses two bits at her. "The McAllister and Haight Street lines are down the road."

"You're sending me home on the streetcar?"

He grabs her by the wrists. "Get dressed."

"What makes you so good? I've got to pee I told you, or don't your fat ears work neither?"

"I can hear the viz, Joy Spot."

He points under the bed. Her nose crinkles again. "Get it for me. I 'twouldn't lay a hand on a man's thoonder mug."

Casey longs to take the hoodoo by her hair and make her crawl after the piss pot, make her squat until her legs cramp. If she ever got around to filling the pot warm, he'd at last let go of her hair. He'd turn the pot upside down over her head and listen to her disgust echoing inside the china. He'd take the emptied mug in one fist, pissy brown mane in the other, and toss everything outside with the banana slugs. He would, but his shoulder screams.

There are a dozen bats positioned in the bedroom. He considers grabbing one and chasing her naked to the streetcar. That would be a show. But it would make the papers, and so he's on his knees and retrieving the pot as if he were the mascot Clarence.

The hoodoo must sense that his anger has started to boil, and she makes nice.

"I've never seen a thoonder mug hand-painted with tiny base balls. It's darling."

"Wouldya piss?"

"Once you step out of the room mighty man."

Casey and Hope listen at the door for her water, and barge in before she finishes.

"What's hell."

"You're not such a queen bee with your legs splayed." He throws her dress at her again, left-handed.

She receives it in a catcher's squat. "What will I say if I bump into your company on the way to the streetcar?"

"C'mon, quit lallygagging or I'll have my Chinaman bury you in the garden. Wouldn't be the first hoodoo gone missing from the Tenderloin."

"I might bump into the iceman, maybe. Icemen sell tips to reporters. What should I say."

"You're my cousin. Visiting."

"Course I'm visitin'. I'm no ol' hoor. I'm seventeen, too sweet for the iceman to think things unless he's pervert-minded like you. Visitin' from where?"

"Who cares? Ireland."

"Makes sense." She pushes up her hair in the mirror, looks at her bubs with satisfaction. "No iceman will believe we're relations. You're fat with freckles and my hair's not red."

"Joy Spot, be my base ball coacher if it gets you out a step faster."

"Some of us would get along better if we were not so proud." She dresses and returns to the mirror for another look. "If I had the money, I'd coolor me hair blonde. I bet if I was blonde as straw you'd have been Mr. Somebody last night, sent me into hysteria 'stead of strookin' out. Again."

"You need muskmelons more than hair. I squeezed lemons last night bigger than you. Put on your shoes."

"They're Cromwell. Jimmy Blake bought them for me."

"You know Blake?"

"Jimmy didn't strook out. He knocked the cover off the ball."

Casey feels his face turn red. He finds a basin filled with water and sinks his face in it. When he comes up for air she makes him wish he'd stayed under. "I went to a girls party where we washed our hair in champagne to get it coolored. Cost a pretty penny. Pity, I don't have the pin money for champagne."

Water drips from Casey's chin. He takes a drink of poppy syrup, puts on a dirty shirt. His shoulder screams murder. He digs into his pockets. The rest of his change overflows her cupped hands.

"Isn't much," she says.

"I wasted the rest on beers last night, wasted the whole evening waiting for you."

"If I bump into that iceman, I'll be your niece from Dooblin."

Her shoes still aren't on when Hope lifts an ear.

"Looks like your mutt's hearin' some viz."

"Shut up for one second."

Hope growls. "Horse hooves," she says. "Outside on the gravel. Your company's here."

Casey goes to the wrought iron balcony. A slip of a girl in long skirts rides alone and astride like a man.

"Stay put until the coast is clear," he says.

"I've got to leave. Right now. It's the Lord's Day. I go to Mass or I go to hell. Not much to confess about last night, the priest will be bored pudden-headed, won't want me back. Tell me to say a hundred Hail Mary's—tell me Jimmy Blake's more interesting."

"Follow me downstairs. I'll sneak you out the back."

"The newspapers say you coin money. I need it more than you."

Casey crosses the room in three steps and takes up the nearest bat.

She's unafraid. "Is that the one you strook out with? Every pitcher once feared your bat, now none do."

Casey shatters the pot with a golf swing and piss sprays the mirror. The swing feels good. It doesn't hurt, it slows his pulse, calms his brain. She crosses herself.

"You're a devilfish," he says. He grabs her under her arms and digs thumbs into her shoulders until the surprise in her eyes turns to pain. "I've tried polite." His thumbs dig deeper for tears, then deeper for fear. Her face turns red, erasing the sleep line. A small puddle splashes on the floor, wets her bare feet and the painted balls of the shattered pot.

Casey releases his grip. "You're a slob, pissing on my redwood. That's swell. Look at my pants."

A sob chokes her voice. "Let me finish next time before you boorst in on me."

"Get in the closet," he says, and she obeys. "You'll mop your own piss soon as I get back."

Hope sniffs at the puddle with a rubber nose, then trots out the bedroom door after Casey. He takes the stairs by threes and arrives in time to help the rider from her hired horse. This isn't the same ole, same ole. He recognizes Nellie Bly.

"Morning, truelove." He feels no twinge of pain when he extends his hand to help her down. "Your prince at your service."

"Who is this chivalrous man with the rigorous grip?"

"C'mon, you know who I am." He catches her at the waist as she dismounts on the starboard side.

She flinches at his touch. "Your hands are tough as crocodile skin. A man's man, thank my stars."

Beneath her red velvet wrapper is a blouse of pale blue silk with rich lace around the collar. The colors are nearly gray in the deep fog, but her face glows as if a source of light originates from beneath her skin.

"You alone?"

A smile of perfect teeth. Full lips. "I circumnavigated the world without an escort. I survived ten days in the madhouse. A ride to your lodgings seems well within my capabilities."

Her chest heaves with a deep breath as she takes in Strawberry Hill to the north. It comes in and out of view through the fog. Casey's eyes search down her, hoping for a bare ankle. The horse nuzzles her. She pats it; smoothes her riding skirts. Her chest heaves once more. "I do love the ocean air. You must sleep an easy, happy sleep out here filled with dreams."

She at last meets his eyes full on. Eyes as pretty as any Cap Anson wrote about from Ceylon. "No place on earth is more lovely. Mr. Casey, it is so pleasant to meet you at long last."

She gazes skyward to expose a long, glowing neck from her lace collar. Her arms raise to adjust her hair. "The wear and tear of the road."

"You look like a million bucks. Dressed to the nines."

"You are a dear. My hair looks like a bird will fly out at any second. Until recently I had not ridden since my Pennsylvania childhood. I climbed aboard a horse once or twice on my journey. The saddle invigorated me, I promised to make it a habit."

"I could use a good invigorating," Casey says. She tosses him a good-girl expression and he stammers, "I'm sick of peace and quiet, I'm ready to jump to New York."

"We will welcome you with open arms."

"Here's my arm." Nellie Bly declines it. She's content to stay outside. "I can jump anytime," he says. "To the new Players League. I'll find my way to the Series with the Giants or Trolley Dodgers any day I want."

"I do not understand the jargon of base ball. What does it all mean?"

"Means that I have all the dough I need, but less than I deserve."

Nellie Bly laughs. "I like you, Mr. Casey. I like a man who knows what he is about. Some of us say we are above money, but we all like it. Joseph Pulitzer is wealthier than you and all of your base ball confederates put together, and he carries his lunch."

Nellie Bly is a talker; she runs on like a train without brakes. Again, she peers through the fog at the landscape. "I adore the countryside. You would be foolish to move. Cities are fire traps. The clomping of hooves on stone, bells on vehicles, odors of cellars, dying as the dog dieth."

The horse whinnies. "I bet you have an escort. C'mon, I bet he's looking at us through his glass from Strawberry Hill."

"He is not, but you had better mind your *p*'s and *q*'s." Hope growls. Nellie Bly laughs. "Does the mutt understand conversation?" Hope growls again and runs to a hedge at the side of the mansion. She barks and barks until the hoodoo comes out of hiding. The smutty nymph runs up to Nellie Bly and hugs her.

"Gawd above, 'tis the famous lass from New York. Oh Miss Bly, you're me heroine, you're every girl's girl, spiffin', too utterly utter, just too, too."

"Get out of here," Casey hollers. "I'm sorry, Miss Bly, factory girls sneak onto my property from time to time. My Chinaman can't keep them out."

"Look at him, Miss Bly. Me uncle's smitten with you."

"Your uncle?" Nellie Bly says.

Casey feels his nostrils quiver. "Wouldya get out?"

"We don't get New York papers in the Tenderloin, but we all know of you, Miss Bly," the hoodoo says. "Don't worry, your visit stays mum with me. I'll tell the girls, but I won't tell the iceman, he'd only blab to Wood Dryden."

"Wood Dryden?" Nellie Bly smooths her riding skirts. "Whatever on earth would the iceman pass along to him?"

"Nothin' Miss Bly." The hoodoo winks. "I'm leavin' for town. Me uncle was about to give me money for the streetcar."

"The girl's lying," Casey says. "She's not my niece."

"Of course, she is not," Nellie Bly says. "How does an orphan have any relatives at all?"

The hoodoo holds out her begging hand. "Wood Dryden's the best reporter in the land—except for you Miss Bly."

Hope shows her teeth. "Wouldya get off my land," Casey says.

She smiles at Nellie Bly. "I wager we fit into the same clothes me and you. 'Tis you, Miss Bly, who fell from the same tree. We may indeed be long lost cousins from Dooblin. Utterly too, too. Uncle Casey, have you ever seen a lady as pretty?"

Nellie Bly opens her pocketbook and gives the hoodoo a fortune of ten dollars. Hope bares her teeth and seems ready to go for the hoodoo's throat when she retreats up the road.

"Be careful, Miss Bly. Red hair means a temper." She hollers from a distance. "Take care, Miss Bly. All the girls in my boardin' house worship you. We're all your lovin' cousins. We'd die cryin' if anything happened."

"That girl is on her way to the *Examiner,*" Nellie Bly says. "Wood Dryden will have us engaged by the morrow."

"Imagine our offspring."

"I will imagine no such thing. That would be a sin." Her eyes are up and down him like a flat iron, and he remembers his pant leg is splashed with the hoodoo's piss.

"I'm no sinner. I give a lot of dough to the orphans."

She fires off another facial expression. "Once you quit playing base ball, I am sure you will study for the priesthood."

The sarcasm reminds Casey of Sybil Sanderson, his sophisticated soprano who read novels before being chased off by Wood Dryden to France. Nellie Bly's much like Sybil. She's self-made. The society prudes look down their noses, but they envy her freedom and pluck and the mark she has made. They ooze with envy.

Too bad Nellie Bly has little bubs, just as he remembers them in the grandstand. Yet standing here alone she's lascivious like Sybil. A small town worldly, licentious girl. A rarity. He tries to guess her age. Nellie Bly's soon to be climbing toward her thirties. She's surely experienced. She's probably as smutty as any nymph he's known.

"I'm trying to imagine why you're here," Casey says. "On a Sunday morning, all by your lonesome."

"It was a waste of time to look for you at Mass." Nellie Bly says. "I am on an umpire safari. A hunt for Walter Brewster. Do you remember him?"

"Some joke. I chased after him a year ago in the worst rainstorm ever seen. Kept me from going on Al Spalding's World Base Ball Tour. I'd've been around the world just like you if not for the rat-turd Brewster."

She stares into the fog. "Finding Mr. Brewster means everything to you *and* to me. Perhaps we should team up."

"I'd like to go around the world with you, Miss Bly."

"Was that a double entendre?"

Sybil used to sling around French words like that. Nellie Bly gabbles more than Sybil, but her voice is as pleasant on the ears. He feels lucky that he didn't waste his ammo on the hoodoo.

"I'll unsaddle your horse."

"I will be leaving soon unless I get what I want. Are you certain Walter Brewster has not returned to San Francisco?"

"I'd've known him if I seen him. He'd never slip by me on Market Street—unless you were passing at the same time. You are quite distracting."

"I must look a rag."

"If I happen to see The Ump, I'll beat him into sewer gas. Then I'll find Judge Gold and sock him in the puss. Can you believe it, The Judge trained Brewster. The blind leading the blind. Gold will never win another election. Not in my neck of the woods."

"Judge Gold. Honest John Gaffney. Dick Higham. They are all the same man."

"What?"

"Mere men trying to arbitrate a game played by cocky athletes."

"Athletes are OK, mostly. Except Fleet Walker. The Ump should've cast him out. A jury should've electrocuted him. Juries and umps are not square, juries and umps are the same."

"As I said, mere men."

"Brewster's dead or else your Jew boss Pulitzer would've smoked him out with dough. Brewster's in the cemetery or slinking from cellar to cellar at night with a leaky tub on his shoulders, maggots in his hair, piss running down his leg."

"Your western lexicon is colorful. Perhaps you should not bring it to New York. We would never appreciate you."

"I sound regular."

"Is the umpire as well spoken?"

Casey watches a low-flying killdeer overhead. "Never said much the whole game."

"Except strike one and strike two."

He looks at her in time to see the hatching of a brief, nasty smile. "C'mon. I was liking you but I guess you're a reporter like the rest. Why would I tell you anything."

"I have many flaws, but I can be friendly when I want to be. I was hoping you would take me for a ride to the Poodle Dog for lunch."

He extends an arm, but she refuses it again. "Brewster's either dead or gone insane, one of the two," Casey says. "He wasn't right the whole afternoon."

"There were more sane people on Blackwell's lunatic island than at The Home of the Mudville Niners. Five thousand, every one with delirium except the umpire and me. We were the only dispassionates there. Mr. Brewster seemed perfectly sane and industrious doing his job."

"He ruined the national pastime. I'll extract a pound of flesh. If he's alive."

"Base ball has survived economic panic and war. I suppose it survives a swing and a miss from time to time."

"You're pissing me off. How's that for western lexicon?"

"I am only trying to see two sides. It behooves me to see both sides as reporters are expected to do."

"C'mon, Wood Dryden's a reporter and all he does is take potshots."

"There we agree, though I have never met the man. He treats journalism like a playground, running about knocking children over. The *Examiner* is a gutter sheet. My readers expect more of me than hyperbole. They expect the truth. Remind me. What precisely was the umpire's crime, other than performing his duties?"

"He's blind. Weak in the head."

"For the life of me, no man adjudicates base ball unless he is weak in the head. Or, has a gun to it."

"You'll never see any Tom, Dick or Harry plunk down four bits to watch an ump. You're the only one who's ever defended one. Takes all kinds. Most folks would pay four bits to watch Brewster hang by the balls. That's the truth. C'mon, I'd like to see you writ that down and put it in your pisspaper."

"I accept your challenge." She doesn't bristle at his language. She takes out her pen and notebook. "Lend me your chest." She scribbles a sentence using the muscles beneath his shirt for a firm surface. Her touch is Sybil-like. His eye twitches.

Her breath smells of gum. He wonders if she would resist him. Casey's yet to meet one gum-chewing girl who doesn't love an honest-to-god base ball hero except those who are society prudes. Nellie Bly's only a partial prude, he can tell by her touch. Deep down she's lewd and vulgar, filthy enough to take one or two puffs from a cigarette.

The hardness he lost aboard the hoodoo returns. For the first time since sunset April 20, 1888 his bat has that spark. How long has it been since he wasted Rex Gallagher's painful wad on a girl worthwhile?

"I have it on high authority that you know something that can lead me to him," she says.

"Lead you to who?"

"Is your mind elsewhere? The umpire. Why do you think I am here?"

Nellie Bly *is* a tease, he's sure now, and she's the lucky charm he's been awaiting, the medicine no doc prescribes. She's the meaningful shit he's been waiting to take.

"C'mon inside," Casey says. "I'll tell you everything there is to know."

She at last takes his arm. "I will accompany you against my better judgment. You must promise no histrionics. You were correct about my escort positioned on Strawberry Hill. He will be riding my way the second I step from sight."

Casey detects the quiver in her voice. Girls lie expertly about their age, but they can never lie about their virtue.

"No girl needs an escort when I'm around." He leads her into the frescoed drawing room. Hope lifts a quizzical ear and follows with exactness. Casey touches his forehead. "The Ump will have a scar here, that much I know."

"I know that much as well," Nellie Bly says. "Never has there been such an outbreak of male instinct when Walter Brewster was speared face first into the dirt. It took the united forces of the other players to detach Mr. Reliable Jake, or the umpire might be dead."

"I saved his sissy life."

"Oh, the crosses you bear."

Then, Casey hears Nellie Bly catch her breath. For no reason, she lets out a little cry of surprise, as if she has just now remembered that she has a million bucks hiding in her saddlebags.

"You OK?" Casey says.

"My stars," she says. "It was right in front of my eyes all this time." She loses her breath again as if she's fallen into spinning, icy water. Her gum falls to the floor. "His scar. I must leave this instant."

Her eyes go large and her face turns white. Her legs buckle. Casey catches her. She's as light as a speck. "Easy, Miss Bly." She isn't faking.

"My dear Lord," she says. "He is much more than my letter writer. I know where he is. The umpire. I know where he is at this precise second."

"Brewster?"

"The Marine Hospital that Houses Crazy Seamen."

"The bughouse? Makes sense. Where else would he be?"

"He is with his dear mother. I must leave. Thank you, Mr. Casey, you have been of great service."

"Sit down, Miss Bly. Let me get you some lemonade. I squeezed it myself this morning. I'll sweeten it, you need a pick-me-up."

"I really must go. He confessed who he was to my face"

"Who?"

"The umpire. I did not believe him. He is such an odd man, but I am the fool."

"You visited The Ump in the bughouse?"

"He confessed in Judge Gold's chambers. I thought it too preposterous to listen. I don't know why, he always tells the truth." She mumbles the names Honest John Gaffney and Dick Higham. "They are one in the same. I figured that out but the other truth escaped me. The important truth. He had that scar from Day One, the day I set sail around the world. I am not fit to be a reporter."

"C'mon. You're making no sense."

"Mr. Ponsonby is Mr. Brewster."

"Who's Ponsonby?"

"The typesetter. My letter writer. My escort."

Casey scoffs. "Your escort's on Strawberry Hill."

"Claude Ponsonby is Walter Brewster. He confessed, but I did not listen."

"You're not well. Squishing up everyone's names."

"He always said that pill bugs are underfoot if only we bother to lift a rock."

"Pill bugs? All I know is you're white as a termite."

She pinches her cheeks to make them red. Casey keeps ahold of her sleek arm. He lets her go outside for air, but he won't let her get on her horse. "I don't know about Gaffney and Higham and those clown umpires clambering about in your head, but if the bunghole Brewster's in the madhouse, he's not going anywhere. He'll be there tomorrow."

Casey's eye twitches. Then his sphincter. Why does he always wind up with nutty girls? "You're not going anywhere. C'mon, you're in a state. A fragile state. I'll get you a lemonade. Or, a ginger ale with kick."

"Mr. Brewster left me at Cap Anson's stoop in Chicago. He knew Mr. Anson would recognize him."

Casey laughs. "The Ump's your escort? C'mon, that's impossible. That's a good one. You're out of sorts, dazed just as he was that April day. I like girl reporters, they have quite an imagination. C'mon. We'll go inside. Put on the feedbag. I won't let you shove off until you're up to snuff. I'll ride alongside you to the bughouse. Casey will be your escort. A real escort, not an imaginary one. Mighty Casey is at your service."

Abbott: "You throw the ball to first base."
Costello: "Then who gets it?"
Abbott: "Naturally."

February 9, 1890, 10:47 a.m.
It's a Sunday

CHAPTER TWENTY-ONE

one year and two hundred ninety-five days after the strikeout

Alone with Casey inside his mansion, Nellie Bly is less apprehensive than she ought to be. She's embarrassed for overlooking the umpire in plain sight. She feels like a simpleton who pulled the wool over her own eyes. A stunt girl as her critics suggest and incapable of rudimentary journalism. She doesn't fear Casey, she fears that little Nellies everywhere will be ashamed to be her namesakes.

Only slowly, she begins to fear for her safety. And yet, she feels odd relief that her dear escort has chosen to take a day off for the first time. He's gone to visit his mother at The Marine Hospital that Houses Crazy Seamen. Just when she at last needs him, she's grateful that Claude Ponsonby—the umpire Walter Brewster—is safe. Knowing that gives her some serenity in the face of vulnerability.

Yesterday they had attempted to take a stroll together. At first he walked fast and waited on her. Then he walked so slowly that she waited on him. He couldn't get himself synchronized. Today he had invited her to come along to meet his mother; he said Nellie Bly's presence would brighten an old lady's day and perhaps spur the construction of the Great Asylum for the Insane over by the Lick paper mill in Agnews. Nellie Bly chose to relax at The Palace Hotel instead, free of her barnacle. He didn't trust her to stay put, and so he went to the hotel desk and came back with a borrowed revolver to tuck into her valise. She accepted the firearm to get him on his way.

The minute her trusty escort rode out of sight she, too, decided to go for a ride. She steered her hired horse toward a hint of morning red breaking through the fog. Without Mr. Ponsonby along, she cantered at the perfect pace toward Golden Gate Park and when she came to the largest mansion on the outskirts she whispered a promise that she would stay outside. The revolver made her valise appear thick and clumsy and she moved it to the saddlebag.

Now she's inside Casey's manor house of redwood, unarmed and the bullseye of twitching stares from base ball's has-been and his evil she-dog. It's best that her escort is not along. Walter Brewster is poetry lore, a slice of Americana, who Casey would pummel, even murder and get away with it. She's America's most beloved girl. He will not dare touch her, though she wishes the revolver was in reach.

She feels stupid more than afraid. Fleetwood Walker had recognized Walter Brewster the instant they walked into the killer's jail cell. They tossed that horrible ball back and forth to taunt her with a game of mental fungus. When it came time to visit Cap Anson in Chicago, the umpire excused himself with a convenient chore. How would she ever explain away all of this to her readers. They will think her a village idiot.

Casey steps to the kitchen to get her a glass of lemonade. It's her chance to dash out the door to her hack, hop aboard, and gallop away. But Hope is a prison guard; the bitch stares with dull eyes and fails to wag her tail. Nellie Bly puts a fresh stick of gum in her mouth. She pets Hope. Still no wag. Though no growl either. Nellie Bly pities the emotionless animal.

"This will help you feel better," Casey says, handing Nellie Bly the glass. "What were you saying about the cheat Dick Higham and Honest John Gaffney and The Judge? Is The Ump in the madhouse, or were you delusional about that, too?"

She says nothing. She's still trying to come to grips with her revelation.

"The color has returned to your cheeks. I think you're yourself again. Drink up and I'll give you the grand tour."

"Who can imagine why a bachelor needs all of this."

"I've done alright. I'd have a telephone, but I'm too far out in the countryside. No place is more isolated. Sacramento politicians should've given me a house in Nob Hill where I could've phoned anyone I pleased."

Casey repeats "Nob Hill" and, without permission, takes her hand and leads her toward the stairs. Dozens of base ball bats litter each room. She keeps her resistance light-hearted. "I traveled the world without a gun. Will I need Smith and Wesson along?"

"San Francisco's less hoity-toity than New York, but girls survive me without munitions."

"Be that as it may, I will remain downstairs. I was not long enough in France to acquire French morals."

"I'd've been to Paris except for the spastic Ump." Casey takes a plum from a bowl, puts it whole in his mouth. She puts her lemonade glass down and pulls a notebook from her valise. She scribbles some nonsense to calm her scrambled mind.

"What are you writing about me?" Casey says with his mouth full of purple.

She doesn't answer. She turns her attention to a vase of roses on the piano, buries her nose in them. "The perfume is stronger here than in the east. On my ride, I saw them in great flocks."

"Roses are weeds in California, they grow thick in the yards of the poor. C'mon, I've got flowers galore upstairs that match the colors of your eyes."

"Not until my escort arrives any minute."

"You said your escort is The Ump Brewster and you said Brewster's in the nuthouse. Remember?"

"His mother's locked away. He's quite sane and able and positioned on Strawberry Hill."

"He ain't coming. He's let you down. He lacks all courage, which proves he is The Ump, just like you said." Casey uses his tongue to move the plum pit around in his mouth. "Why do you keep bringing up that dolt? Have you and he—reconnoitered?"

His question deserves no answer.

"If he had courage, he'd never let you come alone."

"He always appears when I need him."

"What if he barges through the door right now? What will he do?"

"There is more to men than bravado and bare knuckles."

"The Ump's dumb, but he's smart enough to be swigging courage in a groggery by now. If he sets foot in here uninvited, I'll drag you upstairs by the ankles. He won't do a thing."

"Are you trying to frighten me?"

"Do you want to be frightened? Do you want me to scare the bejesus out of you?" Casey laughs. "Some girls like to be scared. C'mon I'll give you the nickel tour. I can have the girls I want, I don't force nobody."

She takes a seat on the piano stool, dangles her pen between her lips, plays a measure to stall. A measure she remembers from childhood. She feels nine again, plotting against the war hero. Casey is an athlete, far more capable than the limping Jack Ford. She stops playing and pouts as if the piano requires tuning. A moment to think. She has yet met a man she couldn't handle. The grandfather clock sounds the time. Eleven. The fog may never burn off. She wants to disappear into it, but the sheepdog will track her.

"Is that a base ball bat?" she says. "I've never gripped one. May I?"

At first she imagines it to be a weapon, but it will lend no aid. Casey's a lion of a man, but lions have thorns in their paws. Her best chance is to turn what he wants against him. She smiles. If he thinks her willing, he will woo and plead. She leans the bat handle on her breast while she scribbles in her notebook. Another stall to clear her mind and ready herself for the challenge at hand.

"I will write a long yarn about you and your bats. I thought they had all been burned in a bonfire."

"Just the one. Rex Gallagher's at the bottom of the Bay—but he's surfacing now."

"Never think about the ocean floor. It gives me the shivers. A million men must be down there. Why is this bat branded .388 on the side?"

"My portion of hits. That bat won the Niners our last banner."

"You hit the ball less than half the time? I was under the impression that you had more luck than that."

"It ain't luck."

"I suppose you have umpires to blame."

"Saying strike is easier than hitting one."

"Excuses, excuses. I must negotiate with inept editors everyday, and yet all of my items are published on the front page."

"Wouldya try it? Take a swing."

She runs her hands along the bat's grain, smiles more lies into Casey's eyes, then lofts it to rest on her shoulder. "Such heft, I had no idea."

Casey rakes red hair with his left hand. "C'mon, weighs no more than a dozen apples. It isn't kiln-dried like Flynn's and Blake's, it was seasoned for two years."

He circles behind to begin an uninvited lesson. His breath is warm on her neck as he reaches around. The naked plum pit slobbers his speech. "I'm strong enough to swing a sequoia." She feels his spittle.

He reverses her grip, puts her right hand above the left on the bat handle. "You're right-handed, I noticed you writing. I notice lots of things."

"Girls are a science of yours? I will alert the Royal Society."

"I stopped Old Reliable Jake from killing your Brewster. He owes me his life. If you're kissy with him, then you owe me too."

"The bat handle is rough as a horned lizard," she says. "Holding it is an act of pure devilry."

"Holding *you* is an act of pure devilry." Casey slides her top hand up the grain to where the barrel spreads fat, then slides it back. "Hitting's about fast hands with a soft wrist cock. My wrists go soft when there's nothing else soft on me. That's the secret." He whispers hot breath into her left ear. "More care's been given to my bat than to any wood that has ever been shaved. Free of knots and imperfections. Oriental finish, lathe polished. The grain spirals down to the handle."

"You are talking filth."

"You enjoy it. You're that type." He slides her hand up and down in an untoward way. The breath from his nose is warmer than it was even seconds ago. "I've a stereoscope upstairs with filthy pictures."

She stalls. "You must wait until dark. I have a reputation to protect."

"Newspaper girls have no reputation. You're a stunt girl. I look forward to your stunts."

"I must confess a truth about me that has gone unreported. I once testified in a courtroom that my stepfather dragged me into a mop closet." She has never told anyone that, only Mr. Ponsonby—Mr. Brewster. Her mind remains scrambled. She's still coming to grips. Nothing is as it seems. She prays that raw honesty will make her seem human to Casey and slow him down a step. He still has ahold of her from the backside. Her honesty will force him to back away from what he has planned. Her honesty will make Casey someone he is not.

"I prefer a girl who knows the seamy side of life. I prefer a girl with pluck."

"I lied to the magistrate to win my mother's divorce." Her back to Casey makes it easier to speak the truth. "Jack Ford never caught me. No one has. It behooves me to tell you, to give you a chance to do what is right."

"I always do what is right." Casey laughs in her ear. "C'mon, how old are you?"

She tells the truth. "Twenty-five."

He pulls her tighter. "Why do old maids say they're unspoiled? Twenty-six is the oldest nymph I ever had."

"I had a million opportunities to be married, but the eighteen nineties arrived while I was abroad."

"A mop closet? Christ. C'mon, you're like a pitcher who throws at my head to get me off-balance." Casey calls his she-dog to his side, scratches her ears, keeps Nellie Bly's back tight to him with his one arm. "We'll let Hope decide." The dog at last wags her tail. "See, Hope knows you're a gum-chewer. Gum chewing is a telltale sign, like novels on Sundays. There's no shame. All girls want it from mighty Casey. Same ole, same ole."

"Be that as it may, we must all control our appetites." She motions to the dog. "Distance ourselves from the animals."

"I think you reconnoiter with any swinging dick who gives you something to write about."

"I will write endlessly about what happens here."

"Nobody'll believe a word. Not even rat-turd New Yorkers. What kind of girl finds herself unescorted to Casey's mansion? You came alone and unannounced; you knew what you came for."

"I will give you a scratch on the cheek so they will believe me. The world will know. I promise."

"C'mon, no newspaper publishes smut."

"Joseph Pulitzer's newspapers do."

Casey laughs. "You're probably right about that. He's a smart old Jew. He must've caught you a time or two."

"He will commission an illustration. I have a hidden mole, the world will know. Your deed will fill columns. It will be as if Buffalo Bill defamed Annie Oakley. The presses will run out of paper. The earth will run out of trees. You will fall even lower in public opinion."

His one arm loosens as he tries to view more of her face and she seizes the slack to escape.

"C'mon. I never employ force. Never have, never will. Never once, I toldya."

"Good. I receive too much mail as it is."

Nellie Bly's won. She feels giddiness in the way that hiding in the hamper was exhilarating. "Base ball athletes are ruffians in general. Thank my stars you are better than that."

"Sure I am. I wouldn't want you if you didn't want me."

She feels a nine-year-old's victory. Her face flushes. She clings to the bat. Her eyes come alive, she can feel them sparkle.

"Girls appear in my garden every night. You saw, sometimes there are two or three. I don't want them. I shoo them away, but they come back. I bat .999 with girls I want. The only girls who don't want me are society prudes and goody two-shoes. You'll come around. If not, you'll have regrets."

She laughs. "I can live with regrets."

"I can't. Nope. Been trying for two years. Regrets for swinging at Strike Three, which shoulda been ball three. C'mon, let's shoot pool."

She smooths her riding skirts and makes light. "I told you, I have yet shot pool with any man."

Casey laughs and laughs. "Christ you're funny. I'm talking about billiards. I'm patient. Letting you play out your game. Got all day, all night. Extra innings. Come and see my table. Cost a fortune. Cost more to have it shipped."

Casey takes the bat from her, flips it one-handed to the fat end, then flips it again to grip the handle, puts it over his shoulder as if it weighs no more than a chopstick. "Don't forget your lemonade," he says. "I can squeeze juice from the hardest lemon. I can squeeze love from any dry old doe." His eyelid spasms. He laughs when she notices.

The pool room is small and smells like stale smoke. "I prefer piano," she says.

"Nope. I've had it up to here with music." He raises his right hand over his head. He winces in pain and grabs his shoulder. "That's Sibyl's piano. The pool table's mine."

The table is enormous, like a giant table in *Gulliver's Travels*. Casey hands Nellie Bly a cue. He circles around her. "Time for another lesson." His hot breath is in her ear again. "I knew you had some slugger in you when you rode up astride. I wouldn't want one that wasn't a slugger."

She steps quickly from his reach. Casey holds his arms wide. "See. I'm safe. Upstairs safe." He laughs. "C'mon. Relax, wouldya? Girls dream of being shipwrecked with mighty Casey."

"Please, I asked you not to speak of the seafloor."

"A feather bed is what I had in mind."

"Then, it will be one more strikeout for you." She meant it as another joke but it cuts deep. For the first time, Casey's expression turns mean. The cue in her hand is lighter than a bat, no weapon at all.

"Pool ain't my strong suit," he says, sucking his plum pit, using poor grammar and mixing metaphors. She can feel his breath from a distance. His breath is like a dragon's. "Pool's all finesse. Pool's about angles. I like games of raw force. Pool and piano ain't my style. Nope."

Her hack neighs outside. "My escort has arrived," she says, but they both know he has not. She hears begging in her voice.

Casey laughs. "Walter Brewster hisself?"

"Himself."

She starts for the door. Casey catches her in three steps, turns her by the shoulders to face him, grabs her about the collar. "Let's have a look-see." He rips down the front of her pale blue dress with rapid wrists. One instant she's proper, the next she's half naked. Another person altogether. He winces, grabs his shoulder. When the pain subsides, he stands looking, rakes his hair with his left hand.

"There ain't no mole. There's no room on those bubs."

Hope comes out of her curl to stand. Nellie Bly breaks the cue over Casey's head. He laughs. "Christ." He lets her take up a bat. She chops it at him. She prays it's a magic bat, as strong as the vortex of a waterfall, but he catches the barrel and twists it one-handed from her grip.

He lifts her without effort. She spits gum in his face. He walks her out of the pool room to the piano and drops her rear on the keys. It doesn't hurt, all her clothing is folded about her waist, but a tremendous musical chord shakes the mansion. Petals fall from the vase of roses.

"Lucky I didn't waste my viz on no hoodoo. I've got viz up to my eyeballs. If you're unspoiled like you say, well then, we'll both be at the top of our game."

Nellie Bly screams only once. It's futile inside a hundred acres.

"The pinnacle of our game." Hope wags as Casey reaches into her skirts for her underthings but she clamps her legs. He carries her back to the pool table. It's smaller than it was a minute ago.

She swings wildly, missing his face. She swings at air until she gives up in exhuastion. She feels her first tears since Mr. Ponsonby removed the spark from her eye aboard the train west. These are her first tears of true emotion in years. Since her Daddy died.

"Please, I will not write a word."

"C'mon, time we circled those sandbags."

He sets her prone on green felt. The pool table shrinks more. She hears clacking as she kicks around the balls. She kicks him in the jaw as he climbs onto the tiny table. He laughs "Christ a'mighty," and climbs off. He racks the balls. She hears thunder, an impossibility in San Francisco's winter. It's the break between her legs.

"The shit-house beast," she says tearful.

"Right as rain," Casey says. "Right as rain." His speech is otherworldly. He spits the plum pit from his mouth. "Christ." He finds the pit on the felt and puts it back. "Hope, stay here," he says and he leaves her for a while and goes upstairs. She doesn't know how long.

Nellie Bly is alone aboard an empty train. She longs for the next destination, longs for a platform with loved ones waiting. Platform after platform is empty.

He returns larger with his size thirteen steel-plated spikes on his feet. The table shrinks smaller. "I outweigh you a buck fifty, a buck seventy," he says, and he sprawls over her with every ounce of advantage until it's impossible to breathe.

"Time to go to town." He inhales her scent and whispers, "Mighty Casey, mighty, mighty Casey."

Walter boards and sits across from her and tells her about quail hunting with his father. He has never mentioned his father before, only his mother. He describes how quail are sometimes merely wounded by shotgun and the humane way to put them out of their misery is to suffocate them by squeezing the air from their breasts. He says he sometimes wonders if he could have squeezed the colic out of his baby sister, but her bouts of crying ended once their father left.

"You didn't fall from the same tree as that hoodoo. It's me and you who are one in the same." Casey thrusts.

Walter leaves to get her a bun and a cup of coffee. She goes looking for him. She steps between cars. The roar of the train turns hollow as it crosses a high trestle. "Where are you?" she cries into the cry of escaping steam.

"Mighty Casey. Mighty, mighty Casey."

The only light is the red glow of a warning lantern. She reaches to smooth her skirts, but she has no skirts. She runs to her berth and falls asleep, naked. Walter climbs down from where he is pretending to sleep. She kisses him as the train jostles through the endless tunnel. She cries happy tears. Going around the world with Walter is the happiest time of her life.

"Do you fear dying?" she asks Walter.

"I'll gladly die saving you, so that my life will have meant something. I love you Lizzie."

"I despise Lizzie," she says.

She cries aloud. "Where are you?" She squirms, she turns her head away from sewage breath. "Where are you when I need you?"

"I'm right here, Joy Spot," Casey says. "I toldya. Lucky you. There are so few real men left." The breath of his nostrils is smokestack smoke. Nellie Bly closes her eyes against his sparks. "Lizzie, Lizzie, Lizzie," Casey says as he motions like a train building speed.

When it's over, she is face up on green felt and naked, gasping for air. Casey is back on his feet with her riding skirts in his hands. He's hard and proud, sucking the pit. He spits it to the floor for Hope to sniff. Hope chews it like a bone, but Casey removes it from the dog's slobber and puts it back in his own mouth.

He rolls a billiard ball between her legs; it rolls all the way to the spent part of her spirit. She can feel the cold, hear the one clack, as it strikes another ball about the pocket of her thighs.

"Strike three," he says. "Now you know how I felt that day. A little bit."

He adds poppy syrup to her lemonade and drinks it. Spits the pit into the empty glass. "Lucky I'm not drunk. I get fighty drunk." He removes his spikes. "There's green lint in your belly button." He removes it. "It's me and you who are one in the same. Poetry and all. That's right, I know a poem about you, too," he says and he recites it to her.

> *"Nelly Bly! Nelly Bly! Bring the broom along,*
> *We'll sweep the kitchen clean, my dear,*
> *And have a little song.*
> *Poke the wood, my lady love*
> *And make the fire burn,*
> *And while I take the banjo down,*
> *Just give the mush a turn."*

Elizabeth Jane Cochran has nothing to hold onto. Casey gives her half of the broken cue. She hugs it and whimpers for Walter.

"Life is a tragedy full of joy."—Bernard Malamud

December 18, 1955, 10:39 p.m.
It's just another Sunday night in front of the TV

CHAPTER TWENTY-TWO

sixty-seven years after the strikeout

W*hat's My Line* is on Channel Two. The Judge snores in his chair, the one with the broken spring, his half-eaten Swansons cold by the phone on the end table. Food is touching other food. Walter's across the way on the chesterfield, awake with eyes closed. He watches TV the way he listens to the Giants on the radio. Russ Hodges, 570 on the dial. Walter's hand moves involuntarily. He squeezes a phantom baseball. The real one's buried with Nellie Bly in Woodlawn Cemetery.

The *What's My Line* contestant is a young, female lighthouse keeper. Walter opens his eyes. He envies her; he envies her line of work. His eyes stay open for Geritol, because the horizontal lines stop flickering for commercials.

By some miracle, the flicker stays at bay when the face of the host John Daly returns to fill the screen. Then, a wide shot of Fred Allen, Arlene Francis, and Dorothy Kilgallen. They're blindfolded. "Will you come in mystery challenger and sign in please," Daly says.

A tall, fat, feeble man limps on stage, a baseball bat over his shoulder and an ancient Niners cap balances aboard a shock of white hair. The studio audience claps politely. It doesn't recognize him as he shuffles to the chalkboard, but erupts into gasps when he scribbles C*A*SE*Y* in huge, shaky letters. He doffs his cap and the audience roars.

A dormant anger bubbles up in Walter. He hits The Judge with a *Sports Illustrated,* thrown all the way from the chesterfield. "Now, Walter," The Judge says trying to wake up. "Now, Walter, that's just terrific."

Walter shushes and points to the screen where there's a smile beneath the blindfold of Arlene Francis. "Nobody's ever received applause like that—except Marilyn Monroe," she says.

"Are you in the theatrical field?" Fred Allen says.

"Nope." Casey makes no attempt to disguise his voice, his last interview was decades before radio.

"One down and nine to go," John Daly says.

"Never thought I'd see him on TV," The Judge says. "Lucky that Fleet's not still living here, he'd have a heart attack."

Fleet Walker moved in with the umpires when Arabella died of cancer at thirty-two. He had the house at 432 Lake Laberge Boulevard to himself for a year while Walter and The Judge were in the Yukon after the strikeout's 10th anniversary. When Walter and The Judge returned, Fleet and The Judge argued about this, that, and the other, about the Pygmy Ota Benga in the City Zoo, about the first black heavyweight champ Jack Johnson. They agreed about Jim Crow but they argued about everything else; they argued about the Yellow Kid in the color comics. Fleet got furious when the fiftieth anniversary of the Emancipation Proclamation went unmentioned by the press in 1913. When the twenty-fifth anniversary of the strikeout rolled around four months later, reporters wrote on and on.

Fleet stewed and stewed about that. "I hate living with two white guys," he said. A few days later he said, "Umpires are supposed to make order out of chaos."

"That's the job of the Almighty," The Judge said.

Fleet slammed the door for the last time. "I can't stand living with you two. I'd rather live with Martians."

Fleet was in the newspapers a few years later. He learned how to talk dastardly to reporters, how to say things to get their attention. He told them he was the black Moses appointed by God to lead the Negroes out of bondage.

The papers ate it up, but Fleet never went to Africa. He moved to Cadiz, Ohio, ran an opera house where the coloreds sat in peanut heaven. Got rich. On the December before he died, he sent a Christmas card to 432 Lake Laberge Boulevard. On the front it said, "Hoping you the best this season." Inside he wrote, "Because umpires sure do have ass-shit summers."

Life is odd. Walter and The Judge froze their butts off moiling for gold in the Yukon but never even caught a cold. Pneumonia got Fleet on a warm day in May. He was sixty-seven.

There was endless door knocking and phone ringing on the strikeout's fiftieth anniversary in 1938 even after Babe Ruth retired and Europe geared up for another war. The Judge was eighty-six and spry and up to the task. He answered the phone. He opened the door in his poorhouse duds. He told reporters he was Judge Gold, and when they didn't recognize the name he said Honest John Gaffney and then he said Dick Higham, but the hotshots didn't know any of those names. They hadn't done a lick of research.

The Judge hollered at them, "I'm done talking to mugwumps. I'd rather have a sharp stick in the eye." Then he'd slam the phone or the door.

"Miss Kilgallen," John Daly says from the TV.

"Are you in the literature field?" she asks.

"They'll never guess," The Judge says. "Casey sounds like any old codger. I thought he would sound different."

"He *looks* different," Walter says. "Smaller, even though he's obese."

Daly negotiates the fat folds in Casey's neck to whisper in his ear. "I was once well-versed in poetry," Casey says. The audience laughs.

"You sound more like a boxer than a poet," Dorothy Kilgallen says. "Back when boys fought bare-fisted."

"C'mon. I'm a lulu, I'm a cake." The audience laughs. Walter's anger simmers like a pressure cooker.

"Two down and eight to go. Mr. Cerf."

"Are you an athlete?" Bennett Cerf says, and the audience cheers. "Were you ever with one of the New York teams?"

"Nope. Could've jumped east, could've made Washington first in war, first in peace *and* first in the American League."

The audience laughs at the pilfered line. "Three down and seven to go."

"C'mon. Good thing you bums get ten strikes in this blame game," Casey says.

"He wants them to guess who he is," The Judge says. "He's afraid he's been forgotten like the rest of us."

Tears of memory stream down Walter's face. If the baseball he squeezes were real, he'd throw it through the TV screen.

"Now, Walter, let's change channels. You haven't bubbled up like this in years."

"I bubble up like this every week. What do you think I do Fridays when I visit her at Woodlawn?"

Arlene Francis never asks a question. Casey's face goes as white as his hair. His collapse to the floor jolts the TV lines back to a flicker.

"Fix the rabbit ears, fix the knobs," The Judge demands, but there's nothing on the screen except a test pattern and the words **Please Stand By**. Life plays out like a flickering channel. No matter what knobs are turned, no matter how the angle of the rabbit ears are rearranged, all channels flicker and then they go off the air.

"Guess we'll learn what happened the old-fashioned way," The Judge says. "We'll read about it in the papers."

Walter wipes his cheeks and helps The Judge to his feet. They shuffle away to the bathroom. Walter stands behind his feeble friend at the sink. He's there to catch The Judge in case he falls. The Judge puts his teeth in a glass. Over The Judge's shoulder, Walter sees himself in the mirror. His face is camouflaged in tiny veins that cover his cheeks in a purple spider web. He still has his own teeth, he can feel the wiggle of his incisors at the touch of his tongue. Beneath the scar on his forehead are red eyes. Red like his father's were the evening he walked out. Red like that sky. It's been years since he last saw Papa's reflection in himself.

Walter last heard from his sister Annie Katharine when she was in Florida, about the time Pulitzer and Hearst started the Spanish-American War to sell papers. Walter still gets nauseated at the clang of cow bells, or a screaming baby. They invented a vaccine for polio two years ago, but babies will forever scream with the colic.

The Judge spits Colgate into the sink. "A woman is only a woman, but a good cigar is a smoke." He quotes Rudyard Kipling whenever he suspects Walter is thinking about Nellie Bly.

Walter escorts The Judge to bed and continues in an odd, ancient gait to his room down the hall, the room where he wages nightly war against regrets. If only he'd never declared two strikes on Casey. If only he'd escorted her to Casey's mansion. She said that she died partly on the green felt. She died for good thirty-two years later of pneumonia, two years before Fleet. It was a Friday, the time of death was 7:37 p.m. precisely. Before TV. Before radio. Newspapers reigned like trains, their gradual declines about to begin.

She was 57. All the slowly dying newspapers said she was 56 or 55 or 54. Walter was bedside at St. Mark's Hospital. He hadn't seen her since she was 25 on that Sunday morning when he left her at the Palace Hotel to visit Moms in The Marine Hospital that Houses Crazy Seamen. He left Nellie Bly with a revolver, but it wasn't enough.

It was the worst call of his life.

Months later, Moms was moved to the Great Asylum for the Insane over by the Lick paper mill in Agnews. It cost $750,000 to build only to collapse in the San Francisco earthquake of 1906. Walter's mother's in a mass grave with 116 others. Nellie Bly sent Walter her condolences. She was a young widow by then, she never remarried.

She loathed May-December relationships and Walter found it curious when she married industrialist Robert Seaman in 1895. The Judge said that it was chemistry. "He is stinking rich and she's pretty, you know what."

Walter didn't know what; he didn't know what stinking rich meant because rich people usually smell better than poor people. He read up on it at the library. A long time ago, rich Europeans paid to be buried inside the cathedrals so that they could be closer to God. Their corpses started stinking, and that's why they're called the stinking rich.

There were rumors in 1898 that she was coming out of retirement to find Jayson Kelley, the *New York Journal* reporter who was accused of fabricating his own death aboard the USS Maine. But they dredged up Kelley's body from Havana Bay and there was no one left for her to find.

Walter saw her picture in society columns, they wrote on and on about Mrs. Seaman. She was trapped in a joyless marriage. She was forty-two years younger than her husband and they had no children. She was often seen dining at Delmonico's without him.

When Robert Seaman died, Nellie Bly Seaman took over his businesses, patented an invention, and wrote a novel about a young woman with a snake-charming smile who turned down multiple proposals from a handsome, shy man. Walter never reads fiction, but he read her novel three times. He didn't understand it. The pages were filled with colloquialisms. Literary critics hated it, they said her characters were flat and forced into improbable incidents.

She at long last returned to journalism in 1920 to be the first woman to witness an electrocution at Sing Sing. The warden let her sit in the chair. The straps were unpleasant, she wrote, but it was her duty to tell her readers what the murdering rapist Gordon Hamby would suffer when he was jolted with ten cents of current.

Two years later, she was dead, eulogy at the Church of Ascension by the Reverend Percy Stickney, attended by the famous, the movers and shakers, the stinking rich, burial at Woodlawn. Walter wasn't there for the eulogy or burial; he wasn't a mover or shaker, but he was the only one bedside at St. Mark's.

She sent for him, the first time he'd seen her since that Sunday in 1890. Pneumonia, the doc said, she had the same gaunt face as Mouse Mathews when Walter last saw the pitcher penniless in Baltimore. Walter squeezed the baseball, the last baseball Mouse Mathews ever threw, as Nellie Bly told him everything about that day in Casey's mansion. "The pool table was as tiny as a postage stamp," she said over and over until Walter was overwhelmed with shame. Shame for leaving her undefended. Shame for letting her down.

When she saw his shame, she tried to reassure him. "You saved me," she said. "You were in my heart and that saved me."

"My duty was to protect you—and you protected me. You knew that I was the umpire and never wrote a word about it."

"I left that stunt to Wood Dryden."

Walter started to sob because he didn't deserve to be forgiven. Nellie Bly told him to lie down with her on the hospital bed. She took his hand and died as he wept. Love, he decided, comes with the pain of letting loved ones down.

Walter's father used to say, "God is great, God is good" at the meal table, but the part about being good is not obvious. God is a channel that flickers. God is three words on the screen that say, "Please stand by." God is a borderline pitch. Too close to call. Walter kissed Nellie Bly's cheek. He put the baseball in her hands and left without telling the nurses she was gone. He took French leave.

For a moment, Walter is unsure if *What's My Line* has been a dream. He was awake all night. He'd fallen asleep minutes before the morning paper crashes into the screen door. The milkman rarely wakes Walter with his bottles, it's always the *Herald Tribune* with Red Smith's column deep inside.

The newspaper kid has a better arm than Don Newcombe. Newspapers slap-land on icy cement porches on down Lake Laberge Boulevard each morning like the slow chug of a doubleheader train escaping inertia. Walter sits up in bed and pain rolls from his lower back to his left hip. Nights are emotionally painful. Mornings are physically painful. He shuffles down the hall past The Judge's snoring. The headline's big enough to read through the screen door.

Mighty Casey
Strikes Out
For All Eternity

"All eternity is redundant," Walter mumbles as he rescues the newspaper from the cold and guides himself back inside by the porch railing. From his seat at the kitchen table he takes ahold of the magnifying glass with the shaky grip Casey had last night on a stick of chalk.

> The slugger made immortal by a poetic Strike Three died on live television Sunday. He was 97.

Walter skims for his own name and is delighted he doesn't see it.

> Born July 4, 1858, twelve pounds...one of the last of a generation that saw the world on horseback...raised in an orphanage...among the first class of players elected to the Hall of Fame in 1936 with Ty Cobb, Walter Johnson, Babe Ruth, Christy Mathewson and Honus Wagner, who died five days ago at 81... Casey will always be the one Hall of Famer never to have played Major League Baseball...

Mouse Mathews never got to 300 wins and he never got to Cooperstown. He's the winningest pitcher not in the Hall of Fame.

> Casey retired in 1890 when the Mudville Niners sold his contract for a dollar...he lost his personal fortune wagering on dog fights and investments in ginger beer...memorial service at Yankee Stadium, to be flown to San Francisco for burial in his goldenrod jersey and polka-dot stockings...

The phone explodes next to the broken-spring chair. Walter always gives callers a chance to change their minds, but when the ring goes off a second time he prevents it from exploding a third.

"Mr. Brewster, please. Long distance." A reporter's voice, he's mundane, in no hurry, sounds like one of those war pilots who fly for TWA. "Is this New York? Yukon 3-2657?"

"It ain't Sam McGee."

"Is this Walter Brewster?"

"Gone fishing." Somewhere, somehow, Walter's learned to lie. "The Adirondack."

"In winter? At his age? When do you expect him?"

"Take a message? Wait, I need a pencil." Walter lets expensive seconds tick by to get the reporter antsy. "Damn, I can never find a pencil."

"J. Roy Stockton, *St. Louis Post-Dispatch*. Looking for a statement. About Casey. Passed last night, out like a light, did you see Dorothy Kilgallen's face?"

"We knock off early most nights. Knock off means go to sleep."

"I can't find anyone who knew Casey back when, nobody left. Hell, I'm an old-timer, but born after the strikeout. Been a sportswriter forty-some years, never met a soul who saw Casey at the bat."

Walter's end is quiet.

"Need a quote, something like 'He was better than Ruth,' 'loved by all,' blah, blah, don't want to put words in anybody's mouth. Don't say he was better than Musial, readers in St. Louis won't cotton to that."

"I thought Casey was dead already."

J. Roy Stockton laughs. "Everyone on the sports desk said the same, but there he was on TV. Last of the greats. None left."

"Cobb."

"Say, you're right. Guess I'll call down to Georgia. They go in threes, you know. Singers. Politicians. Movie stars. They all drop in threes."

"Like strikes at the knees."

"Honus Wagner and Casey make two in a week. Cobb may be next. Nobody bigger than Casey has died in 1955."

"Einstein," Walter says. "He deserves a poem but nobody wrote one."

Stockton laughs. "You're a hoot. I wanted to call last night, too late back east by the time I found a number."

"Pretty early back there now."

"Sure it's early, wife got frosty when I crawled out of bed, but Casey's a big deal. A prince of a man, unlike the S.O.B. Cobb. I wanted to reach Brewster before he got sick of calls from the TV and radio guys. Frigging broadcasters have made life miserable. Walter Brewster's an old newspaperman himself."

"Typesetter."

"That so? Typesetters will one day be long gone. There will always be reporters. The public needs someone to hate."

"Umpires."

"Two hopeless lines of work," Stockton says.

"Typesetters have peace and quiet. They mind their *p*'s and *q*'s."

"Is that where that saying comes from? Peace and quiet?"

The Judge's holler echoes from his room. "Are you off the damn phone?"

"Silver bells to you, too," Walter hollers back.

"Whose that?" Stockton says over the phone.

"Honest John Gaffney."

"Who?"

"Dick Higham."

"Who are you?"

"Avocado Jones. Look at the time, I'd better be shoving off."

"I need to find Brewster, it's important."

"Look under a rock." Walter hangs up.

The Judge is on the pot. "You have the gronk again," Walter says. "I can tell by your tone."

The Judge strains with his eyes wide, they stare at Walter as if a stranger stepped into the bathroom. The Judge has lost most of his hair and most of his sense of humor. He's the last man on earth to have dundrearies. He feels poorly, and his temper flares hourly. Walter never loses patience, not even on Tuesdays at 10 o'clock when The Judge orders him to stand there holding the rabbit ears for *The $64,000 Question*. They don't get Channel Two very good.

The Judge hides himself with a *Life*. The magazine's cover is about the coming Jet Age. The death of trains. "I hope your legs are strong enough today to get off the pot by yourself," Walter says, but it's been some weeks since The Judge had one of those days. He gets smaller all the time, but he weighs enough to be a bother.

The Judge extends his hands straight out. Walter takes them and leans back, uses his weight to pull his friend upright. "Santa Cruz," The Judge says. He says Santa Cruz whenever Walter sees him with his pants down.

Walter's eleven or twelve years younger than The Judge, who will be 104 on New Year's. He's been singing Sinatra's *and if you should survive to a hundred and five*. He can whistle songs that date back to the Civil War, but he's already forgotten *What's My Line*.

The Judge stops singing. "Did you have that dream again?" His voice is a pickup over gravel, it got worse when he survived the pandemic. He never caught cold in the Yukon, but he's been coughing like Pulitzer since 1918. Each morning Walter stirs salt and iodine into warm water. The Judge gargles it on the toilet and spits between his legs, he likes salt and iodine better than the Listerine advertised on *The Perry Como Show*, 8 o'clock on Saturdays. Good reception on Channel Four.

They bought a TV after they missed Bobby Thompson's appearance on *Perry Como* the same night as the shot heard 'round the world. It doesn't take seventy-two days to get around the world—only an instant or two.

"Casey's gone." Walter says.

"Who? No shit," The Judge says. "The shit-house beast caught Casey?"

"Last night. Come to the kitchen, I'll read it to you."

The Judge moves faster than in some time, but Walter's in no hurry, he slices The Judge a piece of rhubarb pie, pours him a bowl of Sugar Frosted Flakes. Two teaspoons of sugar get sprinkled on the pie and three more on the cereal. The Judge says he has a sweet tooth, but it's the cereal that's sweet. Walter picks up the magnifying glass. Walter starts reading from the middle, The Judge never cares.

> Casey's exit ushered in the most disastrous decade in baseball, historians call it the lost decade of the 1890s. Attendance crumbled, three Major Leagues consolidated into one.
>
> No footage exists of Casey taking a swing, no newsreel will keep him forever young. Casey batted from the right side, but some old-timers swear it was from the left and a few believe he switched sides depending on the shadows.
>
> There remains a recording of DeWolf Hopper. He recited the poem 10,000 times on stage over 45 years before dying of a heart attack at 77.

"Each recital took five minutes and forty seconds," Walter says. "Precisely." He resumes reading.

> Earnest Thayer was paid $5 for writing the poem. He also died at 77.

"Thayer got trimmed like I did in Santa Cruz," The Judge says.

> Four known photos exist of Casey from the olden days. All are grainy; none show him in action. In one he holds a ten-thousand-dollar check, another has him reading the poem on a vaudeville stage alongside Hopper. A third is from a long-ball throwing contest the day of the strikeout and a fourth is squirreled away in the Hall of Fame archives. It's of the twelve-man championship team of 1887.
>
> Historians who have seen that photo say Casey, in his prime, holds the pennant in one hand and extends a middle finger with the other hand in a manner that explains why the photo was never made public.

"Bet you wished you kept that baseball," The Judge says. "Worth a fortune the second Casey hit the floor."

> Glacial statistics are all that remain of Casey, the only evidence that he took to the field at all.
>
> There is no way of knowing how he would fare against a modern pitcher like Warren Spahn. Cy Young's rookie season was 1890. Casey's last season was 1889, he never took another swing, not even in an old-timers' game.
>
> Where Casey ranks among the greats, how he compares to the legends, is left to the barroom. In the end, Casey's skill and talent matter little. Like Gunga Din, he will forever be remembered in verse.

The Judge smiles at the Rudyard Kipling reference. "Strike two was your *High Noon*." A matinee, two summers ago at The Roxy, when the Giants got rained out on the radio. The Giants were in a slump at the time, and The Judge had said few words in five days. The next day the Giants lost again on a Willie Mays' error. The Judge stayed quiet another two days until they won. The force of baseball remains deep and sweeping. And personal. Walter and The Judge feel diminished by any Giants' defeat. Like other fans, they need victories to feel good about themselves. The New York Giants are as important as air.

"You're no Gary Cooper," The Judge says. "You're no James Arness, either." *Gunsmoke*, Saturdays at 10 o'clock. "Where's Muddy?"

Mudville was a Labrador Retriever, who went from a chewing puppy to an old cripple who crapped dry turds on the kitchen floor in a shaking squat. The other eleven years she heard a lot of baseball, she learned not to cower when The Judge cursed every at-bat that ended in disappointment.

They expected to see Fleet Walker's name in the papers when Jackie Robinson made the Dodgers in 1947, but they never did. They despised the Dodgers, but rooted for Jackie Robinson his rookie year when he never argued with an umpire. He got into shouting matches with them the next season.

"He can kiss my ultimatum," The Judge said when Jackie Robinson kicked down the umpires' dressing room door in his third season. Threw a haymaker.

The Judge slurps the sugary milk left over from his sugared Sugar Frosted Flakes. His stomach makes a racket.

"They haven't hired a colored umpire yet," Walter says.

"Now, Walter, black *and* blind is just too much to swallow. We won't live to see that. We're in the ninth inning."

"Bottom of the ninth. Two outs, two-strike count," Walter says. "The game will end soon."

"Swinging or looking?"

"Does it matter?" Walter says. "Swinging I hope."

"My only hope is that you don't go first. Who will be around to pull me off the crapper when I've finished my stint? Have you given thought to that?"

"They're tearing Pulitzer's Golden Dome down to make way for a car ramp to the Brooklyn Bridge. Walter O'Malley's thinking of moving the Dodgers to California."

"I'll slip into the bowl back assward, leave this world the way I came in."

"You'll outlive the H-bomb, you and the roaches."

The phone explodes when Walter says H-bomb and The Judge jumps. Walter picks it up and says, "Everything known about Casey's been written." He hangs up, then picks up and says, "Most everything" to the dial tone. Walter hangs up again. "We're going to Casey's memorial at Yankee Stadium."

"You hate hoopla. You despise it more than the Yankees."

"I'll demand my turn at the microphone. I've got a eulogy for Casey that'll make the papers."

"Good for you," The Judge says. "Casey was the all-time ass-shit."

"I'll tell the world that maybe I missed strike one," Walter says. "Maybe I missed strike two. Maybe I missed one of them, maybe both. I could've called them balls. They were that close."

"So many strikes are ball-like," The Judge says. "So many balls are strike-like."

"The third one was a ball for sure, but he swung. With two strikes, he had no choice."

"The fud had a choice," The Judge says. "We all do, except for you. If you'd gone with her to Casey's that day the shit-house beast would've had a field day with the both of you. You'd have woken up dead."

"You don't wake up if you're dead."

"Now, Walter, I did this morning."

"Leaving her alone that Sunday morning was the worst call of my life." Walter starts crying. "I was supposed to protect her. In the end, she protected me."

The Judge stays quiet for a long time. "Umpires are the easiest people in the world to please," he finally says. "If we don't get our cow bells rung, it's a blessed good day."

Walter starts laughing. The Judge joins in and they laugh until they weep. "I whiffed like Papa did," Walter says through snot rheum.

"We all whiff," The Judge says. No matter how old we get, we're all bucket-assed kids. Now, Walter, we can't crawl under a rock for being mere men. Without swings and misses, without ball-like strikes and strike-like balls…."

Walter finishes the sentence. "…without kicked calls, without piss-poor angles, there is no ball game."

The Judge is about to say something, but Walter shushes him. Walter Brewster has the last word.

ABOUT THE AUTHOR

Del Leonard Jones lives near Washington D.C. with his wife Dianna. He was a reporter at USA Today for eighteen years where he was nominated for a Pulitzer Prize in beat reporting. He officiates high school and collegiate sports. His first historical novel, *The Cremation of Sam McGee,* is based on the Klondike gold rush ballads of Robert W. Service and set during the 1898 heyday of yellow journalism. *Wild West Magazine* says the "marvelous book is part historical fiction and part historical fable." Please leave ratings and reviews for all books you read. They are the lifeblood for authors.

A number of baseball historians were interviewed while researching this book, but none had seen this original published in the *San Francisco Examiner,* June 3, 1888. Note that the baseball player named Blake is Jimmy Blake in one stanza and Johnnie Blake in another, indicating that the ballad was written and edited in a hurried manner to fill a hole at the bottom of Page Four.

CASEY AT THE BAT

A Ballad of the Republic, Sung in the Year 1888

The outlook wasn't brilliant for the Mudville nine that day:
The score stood four to two, with but one inning more to play,
And then when Cooney died at first, and Barrows did the same,
A sickly silence fell upon the patrons of the game.

A straggling few got up to go in deep despair. The rest
Clung to that hope which springs eternal in the human breast;
They thought, "If only Casey could but get a whack at that—
We'd put up even money now, with Casey at the bat."

But Flynn preceded Casey, as did also Jimmy Blake,
And the former was a lulu, and the latter was a cake;
So upon that stricken multitude grim melancholy sat,
For there seemed but little chance of Casey's getting to the bat.

But Flynn let drive a single, to the wonderment of all,
And Blake, the much despised, tore the cover off the ball;
And when the dust had lifted, and men saw what had occurred,
There was Johnnie safe at second and Flynn a-hugging third.

Then from 5,000 throats and more there rose a lusty yell;
It rumbled through the valley, it rattled in the dell;
It knocked on the mountain and recoiled upon the flat,
For Casey, mighty Casey, was advancing to the bat.
There was ease in Casey's manner as he stepped into his place;
There was pride in Casey's bearing and a smile on Casey's face.

And when, responding to the cheers, he lightly doffed his hat,
No stranger in the crowd could doubt 'twas Casey at the bat.

Ten thousand eyes were on him as he rubbed his hands with dirt;
Five thousand tongues applauded when he wiped them on his shirt;
Then while the writhing pitcher ground the ball into his hip,
Defiance gleamed in Casey's eye, a sneer curled Casey's lip.

And now the leather-covered sphere came hurtling through the air,
And Casey stood a-watching it in haughty grandeur there.
Close by the sturdy batsman the ball unheeded sped—
"That ain't my style," said Casey. "Strike one," the umpire said.

From the benches, black with people, there went up a muffled roar,
Like the beating of the storm-waves on a stern and distant shore;
"Kill him! Kill the umpire!" shouted someone on the stand;
And it's likely they'd have killed him had not Casey raised his hand.

With a smile of Christian charity great Casey's visage shone;
He stilled the rising tumult; he bade the game go on;
He signaled to the pitcher, and once more the spheroid flew;
But Casey still ignored it and the umpire said, "Strike two."

"Fraud!" cried the maddened thousands, and echo answered "Fraud;"
But one scornful look from Casey and the audience was awed.
They saw his face grow stern and cold, they saw his muscles strain,
And they knew that Casey wouldn't let that ball go by again.

The sneer is gone from Casey's lip, his teeth are clenched in hate;
He pounds with cruel violence his bat upon the plate;
And now the pitcher holds the ball, and now he lets it go,
And now the air is shattered by the force of Casey's blow.

Oh, somewhere in this favored land the sun is shining bright;
The band is playing somewhere, and somewhere hearts are light;
And somewhere men are laughing, and somewhere children shout,
But there is no joy in Mudville—mighty Casey has struck out—Phin

Made in the USA
Coppell, TX
03 September 2021

61738061R00144